Lucienne Boyc_____ıd now lives
in Bristol with _____ ks. With its
exciting marit_____ or many of
her stories. W_____ est walking
around the historic city and the surrounding countryside
gathering ideas and inspiration.

To the
FAIR LAND

Lucienne Boyce

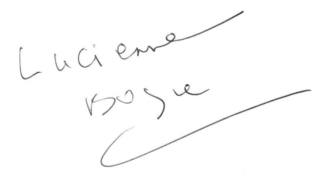

SilverWood

Published in paperback 2012 by SilverWood Books, Bristol, BS1 4HJ
www.silverwoodbooks.co.uk

ISBN 978-1-78132-017-4

British Library Cataloguing in Publication Data
A CIP catalogue record for this book is available from the British Library

Set in New Baskerville by SilverWood Books
Printed on paper sourced responsibly

Men with one foot, indeed, Cyclops, Syrens, Troglodytes, and such like imaginary beings, have almost entirely disappeared.

Anders SPARRMAN
Botanist on Cook's second voyage
13 July 1772 to 30 July 1775

COVENT GARDEN THEATRE

This evening *Tuesday 7 June 1789* will be presented
A new Piece called

The Life and Death of
Captain Cook.

CREW, NATIVE DANCES, MARINES, ETC

Pt 1   On board the *Resolution*

A storm. Thunder and lightning. Rush of waves. The uncommon exertions of the officers and crew. *With appropriate rigging, sails, guns mounted, capstan etc.*

Pt 2   The *Resolution* arrives at Hawaii

Disembarkation of the English. The rapture of the Natives. The ceremonies observed at entering into a Peace with the Natives. *Preparation for a human sacrifice.*

Pt 3   The Death of Captain Cook

The Assassination. A Representation of the Naval and Military Honours observed by the officers of the Resolution. The ceremony performed on the same occasion according to the manner of the Natives of Hawaii. *To conclude with a representation of a Burning Mountain.*

Cook ever honour'd immortal shall live

The music and overture by Mr SMITH, the scenery by Mr KETTLE, the Dances by Mr MORRIS, the dresses by Mr TOWNLEY and Mrs BALDWIN, the Machinery by Mr TINKER, the properties by Mr BLAKE, the Fireworks by Signor MORTRAM, the whole produced under the direction of Mr LEWIS.

One

"No, Father, I beg you!"

The girl, her terrified face turned towards his, struggled to wrest her hands free of her father's grip. She threw all her weight backwards, dug in with her bare heels, squirming and twisting, the swirling fronds of her grass skirt revealing her straining muscles.

"You should be proud of this!" her brother hissed.

The High Priest stood behind the stone slab, his frown of disgust emphasised by the fierce red streaks daubed across his cheeks and forehead. The tall feathers on his headdress quivered angrily. An impatient shrug of his shoulders caused the triple necklace of dogs' teeth and sharks' teeth and – who knows? – human teeth to rattle against his bare chest. Around him a semi-circle of sacerdotal officials glared at the father and brother. In their shame they redoubled their efforts to subdue their rebellious kinswoman and succeeded in lifting her onto the altar. Here the hopelessness of her situation overcame her and she sank back sobbing.

The Priest pushed his cloak back from his shoulders, the tips of its red feathers forming a gory nimbus about himself and his victim. He clapped and an assistant stepped forward, bowed, and handed him a dagger. He gripped the hilt in both hands and slowly raised the weapon above the girl's heart. Her time was ebbing away, she knew it, and her pleas for mercy trailed into silence.

Every eye was fixed upon the blade, every faculty strained towards the awful moment when it would plunge. No one heard the footfall or noticed the slight disturbance on the fringes of the glade. Then, "Captain Cook!" someone whispered, and quickly the words *Captain Cook...! Captain Cook...!* spread through the crowd.

The tall man in white breeches and braided blue jacket stepped fearlessly into their midst, his hands held out to show that he was unarmed. The High Priest lowered his arms and cursed, but he shrank too, his authority flying from him in the presence of the naval officer. With a calm, unhurried step the Captain advanced to the altar, where the girl struggled into a sitting position. He held out his hand. "Madam?" Trembling, she placed her fingers in his.

A collective sigh rose up, but it was not enough. Fine emotions had been roused in breasts that were not perhaps accustomed to them, and those emotions must be vented. The cheering, stamping, whistling and hooting went on for so long that Cook and the girl were obliged to remain frozen in position, hand in hand before the altar. At last the racket died down and she fell to her knees before her saviour, declaring, "I am yours for ever!"

There was a brief pause, then the girl scrambled to her feet, the High Priest skipped out from behind the altar, the lesser priests grinned and slapped one another on the back, Captain Cook winked at the auditorium, and the stage emptied.

Immediately a hubbub of voices filled the hot, heavy air. The people in the upper tiers stamped their feet to rid them of pins and needles. Gentlemen flitted between the boxes, courting ladies, propositioning women of the other sort. The men and women in the pit rose from the benches to relieve their aching backs and cramped limbs. There was a constant flow of people back and forth across the rows, and their neighbours' toes. Some, having had enough of *The Life and Death of Captain Cook*, made their way out of the Covent Garden Theatre and hurried off to catch the end of another play. At the same time there was an influx of half-price latecomers, red-faced from their chophouse dinners and cheap tavern wine.

A scuffle broke out: someone had been foolish enough to leave his seat and another had claimed it. Behind the combatants two young men dodged the flailing arms and legs, steadfastly holding onto their own places in the confusion. The usurper won easily by muffling his opponent in his own jacket and beating him down to a semi-conscious heap under the disputed place.

"I hope the fellow is able to disentangle himself from his coat," remarked one of the pair, nodding at the twitching figure on the ground. "He's likely to suffocate in this heat."

His friend, who was humming the chorus of *Loose Ev'ry Sail* from the first act, shrugged. "Ben, when the play ends I'm going to the dressing rooms to try and strike an acquaintance with that Sacrificial Maiden!"

"You'll get the pox."

Campbell grinned and patted his jacket pocket. "No, I won't. I've taken your advice and got myself some armour."

Campbell the Scottish Poet – for that was how he wished to be remembered by future generations – had very unpoetic habits. His frizzed wig was powdered in uneven patches. Evidence of his most recent meals speckled his plum-coloured jacket, his black breeches were crumpled from spending their nights in a heap on the floor, and one of his shoes had a buckle missing. His scant resources might have been put to better use than a night at the theatre, but when he had money he spent it on his appetites, not his appearance. For all his slovenliness, he often succeeded in obtaining satisfaction. Women, it seemed, liked his carelessness, his supple, loose-limbed figure and his easy laugh, even if he could provide them with little more than a tavern dinner and a bottle of sack.

Ben Dearlove, on the other hand, went to great lengths to disguise the fact that he lived not exactly in poverty but within a budget. He brushed his clothes and hung them up every night, he combed his wig, buffed his shoes, and changed his linen often. He was not above rinsing out his own stockings in the privacy of his room. But then Campbell was not all that fastidious, Ben reflected, as the woman slipping into the seat on his right pressed herself against his shoulder. A Covent Garden Nun looking for business. He waited for the whispered price, knowing that he would refuse it, the woman would move away, and good riddance to her.

Seconds passed and she did not speak. Ben's hand flew to his pocket, but his old-fashioned watch and his coins were safe. Puzzled, he risked looking at her. She was not attempting to catch his or any other man's attention. She gazed at the empty stage, as if with the intensity of her look she could compel the actors to return and finish the piece.

She was not young – in her thirties – and her dress was an old-fashioned sackback gown such as women wore twenty years ago. If she were cheap enough that would not prevent her from obtaining business, but she did not seem to be in that trade. The faded garment was second-hand and hung off her, but it was clean. A linen neckerchief covered her shoulders, and the hood of her flimsy summer cloak was pulled up modestly over her hair. If her face had not been so thin and sunken she would have been handsome. Her eyes were large and lustrous, and there were red circles on her cheekbones that had not come out of a cosmetics pot. Yet the colour looked high and unnatural. He wondered if she was suffering from the stuffiness of the pit.

Campbell nudged his arm. "What's next?"

Ben retrieved a programme from the floor, straightened out the crumpled sheet and read out, "*Part 3: The Death of Captain Cook. The Assassination. A Representation of the Naval and Military Honours observed by the officers –* "

"Hush! She's on again."

The third act opened with the grateful Maiden's nuptial dance. Ben had watched more lascivious performances without embarrassment, but throughout this one he was uncomfortably aware of his neighbour casting indignant glares at the drooling men and tittering women around her. Had she mistaken this play for another, more moral entertainment? He sensed her growing agitation, yet the play proceeded and no escort returned to remove her from her painful predicament.

The gallant Captain bounded out of the wings to explain that he was already married, and it was not the custom in his country for a man to take more than one wife. The Maiden took her disappointment remarkably well and Cook handed her over to a love-struck young prince. The woman at Ben's side swayed and pressed her hand to her head. An ominous sign… was she about to swoon?

The nobles and officers cleared the stage for the Tars to dance a hornpipe and sing one or two comic songs. Their antics attracted the young men of Hawaii, and all was harmony and good humour while they learned one another's dances, swapped jackets for grass skirts, and shared intoxicating beverages. But suddenly there was a cry of "Stop thief!" One of the Hawaiians had run off with the carpenter's tools. To the sailors' annoyance, his friends refused to hand him over. After an acrimonious exchange, which involved much stomping and folding of arms by the Hawaiian warriors, the sailors were forced to retreat.

Ben applauded with the rest of the audience. The woman beside him wrung her hands and mumbled a long, delirious stream of complaint. Alarmed, Ben recollected how bright he had thought her eyes, how flushed her face. It was clear by now that she had no escort, and he examined her with impunity, trying to remember what he had been taught of plague symptoms. She was not shivering and there were none of the red spots his father called 'tokens' visible on her skin. He concluded that she was more eccentric than contagious, and this talking to herself was the habit of someone who was often alone.

On stage, events in Hawaii were reaching their tragic conclusion. Captain Cook visited the King and demanded the surrender of the thief and the stolen property. That portly monarch responded with a declaration of war. Reference was made to the Canoe of the Gods and the military prowess of the Mighty Ancestors. The English prepared for battle with a rousing song, the Hawaiians with drums and ferocious capering.

The woman leaned forward, her hands gripping the seat as if to stop herself springing at the stage. "Gibberish!"

Ben edged away.

In a daring raid on the *Resolution* the Hawaiians made off with the cabin boy. The warriors, dressed in protective mats, their faces daubed with red paint, rubbed their bellies and pointed at the boy, while the priests kindled the cooking fire.

"Nonsense!" The woman next to Ben clenched her fist.

Undeterred by their superior numbers and terrifying appearance, Captain Cook and his marines went on shore to rescue the boy. The lad broke free and ran to his beloved Captain's side. The Captain sent him back to the ship. Stupefied, the Hawaiians watched the boy retreat to the safety of the *Resolution*. Then, howling with rage, they turned on Cook and his men.

"Rubbish!"

A few people turned to stare at the woman next to Ben. He leaned away, hoping they did not think *he* was her escort.

Despite putting up a brave fight, and even though the audience offered all the assistance it could with shouts of "There's one behind you!" or "Now – fire now!", the marines were slain one by one. Cook was left alone amongst his enemies. It was a unique moment in theatrical history: the audience was silent. Even Ben's neighbour stopped heckling.

The Captain flung back his head and announced at length that he was proud to die in the service of his country. Then he ran through a couple of the foe for heroic good measure. His screaming enemies flung themselves upon him and he went down in a flurry of clubs and spears.

The curtain descended and pandemonium broke out. Wailing women flung themselves into one another's arms. Men were not ashamed to be seen wiping their eyes, or blowing their noses on their sleeves. The spectators in the galleries applauded so enthusiastically it was a wonder there were no broken arms. The theatre echoed with cries of "Cook for England!", "Bravo Captain Cook!", and "God Save the King!"

Inflamed by the atmosphere, the front rows rushed the stage, where the boldest and most agile attempted to climb over the spikes, perhaps intending to slaughter the Hawaiians. It was a hot, affecting moment, and Ben and Campbell were on their feet with the rest.

"I'm off backstage before someone else gets there!" said a voice in Ben's left ear. "Captain Cook was a fool," hissed another in his right.

"What?" He turned in confusion from side to side.

"You know, the girl the Captain turned down. Catch me turning her away from my bed!" That was Campbell to Ben's left.

"Captain Cook's discoveries! A fool's discoveries – little islands and barren shores. I wouldn't give you that for Captain Cook's discoveries!"

The thin woman to his right was a picture of madness, talking, gesticulating, her voice growing shriller and louder. Ben frowned a warning, willing her to be quiet, but she was oblivious to all hints of danger.

"What did she say?" shrieked a female in the next row.

"Why, she says Captain Cook's a fool!" rejoined her gossip. "D'ye hear that, gen'lemen?" This to their escorts. "'Ere, Mr Timmins, ask her what she means by it."

"I ask her? Why don't you ask her yourself?"

There was no need to ask her anything. She had no thought of keeping her heresies to herself. "Captain Cook found nothing, nothing at all… yet they make a hero of him. A hero of that blunderer!"

"Lookee, miss, don't you go mullironing a brave and a gallant gen'leman in my 'earing," cried the first woman.

"No, shut your mouth, you damned bitch!" added Mr Timmins.

"Ay, Mrs Harridan, you can keep your pinions to yourself," put in a gen'leman in the row behind, leaning forward to give the woman a shove in the small of her back. She stumbled and looked about her in bewilderment. It was only natural for the Timmins ladies to feel that she committed a further outrage with her "obstropolous" look. They appealed to the pit at large: "Did you hear what she said?"

"Yes, and I saw her laugh with the murdering savages."

"Who does she think she is, coming in and upsetting decent people?"

"Give her a ducking in the water trough!"

"No, roll her in the kennels."

Heedlessly, Ben's neighbour babbled on. "He turned back too soon. He didn't find it. What a mercy is a fool! What would have happened to them all if he had?"

Ben grasped her arm. "Madam, for your own sake, be quiet!"

An orange hit her in the back and she staggered into him. He spied another piece of fruit flying through the air and put his arm around her to ward it off. He missed and it caught her on the shoulder before smashing on the boards at her feet. She looked down at the pulpy mess in astonishment. Gradually it dawned on her that she was under attack. He felt her sudden, panicky resistance to his encircling arm. Before he could assure her that he was not one of the crowd, Campbell tugged at his sleeve.

"Come on, Ben!"

"I can't," he said helplessly.

"Why not? Od's bobs, leave her!"

"They'll tear her apart."

"It's only a Billingsgate fight. Leave them to it."

Doubtfully, Ben relinquished the woman. Unexpectedly deprived of his support she slumped onto the bench. Campbell was already pushing his way out of the pit. Ben followed. A raucous howl made him look back.

"Damn me – she's got a tattoo!"

"A tattoo? She's a Hottentot herself!"

"Has she got one on her bum as well?"

"Let's have a look!"

With one hand the woman feebly beat off the coarse, clutching fingers; with the other she tried to twitch her cloak around her. Her neckerchief was torn; in the dim light her exposed skin glowed palely, the design on it starkly delineated.

17

Ben had shuddered at travellers' tales describing how the peoples of the South Seas used sharpened shells to pierce their skin then injected dye into the perforations. He had seen prints of the Maori warriors of New Zealand with elaborate swirling lines on their faces, and the Tahitians with their blackened buttocks. But the red bird on the woman's shoulder with its high crest and long tail was as delicate as a drawing from a monkish bestiary.

He stared at it in astonishment. How could she have come by such a barbaric ornament? But this was no time to speculate.

"Hell and damnation! Campbell – give me a hand!"

Campbell had gone. Ben hauled the woman to her feet, pulled her close, and forced a way out of the pit. They were pursued by boos and catcalls, pelted with peel, nut shells, and blows. The noise was deafening; it was as if the world was exploding around them. The air was filled with bright lights, green, red, blue, and the hissing of a thousand cats. A cry of "Ooh!" went up and suddenly the bombardment stopped, the pursuit fell back, their assailants barged back to their seats.

They had been saved by the Burning Mountain.

Two

In the piazza, when he was sure that no one was following, Ben stopped to get his breath back. He propped the woman against one of the columns while he straightened his hat and checked his jacket for damage. Her knees sagged and she slid towards the ground. Behind them someone laughed.

"Overdo the wine and spoil the pleasure!"

He caught hold of the woman, glaring at the pair of giggling bucks pattering by on their high heels. Her head lolled on his shoulder.

"Miranda!" she mumbled into his ear.

"What did you say? Is that your name?"

Her head rolled back and she laughed. He did not think the question such a ridiculous one. Annoyed, he shook her. "Who is Miranda? Someone at home? Tell me where she is and I will take you to her."

Her laugh ended in gurgling sobs. "I don't know where she is."

More footsteps. Two couples, staggering up a flight of steps from the bagnio, pointed. "First time?" jeered one of the men.

"Don't worry, sweetheart. It will *come* with practice!" shrieked his doxy.

Ben gritted his teeth and said nothing. Ribaldry had never been one of his strong points. Luckily, the woman did not seem to have heard the chaffing, and if she had he did not think she would have understood it. She was not a whore, of that he was certain. She spoke nonsense but she spoke it with a gentlewoman's accent, and whatever it was that had loosened her tongue it was not drink.

He stepped experimentally away from her. She swayed, but did not fall. "Will you be able to get home?"

"Home. Yes."

"Goodnight, then." He took another step backwards.

She tried to cover her dishevelled hair with her hood, but had no strength and her hand fell to her side. She shrank back, looked despairingly about her. The piazza would fill up as the theatres emptied; if she were still here on her own, she would not be able to defend herself from nuisance.

Ben hesitated. There were rows of chairs on the other side of the square. "Shall I get one for you?"

She smiled weakly. "I could not pay for it. Thank you, but no."

Well, thought Ben, that sounded more rational. The fresh air must have revived her.

"Have you far to walk?"

"I have lodgings in Poland Street."

"Not far, then," he said encouragingly.

She could hardly hold herself upright, let alone walk, and Soho was far enough. If he left her he would lie awake all night wondering if she had fainted in a gutter or been molested and left for dead in a doorway, her corpse to be swept away with all the other rubbish when the dust-cart came round. He would be haunted by her gaunt face, imagining a myriad possible fates, all of them dreadful. For only a little effort he could spare himself the torment.

"I will walk with you."

"Thank you," she answered, and fainted.

He had to hire a carriage, though the commission irritated the driver, who resented leaving Covent Garden just before the post-theatre rush. He dropped them at the top of Poland Street and, too impatient to argue over the size of the tip, almost knocked them over as he wheeled away. Luckily the street was dry, otherwise they would have been spattered with dirt. In the vehicle the woman had revived long enough to give Ben her address, and he half-carried her to the court where she lived.

It was not one of those nasty rookeries thrown up only to crash down on the occupants' heads a few months later, but a solid old place built around a paved central courtyard. Perhaps the square had been lit once; perhaps the entrance had once boasted a gate fastened at night by a gatekeeper. No gatekeeper watched now that the houses had been subdivided and let. Ben and his charge stumbled between the disused chain posts, disturbing a scavenging cat which howled its displeasure before slinking away.

The woman drifted in and out of her senses, but never remained unconscious long enough for him to search her pockets for a key. It would not be easy to explain himself if she should revive and in her confusion cry "Robbery!" so he knocked on the door and prayed that he would not wake the whole neighbourhood.

The cat glared at him from the shadows but no light appeared in the tall building. His burden, light though she was, was onerous. He wished only to deposit her with her own acquaintance and hurry back to The Shakespeare at Covent Garden, where he expected to find Campbell either celebrating his success with the actress or drinking away his disappointment.

Exasperated, he knocked more loudly. A sash window flew open, an aged head appeared against the stars, and a toothless female shrilled, "What'sh all that noishe?"

He peered up. "Your lodger has been taken ill."

"It'sh not my houshe," the woman replied, leaning out to take a closer look. "Firsht floor landing," she added.

"Could you let her in?"

Some seconds passed. Then the crone said, "I'll get her shervant."

Servant! How could a woman in these lodgings keep a servant? Nevertheless, a servant there was, who appeared at the door, shawl over shoulder and candlestick in hand, a few moments later. Her face was in shadow, but from her figure Ben thought she could not be more than twelve or thirteen. His hopes of draping the swooning female over the girl's shoulders were dashed – she did not look strong enough to take the load. She signalled him to follow her into the house and grudgingly he obeyed.

Firsht floor landing comprised two rooms. The first contained a shabby sofa, one or two chairs, a threadbare rug, and a table by the window. A light burned on the table, by no means brightly, but sufficient for Ben to see that the servant was not a child for all the slightness of her frame. She was a grown woman, though slender and small, with tiny hands and shapely, bare feet. Her tawny eyes reminded him of the cat's a few moments ago. Her hair was long and dark and gleaming, loose about her shoulders. He had never seen hair that looked so liquid and undulating, that moved like a waterfall when she turned her head. A fashionable beauty had hair full of powder and grease, plastered to her head and left to set stiffly for weeks between washes.

She padded on ahead of him, paused at the door of the bedchamber and turned to face him with the candle held aloft. For an instant her skin shone pale gold, then she lowered the light, opened the door and motioned to him to go in. He followed the young woman into the room and lowered her

22

mistress onto the bed. She fell back with a low moan. He lifted her bony wrist to count her pulse but the servant, whispering something that sounded like "ashlackticcytak" into the woman's ear, bustled him out of the way. Not recognising the language he hesitated, wondering how to take leave of the pair, one senseless, the other a stranger to the land. But, "Wait!" the servant said, nodding towards the open door. He backed out of the bedchamber, the music of that low "Wait!" reverberating in his head.

He considered what to do next. After all, why should he wait? He had got the patient home; it was no concern of his that she had only a foreign woman to care for her. Since leaving the heat of the theatre all the symptoms that had made him suspect fever or infection had vanished. She lay on the bed, cold, weak and thin. He wondered if the little woman with the magical voice was capable of diagnosing the all too obvious malady that afflicted her employer.

But why should he concern himself with these women? They were a pair of curiosities, to be sure, but London was full of curiosities. All the same, the maid had asked him to wait... she had pretty eyes... she might not know what was needed.

The light on the table drew his eyes. It was covered with pens, ink, paper and drawing materials which must have cost more than the rest of the furnishings put together. There was a newly-finished painting pinned to a drawing board. A wading bird with legs like twigs; it was a wonder they did not snap under its great, round body. Its plumage was a startling orange and along each eye was a vivid, peacock-blue stripe. No such bird had ever landed on British shores and he might have thought it nothing more than the product of imagination had not the drawing been so meticulously rendered and bordered by diagrams of barbed feathers and webbed feet. A handful of studies of the same subject lay nearby. They had been roughly and hastily executed, with scribbled notes indicating which colours should be used in the final drawing. He supposed these must be the sketches, made in the field, of some well-travelled natural historian.

If the picture had been made by a traveller, then where was that traveller now?

There was a noise at the door. He whirled round. In his imagination a fearful giant of a husband, bristling with pistols and reckless with jealousy, burst in. Ben saw himself lying on the floor, whispering his innocent explanation to his remorseful murderer with his dying breath... but no one burst in, and a moment's reflection brought to mind that he had seen no boots, wigs or snuffbox. This was a spinster's domain.

Ben went back to examining the books on the desk. *A Natural History of British Birds*, a conchological study and a botanical dictionary. They were expensive volumes, and Ben doubted that they belonged to a woman who could not pay for the hire of a chair. Natural history books were popular, but very few people could afford to buy an original. They made do with poor quality imitations produced without permission of the author. He revised his conclusion: the rough sketches were her first attempts at reproducing someone else's pictures. So that was how she made her living, such as it was. She was one of the hack-artists employed by some Paternoster Square tradesman who had lent her these exquisite books, and no doubt docked the money for her materials from her wages, so that she could copy the drawings for his own cheap editions.

The servant stepped out of the bedroom, softly shutting the door behind her. "Sleeping."

"You do know what is wrong with her?"

She stared at him.

"Your mistress. She needs food. Do you understand me? Eat. She must eat." He mimed the act of bringing food to his mouth, chewed, smacked his lips.

"Food, yes," the girl said. The light in her hand flickered.

"And when did you last eat a proper meal?" He might as well have been talking to himself, for she did not seem to understand him. "I don't suppose either of you will eat if the lady is unable to work... Damn! It's all I have. Buy some food. Bread. Broth. Do you understand me?" Ben laid some coins on the table, abandoning the prospect of a pint of wine with Campbell. He waved his hand, meaning to pre-empt her expressions of gratitude. Surprisingly, these were not forthcoming. A little disconcerted by her matter-of-fact acceptance of his gift, he reached for a pen and paper.

"This is a recipe for a restorative," he said, scribbling. "A cordial. Something for the lady to drink." He replaced the lid on the inkpot, folded the paper and held it out to her. "Give this to your mistress. She will explain. You must take it to an apothecary. He will make it up for you. It's for her to drink. Drink?" He raised an invisible glass.

She took the sheet from him. He hesitated, but as no 'thank you' – no words at all – left her lips, he picked up his hat. "Remember," he said. "Food and drink."

Then he was in the corridor listening to her fasten the bolts. A few seconds later the line of light under the door disappeared. He turned and groped his way down the stairs and out of the house.

Three

It was a month later. A whole month! Eighteen of his months had gone. An entire morning had gone, and he had not written above twenty words. He lowered his pen, leaned back in his chair, pinched his lower lip between his thumb and forefinger and eyed his work.

His father had agreed to pay his way in the capital for two years. ("It has to be London, Father, for that is where all men of letters reside.") Father could afford no more, and at the end of that time, if he had not succeeded as a writer, he must go home and resume the career to which he had been born. An apothecary! Measuring out powders and potions for the querulous old, the whimpering sick, the vomiting young.

But these thoughts always made him uneasy. Was his father's not an ancient and honourable profession? Was his father not an honest and generous man? Ben stifled his unfilial opinions and tried to concentrate instead on his catalogue of good fortune.

It was not write or die for Ben. He had his allowance every month. He also had the cheeses, cake and wine his father sent him, and the extra blankets for his bed that Mrs Shackleton had insisted he take with him – for no London housekeeper could air bedding as well as she – and all the other little comforts that they pressed on him whenever he went home, which was not as often as it should have been. He excused himself with his work: it was proceeding apace, it was at a critical stage, he was expecting to meet a man who would help him break into the profession.

He was roused from his brooding by the sound of bells and the patter of feet hurrying past his door. His pious landlady on her way to church. She was, as she never tired of telling him, a clergyman's daughter, brought up in the ways of the Lord with such thoroughness she never could deviate from them. Storm, sickness, servant problems – no calamity kept her from sermons on a Sunday.

Still, his lodgings were comfortable and clean, his laundry was done regularly, his fire was lit for him, he could order dinners when he wished and they were always generously portioned and hot, if bland. He had two rooms, his bedroom and this where he wrote, read, ate his breakfasts and suppers. They were not furnished to his taste. There was too much of the fussy woman in the elaborate covers and irritating china knick-knacks – too many fiddle and flute-playing monkeys, birds on stumps, and pot-bellied Cupids. But the rooms were reasonably priced, and very far from being a garret.

He might, at this point in his musings, have remembered the women in the dismal Poland Street quarters, but he had long since forgotten them. In the week following the encounter, he had wondered about them once or twice. He had told Campbell simply that the woman had been ill and he had taken her home. Laughingly, Campbell gave the tale his own conclusion. Ben protested, saying it was not like that at all, which only made his friend tease him more. Since then, the subject had been dropped.

Tonight, it was Campbell that Ben was thinking of. Campbell in a damp, dingy room hunched over his work, forced to abandon poetry for long periods so he could earn enough to live on. His latest commission had plumbed new depths of drudgery – he was indexing a reverend enthusiast's *Illustrations of Obscurities in Shakespeare*. "And I wish they had stayed obscure," Campbell growled, "for no duller work has ever been written." But that was what hackery was all about: indexes, pamphlets, articles, all scribbled anonymously to order.

Ben looked gratefully about him, but caught sight of himself in the mirror over the fireplace. He looked ridiculous, like a baby in a bib, with that towel draped across his shoulders, protecting his frilled shirt from ink splashes. He rose to his feet, pulling the towel away, and went into his bedroom to finish dressing. The jacket of his best suit hung on the back of the chair, his shoes were polished, his wig waited on its stand on the dressing table.

Today he was promised a feast of beef, pudding, potatoes, and port. He had been invited to one of Mr Dowling's Sunday dinners. There had been a time when an invitation from Mr Dowling filled him with excitement. Mr Dowling, the bookseller, had shown an interest in him! He would become part of a literary society. Its members would welcome him into their world. In their selfless love of literature they would help him make his way, though he could give them nothing in return...

It was only a short walk from George Street to St Paul's Churchyard where Mr Dowling kept his shop. When he got to Blackfriars Bridge, he realised that he was early. He stopped in an embrasure to watch the skimming boats full of people in their Sunday best. A swirl of colour caught his eye. A woman in a red skirt approached, her glazed eyes voraciously fixed on him, her sore-encrusted lips puckering greedily. He remembered his landlady had told him that before the bridge was built, Blackfriars was a den of prostitutes and thieves, gin shops and brothels. It seemed that things had not changed that much.

"Not now, thank you!" Ben cried and hastily strode on.

Mr Dowling's house was tall, squeezed with its neighbours into one of the lanes encircling St Paul's. The street was too narrow for wheeled vehicles, and was made even narrower by the shops' protruding bow windows. Mr Dowling's blinds were down, a sure sign that this was the Sabbath. Although his place of business was separated from his home by only a single flight of stairs, Mr Dowling made it a rule never to set foot in the shop on the day of rest. It was not so much a rule of religion as a rule of relaxation.

Ben rang the doorbell and was admitted by Tom, one of the apprentices, who led him at a run between the shadowy bookshelves. Tom, anxious to get out and start his day of freedom, veered off at the foot of the stairs leaving Ben to make his own way up to the dining room. The others were already gathered, squeezed into the narrow spaces between the long table, the high-backed chairs, and the dark green walls – the old, dark country furniture had been made for a bigger hall. There was a parlour across the landing, but it was exclusive to the use of Mr Dowling's sister when he entertained. Miss Dowling would issue forth from time to time, whispering instructions to the servant passing up and down with the dishes.

One glance around the room showed Ben that there had been no additions or losses to the company since their last meeting. The guests nervously sipped their sherry, trying not to look too obviously at the table or their host, though every one of them wanted the same things – their dinner, and a publishing agreement with Mr Dowling.

Ben worked his way through them, greeting and shaking hands. Mr Barlow's hands were huge and fat, like his belly, his voice, and his opinions. Dr Johnson might be dead, but here was his successor, the worthy inheritor of the doctor's pompous certainties. Barlow squinted condescendingly at the young man, for he was a critic and in this society that put him on a level equal to Mr Dowling's and a long way above the rest of the company. Ben always engaged in tortuous manoeuvres to avoid being seated next to Barlow.

Rigg, the poet, was another man Ben avoided, and not just because of the nastiness of the man's nature. Rigg had a private income, which was fortunate, for he made no living from his verses that savaged every human creature, living or dead, save himself. His remarks were irritating because they were mean, but when a man judges everything to be bad, it is clear that he is not to be taken seriously. It was not the dark little man's sibilant spitefulness that bothered Ben so much as the fountains of spittle that drenched anyone who happened to be within range of his criticisms.

Mr Hart was a bent, whispering fellow in his sixties whose face was lined by long years of struggle, lightened only by the near success of the days when he dined with Mrs Thrale and Dr Johnson at Streatham. He was harmless enough, in spite of his political views, though he was too out of touch with the times for his writings to contain anything of relevance or danger to the commonweal. He acted as the death's head at the feast, a poignant reminder of what could happen to a man when his dreams elude him, and for that reason he made Ben uncomfortable.

Then there was Parmeter, the engraver, poet and fabulist. He looked like a parson in his dark suit, plain shoes, black stockings and white shirt. Or he would have done had he not been wearing the largest, most alarmingly patterned cravat Ben had ever seen. It was a nightmare of blue and yellow stripes that made him go cross-eyed to look at. Parmeter had a way with colour. His landscapes were strange wildernesses painted in wild hues under a jagged yellow sun; his figures pale, gaudily robed ungrounded beings, hovering like angels. Ben was sure that Dowling only invited him out of pity, for no one in their right mind would allow their work to be illustrated by Parmeter. Yet, out of all of those present – even, sometimes, Campbell – Ben liked Parmeter best. Nervous, emotional and unselfconscious, the man's earnestness and dedication appealed to him. "Whatever inspiration I have is given to me," he had declared once, "and it is my privilege to struggle to realise it."

But Parmeter could not help Ben's career. No one here could, except Dowling himself. It was only for the sake of his acquaintance with the publisher that he endured these gatherings of literary might-have-beens or never-would-bes. It was the same for Campbell and, of course, the two young men fervently hoped that they would not remain long in these literary doldrums.

If Mr Dowling himself was sometimes made uncomfortable by all these ambitions and desires seething about him, he did not betray it. He was a thin, active man in his fifties who owed his success to his policy of buying only what would sell. That did not mean that he was beyond appreciating what would not, but he was a businessman and, while he might praise, he would rarely buy that which he was not confident of profiting from. Yet he liked, indeed admired, many of the writers who applied to him and, if he could not place them, he would offer what help he could – in the form of these dinners (he doubted if some of his guests would have eaten a square meal from one month to the next without them), or introductions to publishers who might be able to employ them. Also, the company of his sister did occasionally need alleviating.

Mr Dowling summoned everyone to the table, where Ben's sidling about the chairs was rewarded by finding himself between Campbell and Parmeter. The dishes were brought in, the covers removed, and the guests gazed in awe at the boiled beef. Once their plates were filled, however, the conversation grew lively. Ben leaned forward to listen to Mr Hart whispering the most bloodcurdling passages from his latest pamphlet, *Reflections on false English liberties and the true liberties of the Revolution in France*.

Mr Dowling shook his head. "Too hot for me to publish, my dear! You'll have to try Jo Johnson round the corner."

"I have tried him," Hart lisped sadly.

"Well, I'll have a word and see what his objections are."

"Perhaps you are not radical enough!" giggled Mr Rigg. "A few more heads on spikes ought to do it."

"Heads on spikes, sir!" boomed Barlow. "Let any of your damned Frogs try to put John Bull's head on a spike and he'll see how we gore him."

Parmeter tilted his head to one side, raised his hand to his chin, and looked as if this suggested a picture to him.

Dowling, rising to bring another bottle from the sideboard, smiled over his shoulder. "And tell me, Mr Barlow, what do you make of my literary sensation?"

"Literary sensation, sir! Literary *shamble*, more like. What I want to know, sir, is, is it poetry or is it prose?" He reached into a deep pocket and drew out a notebook. "I copied this out of your *literary sensation*."

As the familiar notebook made its appearance, Campbell smirked at Ben. Ben looked away, trying not to laugh. Barlow never bought any books of his own, instead treating Mr Dowling's stock as his private library. Barlow flicked through the papers with his monstrous fingers, found his place and read, his breathing heavy and in the wrong places.

With the stars twinkling through the masts, and the moonlight turning the dark wood to silver, the ship would sail and sail and sail into the night, under the stars and the black sky, until the black turns to grey and the sky is pearl white and soft pink and pale yellow, and rainbows dance in the white foam around her prow. And then the water changes colour, from deep blue to pale green, and birds wheel around the mast, and ahead lies a long, low purple belt of land, and drawing closer they see snow-capped mountains and ancient forests, golden meadows and green pastures, beaches of black sand, cities of dazzling white stone. Smiling people garlanded with flowers wait to greet them; there is music, laughter, and no going back.

"There!" Barlow cried, triumphantly banging the book into the puddle of gravy by his plate. "What, sir, is that, sir?"

"What is it?" cried Rigg, foam flying from his lips. "It is exquisite, that's what it is. I have never written a panegyric in my life, but I shall pen one now!"

"Oh!" creaked Hart. "It is wonderful, wonderful!"

"It is the best thing I have ever read in my life," Parmeter said solemnly. "It has already inspired me to make several drawings, though nothing of mine matches the author's illustrations."

"I have never been amused by anything so much as Mumps, the melancholy sailor." Campbell threw back his head and sputtered, "*He advanced slowly with a pig on his shoulder!*"

"And," roared Rigg, "the way the man speaks! When he's telling his mates how he was robbed in a Janeiro brothel: *The punk came at me with a pair of pops in her paws and grabbed me Portugal pieces!*"

"And yet," said Dowling, wiping the tears of laughter from

his eyes, "how the author teaches us, by the power of contrast, what it is to be a gentleman."

"You mean Mr Noble," said Campbell quickly.

"Braveman! Mumps! And I suppose the villain is called Mr Bad or Jemmy Wicked or Mr Slysneak," growled Barlow. "I wonder there isn't a place in it for Dearlove."

Ben did not know why Barlow turned on him, for he had no more idea about what they were talking about than the man in the moon. There was little he could do about the jibe, however, except laugh and pretend it did not trouble him. In truth, he was very sensitive about his name. It was exactly like the surname of a character in a novel, a female novel, of the most sentimental kind. Yet he refused to change it. He could not disappoint his father any more than he already had by adding abandoning the family name to turning his back on the family business. So Dearlove he was, but he had to believe that one day he would be a respected man of letters, and his name would be respected too.

"Ha! Ha!" Ben affected. "But what is this literary sensation you are all speaking of?"

"Ben, where have you been all week?" Campbell cried. "Why, it's the book of the year."

"Of the decade."

"Of the century."

"Of all time." This last from Parmeter.

"But what is it?" Ben persisted.

"It is a book about a voyage to an imaginary land. A land where there are no politicians or lawyers," murmured Hart. "No Newgate and no Marshalsea, for there is no crime and no debt where there is no poverty, and where it is every person's greatest joy to serve his fellows."

"A place where beauty in art and architecture is sacred,"

said Parmeter dreamily. "A land where poets are honoured."

"And the women!" Campbell winked. "Amorous *and* beautiful."

"You mistake the author's purpose if you think it is to arouse low sensations," Dowling gently rebuked the Scot. "The book has a serious intent."

"Another of your Gullivers?" sneered Barlow.

"I suppose it is," the publisher answered. "But superior, I think. The author takes us from extremes of savagery – you have only to think of the poor fellows they meet in Tierra del Fuego, clad in nothing but sealskin, with such a degraded notion of decency that their mode of greeting is to display their manhood to one another – "

"What Mumps might call a Pagan playing with his pizzle!" hooted Campbell.

When the laughter had died down, Dowling smilingly continued, "I say, he takes us from these extremes to the ideal of a culture and civilisation far above our own."

"Pooh!" said Barlow. "We're British, aren't we?"

"And the whole is presented as if it is an account of a true voyage," added Rigg. "I have never read so convincing a tale."

"Pah!" Barlow again. "Your author's a charlatan. A book is fiction or it is fact, it cannot pretend to be both."

"But who is the author?" Ben asked.

"No one knows," Campbell answered. "Not even Mr Dowling."

"Mr Dullwit, I suggest." Barlow chortled at his joke, which the others ignored.

Ben stared at Dowling. "You are the publisher! How can you not know?"

"All my dealings with the author were care of Will's Coffee House. I sent my letters there and he sent someone to collect them and deliver his proofs. I had no idea the book would sell as well as it has. I could have done it more cheaply if I had refused the illustrations. However, I think they have increased the book's popularity. I shall have to do another print run for the shop at the week's end and I have a long list of circulating libraries demanding copies."

"If the book is such a sensation, surely the writer must desire the acclaim that goes with it?" Ben wondered.

"It would appear not. Since publication, I have had no communication from the gentleman, and my inquiries have failed to discover him. I do very much wish to find him before another publisher does." Dowling put down his glass and stared gravely at the company. "If I knew who the author of *An Account of a Voyage to the Fair Land* was, I would not only shake him by the hand. I would offer him a thousand pounds for his next book."

A hush fell around the table. They all tried to look as if they might have been the author, but none of them owned up to it. Ben knew better than to ask his host to allow him sight of this stupendous book on a Sunday. He would have to come back in the morning when the shop was open.

Weaving home with a belly full of punch and beer, he thought not so much about the thousand pounds but what it would mean to be revealed as the author of a literary sensation. Lionised by the best society, painted by an Academician, introduced at Court – he could not understand why any author would turn all of this down.

No women approached him on Blackfriars Bridge, or if they did he was too preoccupied to notice them.

Four

Who would have thought that book lovers could be so warlike? They jammed themselves around Mr Dowling's door, ignoring the fact that six people could not pass through a space wide enough for two, dealing out spiteful jabs and sly blows to one another. The stationer, watchmaker and music seller stood on their own doorsteps complaining loudly about the crowd that made it impossible for their customers to pass.

Ben joined the fray and, taking advantage of the small gap created as two men burst out of the shop, managed to squeeze inside. He squinted through a mass of bobbing heads, crooked wigs and clamouring mouths until he located Dowling sheltering behind his table. The shop did not have a long counter, which might have made a more effective barricade. The pressure of people had pushed the table back and, if it had not been rammed against a small bookcase, there would have been no sanctuary for the bookseller at all. Crushed in beside him, Tom and his fellow apprentice, Sam, struggled to keep hold of a dwindling pile of books.

"I am sorry, Your Lordship!" Dowling shouted hoarsely. "These copies are all reserved. If you would care to add your name to the list, I will personally deliver the book to you as soon as it is available. Sam, make a note of His Lordship's address."

Sam pulled a quill from behind his ear and added it to the entries in the book on the desk.

"But you are putting his name before mine!" bawled a city

merchant, jostling His Lordship's elbow. "Is my money not as good as his, though it's earned by my own labours?"

Sam looked scared and doubled his writing speed.

Dowling waved the complainant aside. A young servant girl timidly held out a purse.

"Did your mistress not send you with a ticket? I am sorry. I cannot release the book unless you bring me the ticket."

"But I've got the m-money," the girl whimpered.

Dowling had already turned away from her to deal with someone else. She burst into tears, adding a dreadful keening to the uproar.

By this time, Ben had reached the front of the queue. He ducked down and crawled under the girl's skirts, at which she set up a greater shrieking than ever. Emerging on the other side of her lumpy knees, he slithered under the table, struggled to his feet, snatched *An Account of a Voyage to the Fair Land* from His Lordship's footman and clambered onto the table.

"Ladies and Gentlemen!" he bellowed. "If you have a ticket, please wait on this side of the shop. If you have not yet put your name down for a copy, please move to the right and Sam will come round and make a note of your details. Tickets only on this side... Yes, sir, every printing machine between here and London Wall is rattling off copies as we speak... No, madam, to the right if you wish to put your name down."

"Mr Dearlove!" Dowling gazed up at the young man in grateful surprise. "Thank heaven! I did not think I could withstand the siege much longer."

"After all your kindness to me, it's the least I can do," Ben said cheerfully. "Sam, take their details. Tom, stand in front of the table and get them to form a line. Don't hand out any more books until they have."

The boys, following Ben's route, scrambled off. Ben jumped

down and squeezed himself in beside Dowling. Gripping the table, he firmly pushed it forward to make enough space for Mr Dowling to sink into his chair.

Once order was restored, the customers settled down to wait patiently. This was a bookshop after all, and there was plenty to occupy the mind. Some browsed through poetry, novels or history, some leafed through magazines, some ran their eyes over the shelf they happened to be standing by, content with reading the titles.

Ben noticed two men a few places back in the line on the right. He felt that they were behaving very oddly, but he could not decide what gave him that impression. They were both large men. One of them was dressed in a dark brown suit, the seams strained about his shoulders and upper arms. His tricorne hat was devoid of button or braid – plain, almost anonymous clothes. He had a long, large face set on a broad neck, but his mouth and eyes were disproportionately small. This meanness of his features gave him a cruel aspect, though not an unintelligent one. There were brown stains around his nostrils, and when he raised his hand to tug at his collar Ben saw similar staining on the thumb and forefinger. He also saw that he had mighty knuckles and strong, thick fingers. As he drew closer to the table, Ben caught a whiff of the peppery smell of snuff.

The other man had tucked his black, beribboned hat under his arm, revealing thinning hair tied back in a wispy pigtail. Though slighter than his companion, he was more muscular, with a boxer's physique he was evidently proud of. His well-fitted blue jacket was enlivened by an embroidered silk waistcoat emphasising the flatness of his stomach and the breadth of his chest.

If Ben had seen them in a quayside tavern, he would not have looked at them twice. But here they stood, books behind them, books to the side of them, books before them – and not one glance did they cast upon the shelves. 'Pigtail' pulled a knot of tobacco from his coat pocket. Ben caught a glimpse of a small knife in his other hand. 'Pigeyes' shook his head. Sighing, Pigtail put the blade and chaw away. Assuredly, the pair were out of place in a bookshop!

Ben had averted a riot and was now at liberty to study the literary sensation. Mr Dowling smiled in assent when he took up the display copy, with its pages already cut. He leaned against the wall behind the bookseller's chair, opened the book and read:

An Account of a Voyage to the Fair Land
by a Gentleman

There can be no greater undertaking for a man of courage than to set off on a voyage of discovery into uncharted or partially charted seas, with only his gallant ship between him and the awful depths, the hearts and sinews of an untried crew to sail his vessel, and the fidelity of his friends and companions on the voyage to keep his purpose alive. A leader of men he must be, a good man and brave he must be, a man of hope and wisdom, a man able to endure the smallest discomforts and the greatest dangers. Such a man was Captain Braveman.

Of the other gentlemen on the voyage, only Mr Noble was his equal in courage and determination, although, as Braveman generously acknowledged, his superior in education, having long ago surpassed his teachers in mathematics, languages and natural philosophy. With Mr Noble travelled his draughtsman and secretary, young men both, and entirely dedicated to their master's restless cause. Such were the men who, many years ago but still in living memory, set sail from England in the Miranda.

Miranda! Ben thought. Where have I heard that name before? It's the name the woman in Covent Garden called out when I was trying to shield her from every buck on the Piazza. Well, well, what a coincidence.

"What name shall I put?" Sam's voice piped.

"Mr 'Ay," rumbled back the answer. Ben looked up and saw that Sam was talking to Pigeyes.

"Mr Hay," Sam repeated. "And the address?"

"No address. We'll collect it. When do you say it will be ready?"

"Thursday." Sam handed over their ticket. Pig… Mr Hay held it close to his face and examined it as if he suspected a cheat. His friend looked on, nodding wisely at the paper. Ben guessed that Pigtail could not read or that reading was a great, slow effort for him.

Ben had not marked his place with his finger and his attention was called back to the book, where the stiff new pages fanning softly shut sent out flickers of colour. The book was illustrated. He remembered Parmeter had praised the pictures. Ben leafed through the prints of fabulous creatures invented for a fabulous tale, all very cleverly contrived to look like genuine botanical plates. Who had ever seen a blue fish? Could there exist such enormous, fierce-looking blooms as these, spotted as if with a hundred cruel eyes, the stamens hanging out like slavering tongues? These writhing sea-dragons and snakes were straight from Hakluyt. And this orange wading bird, with its impossibly brittle legs and the peacock-blue stripes around its eyes…

"It seems to be in order," Hay said, pocketing his ticket.

He turned away from Sam but when Ben gasped, "I know that picture!" he stopped and stared at the young man. Perhaps Hay believed that he could hear Ben's thoughts if he stared hard enough. If he had had that power, he would have struggled to understand the barely coherent tumble of ideas passing through Ben's mind.

This is the picture the sick woman at the play was working on, Ben thought excitedly. She wasn't copying those natural history books – she was studying them to make her drawings more authentic. But my word, what a skill she has! And how they exactly match the descriptions in the text! She actually read the book – how many illustrators do that? The manuscript must have been in her possession while she was working.

So the author – this secretive, shy author who won't even reveal his name to his publisher – entrusted her with his work. Would he put his work in the hands of a hack he didn't know if he wanted his secret kept? He wouldn't. The secretive Gentleman and the artistic Lady must be known to one another. Friends? Lovers? No, it would be like caressing a sack of bones. Friends then. Acquaintances at the very least.

Ben's reasoning brought him to a triumphant conclusion: she knows him! She knows the name of the author of *An Account of a Voyage to the Fair Land*. And she's living in a hovel and Dowling will pay a fortune for the next book. She could name her own price for doing the illustrations for that. And, anyway, I helped her once so why shouldn't she tell me in return who he is? And I won't have to go home when my allowance stops – I won't have to be an apothecary – I can stay in London!

"Mr Dowling," he cried, "you said that you wanted to know the author! If anyone were to discover his identity, could he expect to earn a reward?"

"Discover his identity?" Dowling repeated, twisting round in his chair. "Why should anyone discover his identity but the gentleman himself?"

A shadow fell across them and Ben was startled by a pair

of tiny eyes gleaming at him from under the brim of a hat. Impertinent, he thought, and shifted irritably to shut out Hay.

"But if he is too shy, surely the person who led you to him would deserve some compensation for his troubles?"

"Yes, I suppose he would. But, Dearlove, you aren't saying that..."

"Sorry, Mr Dowling! No time to talk now. I shall be back later this afternoon!"

In the daylight, the courtyard appeared squalid, full of litter, the cobbles splashed with dubious stains. In one corner, a rubbish tip attracted scavenging dogs, cats and rats. Children played around the water pump, women gossiped over their washing lines. There were few men around – these were not families who had sunk to the lowest level of poverty. There was still a breadwinner, even if bread was sometimes all he could put on the table.

The door to the house where the women lived stood open. Ben pushed his way past the grubby children sitting on the step, ignoring their pleas for money. The hall and stairs were not much lighter in the daytime than they had been the first time he saw them. He ran up the stairs, remembered that theirs was the door in the middle of the landing, and knocked loudly. There was no reply, but he fancied – for no other reason than he was impatient of disappointment – that there was someone inside. He knocked again.

A door in the murk at the end of the corridor opened and a woman glared out at him. She was a threadbare person with faded hairpieces attached to her own worn-out hair, patched shoes and a napless woollen skirt.

"What do you want to make all that noise for? They're not in."

Ben took off his hat. "Do you know when they will be back?"

The woman curled her thin lips. "Do you think I stand here all day watching their comings and goings?"

Ben thought it very likely. "Would you give them a message?"

The woman shook her head and stepped back.

"Here's a shilling for your trouble," he cried hastily, resigning himself to its outlay by regarding it as an investment to be amply realised when Dowling had his author. She snatched it from him and dropped it in her pocket. "Tell her that Ben Dearlove called with a message which is greatly to her advantage. I will call tomorrow at the same time and will be much obliged if she will receive me."

He was sure the woman had not grasped the polite tone of the message, but she had the substance of it and that would have to do. She returned to her room and he left the house. He did not see the man who stepped out of the building after him, spitting a plug of tobacco in a high arc over the children's heads.

When he entered the corridor the next day, he noticed a faint strip of sunshine coming from under the door, the line broken into a restless pattern of dark and light. There was someone moving about inside. Good! He raised his hand to knock.

"Bugger it. She's run, Beale."

Startled to hear a man's voice, and such a rough one, Ben hesitated. The voice carried clearly – the door was ajar. In fact, it could not be fastened for the lock had been unscrewed with the plate, lock and handle removed. Housebreakers, at least two of them. This was no time to play the hero, even if he had been inclined to do so – which he was not. But neither was he inclined to tiptoe away and call for help.

"Just haul out this table," the man said.

Grunts and the scraping of furniture. A pause. Then, "What now?" Beale, presumably.

"Back to the office to see if His Lordship's got any more orders for us."

Just in time, Ben dodged into the shadows at the end of the corridor. There was nowhere to hide, but the men did not look around as they pulled the door behind them and moved off. He crept after them and peered into the stairwell at the descending tops of a triangular brown hat and a black hat with a pigtail beneath it. The front door was open and the pair left the house as they had arrived, without being seen by anyone else.

Ben pushed open the damaged door. Like professional burglars, the men had left the cupboards and drawers gaping open after looking inside them. He saw at a glance that they were all empty. There was not one scrap of paper, torn receipt or crumpled sketch to give any clue as to where the women had gone.

But he knew who the men were. They had been in the shop yesterday when he told Mr Dowling that he could find out the identity of the author of *An Account of a Voyage to the Fair Land*. They were Pigeyes and Pigtail – Hay and Beale. They had eavesdropped on his conversation and they had followed him here with the intention of discovering the author before he did. They had beaten him to one discovery at least – the women had disappeared.

Five

"But why, if they followed me from the shop to Poland Street on Monday, did they wait until Tuesday to search the room?"

"Mmm," mumbled Campbell. "Do you want that bread?"

"I've got an idea about it. They said they were going to see if 'His Lordship' had any more orders for them. 'Any more orders', d'ye see? They were acting under orders. On Monday, they didn't have any instructions to search the woman's lodging, but by Tuesday, they did. I knew they weren't at the shop buying the book for themselves. Gin shop, yes. Bookshop, no. I doubt the lesser brute can read. His Lordship sent them to the shop, and His Lordship sent them back to Poland Street. So, who is His Lordship?"

Campbell, busily dipping the bread into the gravy on Ben's plate, shrugged. "London is full of Lordships, both foreign and home-grown."

"Ah, yes, but what if he isn't really a lord? What if 'His Lordship' is the alias of a master criminal? Those men looked like desperados to me."

Campbell laughed. "I don't think master criminals and literature go together. There's no money in books as a general rule. More beer?"

"No. Yes… and now the woman has gone, and without her I'll never know who the author is."

"Parmeter said the illustrator was the author."

"Oh no, she couldn't be."

"Women do write books, Ben. I wonder how often Anon turns out to be a woman? They're not above lying about their sex either."

"No woman ever launched a volume on the world without apologising for it first. 'Took up my pen with no thought of publication... Nothing but the necessity to provide for a young family could have induced me to lay this trifle before the public... Beg the reader will look kindly upon it for all its demerits.' There's no hint of that in *A Voyage to the Fair Land*. The style is too bold, too rational, the scope of the book too wide. This is no female epic of lovers, fops, thoughtless heiresses and foolish parents. That pagan pizzle – no, no woman could have written that."

"Or only a very interesting one."

"Not the woman I met."

"The woman who was on her own in the theatre and persuaded you to take her home and give her money? If you say so. Anyway, you're no worse off and they're no better off, and that's the end of it."

The maid brought their second jug of beer and carried off the plates. Campbell refilled their glasses and leaned back with a sigh of contentment. "There's nothing better than lingering over your dinner when there are people waiting to get in!" he crowed, raising his drink to the legs and ankles on the other side of the barred window above his head. The queue extended out of the basement chophouse all the way up the staircase and straggled along the street. There was a constant movement up and down the stairs as those who had finished their meals squeezed past those who were waiting to eat, risking lost buttons, tangled swords and dishevelled wigs.

Ordinarily, Ben would have agreed with Campbell. Having had their turn of sniffing hungrily at the hot food, there was something pleasant in relishing their hard-won place at table. Instead, he said, "Perhaps His Lordship is a wealthy connoisseur, anxious to find the author of *A Voyage to the Fair Land* and offer him patronage. Or a publisher, trying to poach him from Dowling. Only then you'd think they'd call him 'The Publisher', not 'His Lordship'."

Campbell banged his glass on the table. "Ben, I really can't endure much more of this. If you are so anxious to know more about your spies..."

"Spies! That's it, they are spies. The woman must be a spy too – she's got a foreign servant. She's in the pay of the French..."

"And I expect *A Voyage to the Fair Land* is a coded description of every British ship of the line, including number of guns, crew, tonnage," Campbell snapped.

The men at the next table turned their startled faces toward the Scot. Someone muttered, "Jacobite."

Campbell lowered his voice. "What I was going to say was, if you are so interested, why don't you go to the shop and wait for them to come in and collect their order? You did say Thursday, didn't you? Then you can follow them and find out who their mysterious employer is."

"Of course!" Ben jumped to his feet. "Aren't you coming?"

"Not while there's ale left in the pot. Don't worry about the bill. I'm rich now, after the sale of my poem."

Ben did not insult his friend by refusing the offer. He had paid for Campbell's dinners on many occasions and knew that, although Campbell played the part of careless scrounger with such apparent relish, his dependence on the generosity of others was a secret humiliation. Besides, he understood the nature of Campbell's wealth. In a day or two, his money would be spent, new bills contracted for old, and paying for cooked dinners would be a thing of the past. Ben left him to his transient enjoyment.

The shop was empty except for the apprentice, Tom. He was slumped in the chair behind the desk, his legs thrust out under the table and crossed at the ankles, his hands trailing on the floor and his mouth in a sulky downturn. He sat up when the doorbell rang, but when he saw it was only one of Mr Dowling's authors sank back again.

"Oh, Mr Dearlove, it's been non-stop this morning," he complained. "This is the first opportunity I've had to draw breath, and Mr Dowling has only just gone out to snatch a bite of dinner. It's very late for him, which doesn't agree with his constitution, so I expect he'll be bilious this afternoon."

Ben, frowning sympathetically, picked up a copy of *A Voyage to the Fair Land*. "This is the second edition, eh, Tom?"

"Came in this morning, and most of them have gone already. Sam's been out making deliveries. Trust him to get the easiest part."

"Well, you have the best manner with the customers." Ben looked down at the order book, twisting his neck to read it upside down. Most of the names were crossed through. "Have all the books that were ordered been collected?"

"Mostly." Tom yawned.

"It looks like an efficient system. I presume these names with lines through have been for their book?"

Tom grunted assent and watched apathetically as Ben turned the pages.

"I notice," Ben said in what he hoped was an unconcerned manner, "that there is a cross through Mr Hay's name. He has already been in?"

"Don't remember him in particular."

"A big man. Came in on Monday to order his copy."

"I don't remember anyone of that kind."

"Well then, was it a pugilistic man in a patterned waistcoat?"

Tom shook his head. "Don't remember anyone of that kind either."

"But their book has gone? So someone has collected it. I don't suppose you have any way of knowing who it was, or where the book went?"

Tom pulled the book towards him and perused the entry for a moment. "Oh, that one." A sly look came over his face. "But I don't know if I ought to tell you, Mr Dearlove."

"Buy yourself a drink, Tom," said Ben, handing over the money he would have spent on his dinner had it not been Campbell's treat.

"Thank you, Mr Dearlove. A messenger called for their book." Tom glanced down in disgust at his own drab jacket. "Lovely and smart he was in his livery, and in such a rush too." He looked wistfully at the door. "Running here and there all over the town."

"A messenger? From where?"

The doorbell jangled. Tom rose to attend to the lady who entered with her footman. "The Admiralty," he hissed over his shoulder.

The lady picked up a novel and peeped at Ben over the pages. "Do you have Miss Lee's novel, I mean Miss Sophia Lee?" she cooed. "I believe it is entitled *The Recess*. I think there can be very few historical characters as romantic as Mary Queen of Scots."

Her honeyed tones disturbed only the air about her lips. Ben's head was full of harsher voices. "Let's go back to the office to see if His Lordship's got any more orders for us," Hay had said while he and Beale searched the Poland Street rooms.

An Admiralty Lord? What interest could an Admiralty

Lord have in the book? *An Account of a Voyage to the Fair Land* was nothing but a fabrication from start to finish. What Admiralty official would be interested in a voyage that had never been made, in a ship that never existed?

A delirious woman had murmured, "Miranda," and he had demanded, "Who is Miranda? Someone at home?" A servant, or a sister, or an aged aunt? A close friend? A landlady? A daughter... Or a ship?

"Do you know any sailors, Campbell?" Ben pushed his empty cup away, the drink swallowed but not tasted. It was early evening and they were sitting in a booth in the Chapter House coffee shop.

"Why, you're not thinking of running away to sea, are you?"

"No. I'm interested in a ship though. Well, a possible ship."

Campbell laid down his newspaper, picked up his dish and blew on his coffee. "What is a possible ship?"

"I want to find out if the Navy owns a particular vessel."

A red, spotty face appeared at Campbell's shoulder. "Have you finished with that paper, sir?"

"No, I haven't."

"Well, Oatmeal, you aren't reading it," the stranger snarled, thrusting his erupting face closer.

"And I doubt that you *can* read it."

"Don't be so uncivil to your betters, or I'll give you a thrashing you won't forget."

"Better at what? Fuddling your head?"

"Give him the paper," Ben said. "Can't you see the man is drunk?"

"Drunk?" roared Pimple Face, tottering towards Ben in a spirituous haze. "Do you call me drunk?"

"Campbell," Ben pleaded.

"Really, the people they let into the Chapter House these days. Very well, take the paper." Campbell thrust it into the man's hand. "And have another glass of punch," he added. The man, pleased with his crumpled acquisition, ignored this parting shot and rolled off to the next booth to fall asleep over the news.

"The sailor?" Ben prompted.

"I do happen to know a sailor. He's a half-pay lieutenant who spends most of his evenings in one of the taverns near the Navy Office in Broad Street. I'll introduce you if you go and get me a copy of the *Gentleman's Magazine*. It's your fault I have nothing to read now."

Ben fetched the publication from the other side of the room.

"Mrs Seward is at it again!" Campbell grimaced, scanning the contents. "Tell me, Ben, which side do you take, Dryden's or Pope's?"

"Neither... when can I see the lieutenant?"

"But you must have an opinion. Mrs Seward's defence of modern poetry is engaging the keenest minds in the land." Campbell smirked. "You don't want to look like an ignorant oaf when *this* subject comes up at Dowling's dinner table."

"I don't care what Mrs Seward thinks of Dryden. When can I see him?"

"You don't care what Mrs Seward thinks? Mrs Seward, the Swan of Lichfield? The Queen Muse of Britain? The friend of Dr Johnson? The celebrated author of an *Elegy on Captain Cook*?"

"Campbell!"

"What do you want to see a sailor for anyway?"

"I discovered that the men who followed me are connected with the Admiralty."

"I thought it might have something to do with that."

Campbell sighed and put his journal aside. "Very well. What is your reasoning now?"

"That it explains 'His Lordship'. Someone at the Admiralty wants to find out who wrote *An Account of a Voyage to the Fair Land*. Now, why should an Admiralty Lord be interested in the book?"

"For the same reason you are. To make a bit of money by discovering the author."

"An Admiralty Lord is hardly likely to be that short of money. No." Ben crossed his arms on the table and leaned forward confidentially. "Imagine, Campbell, what it would mean if a British ship had discovered a new country in the South Seas. A country rich in timber, spices, foodstuffs... silver and gold for all we know! Now, further suppose that the ship was called *Miranda*, but she never came home with the news of her discovery. Then one day – no, hear me out – a book appears telling the story of the *Miranda*. Someone in the Admiralty reads the book and recognises the name. So, it seems that someone survived the voyage to write about it. Who is going to be more interested in finding out who he is than the Admiralty?"

"I think your imagination has caught a distemper from preposterous Parmeter."

"But the men were reporting to His Lordship."

Campbell leaned back in his chair with the air of a man settling down for a long and difficult debate. "Very well, if there was a voyage and if there is a survivor, why all this secrecy? Why pretend his book is fiction?"

"I don't know. Perhaps he's a deserter. Perhaps he has debts. Perhaps he abandoned his wife and children. Perhaps he's a murderer."

"Then why write the book at all?"

"He needed money? Voyage narratives always sell well. He just dressed his up as fiction so no one could discover him."

"Then why use the ship's real name?"

"An oversight? An author's attachment to some veracity in his work? He ran out of ideas for names and he didn't think anyone would notice?"

"Ben, not only is *Miranda* a made-up name, it's a damned plagiarised one too."

"What do you mean?"

"Shakespeare. *The Tempest*. Trust me, I have come to know a great many of the playwright's obscurities over the last few weeks."

Ben shook his head. "Dowling will pay a fortune to be the one who publishes the author's next book. If I can find the ship, perhaps I can find the author too."

"Find the ship and sail to the moon in her as well I suppose? Bless me, you are a numps sometimes!"

"For the sake of asking one simple question, Campbell," Ben pleaded. "It's not as if you are averse to spending a night in a tavern. I'll pay for the drinks. And if I discover that there never was a ship called *Miranda*, I promise I will never mention it again."

Campbell laughed. "I'd make a wager on the outcome but I'd only be robbing you. Very well. I'm engaged tonight, but I'll take you to The Three Bells tavern tomorrow."

They say that the noise of the guns on board a ship can deafen a man. Entering The Three Bells the following evening, Ben felt much as those gunners must feel – locked into a confined space with a hideous din. Every seat was taken by a naval man, every naval man had a brimming glass before him, and every naval eye was turned towards a red-haired, freckle-faced Scot who stood in the middle of the room beating time with an empty mug. The one exception amongst all these attentive mates, midshipmen and masters was a fat surgeon lolling between his companions on a long bench. He was dead to the world, and oblivious to the cork moustache daubed on his face.

The Scot was bawling a song:

Sailors they get all the money,
Soldiers they get none but brass;
I do love a jolly sailor...

"Now squawk it out, boys!" His tuneless choir opened their mouths, revealing the most uneven distribution of teeth Ben had ever seen. One pair of sailors, arms linked in comradeship, had only one incisor between them.

And soldiers they can kiss my arse!

The maestro caught sight of Ben and Campbell, the only two landsmen in the place. His red-rimmed eyes widened with blood-freezing effect. "Here's a couple of lubberly sons of whores! Come in here, would you, you blockheads? Well, gi'us ten shillings to buy the company a drink and perhaps I'll let you pass."

This did not seem a particularly friendly greeting between fellow Scotsmen but Ben supposed it was nothing more than badinage. "Your friend doesn't seem to remember you," he muttered.

"He's not the man we've come to see. I've never seen him before," Campbell whispered back. He raised his voice. "I'm looking for Lieutenant Brine."

The singer winked at his audience. "He's the shaver that's busting his hoops over there." The men laughed, the surgeon slobbered, and the Scot stepped aside to reveal a shabby, middle-aged man hunched in the corner by the bar. He was far from busting his hoops or anything else with merriment. Nature had fitted out his long, lugubrious face for misery; temperament and circumstance had perfected the image. Recognising Campbell, he raised his glass forlornly, and with an apathetic wave of his hand invited them to approach his table.

"I warn you, he likes his grog," Campbell hissed. "Don't try to match him drink for drink. I don't want to carry you home... Mr Brine! How do you do?"

"Very well, Mr Campbell," Brine answered, in the tone of a man whose physician had just told him he has a week left to live.

"Right, lads!" the musician behind them bellowed. "*I hate this damned watching and trudging the deck...*" and another song began.

"Will you take a drink with us?" Campbell asked.

"Rum and water. Make it half and half," the lieutenant added as the landlord reached for the glasses.

Ben glanced at the landlord, but quickly turned away for fear of giving offence. The man's face and hands were a grisly mesh of scabs and scars. He looked as if he had been in more battles than every sailor in His Majesty's Navy put together.

"My friend here has a question to put to you," said Campbell after the introductions had been made.

Ben wiped away the tears the rum brought to his eyes. "I'm trying to find out about a ship I have recently heard of."

"That's easy," Brine answered, pulling a battered book out of his pocket. "Steel's List. Every ship in service. As you see," he added bitterly, "it's a thin book. There aren't many vessels in commission at the moment. I buy it every month, hoping to see my name move up, but I'm no closer to getting a ship than the day I passed my lieutenant's examination ten years ago. It is just my luck to be caught in this damned peace. While there's no war, there's no chance for promotion."

"Your turn will come, I'm sure of it," Campbell soothed. "The other fellows can't hang on forever. You'll be an Admiral before you know it."

Brine grunted. "What's the ship called?"

"*Miranda*," said Ben.

Brine flicked through the pages. "No, not listed."

"I think she was lost some years ago."

Brine put his book away. "Can't help then."

"I think you can. The Admiralty keeps records of all its ships?"

"Of course."

"It's impossible for me to go and look at those records. But you're a naval officer. You could go and look for me."

"I go and look?" Brine repeated. "I go to the Admiralty without an appointment? I go to the Admiralty without being summoned? D'you think that their Lordships would let me, a mere half-pay lieutenant, grub amongst their papers? I have no interest with the Board and even if I had, I cannot afford to pay the price the porters would demand to let me in. The highest, most arrogant sons of bitches in the Navy… it can't be done. His Majesty's ships are His Majesty's business. There's nothing to be done."

Ben could not face Campbell's triumph. He stared glumly at the guttering candle on the table.

Brine took a swig of his drink. "You could try Lloyd's."

"Lloyd's?"

"If she was lost at sea, it might have been reported in their shipping lists."

"It's a good idea," Ben said. "But how much do you think they are likely to charge me to look at them?"

"Charge you? Nothing. I'll write to my cousin. He's a subscriber. On the rich side of the family, though his grandfather was born on the wrong side of the blanket. By rights, the money should have stayed with our branch. Lawyers! I'd put every one of 'em in a ship and scuttle her, so I would."

Ben, fearing that Brine was about to settle into a long, ranting family history, signalled to the landlord to refill the mariner's glass. "It's very kind of you. Are you sure your cousin won't mind?"

"Not he. Likes doing me the occasional favour. Eases his conscience after stealing my inheritance. Where can a letter reach you?"

"George Street. Thank you, Mr Brine."

Six

When thinking of London's attractions, many people listed Covent Garden with its theatre and coffee houses, where they could eavesdrop on famous actors, opera singers and impresarios. Or they contemplated a stroll down Oxford Street, especially at night when it was lit by double rows of lamps and they could saunter from window to window ogling arrangements of guns, china, glass, silks, shoes and watches. Or they might think of the magnificent westerly squares built by the nobility, where by night and day lacquered coaches flitted from dinners to card parties to routs.

But Ben liked the City. For him, London's greatest attractions lay in the shadow of St Paul's, where every other person he passed in the street was a printer, poet or bookseller. There, in St Paul's Churchyard was Mr Dowling's shop, and in Paternoster Row the Chapter Coffee House. He even liked those parts of the City where literature had no place. He enjoyed the atmosphere of industry and enterprise, watching people hurry from office to coffee shop and back again.

The Royal Exchange, wedged between Cornhill and Threadneedle Street and surrounded by a network of alleys, yards and courts, was a bottomless source of interest for Ben. Walking around the Exchange's vaulted colonnade, he indulged himself in his usual game of guessing what business brought people here. That merchant with the ferocious face, striding out of the shadows, had just discovered the bill in his hand was a forgery and he was ruined; the penniless lord with whom he had contracted for his daughter's hand would not honour the agreement now. A mean-looking fellow sitting on a bench, rubbing his hands and chuckling to himself, celebrated the news that a wealthy relative had just died and left him enough to keep his crooked business afloat for another day. The messenger boy with a bundle of papers under his arms, the seals clacking as he clattered down the steps from the upper gallery, ran so eagerly at his master's bidding now but dreamed of being the captain of a ship in the future.

Ben's inventiveness, and almost Ben himself, were brought to a sudden end by an advancing chair. He skipped out of the way as, with a great deal of bumping and scraping, the chairmen manoeuvred into Lloyd's Coffee House. An outraged shriek drifted from the building. "No chairs! No sedan chairs in the Rooms!"

"What do you mean, no chairs?" came the answering drawl from inside the conveyance. A panted "Where the 'ell shall we put it then?" came from the front. The sweating, swearing chairmen backed out of the doorway, their fare exhorting them to "Have a care!" and "Don't bump so!" They were followed by the doorman, shaking his fist at the ousted vehicle.

Ben slipped into the building and waited for the doorman, still bristling from the altercation, to return and despatch a giggling boy to fetch Lieutenant Brine's cousin. Five minutes later, the underwriter skipped lightly down the stairs, a notable achievement for a man of his rotundity. Whereas the Lieutenant had been ponderous in his gestures and slow and heavy in his speech, Valentine Brine danced and chattered as if he was the merest slip of a thing.

"Delighted to be of service, Mr Dearlove! Roderick... excuse me, I call him Roderick because we were closer than brothers when we were boys, closer than brothers… Roderick told me that you wished to consult our archives. Of course I told him they are as open to you – and by extension your friends – as my mother's mansion was when we were children. The Lord knows it did him good to get away from that insanitary little terrace in Portsmouth. Taylor, have you signed our young friend in? Then let us go up."

Under the high ceiling of Lloyd's Coffee Room, waiters scurried back and forth with jugs of coffee and chocolate, armfuls of paper and writing materials. Counting-house clerks ran in and out with messages for their employers. Each of the booths around the wall had its complement of men talking, writing or reading the newspapers. The honest men leaned back in their seats, puffed comfortably on their pipes, conversed unashamedly of percents and profits. Others huddled together and bartered insurance policies on ships that had already sunk, valued a cargo of brimstone as a cargo of silk, or declared a rotten hull and defunct equipment A1.

While Ben was making sense of the noisy, crowded chamber one of the wall clocks struck the hour. The door through which he and Brine had just entered burst open and a boy pelted in waving a sheaf of papers. Behind the lad trotted a waiter ringing a handbell and shouting, "Silence! Silence!"

The youth ran up wooden steps into a pulpit-like arrangement beneath the still-chiming timepiece. As the last note died away, his high voice broke the obedient hush. "Just in from The Downs. The *Swift* has gone down off Tenerife. Cargo lost. Thirty drowned."

The room echoed with groans. Ben was about to remark on the gentlemen's compassion when Brine stopped in front of a door. A sign read 'Subscribers and their connections only are to be admitted into the within room'. A waiter stood sentinel in front of this impressive portal, making sure that only those who had paid for the privilege gained entry. He turned the handle and let Brine and his guest through. The door shut behind them on the investors' continued lamentations. "We'll have to pay out, we'll have to pay out!"

The noise of the crowded public room scarcely penetrated the subscribers' sanctum. Here, orders were given in whispers, waiters tiptoed to obey them, and the loudest sound was the occasional rustle of a newspaper. It was an opulent chamber, more like a gentleman's library than a place of business, with cushioned armchairs, elbow tables, sideboards and bookcases. Silver and glassware glinted on the polished surfaces. Three chandeliers hung from the ceiling, the crystal canopies reflected in a gilt mirror over the fireplace. On the wall by the door hung a list of the subscribers' names, printed on vellum and framed. A large green book lay open on a stand.

"*The* book," Brine explained in an awed whisper, "in which all ships' losses and arrivals are recorded."

They crept past the dozing capitalists into a committee room with a long, gleaming table. No one was sitting there now, but from the walls paintings of the committee members kept watch over their places. From here, an obscure door opened into a bare room, uncarpeted and uncurtained, with a couple of cheap candles on a dusty mantelpiece over an empty hearth. Deed boxes were piled against the wall under an ugly, loud clock. The only furniture was a high, battered desk with a hard wooden chair fixed to it where a clerk scratched his way through piles of letters and insurance agreements.

"Creech, here's that friend of Cousin Roderick's I told you about. You are to give him all the help he needs."

"Oh yes, sir, Cousin Roderick's friend, sir."

The old man clambered down from his seat. Although naturally tall, years of being crammed into his desk had bent his back and bowed his legs. He spoke with the dusty wheeze of a man who breathed nothing but particles of paper and parchment. His eyes, weakened by straining in poor light, focused slowly on Ben.

"What is it *precisely* that you want?" Creech said 'precisely' lovingly, lingeringly, as if in that one word was epitomised his entire creed and philosophy.

Ben had devised a story that he thought more plausible than the tale of the *Miranda*. "I'm writing a history of trade in the South Seas. I'd like some information about the vessels that sailed there, where they were built, their construction, crews, that sort of thing. It would give my readers some background to our great British endeavours in the southern part of the globe."

"You won't find much of that sort of detail in the Register," Creech said doubtfully. "They only record a ship's movements, nothing of her origins."

"It's a good place for me to start," Ben answered. "Once I've got a few names I can find out more later." This was true, though there was only one name he was interested in.

"I have business to attend to," Brine interposed. "If I could leave you with Creech, Mr Dearlove?"

When he had gone Creech took Ben into a dim inner closet. It contained a table and chair and was lined with roughly-made shelves piled high with papers – rolled-up maps, age-spotted notices of auctions-by-candle, yellowing newssheets and mouldering broadsides. What odd things people argue about, Ben thought, ruffling through the pamphlets. The vices of Irish haymakers who flocked to the capital on the pretext of looking for work, objections to a charity house for exposed girl babies, demands for the banning of pig keeping in Charing Cross, diatribes on the overcrowding of London's graveyards with their stinking, half-covered burial pits...

Ben tore his gaze away from these tantalising subjects when Creech, who stood by a shelf that sagged beneath a number of thick ledgers, said, "Here are the shipping Registers, bound into volumes by date. Of course, our records only go back as far as 1769. If you wanted anything before that you'd be looking at Old Lloyd's. Their shipping list started in the 1730s."

Ben stared at him blankly. "Old Lloyd's? Do you mean there are two Lloyd's?"

"We are New Lloyd's. The original Lloyd's was established by Mr Edward over a hundred years ago. It remained a family business for some time, but when gambling was introduced to the Lombard Street premises in the 1760s our Subscribers set up their own establishment in Pope's Head Alley. But that house was most unsuitable for our Subscribers. We moved here in '74."

"Is Old Lloyd's still in Lombard Street?"

"They went out of business four years ago."

And Creech's books only went back twenty years! It would not be much of a Pacific history that started only twenty years ago. Ben was not much of a historian either, for surely he should have found out about New and Old Lloyd's before he came. He had the uncomfortable feeling that these were Creech's thoughts too. He turned away to hide his embarrassment, hung his hat on the corner of the chair and said briskly, "I shall begin."

"I shall be next door. Summon me if you require anything."

"Could I have a light?"

"No candles are allowed in here."

Left to himself, Ben rubbed a circle of grime from the window with his sleeve. It left his cuff filthy, and let in very little extra light. He glowered at the numbers on the spines of the registers.

"Dates!" he muttered. "I never thought about dates. All I know is that if there was a ship called *Miranda* she set sail, according to *A Voyage to the Fair Land*, 'many years ago but still in living memory'. But whose living memory? Mine? Creech's? He looks as if he's been here since Mr Edward's days."

In the other room, a metal box scraped over the wooden floorboards. A lid creaked open, papers rustled, a lid clanged shut. It occurred to Ben that his own silence would arouse the clerk's suspicion. For want of a better place to start, he pulled down the first volume.

The table groaned under the weight of it, as did Ben himself after a brief examination. Each newssheet gave on its cover financial information such as the exchange rates, interest on annuities and the price of stocks. Then came the weather news. Over the page were announcements of shipping arrivals and departures, together with details of naval manoeuvres, shipwrecks and prizes. The first New Lloyd's List had been issued from Pope's Head Alley and was dated Tuesday 28 March 1769, a few days after the secession from Lombard Street. Since then, a new List had appeared every Tuesday and Friday. There were one hundred and four Lists a year. If he started at the beginning – and where else could he start? – Ben would have to read two thousand and eighty newssheets to bring himself up to the present day.

As if that was not daunting enough, the shipping information was listed by port of embarkation. Ben had no idea where the *Miranda* had sailed from, so he would have to read the entries for ports from Hull to Dover. He imagined Campbell's mocking accent, "Try the Royal Port of Lilliput."

The light had all but gone when Creech appeared to tell him that it was time to lock up. Ben raised his aching eyes from the book and slammed it shut. Slotting it back onto the shelf, he noted how many volumes were still left to read. But he had come to a decision. He would not waste any more time on this ridiculous quest. He thanked the old man, took a last look around the room and left, vowing never to return.

*

The next morning he requested a mug of coffee to keep him awake while he worked. He had slept badly. All night long he had been haunted by the ships he read about in the Lists. When he shut his eyes, their names floated before him. *Queen*, *Drake*, *Cabot*, *Minerva*, *Miranda* – no, there had been no *Miranda*. But what if hers was the next name to appear? What if he had abandoned the search when he had only one more page to turn before she would be revealed?

He had turned many more pages by the time the coffee pot was empty. He did not think his constitution could stand any more of the stimulating brew, nor could he concentrate for very much longer on the information before his misted eyes.

Surely I am coming too close to the present day, he thought. *'Many years ago'* must mean further back than this. Campbell was right, I really am a numps sometimes. Of course it's all a fiction and *'Many years ago'* means as much as *'Some few years since'*, *'It was a wild and stormy winter's night'*, or any of the other stock phrases used to open a novel. I'll read just one more sheet... Two more. Five more and then I will give up.

Ben glanced down at the sheet of paper and read, "*The* Bellona *arrived... The Boulogne packet arrived... A Dutch East Indiaman arrived...* Wait! The *Bellona*! *The* Bellona *arrived at Deal from Cape Town, reports that the* Miranda *of Bristol was lost six months ago off Madagascar...* She's here! The *Miranda* is here!" He flicked back the page to the front of the issue and checked the date, read it in a whisper, "Friday 25 August 1780. *'Lost six months ago'* – she must have gone down in March."

He turned back to the shipping page and searched it again as if he feared the lines might have vanished while he was not looking at them. He tilted the book up to his nose, lowered it to the desk, looked away then quickly looked back. The entry was still there. Too excited to sit still, he rose to his feet, crossed the room and repeated the words out loud to the windowpanes, "*The* Miranda *of Bristol was lost six months ago off Madagascar.*" A blank blue sky stared back at him through the glass. "There *was* a ship!" Ben insisted to the firmament. "And she didn't belong to the Navy."

If only the List gave the name of the *Bellona*'s captain or her owner. But who kept lists of captains, except the men or consortia who employed them? Ship owners went in and out of business all the time. Even if he found out who had owned the ship, even if they had records of the captain's name, who was to say Ben would be able to find the captain? He might be dead by now. Or half way around the world commanding another voyage and who would know when, or if, he would be home? And perhaps, after all that, he might have no memory of how he came to report the loss of the *Miranda* nine years ago.

Without that captain Ben was stuck with nothing more than the certainty that the ship had existed. Where had she been? Who had been on board her? If he just had some names it might help.

There was one other place he could look for information about the *Miranda*. Ben frowned at a passing white cloud. "I shall have to go home."

Ben went directly to the coach office and booked himself a place for the following day. He spent the evening packing and putting his rooms in order, and in the morning went to the bank to withdraw next month's allowance. Finally, he called at Mr Dowling's bookshop.

Although he did not expect to make any profit from it, Mr Dowling gave the author a friendly greeting. For once his good nature was rewarded. Ben had come in to make a purchase.

"I have one copy left," Mr Dowling said. "But it is for another customer."

"When will the third print run be ready?"

"At the end of the week."

Ben's face fell. "I have to go away tonight. I really needed to take the book with me."

"I could send you a copy if you leave your address," Mr Dowling suggested.

Ben sighed. "Yes, I suppose that is the best I can do."

He looked so disappointed that Mr Dowling, after a moment's reflection, said, "The book should have been collected two days ago. Her Ladyship has evidently forgotten about it… I could have sold it a dozen times over by now. Why don't you take it and I will put one by for her out of the next lot?"

"Thank you, Mr Dowling!" Ben cried. "One other thing – would you still be willing to pay a fee to whoever found the author?"

Dowling smiled. "Ah, yes. I remember you asked me the other day." He paused. "If the sum demanded were not immoderate."

"What would you consider a moderate amount?"

"What would you?"

"Fifteen per cent of whatever you're going to offer the author?"

"I'm sure we could come to an agreement."

To while away the hours until his coach left at eight o'clock, Ben went to the Chapter Coffee House in search of Campbell. He found his friend sitting in a corner drinking a glass of wine spiced with cinnamon and pepper. If Ben had not been so excited about his own affairs, he might have noticed that the Scot was not engaged in either of his usual coffee house pursuits – reading a newspaper or scribbling.

"Campbell, you will never guess what I have discovered!" Ben cried as he sat down.

Campbell shrugged.

"There was a ship called *Miranda*. She was lost in 1780, but I don't know how or where she had been or who sailed in her, but I know that she was from Bristol, so I'm going home to see if I can find out anything else about her."

"Going to Bristol, are you?" Campbell repeated dully. "Are you sure that is a good idea?"

"Why, what do you mean?"

"Your man does not want to be found. If he did, he would not have written his book anonymously. Why not leave him in peace? You might do him harm with your meddling."

"But I only mean to do him good. As soon as I tell him about Dowling's offer to publish a second book, he'll thank me for it."

"And if he still does not want anyone to know his name? Will you betray him to Dowling then?"

"No, of course not. In that case, I'll keep his secret, but I'll offer to act as go-between for him and Dowling. But I don't see why he should object to being made a wealthy man. Would you?"

Campbell merely looked sullen. At last Ben realised that something was wrong. "What's the matter?"

"I've just come back from Bodley's. I sat up all last night to finish my *Shakespearean Obscurities*, but Bodley refused to pay me this morning. He said no one had asked me to finish the work ahead of time, and it was not convenient to pay me before the due date. I'm out of money."

Ben, who knew Bodley's dingy little bookshop and its owner's stingy nature, was not surprised. It was only luck and no merit of his own that meant Ben's allowance spared him the indignities the impoverished hack had to suffer – and here he was about to set off on a venture that could make him more money in one stroke than Campbell had earned in all the years he had been in London. If anyone deserved good fortune it was Campbell who, having no family to back him, had taken a bigger risk than Ben when he left Edinburgh. The situation was unjust, but Ben had it in his power to redress it.

"Why don't you come with me? We can work together and share the profit."

"There might not be any profit," Campbell said gloomily.

"Perhaps not. But it's an adventure, if nothing else. We'll treat it as a holiday. Come on, Campbell. Come to Bristol with me."

Campbell gulped the last mouthful of his wine. "I can't."

"If it's the fare – "

"You want to make money, not spend it."

"You could pay me back when – "

"No. You're generous, Ben, but I'm poxed. I shan't be going anywhere for the next few weeks."

"Poxed?"

"Gleeted and heated."

"Do you have any medicine?"

"A paste that cost me all the money I had. I'll have to throw myself on my landlady's generosity while I'm confined to my room." He glanced woefully at his empty glass. "I was having a last drink before I went back to start my treatment."

Ben knew how sick Campbell could expect to be. Apart from the discomfort of the sores on his genitals and inflammation of the testicles, he would feel weak, shivery, nervous and low-spirited. He would need tea and fresh water to drink, wholesome food to eat, a fire, his linen changed, and his room cleaned and aired. Setting aside the fact that his room had no fireplace and only a skylight instead of a window, his landlady had never provided him with any of these services before and was unlikely to provide them now. If he fell behind with his rent she would evict him – sick or not.

Ben stood up. "Come on, Campbell. You're coming with me."

"I told you, I can't go to Bristol."

"I'm not taking you to Bristol. You can stay in my lodgings while I'm away. Any tea, coal or food you have can be put on my bill. We'll tell my landlady that you have a fever, something you've had ever since you were a child, not contagious. Whatever you do, don't go interfering with the maids. You are to stay indoors, go to bed early and rest during the day. As for that paste, I expect you bought it from some quack who promised a quick cure. It's probably mostly mercury, mostly lead or mostly rat poison, and it won't do you any good. As soon as you're settled in George Street, I'll go to the apothecary's and get him to make up something better."

"All settled outside and in!" cried the guard, slamming the door. The vehicle swayed as the driver clambered up into his seat. The fat woman settled across the seat, casting her huge shadow over the page of Ben's book. Why, Ben wondered, squashed into the corner, must there always be a fat woman? It was his first opportunity to read that day. There was the business of moving Campbell's belongings to his chambers and paying off his protesting landlady. Then the time spent persuading the Scot to allow Ben to examine the affected parts. After that, the lengthy argument with the apothecary over the proportion of mercury Ben wanted in his prescription – a much smaller amount than was usual. Finally, Ben had ordered an early supper for them to share, by the end of which Campbell had stopped bewailing his ill luck and the weeks of sexual abstinence his infection imposed upon him, and begun to look forward to time to write and read in peace and comfort.

Ben held his book up to catch the square of light that fell through the small, open window and began to read...

In stature they were as variable as a similar number of Europeans, that is to say that some were tall and some small. In colour too they differed as much as any London crowd; those who were obliged by the exercise of their professions to be much exposed to the sun were a darker brown than others. There was much variety in the appearance of their hair, though in colour brown predominated, and in texture smoothness, yet all men and women, whether curled or straight, wore their hair long – the men to the shoulders, the women longer. Some fastened it back with ties ornamented with shells, coloured stones or feathers, but this seemed to be a matter of preference only, not depending on sex or status. All were covered with a fine cloth of a manufacture new to the ship's company, with hems richly patterned or fringed. Both men and women wore their robes tied at both shoulders but lengths differed, though never beyond modesty; this again seemed to be a matter of preference, as they seemed ignorant of any sumptuary laws.

Only in their variety did they resemble the inhabitants of our chief city. They were all excellently made and handsome, none of their workers exhibiting any of those defects of lameness and blindness, enfeeblement and asthma, which renders the sight of any London street a mournful one. Nor were those who toiled treated with any of that inferiority that our labourers meet, but stood shoulder to shoulder with their leaders.

The sailors dragged the boat onto the strand. The marines disembarked and rapidly formed a line of muskets beyond the reach of the foamy waves. Captain Braveman boldly stepped forward with Mr Noble beside him and beckoned to the men to bring the chest of beads and mirrors, the stock much depleted. The majority of the natives watched in silence, though the four at the front kept up a steady chanting, as of prayers or spells. When they ceased, several of their countrymen detached themselves from the group as if by arrangement and advanced towards the explorers. One of the sailors flung his musket to his shoulders but the Captain angrily knocked it from his hand. And indeed the natives were empty-handed, carrying neither weapon, nor staff, nor branches as they offer in welcome on King George's Island (which the inhabitants call Tahiti), nor livestock to barter. So profound was their isolation that they had no notion of trade.

The natives approached to within a bayonet's length but the Captain stood his ground and bade his men do the same, even when one of the natives, a young man much the Captain's own age, planted himself in front of the Captain, though whether with belligerent intent was not at first evident. He seized Braveman by the upper arms and caught him in a close embrace, smiling and repeating the same phrase over again. Mr Noble found himself imprisoned in a similar grasp by a tall man whose height, bearing and movements were as elegant as any courtier bowing to the King. The remainder of them divided and ran amongst the crew imitating the gesture and the words. Their voices were gentle and melodious, sweet and tuneable. The Captain, released from the embrace, shook the fellow's hand, ordering the rest of his men to follow his lead and return greeting for greeting. Then each took his Englishman by the hand and led him up the beach to the others. There was one native for every one of the ship's men – the chanting had been the sound of them counting out their ambassadors.

*

"Let them go!" roared the guard. Ben jolted in his seat as the coach started to move.

The man opposite Ben had his face muffled in a scarf although it was the middle of July. "Do you think we could have the window thut?" he said, his voice thick with pain.

Toothache, Ben guessed, either untreated or, more likely, just treated. He hurriedly complied with the request to shut out the tormenting draught, and with it the light. He closed his book and settled down to sleep through the long miles. Once his eyes flickered open. The sufferer was staring at him balefully, as if the agony in his jaw had driven him into a murderous rage. Beads of sweat sat above the fat woman's peevish lips. A thin, young man in the far corner tilted back his head, took a swig of brandy and belched. Ben shut his eyes again and, with very little effort, conjured up the bright, handsome faces of the ambassadors at the edge of a blue ocean, smiling their welcome to men worn out from their perilous voyage.

Seven

At midday, Ben got down from the coach at The American Coffee House in Broad Street and in a few minutes he was on the Quay. As ever, there was an air of hurry at the edge of the murky, lapping water. Ships had to be unloaded quickly, not only to make room for newcomers, but because the vessels were unprotected from the tides and the weight of their cargo could overbalance them as they sank into the mud. Ever since Ben could remember, the Merchant Venturers had intended to make improvements – dig canals, rechannel the Frome, dam the Avon, create basins where the ships could remain afloat. The latest scheme – to divert the Avon along a man-made ditch so that a floating harbour with entrance locks could be constructed – was controversial and expensive. Few of the city's inhabitants expected that it would ever come to fruition.

There had been a time when he would stand for hours and watch the porters working the cranes, the landwaiters checking unloaded goods, the customs men sniffing about for excise cheats. Timidly, he would linger at the threshold of the taverns, The Three Tuns, The Three Kings, The Three Mariners, where, swathed in smoke and the fumes of rum, sailors with gold rings in their ears swapped tales of dread and wonder. Now the men rolling barrels from ship to shore, the packhorses with their swaying loads and the laden sleds hissing over the stones were only nuisances to be avoided. The mariners in their worn woollen jackets stained with the salt of a dozen oceans were simply labourers, no less coarse and drunken because they happened to ply their trade on floating boards.

Along the Quay shoe shops, jewellers, silversmiths, watchmakers, glassware and hat shops mingled with chandlers, brightsmiths, shipwrights and sailmakers. There was one apothecary's sign amongst them and it was this sign that drew him. He stopped and gazed in through the window at the ornamental display of Bristol Delft pitchers and flasks. An enormous dresser of dark wood lined the far wall, the shelves reaching up to the ceiling. Every shelf was covered with stoppered glass bottles, lidded jars, tins and boxes all carefully labelled with symbols and abbreviations that only the initiate could understand. Not one of these receptacles, even those that were so high up they could only be reached by clambering up a set of movable steps, was dulled by dust. In front of the shelves was a polished counter with two chairs placed at each end for customers' use.

A door on the left of the counter led into the living apartments, and a plain black jacket hung from a hook on the door. The owner of the jacket, in white shirtsleeves and a green apron, stood behind the counter with his back to the window. He had taken down a selection of containers and was busy weighing out ingredients on a gleaming set of brass scales. Ben watched as the steady hand poured the powders and liquids, deftly adjusting the tiny weights and pausing every now and again to run a finger along the page of a large book that lay open next to the scales. The man closed the book, took a small key on a fine chain out of his pocket and locked its heavy gold clasp. Quickly, he restored the bottles and jars to their places on the shelves. Pausing to brush stray specks of powder off the counter, he caught sight of the figure at the window. He snatched up the volume and, although only a little man, glared combatively at Ben's silhouette until, with a smile, he recognised the spy and ran to open the door.

"Ben, Ben! When did you – ? Why are you – ? How well you… Mrs Shackleton, here's Benjamin, Mrs Shackleton!"

"Good day, Father," said Ben, stepping into the shop.

He followed the smell of warm bread into the parlour. There was the old desk under the window with its rows of pigeonholes filled with bills, receipts and bundled correspondence. He had once spent a happy afternoon rearranging the papers – his father had beaten him when the mischief was discovered. The window overlooked a tiny yard filled with pots of herbs, the outhouse and a gate to the narrow lane that ran between the backs of the houses.

There were the shabby armchairs, one on either side of the fireplace, where he and his father used to sit in the evenings. "What's that you are reading? A novel? And what is that about? See this, Mrs Shackleton, the boy is reading a novel!" his father used to say. There was the tall dresser with its old pewter mugs hanging alongside the best blue and white china. In pride of place were the six plates on which Mrs Shackleton served their Sunday dinner, each one containing a line from a grace: *When thou sit down to meat; Give thanks before thou eat; To him that always gives; The mercies thou receive; That such favours may be; Repeated unto thee*. The plates belonged to his mother, of whom he had no memory.

Mrs Shackleton appeared in the kitchen doorway, wiping her hands on her apron. Ben grinned at the sight of her pursed lips and stooped to kiss her. Once he had discovered that growing into a tall lad gave him certain advantages, he had unashamedly exploited them, and Mrs Shackleton was soon tamed. He only had to seize her hands and whirl her around the room or offer his arm in mock-gentleman style when they walked to church to soften a heart that he knew, for all her grumbling, was already his.

"You've come away on a whim, I suppose?" She tut-tutted.

"Hush! Don't scold the boy," Mr Dearlove cried. "Sit down, sit down, son. Why didn't you let us know you were coming? Mrs Shackleton, his bed will need airing."

She bridled. "His room is always ready." For once, Christopher Dearlove did not attempt to pacify her. He only had eyes for Ben, whose hand he still had hold of.

"You've left the *Recipe Book* in the shop," Ben said awkwardly.

The apothecary hurried to retrieve it. Ben put down his bag, unbuttoned his jacket and sat down at the table. Mrs Shackleton disappeared into the kitchen and returned a moment later with an extra plate, knife and tankard. "You've not got yourself into any trouble?" she whispered loudly.

He laughed. "No, Mrs S, I've not got myself into any trouble."

While aware that London was a slimy pit of sin and ruin for young men, Mrs Shackleton sought to keep this knowledge from Ben's father. She nodded in stern satisfaction and by the time Mr Dearlove came back into the room was innocently clattering about with bread knife and board. Mr Dearlove locked the *Recipe Book* in the bottom right-hand drawer of the desk and sat down.

"You caught the eight o'clock coach last night?"

"Yes, it was a good journey. I slept most of the way."

"And is your book finished?" the old man asked eagerly. "Are Almira and Ethelfreda united at last?"

"Nearly."

In fact, Ben had made no progress on his book since the day after Mr Dowling's last Sunday dinner. He sat down to it often enough, but passed the time trimming his pen and daydreaming about finding the author of *A Voyage to the Fair Land*. In his imagination, he had tracked the elusive genius to a garret, a cottage or a mansion. He had discovered a lonely bachelor, a widower with ten children or a husband nursing a dying wife. He had envisioned the author as a young man, a middle-aged man or an old man. In every version of the dream, though, the shy writer was always grateful for the trouble Ben had taken to bring him Mr Dowling's offer. In fact, he was so impressed by Ben's acumen and intelligence that he insisted on dealing with him and no one else. He declared that Ben must be his man of business. Ben must be his amanuensis. He was astonished to learn that Ben's talents had so far been ignored, and promised to use his considerable influence to rectify matters. They forged a literary friendship, the like of which the world had never seen before.

"And who knows?" Ben's musings usually ended. "One day, the reclusive, brilliant writer and explorer, Anon, will be the subject of the greatest biography of the age, written by his lifelong friend and fellow man of letters – a decent interval after his death, of course. I shall have to keep a diary."

While Ben was revisiting these happy dreams, a troubled expression crossed Mr Dearlove's face. He had heard *nearly* many times. "You said that two years in London would see you an author."

The words jolted Ben out of his daydream. "I still have six months left!"

Mr Dearlove gazed at his son. "Of course," he said gently.

Crossing Queen Square the next morning, Ben was optimistic. He knew that the *Miranda* existed, that she was a Bristol ship and that she had been lost in 1780. He also knew – what man brought up in Bristol didn't? – that the Customs House men were easily bribed, and he anticipated no difficulties in being allowed access to the port records. Even when the clerk who accepted his money warned him that compulsory registration of ships had only come in three years ago, Ben remained hopeful. Other records had been kept before 1786 – records of cargoes, of ships leaving and entering the port, of dues paid and dues avoided. There would be mention of the *Miranda* somewhere.

His only misgiving came when he watched the greedy fingers close over his money. His father's money. They had been sitting in their armchairs after supper when his father said, "Let me give you the money for your fare, son. You can't afford to spend such large amounts of your monthly allowance." A small argument ensued, which Ben lost. If Mr Dearlove could see how he was spending the gift! He knew how laboriously the money was earned. He had tried many times to persuade his father to employ an assistant during his absence. But Mr Dearlove did not want anyone to take his son's place. Ben reminded himself that if he succeeded in bringing Anon and Mr Dowling together, he would no longer be a financial burden and his father could easily afford an apprentice. He ignored the nudging of his conscience and dropped the money into the clerk's palm.

He was taken through a large room where the clerks were going through the reports brought from the docks by the teams of checkers and weighers responsible for monitoring the unloading of incoming vessels. These reports went first to men who consulted tables of tariffs and scribbled notes on them before passing them on to others who calculated the amount of customs to be collected. From there they went to draughtsmen who drew up the bills to be presented to the ships' owners. Finally, the reports were copied into the large parchment volumes which formed the port books.

In the next room a similar process was underway for vessels leaving the port. Here the owners' applications for passes to sail travelled along a line of workers who checked cargoes and destinations, until they reached the head clerk for final approval. The constant rustle of paper and scratch of pens was punctuated by loud bangs as he stamped the dockets, which he did with a furious air. Like many officials he was offended by the public's temerity in bothering his department.

It was here, in the records for voyages out, that Ben had to do his research, which was no easier than the business at Lloyd's. True, he had a date now. He knew the *Miranda*'s wanderings ended when she went down in March 1780. But when had she sailed? He decided to start with the books for 1777 and work backwards, reasoning that if Cook's voyages to the South Seas each took three years, the *Miranda*'s could not be less.

Though he had his back to the clerks, he was conscious of their whispered resentment. His presence was a distraction that broke the rhythm of their work. After a while, however, they forgot about him and he forgot about them. Each man settled down to concentrate on his own tedious task.

Ben had brought a pencil and paper with him to record his discoveries. The day was well advanced by the time these were made and he at last found an entry for the *Miranda*. She was a Bristol privateer built by James Hillhouse and launched in 1770. She had been purchased in April 1773 by a consortium of buyers. This was not unusual as people often joined together to finance a ship for one or more trading voyages, sometimes directly to the sugar plantations, often on the more roundabout slave routes. The *Miranda*'s backers were listed as banker Jacob Edgcumbe of Bristol; George Fenwick, gentleman, of Gloucestershire; and Mrs Lambert, widow, of Clifton.

They had entered the East Indies as the ship's destination, no doubt to avoid awkward questions from port officials. A ship bound for the Great Southern Continent would have attracted a great deal of attention. Like most investors, they had preferred to keep their trade secrets.

*

"Do you remember the ingredients for a headache, Ben? One that has lasted an entire night and may be accompanied with disturbances to the vision?"

As Ben entered through the shop door, he was almost bowled over by a young servant running out of the shop on his way to some clandestine quarter of an hour's enjoyment while the apothecary made up his mistress's medicine. Mr Dearlove gazed at his son with a confident and proud smile. Irritated with himself and feeling undeserving of that pride, Ben answered brusquely, "Everyone in town takes James's Powders now. It is good for almost anything."

"Rubbish! Full of manufactured stuff and served up stale, not made fresh for each patient. No, no. What is the first thing I taught you?"

"That only the best and the most natural ingredients are to be used," Ben recited, grudgingly.

His father beamed at him. "And so, for a headache?"

"White magnesia calcined, six drachms. Powder of rhubarb, sharp cinnamon, ginger, half a drachm each. Mix together in a fine powder."

"And the dose?"

"The dose? Oh, a teaspoonful to be taken in mint tea every night."

Mr Dearlove clapped his hands together in delight. "And do you want to make it up, Ben?"

No, was his first thought but his father was looking at him with such pleasure he could not disappoint him. Stifling a sigh, he stepped behind the counter and busied himself with the mortar and pestle.

"Do you know anything of Jacob Edgcumbe, the banker?" he asked as he worked.

"I know him by sight, of course. Edgcumbe and Edgcumbe is one of the oldest banks in Bristol. Their offices are on Corn Street. The family have a house on Park Street or George Street, I forget which. Why do you want to know? You have not fallen in love with his daughter, have you?"

Ben laughed. "I don't even know if he's got a daughter. I think I ought to start taking an interest in the city's business, that's all."

It was all he could think of to explain his curiosity but the lie pleased his father. So did his mixture, which Mr Dearlove pronounced perfect.

Their houses, built on wooden frames with walls constructed of sheets of overlapping bark, were long, low and rectangular with sloping roofs in which traps that opened by means of a cord were placed at regular intervals to admit light and air. These were kept open all day and not completely fastened during the hours of darkness, the people fearing no evil consequence from the night air, so that the rooms were always sweet despite the number of dwellers in each domicile. Around the centre of each dwelling were raised platforms divided by thin partitions in which people slept, each in his or her own berth. The central part of the room formed their living space where, when they dined indoors, they gathered to eat, seated on a large rectangular mat. But they often moved the mat onto the veranda and ate their meals there. The mat was decorated around its borders with a series of geometric patterns divided into squares, the middle part where food was placed was left plain, and the people sat on the patterned edges, each person having his or her own pattern as a European would have his own chair.

The houses were not close together but each stood in

its own plot of land where herb or flower gardens and a few edible crops were planted, although most crops were cultivated on the large fields beyond the dwellings. None of the plots were fenced; indeed, there were no fences at all except for the one that was erected around the British encampment which was an object of wonder and curiosity to the people, the children especially. They swarmed up, down and over the wall, nullifying its purpose so that within a short time the Captain ordered its removal.

In the centre of the town was a house larger than all the rest and without sleeping platforms. This was used both for formal gatherings and also as a meeting or resting place for individuals. Anyone could go into the building at any time he or she wished. It was here that the Captain and gentlemen witnessed their first dispute, which was entirely due to this absence of boundaries and seemed to demonstrate how much wiser it is to delineate ownership, both in law and in fact, between properties. An argument had arisen between two neighbours over who had the right to pick the fruit of a tree that grew between their houses. Though hideous to look at, this fruit, about the size of an apple with a thick, knobbed rind of an unappetising brown-green colour, when opened was found to contain a delicious orange flesh. It was considered a great delicacy by the people and, soon after tasting the sweet flesh, by their visitors, who had orders from the Captain always to ask permission before taking any fruit, or cutting down any tree. This permission was never denied.

The debate was carried on with such vehemence it seemed certain that combat would ensue. The elders, family and friends of the disputants were hard pressed to soothe the heightened emotions displayed by the men, who rent

84

their garments, shouted, wept and stamped their feet. At this time, Mr Noble was the most adept at their language and acted as translator to the Captain and others who, not being such accomplished linguists, were not always certain of the meaning of what they heard. Upon informing his colleagues that the most often repeated phrase was 'You must have it!' everyone concluded that Mr Noble must be in error. It was not until later, when acquaintance with the people, their language, laws and customs had improved so far as to render doubt impossible, that Mr Noble was proved to be right. The contest was not for the right to possess, but for the right to give away.

A panelled door opened and Ben, sitting on a hard-backed chair in the corridor outside Jacob Edgcumbe's office, looked up from his book. Edgcumbe, a stout man in a silk coat and embroidered waistcoat, with a magnificent wig curling about his shoulders, stood on the threshold of his office shaking hands with a sea captain.

"The bank will require proof that the vessel is adequately insured."

"I shall go to the insurance office directly," his client answered in a strong Gloucestershire accent. He was a squat, broad-shouldered man in his fifties dressed much like the banker in coat and silk waistcoat. However, the mariner moved like a prisoner in his land togs, shuffling as if manacled by breeches, coat and shoes.

"Will you send an agent on ahead to secure your cargo?"

"No, I shall save money by not using a middleman."

"And when you leave the African coast, where then? Virginia?"

"The Virginian duties are too high, as I found last time. I shall try the Cuban market."

"Very well. I'll have the deeds drawn up. We'll finalise the amount of the advance later today, next door."

'Next door' was the Corn Street Coffee House which, being situated between the bank and the insurance office, meant that the sea captain had not far to go to complete his business.

Ben rose from his seat. Edgcumbe did not even glance at him as he went back into his room, but he did leave the door open. Ben wondered if this was his invitation to enter and took an irresolute step forward. The jangle of a handbell brought him up short and, for a moment, he expected an outcry and prepared himself to repudiate charges of a violent attempt on the banker. It was not an alarm, only a summons for the desiccated clerk who had escorted Ben to the waiting area over an hour ago.

"Will he see… " Ben began, but the little man clacked past him in his sloppy shoes, his shrivelled legs in their baggy white stockings quickly disappearing through the doorway.

"Well, Timothy," Edgcumbe's voice came from the next room. "I don't think the outcome of this investment is in much doubt. It's a scrape-the-bottom-of-the-barrel venture, if ever I saw one. Nothing in the purse for contingencies."

"Then the captain is taking a mighty risk, sir," Timothy, the old clerk, responded.

"Indeed he is. I did warn him before I agreed to the loan. Do what my grandfather did, I said. He started off as a sea captain, like you. He took a risk on the trade, like you. But he knew when to stop."

"Will you lend the captain any extra, sir?"

"He hasn't enough security for that. We will have the ship if he gets back and the insurance if he doesn't. He also has a house in Guinea Street and a fairly well-stocked wine cellar, I believe. Two black servants… here's the list. You know how to word it."

Timothy lowered his voice, "There is one more person

waiting to see you. Ben Dearlove, the apothecary's son."

"The Dearloves? What do they own?"

"Just their shop, as far as I know. It's a solid business. The old man's credit is good. He pays for his stock as he goes along."

Ben ground his teeth at Edgcumbe's assumption that he was here to ask for one of his ruinous loans.

"Tell him to come back tomorrow."

The clerk backed out of the office and closed the door. Since Ben had heard the exchange, as he had been meant to, there was no need for Timothy to do more than raise his shoulders in an apologetic shrug.

"Wait a minute!" Ben hissed as he stood. Towering over the clerk, Ben drove him back against the wall. "Go back in and say to Mr Edgcumbe that I am not here to borrow or beg – which amounts to the same thing. Tell him I wish to speak to him about the *Miranda*."

The clerk bleated, "He said tomorrow!"

"The *Miranda*!" Ben propelled the clerk towards his master's threshold, kept a tight grip on his arm and rapped on the door. Timothy had no choice but to answer his employer's irate summons to enter.

Poor little man, Ben thought ruefully. He was less than proud of his tactic but, a moment later, he was in Jacob Edgcumbe's office. The room was full of Edgcumbes: he felt their acquisitive eyes staring from their picture frames as he crossed the oriental carpet. Captain Edgcumbe, the grandfather who had made a fortune from one slave voyage and then shrewdly invested the profits away from the trade, sneered at him from the largest canvas. In another painting, Jacob's brother Joseph peered with complacent absent-mindedness over a sheet of music. As Ben had learned by gossiping with one of the errand boys before Timothy whisked the garrulous lad away, Joseph had never taken any part in the management of the business other than drawing the income that had enabled him to live in the grand house in George Street. The house was still in the family's possession. Joseph's widow lived there, alone now that her daughters were well married.

There was a painting of a much younger Jacob standing in front of a window, the velvet drape drawn back to reveal a misty background of sailing ships in a harbour. Ships like the ones the hapless Gloucestershire captain had just signed away. Ships like the *Miranda*. Jacob Edgcumbe had not put money into her voyage for the love of discovery, the furtherance of scientific knowledge or the dream of a fair land. He was after what every merchant had sought since the world's first ship put to sea – gold, timber, nutmeg, spices.

The banker, maintaining an intimidating silence, nodded at the chair in front of his desk. The seat was lower than Ben expected and he flopped into it. Feeling at a disadvantage to the man who sat above him like a judge on his bench, he was glad that he had not come to ask for a loan. But how to begin explaining his business?

Luckily, Edgcumbe opened the conversation himself. "You wish to talk to me about the *Miranda*?"

"Yes, I believe you were a co-owner of the vessel, along with a Mrs Lambert and a Mr Fenwick?" Edgcumbe neither confirmed nor denied this. Ben put his book on the desk while he dug in his pocket for his notes. "I copied this from the Lloyd's Register. It's a report of the sinking of the *Miranda* made by the captain of the *Bellona*. Perhaps you already know of it?"

"The report has never been disclosed to me."

"I have reason to believe that the captain's report is incomplete." He doubted that his reasoning would impress this stony-faced man and tried to make his voice confident and businesslike.

Edgcumbe snorted. "The claim was made in good faith.

If your principals are seeking a reimbursement, they will have to bear in mind that the money has been invested and cannot quickly or easily be repaid. That is assuming, of course, that you can substantiate your allegation."

Reimbursement? Substantiation? Allegation? What on earth was Edgcumbe talking about? Ben watched in bewilderment as Edgcumbe snatched up the piece of paper, read it and tossed it back across the table.

"This only proves the validity of my claim. The captain's report was made long before I applied for payment. It should have been investigated before, not after, the settlement. You should have checked your facts, Mr Dearlove. I wish you a good day."

"Good day? But I haven't yet told you why I'm here!"

Edgcumbe frowned. "Are you not the insurers' agent?"

"Insurers' agent? Lord, no!"

"If you are not acting for a subscriber, what is your connection with Lloyd's?"

"I have no connection. I only went there looking for information about the *Miranda*. I've come about this book. It's the story of a voyage to a land the author calls the Fair Land."

Edgcumbe looked at the book as if he thought it might spring open and shower him with turds. "You have come here to tell me fairy stories?"

"I think the book is based on real events. It is a huge success and all of London is agog to know who wrote it. I have been retained by the publisher, Mr Dowling by St Paul's Churchyard, to find out who the author is. Initially, the only clue I had was the name of the ship. So I went to Lloyd's, found this entry in the Lists and came to Bristol to search the port records in the hopes of finding out who sailed on her."

"You have come to see me because a ship in a book is called the *Miranda*?"

"Yes. You see, I think someone survived the wreck and I think that, whoever he is, he is the author I am seeking."

The banker shook his head once, twice, thrice before he finally found something to say. "I do not follow your reasoning. There is no mention of any survivors in the *Bellona* captain's information."

"The report makes no mention of survivors, no. But it does not say that there were none."

"And on the strength of that you suppose your *someone* exists? Mr Dearlove, you do not know much about the shipping business. If a sailor had survived, he would have been back by now to claim his wages."

"I don't think the survivor is a common seaman. An educated man wrote this book."

"Let the man who wrote your book be as educated as you like. He was certainly not on board the *Miranda*. If any of the gentlemen who were had survived, I would know of it."

"How can you be sure?"

Jacob Edgcumbe placed his hands, palm down, on the edge of the desk and contemplated his pink nails. "I can be sure. You see, the captain of the *Miranda* was my nephew, Alex, and Mr George Fenwick, one of the investors, was his dear friend and sailed with him."

Eight

There was nothing left for Ben to do but gather up his book and papers, apologise for intruding on the old man's sorrow and leave. He could still hear the furious peal of Jacob's handbell, the clatter of Timothy's shoes, the clerk's obsequious indignation as the door slammed shut. Could the interview have gone more badly?

Still, at the cost of his embarrassment, he had learned a great deal. He knew the name of the captain and that one of the investors had also been a passenger. If either of them had survived, of course they would have come home. The author, then, was not Alex Edgcumbe or George Fenwick. But there are many people on board a ship who can read and write – officers, scientists, surgeons, perhaps even one of the common sailors. If a milkmaid or shoemaker can be a poet, then why not? And if the banker was too angry to help him, there was still Mrs Lambert.

He walked along the Quay, ignoring the small dog yapping at his heels. In the middle of the busy thoroughfare, two children played seesaw on a plank of wood dangerously balanced across a barrel. Tall masts rose above Ben's head, birds wheeled in the blue sky and ropes flapped against slimy steps. They looked like nothing now, those sail-less ships with their battered paintwork, drooping in the mud of Bristol harbour. But any one of them could carry him a hundred miles, a thousand miles, thousands of miles – to Madeira, the Canary Islands, the Cape of Good Hope, India, China, Batavia... to a fair land.

What was it like to sail to a new land? What if he was not Ben Dearlove walking through the place where he had been born and bred, but a stranger who had just sailed from the other side of the world into an unknown harbour? Nothing would be familiar, not the distant hills that surrounded the city, not the trees on Clifton Hill, not the city's houses or towers or spires. The hills are an unmapped mountain range, guarding an unexplored interior. The trees are a dense, alien forest full of roaring beasts, venomous snakes, and the heady scents and extravagant beauty of deadly flowers. The smoke over the houses rises from native dwellings, the church spires are the outer walls of a cruel king's palace, the conical sugar chimneys are mysterious temples, their flames sacred to an unknown god.

A crash, a scream and the dog's frenzied yelping wrenched Ben out of his daydream. The makeshift seesaw had come apart, depositing two wailing children onto the mucky cobblestones. He came to his senses just in time to avoid tumbling into the calamity. Dreaming again, he thought ruefully. The book must be affecting my brain.

In the morning, he walked up Park Street, passing the girls' boarding school with hardly a glance at the windows. He remembered a time when he thought himself in love with one of the young ladies and used to hang around the house for hours in the hopes of catching a glimpse of her at one of those windows. What had she looked like? Like all the other young girls, no doubt. Certainly he could not recall her face now and by the time he turned left into George Street, he had forgotten her again.

Here, the houses were all fine and well built, preceding

the days of the speculative builders who, in their hurry to throw up buildings for the newly-rich merchants of Bristol, left out details like foundations, roof supports and plaster. The Edgcumbe house was a solid, three-storey building. Its golden stone, marble steps and gleaming front door revealed nothing of its interior life. He walked on to Brandon Hill where he stopped to look down at the property from its side elevation, noting the walled garden, stables and mews. No one was moving about outside and he caught no glimpse of a lady or servant flitting about inside. The house could only repeat the tale of the family's wealth, it had nothing new to tell him.

He struck out across the hill on the Clifton footpath. A few moments of striding along the open brow brought him out above Jacobs Wells, near Limekiln Lane. As a lad he had often gone down the lane to the furnace where half-naked and more than half-drunk workmen toiled with molten glass. They were the most accomplished swearers in the world. He and his friends had giggled over many a half-understood oath. The workmen made bottles for the Hotwell water, which was sold around the country and sent across the world too. Perhaps, at this very moment, a bottle was being opened by some homesick Bristolian in America or the West Indies.

He did not make the detour to the furnace today and soon descended Brandon Hill and started up Clifton Hill. Many of the mansions here owed their existence to lucky investments made by their owners eighty or ninety years ago. Clifton Wood House, Clifton Hill House, Goldney Hall – they had all been built for newly wealthy Quakers who wanted to get away from the cramped, smelly, ill-lit streets around Bristol Bridge. The Goldney story was a typical one. They backed Woodes Rogers in his venture to the South Seas in 1708 and built their house with the French and Spanish gold the buccaneer brought back.

Here, on this hill of Quaker privateers, lived Mrs Lambert. He approached her house and knocked on the door. He was shown into the drawing room as Mrs Lambert came out of her library, carefully shutting the door behind her. She had been a beauty in her youth, was almost a beauty still, though she must be turned fifty he guessed. He appraised the trim figure, the clear, intelligent eyes, and the complexion that need not fear daylight.

She invited him to sit down with a gracious flick of her laced wrist. "You are an author, Mr Dearlove?"

"How did you know that?"

"You have a book in one pocket and a piece of paper poking out of the other. And why else would you be here? However, let me not waste any of your time. I am not one of those who thinks applicants should be teased with *perhaps* and *possibly*. I do not have any patronage to spare at present."

"Patronage? You mistake me – I have not come for patronage. I had no idea that you – " He broke off, regretting the vehemence of his denial. It was too late. The moment to interest her in his work had passed before he was even aware that it had arrived. Resigning himself to his lost opportunity he took the book out of his pocket. "I have come about this."

"*An Account of a Voyage to the Fair Land*? I have read reviews of it, of course, and have a copy on order. You are not suggesting that you are the author?"

"Oh, no."

She placed her elbow on the arm of her chair, rested her head on her hand and gazed with disconcerting steadiness at him while he repeated the story he had told Jacob Edgcumbe. His voice trailed away. He cleared his throat, once, twice.

She moved slightly; there was a crisp rustle of silk. "Have you read Dampier's voyages, Mr Dearlove?"

"No, I – "

94

"Does the name Robinson Crusoe mean nothing to you? You have heard of Monsieur Bougainville's *Voyage autour du monde*? Or perhaps you do not read French?"

"No, I – "

"But if you were planning to write a story about a voyage, I expect you would start by reading these?"

"I... I – "

"Nevertheless you feel sure the author of the book had to make a great journey before he could write about a great journey? You do not have much faith in his powers of invention."

"I know that the *Miranda* is not an invention. I know that she sank at Madagascar. I know that the captain was Alex Edgcumbe and that George Fenwick sailed with him."

"How do you know that?"

"I spoke to Alex's Uncle Jacob yesterday."

"And he agreed to help you?"

He hesitated. "Not really. In fact that was all he told me."

"You are fortunate to have gained so much from him. But really, Mr Dearlove, I fail to see why you connect the *Miranda* of fiction with the *Miranda* of fact."

"I would not have done so if I had not discovered that the Admiralty are also looking for the author."

She glanced towards the library door. "The Admiralty? Why would they be interested?"

"Because if the Fair Land does exist, its discovery is of immense importance."

"Indeed it is, if it does exist. Which a romance cannot prove." She smiled. "It is a charming fantasy, Mr Dearlove, but really a foolish one."

"Not too foolish for the Sea Lords. Think of what it might mean, the opportunities such a discovery might offer. You yourself must have lost a great deal of money in the venture.

Surely the possibility of retrieving something – "

"I lost a great deal more than that," she said sharply. "And the world lost two fine men. Alex had a brilliant career ahead of him in the Navy, and as for George, who knows what he might have accomplished had he lived?"

"Captain Edgcumbe was in the Navy? I did not think that the *Miranda* was a naval vessel."

"She was not. George's father was a close friend of Lord Sandwich, First Lord at the time, and when George said he wanted Captain Edgcumbe to command his South Sea expedition then, as was the way with George's desires, no effort was spared to see it was fulfilled. Alex was released from his normal duties."

"Why did Mr Fenwick wish to go on the voyage?"

"George was a natural historian. He had already made a name for himself with his observations in Newfoundland. He and Alex met on that expedition."

"George Fenwick was a natural historian?"

"And a botanist, an ornithologist, a mineralogist, a linguist, a chemist, a genius in the study of the works of nature and the works of man. If the *Miranda* had come back, there is no doubt that George's work would have surpassed that of Joseph Banks on Cook's first Pacific voyage, and Johann Forster and Anders Sparrman on the second."

Ben hardly heeded her catalogue of George's accomplishments. What did natural historians do? They collected plants and animals, argued about how to classify them, wrote long descriptions of them – and drew them. Here then was the artist who had supplied the originals of those fantastic plates worked over by the woman in London. They were not the products of her imagination, they were his studies from nature, the flora and fauna of a distant shore.

But if Fenwick had survived the loss of the *Miranda*, why had he made a secret of his return to England? Why had he written his marvellous book anonymously? Why not tell his friends he still lived?

Ben tried to sound as if nothing depended upon his next question. "Were there any other artists or draughtsmen on the voyage?"

She looked at him oddly. "No. No one. George's secretary went. I forget his name. But he was no artist."

"Do you know where Mr Fenwick lived before he went away?"

She seemed surprised that he did not know. "George was one of the Fenwicks of Overcombe Park near Painswick."

He thanked her and took his leave. "Thank you for sharing your theories with me," she said, offering him her hand. "They have afforded me much amusement."

She was certainly not easy company for a man, Ben thought when he got outside. Far too learned, and shrewish with it. He glanced up at her window and was surprised to see her watching him. No, the figure's gown was dark and plain. A servant probably, and not looking at him, but at something behind him. He glanced over his shoulder, but all he could see was a group of road workers leaning on their shovels and another man with his back turned, slouching against a tree and gazing down at the river.

Ben had much to think about as he hurried home. What could explain George Fenwick's secrecy? Clearly, he was no deserter. A debtor then? It was possible he had ruined himself by financing the voyage. But then his discovery gave him the means to make good his losses. A man who had abandoned wife and children? Perhaps, if he had secretly married someone of a lower station, as so many young, rich fellows were wont to do on first setting out in life. Or perhaps the answer lay in the circumstances of the voyage itself. Perhaps he had come back maimed, disfigured or diseased. Ben had read that many South Sea islanders suffered from leprosy. What if Mrs Lambert's fine young man had returned with his nose eaten away, his fingers decayed, his face turned to red, rotting, spongy flesh?

There was no way of knowing until the man was found. But how was he to be found? Where would a man who had long been exiled from his home go, if he could not go back to that home? He might go somewhere close to it. He might go somewhere where he could, occasionally, gaze upon the beloved place. Or he might even be there, hidden away by a loving family or loyal servants.

It was as good a place as any to start.

Nine

The Tahitians have their marae or stone temples, often
containing human remains; the peoples of Africa have
their sorcerer-gods, bush spirits and ancestors; the peoples
of New Holland their rain-makers; but on the Fair Land
were no religious houses, and the people who had seemed
to occupy the position of priests or priestesses when the
Europeans first landed were seen, over the next few days,
to be held in no more reverence than the other inhabitants.
Neither they, nor any others, performed any ceremonies that
could be regarded as religious in meaning, nor were any
of the people observed adopting any worshipful attitudes
towards any of the carvings, paintings and hangings that
adorned their homes. The first conclusion was this was a
godless nation. It was some months before the two peoples
attained sufficient proficiency in one another's languages,
which was achieved largely by the talents of Mr Noble
who taught what he more quickly learned to his slower
companions, and their mysteries could be unveiled.

At dinner one evening, Mr Noble asked them if they
had any idea who had made them, who provided them
with the food and drink that came so easily to them in this
pleasant land, who regulated the motion of the stars and
the sun. They said that this was Amraho. Mr Noble then
asked what Amraho looked like. The question disconcerted
them and none answered. Did they have any statues or

paintings of him? Mr Noble pursued. That was the Old Religion, they replied. Amraho had no appearance. "Where, then, do you go to speak to him?" queried Mr Noble. They said they would take the gentlemen to one of the places the next day and Vannir, a middle-aged man who occupied a position as a sage or wise man in their society, was chosen to be their guide.

In the morning, Mr Noble, his secretary, Captain Braveman and his lieutenants, and some of the men to carry food and wine left the town in the company of Vannir. Before long they found themselves at the foot of a wooded hill which they climbed for an hour or more. The trees thinned out as they neared the top and there, in the bright sunshine, they stopped to take some refreshment and examine the view. Behind them lay the town of Mervidir. Outside that, their own shore-side camp, a pattern of circles and moving specks, where the ship lay on her side surrounded by the coopers' and caulkers' workshops. Briefly they looked on the steely ocean, but soon turned their backs on it. Beneath them, pockets of mist still lay in deep copses, brightly coloured birds flitted to and fro. The hills rolled down into a verdant interior, with here and there glimpses of other rivers, towns and fields. In the distance was a line of mountains topped with snow.

Vannir led them down into the valley. Here, after thirty minutes' walk, sometimes on the springy soil at the river's edge, sometimes on large flat stones in the water, Vannir veered off to the right. They clambered after him down a steep slope into a narrow gully which could only be passed in single file. The gully was a dead end so far as they could see, and they began to think that Vannir had lost his way. But, suddenly, he seemed to pass into the wall of rock and, hurrying after him, they discovered a narrow gap. They followed him into a tunnel, the sound of their footsteps muffled by a curious roaring caused, they at first supposed, by currents of air driven through subterranean passages as if through some mighty musical instrument.

They expected the gloomy, damp place to bring them into a cave where they would discover idols, sacrificial remains, and burial chambers. On turning a corner, they found themselves standing not on the threshold of an underground chamber but blinking in the sunlight at the foot of a cascade. A column of water came rushing over the edge of the chasm about a hundred yards above them. Halfway down, it met a steeply sloping rock which slowed its rush by spreading it out into a sheet about twenty-five yards wide. From this scarp, it foamed over massive boulders and was finally tamed in a deep basin before passing on to the sea.

There was a perpetual rainbow in the mist rising from the water. Lesser arcs and bows darted around it so that the air all around them danced with colour. Trees and shrubs fringed the rock face and white trumpet-flowers, nourished by the coloured waters, gave off an exquisite scent. Occasionally, a bird's joyful anthem could be heard above the rush of the water.

Vannir turned and smiled at the group standing, awestruck, on the edge of this tremendous spot. He moved away and, thinking that he was going to perform some religious ceremony, they kept a respectful distance. But he only sat down, gazing peacefully at the beauties all around him, and when Mr Noble asked if his people prayed or made offerings to the gods of the place, he shook his head. "This is only one of the places where we come to meet Amraho. There are many others. Everyone has their own special place. For some, it is in their heart."

No one could say how long they stayed, nor describe how they passed the hours. Not one sketch was made, nor a single flower plucked. By the time they departed, all traces of the fatigue of their walk had left them, and they set off for the long trek home feeling as fresh as they had at the dawn of the day.

That evening Hutan, a young huntsman noted for his proud temper, asked the gentlemen what name the British gave Amraho. Mr Noble explained that the Supreme Being was called God, and that he was Almighty, all powerful, and good. Hutan asked if they had pictures and statues of Him, and Mr Noble said no, but of His Son, His angels and His saints. He described how in Britannia God has many houses, which are made more beautiful than men's houses, where people assemble for prayer and worship led by priests, who also teach them to be good and charitable: that is, to do unto others that which you would have them do unto you. They listened gravely and seemed to have no difficulty in understanding any of this; and it must here be said that in the matter of charity they surpass any nation, for they have no beggars, nor starving nor ill-clad children, nor are the sick and the lame neglected. Every adult regards him or herself as the parent of every child, regardless of birth, and would no more allow the child of another to suffer than they would allow their own.

As they are generous in great things so are they in small things. If they saw a sailor struggle with a heavy burden, a dozen of them would run over to help. If Mr Noble picked a flower then a score of them would hurry off to bring him more. If anyone needed carrying from boat to shore, they would take him on their backs. They were a people who lived to serve one another and to whom service, always willing, always cheerful, was the greatest happiness they knew.

"My husband says that you have ordered dinner."

Ben looked up from his book. A plump woman in a gravy-stained apron, her huge hands greasy from her kitchen work, her peevish face flushed and shiny, stood before him.

"That's right," he said, recollecting his surroundings. The common room of the Falcon Inn at Painswick was an ordinary enough place, with a sanded wooden floor, tobacco pipes above the fire and ring-marked tables covered with splashes of ale. Farmers in muddy boots straddled the wooden chairs and filled the air with smoke and small talk.

"It's too late. Kitchen's closed."

"But it's only eight."

"Kitchen's closed."

He would just have to fill up on beer and hope for a good breakfast in the morning. A poor, or no, meal was not rare, nor the worse thing that could befall a traveller. "Well, can I have another mug of ale – or are the casks closed too?"

"'Nother mug'ale!" she yelled over her shoulder, and waddled away.

He resumed his reading.

"I can get you some bread and cheese," said a soft voice.

This was a pretty interruption to his reading. The girl who stood blushing before him was plump like her mother but, unlike her, neat and pretty. He lay his book aside and smiled. "Could you? I would be very grateful."

The bread was hard and the cheese dry, but Ben did it

what justice he could. The girl glanced cautiously at her father, saw that he was busy behind the bar and lingered to ask Ben if he had everything he needed.

"Yes, thank you. There is one thing, though. Do you know the way to Overcombe Park?"

"Oh, yes. Go along the High Street until you are out of the town and turn left. It's not far."

"Has anyone lived there since Mr George Fenwick went away?"

"Mr George is back now."

Ben stopped in mid-chew. "Mr George is back? Have you seen him?"

"Of course. He's often in the village."

Ben almost choked on a lump of rind. "Often in the village?"

George Fenwick was at Overcombe Park – and, locally, it was no secret! Did Jacob Edgcumbe and Maria Lambert really not know or had they lied to him? No matter. Despite their best efforts, the mystery of the *Miranda* was unravelling much more easily than he had imagined it would. In spite of his grumbling stomach, he slept contentedly.

The next morning was a fine one, so he decided to leave his hired horse in the stable and walk to Overcombe Park. Before he set out, he wrote a letter explaining the purpose of his visit which he would leave if Fenwick refused to see him. With the note in one pocket and his book in the other, he emerged from The Falcon into a street of stone cottages. Half a dozen pigs grunted contentedly in front of the church. In the churchyard, two men were hard at work trimming the yew trees that overhung the garden of the Jacobean mansion. Somewhere in the streets behind the Inn, a donkey brayed. In the narrow byways they were still the only way of shifting bales of wool in and out of the clothiers' houses.

Beyond the village, his path took him through beech woods where he shuffled through dead leaves or slipped on mossy stones. He crossed fields divided by lines of low stone walls. Occasionally, there were narrow brooks to jump over, gates to climb, and patches of dried, hoof-churned mud to negotiate.

His first sight of the house came as he turned a corner in the sloping, tree-shaded track that led down to it. It was a large seventeenth-century mansion, built of grey stone roughened with age and spotted here and there with patches of dull greeny-yellow lichen. The casements were small, leaded and swung outward. Most of the windows on the ivy-grown front were open to take advantage of the mild air. The house was flanked at each end by a gable and there were lines of chimneys in the stone roof that, taken with the stoutness of its construction and the shelter afforded by its position, suggested it was a snug place when gales blew or snow fell. There was a small stone barn on the near side, and on the far side of the house, at a little distance from it was a small and ancient farmhouse surrounded by a muddy yard. Beyond that, the countryside rose again in gentle slopes, dotted with grazing horses and sheep.

He paused at the top of the incline to brush the dust off his shoes and stockings. He was hot from his walk and the walled garden at the rear of the house looked like an inviting place to sit and drink cool elderflower cordial. Around a clipped green lawn, flowerbeds nestled against the old brick. Roses, honeysuckle and morning glory curled about the parapets, and old trees cast their benign shade.

A spaniel shot out of the shadows in pursuit of an arcing stick, leapt into the air to snatch it, skidded down to earth and raced back with its prize to the sound of childish laughter. The stick again emerged from the shaded end of the garden, followed by the dog and this time too by a girl in a sprigged summer dress. Her thick brown hair gleamed in the sun and her lithe figure twirled gracefully over the green.

Ben turned into the driveway between the barn and the house and headed towards the garden. The dog abandoned the game for her duty, which was to fling herself at the intruder and bark wildly. A tall young man ran out after her.

"To heel, Lady!"

The dog obeyed, loping to take a defensive position behind her master. Strictly speaking, both players were past the age of romping. Ben guessed that the boy was about seventeen, his sister a couple of years younger. The girl was still flushed from her exercise, her lips slightly parted and her breath quick. She pushed a lock of hair into place, leaving a smear of dirt along her cheekbone. Ben thought that no cosmetic, no silken gown, no elaborate hairstyle or ribboned bonnet would ever adorn her beauty so well as that black smudge.

As for the boy, he had the same luxuriant hair, the same shapely lips, handsome face and elegant limbs, but his eyes were darker and keener, had more authority than hers. There was a quiet certainty about him that commanded respect. Ben pictured him growing up to be a great leader in whatever field he chose – soldier or scholar, priest or politician.

"Good morning, Mr –? Do you have business with us?" The boy's smile invited candour.

"Dearlove. I have come to see Mr George Fenwick."

"I am George Fenwick."

"You can't be."

The lad laughed. "I assure you, I am."

"But there is another George Fenwick, surely? There has to be."

The boy's smile snapped shut. "There was another George Fenwick, as no doubt you are aware," he said icily. "You had better speak to my father. Come, Rachel, let us escort our *caller*."

He loaded the last word with as much contempt as outward good manners would allow. Rachel, glancing haughtily at Ben, took her brother's arm. Disconcerted by the abrupt change in their demeanour, Ben followed them into the house.

"Wait," said George, pointing to a spot in the hall. Ben might as well have been a piece of the oaken furniture for all the notice Rachel took of him as she stalked away. George disappeared behind one of the doors. No sound escaped through its thick panels. He came back a few moments later, jerked his head at his father's study and said, "Go in."

Antony Fenwick and his steward stood in front of a large, heavy desk, the bay window behind them. "We'll finish this later, Cales," Fenwick said, closing an enormous ledger.

Ben stood aside to let Cales pass, the man's grimaces evincing an intense desire to commit acts of violence against him. Shaken by the growing hostility of the household, Ben shut the door and moved hesitantly into the room. There was a pair of old wooden armchairs on a rug by the hearth. On one wall, a heavy bookcase rose from floor to ceiling with a set of steps next to it. Family portraits hung about the walls and, although much of the brushwork was dulled by age, he recognised several ancestral likenesses to the boy and girl. Everything he had seen of the house, with its well-used furniture and books, suggested continuity and stability. The family had dwelt in this place for generations, yet there had been one restless soul who had left it to travel into the unknown.

Fenwick leaned against his desk with folded arms, a dark silhouette with a face of menacing shadows. "I am informed," he said coldly, "that you wish to see me about my brother, George."

"I...yes. My name is Ben Dearlove, and I am..." Ben hesitated. What was he? An author? An apothecary? A publisher's agent?

"I am acting on behalf of Mr Dowling of St Paul's Churchyard who has recently published this book." Ben drew the volume out of his pocket. The other man showed no interest so, turning the volume nervously in his hands, Ben continued. "The book, which is a work of genius, was published anonymously and as if it is a work of fiction. I think that it is based on fact, and that it was written by someone who had been on the voyage to the South Seas that he describes in the text. You see, his ship is called *Miranda*." Ben paused, but even this name elicited no reaction. "Anyway, I think… I think it is possible – that is, I thought it likely – that he is George Fenwick. The author. Of this book."

"My brother George is the author of your book?"

"Yes. Because of the illustrations. He survived the voyage – "

"Survived the voyage. I see. You are ready to name your sum?"

"Name my sum?"

"It's an elaborate tale, the most original I have heard yet. Others have confined themselves to some trumped-up ancient debt, or produced a child with a passing resemblance to George. You have a talent for invention that I fear will be wasted on a transport ship. I presume you will now offer to keep your part of the bargain and not publicise your so-called revelation that my elder brother lives, so that I may continue to enjoy his property in peace?"

"I am not here to extort money out of you."

"That is just as well, since I do not intend to give you a penny."

"But what I told you is true." Ben fumbled in his pocket. "This is a copy of the entry in the Lloyd's Register."

Fenwick angrily brushed the paper aside. "Be advised, Mr Dearlove, or whatever you call yourself, that your trick will not work. I would give up everything tomorrow if I could have my brother home again."

"But my name *is* Dearlove. My father is a well-known apothecary in Bristol. I can bring letters, testimonials – I can prove that I have not come to rob you."

"Then why have you come?"

"I am looking for George Fenwick, and I thought he might be here. And far from making money out of it," Ben added bitterly, "it's cost me what I can precious little afford up to now."

The door burst open. Cales stood on the threshold, two be-cudgelled farm labourers behind him. "Alright you, time for a dip in the horse pond!"

The men, delighted with the rare treat of some sanctioned bullying, seized Ben's arms, scattering his book and paper. They hoisted him from the ground, twisted him round and hustled him towards the door.

"No, wait!" he cried, desperately trying to find a foothold. "I'm not making it up. Ask Jacob Edgcumbe and Mrs Lambert!"

"Stop!" Fenwick commanded. "You know Mr Edgcumbe and Mrs Lambert?"

Ben, his feet still paddling the air, said, "I have spoken to them. They didn't believe me either. But it's true, I tell you. George is still alive."

"And why would that matter to you, if not to extort money out of me?"

"Because I believe that he is the author of *A Voyage to the Fair Land* and Mr Dowling has commissioned me to find him and offer him a thousand pounds for a sequel."

Fenwick picked up the book and smoothed the pages. "You are here because of this book?"

"Yes."

"And it is a work of genius, acclaimed by those who are the best judges of these things?"

"Yes."

"George could have done it. Whatever he did would be judged the best of its kind. But why would he not come home?"

"I don't know. Perhaps he's concealing a wife, or he's in debt, or he killed someone or..." Ben, seeing from Fenwick's frown how unwelcome these suggestions were, thought better of pursuing the criminal possibilities and instead offered his leprosy theory. The look of horror this brought to the brother's face made a soaking in weedy slime seem inevitable until Fenwick suddenly said, "Put him down."

The men were quick to obey, dropping Ben so suddenly he sagged at the knees and would have sprawled on the floor had they not hauled him up.

"Perhaps, Mr Dearlove, we had better go back to the beginning, with a glass of wine to help us both with the shocks we have sustained."

Ten

Ben told Antony Fenwick about his meeting with the book's illustrator, how he had guessed that she knew the author of the book and how, when he realised that Navy agents Hay and Beale were also on the trail, he began to suspect that the *Miranda* was a real ship and the voyage described in *A Voyage to the Fair Land* had actually taken place. His investigations at Lloyd's had confirmed it.

"I did not know of the *Bellona* captain's report," Fenwick said. "And I do not understand how the *Miranda* came to be at Madagascar. The last I knew of her was that she was about to set out from Batavia where she was delayed by repair work. George sent me the news on a Dutch merchant vessel. He was on his way home after an absence of almost seven years."

"Did he say where he had been?"

"No, he just said he had many marvellous things to relate and told me to keep the packet safe. But I don't understand the role of these so-called Navy agents. You say you are looking for the author because his publisher wants him to write a sequel. But why are they looking for him?"

"Because he is the only survivor from the *Miranda*, and he can tell all about her great discovery."

"What could the *Miranda* have discovered that we do not already know about?"

"The Great Southern Continent."

Fenwick gazed in astonishment as Ben continued.

"The Admiralty sent Cook to look for it. In two three-year voyages he did not find it. Then the *Miranda* went. She was away for seven years. Where was she?"

"Not in the South Land."

"How do you know?"

"Because Cook proved it does not exist."

"Well, call the South Land something else, if you will. But there was a great discovery."

"Then why did Captain Edgcumbe not forward official word of it from Batavia with copies of his logs and charts and so on? That is what naval captains generally do, send reports on ahead in a faster ship. It is what Captain Cook did. But all that came back was George's wallet, and that was not addressed to the Admiralty."

"Perhaps the *Miranda*'s log was lost."

"Captain Edgcumbe could have written to say so, or pieced something together from his officers' private logs and the gentlemen's journals."

"Perhaps he did send his reports home and the ship carrying them foundered."

"You are very inventive, Mr Dearlove."

"I have not invented Hay and Beale."

Fenwick shook his head. "All you have told me so far suggests that they are nothing but common housebreakers and your encounters with them mere coincidence. I find it hard to accept that they have any connection with the Admiralty. Not only do I think it improbable that their Lordships would employ the bullies you describe, I think it unnecessary. If someone at the Admiralty did suspect that George was alive and in England, why would they not simply do as you have done and come here?"

Aghast, Ben stared at Antony. Why not, indeed? He

remembered his conversation with Campbell, when the Scot had laughingly thrown out a hint about spies and suggested that *A Voyage to the Fair Land* contained coded information about the British Navy. And in one sense, it was an encoded document, for its fiction stood for fact. The discovery of an unclaimed continent would be of interest to other nations, and especially to Britain's greatest rival.

"Hay and Beale work for the French! That would explain why George has not been to the Admiralty and why he is in hiding. He would not come back to his family if he thought it would put them in danger." Ben regretted his hasty theorising when he saw the stricken look on Antony's face. He tried to backtrack. "Well, I don't know that there is any danger. Even if there were, I am sure George is safe."

There was an awkward silence. "I used to picture him," Antony said at last, "on a desolate island, burned by the sun, dressed in goatskins, his hair matted and long. Or living amongst natives in a house of ice, going out to fish on the freezing water in a canoe of deer hide. Always he would be looking out for a ship and, one day, a ship would come. And now you are suggesting that a ship did come and he did not perish with the *Miranda*. You have raised a cruel hope, Mr Dearlove. You say leprosy is common in the South Seas?"

Ben shifted uncomfortably. Leprosy was not the only condition that might make a man hide himself away, and George would not be the only traveller to return from the Pacific with syphilis which, as everyone knew, the French had introduced to the islands. He had learned enough about Antony's feelings for his brother to keep this to himself.

But the thought had occurred to Antony. "It would be nothing vicious. George would never do anything to bring shame on himself or Overcombe." He reflected for a few moments. "I give no credence to your Great Southern Continent or French spies. But disease is something that could come to a man, something that might keep him from home. If George thought he would be a burden... his was an unselfish heart. And there is the book. Why give the ship that name of all others? It is coincidence, surely. But if it is not? There is only one way to be sure. The author must be found. I will help you, provided that you agree that if it is George you tell me where he is whether he wills it or not. In return, I will reimburse you for your expenditure to date and pay your future expenses, with a reward of £200 when he is found."

Astonished, Ben nodded.

"Then you must tell me what it is you need from us. But first, I must tell the children what has happened."

"But even if Uncle George was ill he would come home, wouldn't he?" His namesake, who was leaning on the mantelpiece in his father's office, protested a few moments later.

Antony, who had not specified so dread a disease as leprosy, answered, "Who knows what changes his odyssey might have made in him? He would have seen things we cannot begin to imagine, experienced hardships we cannot comprehend. A man might feel that he is a stranger to his friends and family after that."

George glanced suspiciously at Ben, then turned back to his father. "And you think the evidence is strong enough?"

"I hardly know what to think. The likelihood is slight, but I cannot ignore it."

Rachel put her hand through her brother's arm, turned her earnest face up to him. "We must look for him, George! He cannot be left to the care of strangers. If he needs tending, then I shall be his nurse."

The thought of the lovely girl Ben had first seen dancing

over a lawn locked in a sickroom, administering to a man she had never known, a man who might be hideous with deformity or pestiferous with disease, almost made him want to give up the endeavour. But then she rounded on him and cried, "Mr Dearlove, you must help us bring our uncle home."

"Oh, I, yes, of course." They were all looking at him, waiting for him to reveal his strategy. If only he had one! He took another sip of wine, hoping to find inspiration in the bottom of the glass.

"Why don't we advertise in the papers?" George asked impatiently.

The impracticality of the suggestion gave Ben's sluggish mind the start it needed. "You would be inundated by applicants. Mr Fenwick, do you know of any place that was special to your brother, somewhere he regarded as a retreat perhaps, somewhere he had studied, or been happy as a child?"

"George visited many places. I know of no place that he regarded as a retreat. He was not the kind to shut himself away. He studied in Cambridge but he was bored there. And, as a child, he was happiest here."

"What about his friends? Did he know anyone in London? Was there anyone to whom he might turn if he needed help?"

"I know of no particular friends, apart from Alex Edgcumbe."

"You still have your brother's papers?"

"Yes, they are in his room. Of what use are they?"

"At the moment, I don't know whether to set off north, south, east or west. Perhaps they will give me an idea of where to look for him."

It was too much to hope that Rachel would be sent as his guide. She was left to prepare a room for their unexpected guest. It was many years since her mother had died and she was used to shouldering domestic duties. It was hard to say, then, why she spent so much time fussing over the smoothness of the counterpane, dusting the furniture, and arranging flowers from the garden.

Antony accepted George's offer to ride into Painswick to fetch Ben's luggage. He led Ben across the flagged hall to a dark wooden staircase, over which hung portraits and paintings. A battle scene caught Ben's eye, the combatants in the lumbering gear of over a century ago.

"*The Battle of Naseby*," Antony said, seeing his interest. "My grandfather fought there. The King lost the battle and, some time later, we lost our family home."

"This is not the Fenwick house?"

"Yes, it is. We have been on this land since the sixteenth century, with the exception of the period of the Rebellion. Parts of the house are very old, and the farmhouse too. It cost my grandfather dear but he retrieved Overcombe Park and most of its contents, though there was hardly anything left in it when he came home and much of our land had to be sold." They stopped at a door on the second floor landing. "This is George's room."

Ben, who had been expecting a gentleman's bedroom, found himself in what looked like a storeroom. In the centre was a long bench topped by a slab of wood thick as a butcher's block. Underneath it were rows of shelves, some piled with labelled boxes, the labels yellowed and the ink faded. On others were jars, nets, pins, boxes of knives, magnifying glasses, bottles of ink, powders and spirits. The sun, pouring in through two large windows in front of the bench, gleamed on its scored, stained surface.

Behind the bench was a large glass-fronted cabinet. Here were iridescent insects of impossible size impaled on cork boards, papery snake skins, shrivelled lizards, trays of seeds, dried plants faded to a straw colour, pink-tinged seashells, chunks of grey rock split in two to display the gleaming crystals inside. Beneath the display case were shallow brass-handled drawers, specimen trays all labelled in the same faded writing.

Although the room was unused the air was not stale, there was no dust on the furniture, no cobwebs in the corners. It was tidy except for the trunks, bags and cases heaped up in one corner. It was as if they had just been carried into the house, and were only waiting for their owner to fling off his travelling cloak, run up the stairs and unpack them.

"They are the collections George made or bought on his last tour of the West Country," Antony said. "Here is the packet from Batavia." He opened one of the drawers in the cabinet and pulled out a discoloured leather portfolio. It had been damp once and had dried out in stiff, awkward crinkles. The address 'G Fenwick Esq, Overcombe Park, Gloucestershire' was branded into the leather, the letters scorched deep and darkened with age. It was tied with leather thongs, the knots difficult to open.

Antony laid the packet flat on the worktop, inviting Ben to stand beside him and examine the contents. They consisted of a bundle of drawings – anonymous shore lines, maps of harbours and bays, survey readings, and sheets of what could have been astronomical calculations or compass bearings.

"There are no labels or notes on the papers, nothing to indicate when or where the drawings were made," Ben observed.

Antony smiled. "They could be anywhere in the world, but not the Great Southern Continent."

"Even so, it might help if we knew more about them. There's a mystery about how the *Miranda* ended in Madagascar. Perhaps an experienced navigator who understood these figures could tell us something. I know a sea captain in London who could help. Would you mind if I took the wallet with me?"

"Take what you need." He led Ben over to the bookcase against the end wall. Ben scanned the titles. Few could he understand, none could he pronounce: Piso and Marcgraf's *Historia naturalis Brasiliae*; Martin Lister's *Conchology*; Rumphius's *Amboinsche Rariteitkamer*; *Hortus Indicus Malabaricus* by HA van Rheede tot Drakenstein.

Antony pointed to the bottom shelf. "Those are his journals." He ran his finger along the spines of the leather-bound volumes. "These are the earliest, written while he was at Cambridge. This is a journal of a journey to Wales. This one is from his Newfoundland voyage."

Ben took the proffered volume and leafed through the pages. Already, George Fenwick's handwriting was familiar to him from the labels but not his hasty, unpunctuated style. *May 3 Today calm fished with a net out of the Quarter Gallery window caught fucus acinarius and two species of what the seamen call blubbers... May 7 this morn weather moderate a number of birds about the ship which the seamen call penguins... May 9 this morn seven islands of ice... June 1 this even fine walked out gathered some of northern english plants cornus herbacea alsinanthemos trientalis europaea juncus pilosus drosera rotundifolia...*

There were sketches too, though nothing like as accomplished as the drawings in *A Voyage to the Fair Land*. But then these were the botanist's quick, rough drawings made in the field, not the finished plates of a printed book.

"I will leave you to your reading. I have business to finish with Cales."

It was hours after Ben's lunch had been brought to him on a tray and cleared away by the time that he looked up from his work and gazed out of the window at the horses grazing on the hillside. The diaries had revealed little to him, being mainly in the style of the Newfoundland pages – lists of places visited, animals and plants seen and collected, weather conditions. Page after page of facts, but they told nothing of the character of the writer, his friendships, his likes or dislikes, his feelings, nothing but his passion for natural history. Ben had ended by merely skimming the contents and now he closed the last of the journals and pushed it away from him. He had advanced his quest not one bit.

It was late afternoon but, now he was waged for them, too early to give up his labours. He pushed his chair back from the bench, rose to his feet and slotted the book back into the case. This done, he idled over to the display cabinet, pulled out two or three trays and wondered how anyone could think such things worth picking up. He closed the drawer, outstared a desiccated frog, uncorked a bottle, gagged at the smell, put back the crumbling stopper and examined the back of his hand through a magnifying glass. When he grew bored with this, he trained the glass around the room, noting the way it distorted everything – the books, the windows, the boxes in the corner.

He left the glass on the bench and went to have a look at the luggage. The first case contained paper wallets. They rattled when he shook them – seeds. Next was a heavy crate full of sketchbooks. He recognised St Vincent's Rocks, the Bristol Hotwell, a view of the lime kiln beneath the snuff mill on the Downs. He opened a box of shrunken watercolours, then a wooden collecting case with a webbing strap and velvet-lined compartments for jars.

He shifted and opened boxes until, with aching arms, he reached a flat wooden case buried at the bottom of the pile. It was made of walnut and meant for a gentleman's desk, certainly not for travelling as its only fastening was a single brass hook. It was lined with green silk, still bright, and full of letters thrown in unsorted. He rifled through and selected one of the letters. It was addressed to Overcombe Park and dated August 1772. Ben sank back on his heels and read:

George,

I can understand your impatience but I must repeat that the Admiralty has every faith in the abilities of Captain Cook, who possesses in an eminent degree all the qualifications requisite for his great undertaking. However, I know that you are motivated by the highest notions of honour and patriotism and it is not my desire to stand in the way of any discoveries that may be made in the name of King George. If you wish to go any further in the matter, we must have a private interview.

Give my regards to your father. I hope to see you in London very soon.

The letter was signed by the First Lord of the Admiralty, John Montagu, the fourth Earl of Sandwich.

Ben snatched up the case and tipped the letters out onto the workbench. He pushed the leather folder and glass to one side, clearing a space so he could sort the correspondence chronologically. Some papers were undated, being no more than brief notes signed *Alex*. One announced *A ship has been found*. Another that *an advertisement for the crew is made, emphasising the need for sobriety (which must, you understand, George, be no more than a relative term where mariners are concerned)*. Another advised that *fitting out works commenced at Bristol Wapping yesterday*.

There were sheets scrawled with figures, budgets and

lists, some in George's hand, some in Alex's. There were letters setting out terms from chandlers, sailmakers, coopers. Bundles of receipts for wine, beer, salt meat, biscuits, shot, slops, cheeses, raisins, salted cabbage, carrot marmalade, oatmeal and powder.

"But after all, what have they told me that I didn't already know?" he muttered. He rifled through the remaining documents. More receipts and tradesmen's letters. He was puzzling over a sheet covered in symbols when Antony returned to take him to dinner.

"I've found this box of papers relating to the voyage. What is this?"

Antony already knew of their existence, and did not share Ben's excitement. "It's shorthand," he said, glancing at the paper.

"What does it say?"

"I don't know. George acquired the skill at Cambridge. I never learned."

"It's curious. Why is this in shorthand and none of the others?" Ben gathered up the portfolio and the box. "I'd like to take the letters as well, if you don't mind."

"If you think it would help."

All the talk at dinner was about George – how he looked when he left home, how he might look now, what his tastes had been then, what they might be now. Antony told his children what Ben guessed he had often told before – that his first born would have been Georgiana if a girl, how George swept up his baby nephew and kissed him farewell on his last day at home, how closely that nephew had grown to resemble his uncle. All useful information for someone seeking him out, but it did not lodge in Ben's memory so securely as the few words Rachel spoke.

"How old would he be?" Rachel wondered, and Ben found himself wondering exactly the same.

"Forty-five. No, forty-six. Just think if he were home in time for his birthday. We would have such a party to celebrate all the birthdays we've missed!" Antony caught sight of his son's face. "But I am running on ahead. You are right, George. We must not allow ourselves to be carried away. I will need you to take charge of things in my absence," he added. "Unfortunately, I am engaged to spend tomorrow with my man of business who is travelling over from Stroud. I shall be joining Mr Dearlove in Bristol the day after."

"Why does he not wait here for you?" George asked.

"I can't," Ben said. "I told my father I'd be away two nights at most."

The boy shrugged. "Send him a message."

It was tempting, but Ben had made his promise.

Eleven

Ben set off for Bristol in the morning with the Batavia wallet and George's letter box parcelled together and strapped to his saddle. It was market day and it took him a long time to get through Stroud, where he had to dismount and lead his horse through the crowds. The road out of town was clogged with farmers' carts, carriages, people on foot and travellers on horseback coming and going from the chaffering. Gradually, the traffic dwindled and there was no one to be seen but two darkly clad gentlemen on horseback ambling behind him and a group of workers straggling across the fields towards the lane.

The road passed between two high hedges. Ben had not gone far into its cover when he heard the rush of hooves. He glanced back. The two gentlemen were in a hurry all of a sudden. He pulled over to let them pass. The first rider wheeled across his path. Ben's horse, an otherwise placid hireling, shied in alarm. While he struggled to calm the frightened animal, the second man drew up.

"Stand!" he yelled, glaring at him with angry red eyes. Ben gasped in recognition. Beale smirked and plucked at his sleeve. Mr Hay clawed at him from the other side. He felt himself slipping. In a moment, he would be unseated.

Before that moment came they were overtaken by the farm workers, the men's boots heavy with mud from the furrows. There were three women, their identical moon-faces reflecting womanhood in all its stages – grandmother, mother, daughter.

Their skirts were hemmed with the muck of the byre, their sleeves rolled up over arms brawny from dairy work. An empty lunch basket swung from the girl's arm, but the cider jar was still doing the rounds.

They halted, their faces showing a mix of curiosity and suspicion. Hay thrust a hand into his coat pocket, drew out a piece of paper and brandished it at them. "Here's a warrant! It's official business."

They goggled at the document, inclined to be awed by it, yet eager – the girl in particular – to see a villain apprehended. A gentleman of the road perhaps. That she thought Ben dashing enough to be a highwayman was clear from her awestruck gaze.

"Pass on now!" Hay waved the paper.

One or two of the men obediently started to move off, but inspiration had come to Ben. "I won't go back to be flogged and hung from the yardarm!" he yelled. "I won't go back to serve under mad Cap'n Jack! The midshipman he threw to the sharks off Port Royal had a quicker death than I'd get!"

"Why, 'e's a runner," the man with the cider bottle said slowly.

"Aye, and that's the press," growled another.

"Come to tear honest men away from their wives and sweet'arts," shrilled the old crone, who was well past the age when the loss of a sweetheart might concern her.

"You dog!" Mr Hay made an angry swipe at Ben. It was not the best move he could have made in the circumstances.

"Help! He's murdering me!" Ben yelled, adding for good measure, if not consistency, "I'd rather die here than go back to run the gauntlet… and be keel-hauled and… and lashed at the grating!"

Whether or not all of these punishments were likely to be inflicted simultaneously in the Royal Navy he had no idea.

Neither did his audience, but they sounded dreadful enough. The country folk had identified Mr Hay and his friend as representatives of that hated institution the press gang, persecuting a man who had been driven to desertion by his sufferings. With one voice, and that an angry one, they tossed aside basket and bottle and flung themselves at the officers.

Ben spurred his horse. The nag was as eager as his rider to put distance between himself and the melee. The women's cheers sped him on. When he judged he was safely away and could no longer hear the uproar, he slowed down. Fenwick would have to believe him about the danger now!

It was getting on towards the close of the afternoon when he returned the horse to its stable. He hurried home, pausing on the Quay to reassure himself that he was not followed. There was no sign of his adversaries. No doubt they were busy counting their bruises, a thought which gave Ben a great deal of satisfaction. He was relieved that he had not led them to his home. Which is exactly what George is thinking of in staying away from his, he thought, and for a moment Rachel's face floated before him. The idea of those brutes going anywhere near her made him clench his fists. He'd show the devils that they couldn't intimidate him – a resolution which would be easier to keep when Fenwick arrived.

He raced up to his room with the parcel before his father could ask about it, unwrapped it and separated out the wallet and the box. He rummaged amongst the letters until he found the shorthand note. He put it in his pocket, closed the brass hook and started towards the door. Here he hesitated. If he left the Fenwick papers lying around, Mrs Shackleton was bound to see them when she was tidying up and mention them to his father. Awkward questions would follow. What was the boy doing, neglecting his literary work when so little time remained to him? And if he had given it up, why wasn't he settling back into the apothecary's profession as he had promised he would?

Where could he hide the papers? She would sweep under the bed, so that was no good. The chest of winter clothes at its foot was the only place. He took everything out, put the box at the bottom and replaced the heavy woollen coats, scarves and stockings on top of it. Lowering the lid, he caught sight of the leather wallet still lying on the counterpane where he had thrown it. He could not be bothered to take everything out of the press a second time, so he shoved it under his mattress.

"You have not had anything to eat!" Mr Dearlove wailed as Ben ran through the shop.

"I'll be back for supper," he promised, and darted out onto the Quay.

The Godfrey family home and business was in a gloomy court off High Street. Here, parents and son lived in a tall-fronted house that never saw daylight. On the ground floor, they had a shop where customers could taste their wines before deciding whether to buy them by cask or bottle. There were gates across the courtyard so that, at night, it could be locked, an added security to protect the precious goods stored in the cellars beneath.

Ben picked his way over the worn cobblestones, stepping back to avoid one of the vehicles responsible for the icy smoothness of the lane. A tired nag, thankfully relieved of its burden, plodded out of the courtyard gates dragging a long, empty sled. The sour-tempered driver jerked the animal's head and the beast managed to maintain a higher speed for a few paces before yielding to exhaustion. The driver cursed, his voice echoing between the dark, overhanging houses.

Ben found his friend pacing around half a dozen casks piled in the middle of the shop. Two of the warehousemen in stained leather aprons, one leaning against the counter and the other sitting on a crate of empty bottles with his hands on his knees, watched Matthew Godfrey with carefully expressionless faces.

"Just look at how they've left this cargo! No manifest, no paperwork of any kind, and there's at least one that's leaked almost dry. For all I know, the others are more brine than wine. Well, I can't leave them here. We'll have to put them away and argue with the shippers later. Put them in one of the stalls near the front. Don't mix them with the rest of the stock."

"Afternoon, Matthew! Looks like I've caught you at a bad moment," Ben called out.

"Bad moment? I should say! Look at the state of this shop. I've got half a dozen aldermen for a tasting in an hour and – Lord! It's Ben Dearlove!" Matthew grabbed Ben's hand. "Forgive me, my dear fellow... I didn't realise... How are you? How long are you in Bristol? We must share a bottle or two. Damn! I can't leave now. Can you come back later? Say you can. Blast it! Father's expecting me home for supper."

Both knew that Mr Godfrey's arrangements were not to be lightly set aside. Ben patted his friend's shoulder. "Don't worry, I don't want to leave my father alone tonight anyway. Perhaps tomorrow."

Matthew glanced hopelessly at the shipment. "I'm sorry."

"No matter. I'm a bit pressed for time myself. I only came to ask you for a favour, if you can spare five minutes."

Matthew's face brightened. "Ask away!"

They had been friends since their schooldays. Like most of the boys at Colston's, they had been sent by fathers who either had their own business or planned to place their sons in some other man's establishment. In Ben's case, his father was motivated by a desire to give his son the chance of an education he had never had. In Matthew's, his father's sole aim was to mould his son for the family business. Like everything else in his life, his boy's education was an investment and he expected a high return on it. When Ben left the school after a couple of years Matthew toiled on, learning everything a clerk might need to know. It was on these skills that Ben had come to draw.

"I want to know what this says," he said, handing over George's letter.

"Shorthand." Matthew frowned.

Ben's heart sank. "Can't you read it?"

"Mmm? Yes, the outlines are a bit idiosyncratic, that's all. It's Byrom's system."

The man slouching at the counter straightened up and scratched his head. "Shall we start shifting this lot, Mr Godfrey?"

"What, you mean you haven't? Start with that one." Matthew waved vaguely at the casks.

With much cursing and banging, they lifted the first barrel onto a trolley and wheeled the screeching vehicle out of the shop. The cellars were accessed by a double trap door beneath the bay window. There was more banging and cursing while they opened them and manoeuvred the cargo down the dank steps to an underground network stretching far beneath the building. Matthew, oblivious to the noise, pored over the sheet.

"This word here." He pointed to one of the squiggles. "It's a name, I think."

"Alex? George?"

"No. It's addressed to George, here. It's an 'S'. Sir... Sor... Sar... Ah, Sarah."

"Sarah? Are you sure?"

Matthew shrugged. "Not really. It's hard reading someone else's notes. It's not like ordinary handwriting. I'll tell you what I think it says. What it means is another matter. *Dear George.*

*All is arranged. The M… M-something. The M?"

"*Miranda*? It's a ship."

"*Miranda*. Could be. Oh, yes, it is a ship. *The* Miranda *will be towed down the Avon the day after tomorrow and will anchor at Avonmouth. Immediately on receipt of this letter send your secretary to King Road to deliver your equipment and oversee its loading. Follow after in three days. On the night of the third day –* there's another name here, they're always hardest to read. Mrs somebody… *Mrs somebody will meet you in Stroud with Sarah. When you take charge of Sarah –* oh yes, it is definitely Sarah – *conceal her as much as possible, but if you have to account for her, pass her off as a servant and not, I beg you, a mistress.* Lord, Ben, you're not planning an elopement are you?"

"No. Go on."

"There isn't much more. Where was I? Ah! I've got it. Mrs Lambert."

"What?"

"Mrs somebody. It's Mrs Lambert. *Mrs Lambert will meet you in Stroud with Sarah. When you take charge of Sarah, conceal her as much as possible, but if you have to account for her pass her off as a servant and not, I beg you, a mistress. As soon as you are both on board, we will sail with the first favourable wind.* Good Lord, Ben, is it this Sarah you're running away with?"

"What? No, I'm not running away with anyone. Can you write it out for me?"

"Of course. I'll put it on the reverse, shall I?"

There had been a woman on board the *Miranda*. A mistress, Alex said, but whose? Had George helped Alex to smuggle his lover onto the ship, or had the Captain agreed to let his friend use the voyage as a cover for his own affair? Impossible to know from the letter alone. But he knew who the woman was. He had held her in his arms as she sobbed out her grief on the piazza of

129

Covent Garden: "Miranda! I don't know where she is."

And Ben realised he had made a terrible mistake.

He had gone striding into Overcombe Park so sure of himself, so certain that he was right, so proud of the way he had pieced the evidence together. He had been convinced that it was his own insight and not Antony's grief that made his story plausible. He had walked into George's room and found George's things waiting for him just as the explorer left them and, even then, he had not realised the simple truth – Antony wanted to believe that George was alive.

Campbell had warned him that he might only do harm if he persisted in his hunt for the author of *A Voyage to the Fair Land* and now the harm was here. He had seen the author's notes and drawings scattered on a table in London and, stupefied with prejudice about a woman's abilities, he had not seen it. George Fenwick had not executed the drawings. George Fenwick had not written the book. George Fenwick had not survived the voyage.

How was he to tell George's family? How would he answer Rachel's plea, "You must help us bring our uncle home"? How would he explain to Antony that he had raised his hopes only to crush them?

"Here you are." Matthew returned the paper. "The letter seems to have upset you. Are you in any trouble, Ben?"

Ben forced a smile. "No, no trouble. I'm just surprised, that's all."

"You seem to be involved in something very mysterious."

"It's nothing, really."

"Well, if there's anything I can do to help…"

"Thanks. I'd better be going."

"Shall we meet tomorrow?"

"I'll see. I don't know. Probably not."

"Oh. Well, before you go," Matthew grabbed a couple of bottles from the shelf. "Your father is partial to a drop of Madeira, isn't he? Give the old gent these from me. Wait. Have some claret as well. Oh, and this Canary is very palatable."

Ben, the bottles clanking in his pockets, narrowly avoided falling into the open cellar as he stepped out into the gloomy yard.

"The Madeira will make an excellent tonic!" Mr Dearlove enthused when Ben had returned home.

"It's for you to drink, not give to your customers."

"If you say so. Perhaps we should have a glass with our supper?"

"Indeed we should."

Ben helped his father close the shop, carefully checking that the bolts on the front door were drawn. When Mrs Shackleton had served dinner and left by the kitchen door, as was her custom, Ben did not sit down to eat until he had locked and bolted it and the yard gate. He spent much of the evening prowling around the house, checking and rechecking door locks and window catches. His nervousness spoiled his enjoyment of the Madeira and made it impossible to sleep.

He sat up in bed, the note spread out on his knees. He cursed George Fenwick for his carefulness. True enough he had concealed the text of the letter. If only he hadn't been so careful about keeping a copy. Covering himself, no doubt, should questions be asked about his part in the affair later. And what had that part been?

Ben thought of destroying the letter and transcript, but knew he could not. The Fenwicks had a right to know the truth. He too had to face the facts. There was no chance now of earning enough money to stay in London beyond the time allotted to him by his father's selflessness. He could go back and eke out his dream for a few short months, although he knew that he would never finish his book and it was too late to start another one. As for Almira and Ethelfreda, he loathed his characters. They were shabby puppets in a stale adventure. If only he could write a book like *A Voyage to the Fair Land*.

How his London friends would mock if they knew what he was thinking! A book by a woman? No one could admire such a thing. Let it be known that the book was by a woman and see the sublime prose turn to hysterical outpourings, the daring style to incompetence, the frankness to immorality. No woman who had written as boldly as Sarah would dare to reveal herself to the public if she had led an impeccable life. Who would read a book written by a woman who had gone off with sailors? No wonder she did not want to be found, and he no longer wanted to find her. There was no such thing as a literary lioness.

Mrs Lambert could have told him all this days ago! Then he would not have gone to Overcombe. He would not have been attacked by Hay and Beale. He would not have persuaded Antony Fenwick that his beloved brother still lived. He would not have seen Rachel.

It would be so easy to destroy the paper, to tear it or burn it, or both.

No, he repeated firmly to himself, the Fenwicks have a right to know the truth. All the truth. He did not want to find Sarah for himself, no, but it might be some comfort for the family if they knew what had happened to George on the *Miranda*. Sarah could tell, and the trail was not cold yet. He would go to Mrs Lambert tomorrow and he would threaten to tell the whole world that she was nothing but a common procuress if she did not help him find Sarah.

*

Mrs Lambert handed back the note. "Yes, of course I know Sarah is alive. She was here last time you called."

He had seen a dark figure at a window, watching him. She had been there all the time, in the library, peeping, listening, only feet away from him. He started angrily towards the next room, but stopped when he saw Mrs Lambert's smile.

"She is not here now."

"And you've known all these years?"

"No, not all these years. She came to me only recently, because she was ill and unable to earn any money. I wish she had come sooner. There is no point in looking for her. Her indulgence has caused mischief enough. She will not write another book."

"That doesn't matter now. All I want is to know what happened to the *Miranda*."

"The ship sank."

"How? Why?"

"I do not know."

"She must have told you."

"No, she never speaks of it."

"Then I insist you tell me where she is."

"You insist?"

"I know about the part you played in smuggling her onto the ship so that she could be someone's mistress. It is not something that would enhance your reputation, Mrs Lambert."

She laughed. "My reputation, should I be worried about it, is quite safe. Sarah did not go away as anyone's mistress."

"I know she did. Which of them was it, George or Alex? How can she have been in Bristol and not told their families the *Miranda*'s fate? I can understand if it is shame that keeps her away, but she could have written. It was cruel to be so close to them and not tell them what she knows."

"First you threaten, now you wheedle. Sarah has no need to be ashamed, Mr Dearlove. Quite the reverse. Certainly, as far as the Edgcumbes are concerned, it is they who ought to be ashamed."

"How could a woman like that shame the Edgcumbes?"

"A woman like that! You are speaking of Alex Edgcumbe's sister."

"Alex's sister? Captain Edgcumbe helped his own sister elope with George Fenwick?"

"I have already told you that Sarah did not elope. Or do you picture her as one of those unoriginal creatures who dress themselves as sailors and run away to sea to be with their lovers? If she had been, I would not have been interested in her. No, Mr Dearlove. Sarah was not running away with, but away from."

Ben shook his head. "I don't understand you."

"No, I don't suppose that you do. Or that you would understand if I told you."

"I will try. Please. Tell me."

"A welcome change of tone. Bluster does not become you." She thought for a moment. "Very well, I will tell you what I know of Sarah's story, some that she told me, some that I saw for myself. But I know nothing of the voyage, and I will not help you find her."

Twelve

"Perhaps you are too young to remember, Mr Dearlove, how Bristol society used to centre around the Hotwells – the Hotwells theatre and taverns, the Hotwells House where people went to drink the waters. Rather unpleasant water, warm and effervescent and, before the Pump Room was improved, liable to have river water mixed in with it. You would have been a boy when the poky little theatre closed, no longer able to compete with the establishment on King Street. I was sorry for it; entertainment had never come so cheap. The theatre had a window opening into the Malt Shovel Inn next door, a portal the actors took too much advantage of. I will never forget seeing an inebriated Richard III swing his sword with more enthusiasm than the tiny stage permitted and crown himself with one of the chandeliers.

At that time, Bristol was proud of its own Vauxhall Gardens, which was near to the Pump Room. One night, a ball was to be held there. There was to be dancing out of doors, supper under trees strung with lanterns, card games in a rotunda near an artificial fountain…"

Sarah shrank back into the corner of the carriage while her stepmother smoothed her stepsisters' gowns, adjusted headdresses, patted shoulders, hands and arms into elegant postures. Charlotte and Eliza twisted, turned and smiled as she directed them, repaying her efforts by an increase in charm, fascination and vivacity. It was beyond Sarah to look beguiling, although that did not prevent her mother from trying to improve her. But how could she put a bloom into a complexion that beside the other girls looked sallow, or a sparkle into her dark eyes? As for smiling at nothing, Sarah felt it was beyond her. It was achievement enough that she did not articulate her boredom, which was profound.

Hours had been spent discussing their gowns, trying on their gowns, altering their gowns, altering their gowns again, and then again, and then once more. The dressmaker, looking paler and more tired each time Sarah saw her, was in attendance every day. Then there were shoes, ribbons, petticoats, flowers, fans, a hundred and one things to think of! At breakfast, in the drawing room, at dinner, tea, supper, nothing but the ball had been talked of. You would think this was their first ball, Sarah thought, when in fact life was nothing but a round of teas at the Pump Room, assemblies at the Pump Room, dances at the Pump Room.

"There is Sir Clement's carriage," Mrs Edgcumbe cried, as if there were anything unusual in that.

Charlotte tried not to look conscious of her sister's envious glance, but it was impossible to suppress her self-satisfaction. "Your turn will come one day!" she whispered to Eliza, who was not so pleased by the remark as Charlotte expected. Eliza thought that her turn should have come a long time before this. Besides, Charlotte's engagement to Sir Clement was old news. There was no need for her mother and sister to parade their triumph as if it were fresh-minted each time they appeared in public.

Still, with the Spa's constantly changing society, every ball was another opportunity, and her sister's success – a long awaited one, for Charlotte was already twenty-three and Eliza twenty-one – was not without its advantages. Sir Clement knew all the best families and any visitors to Bristol who were worth knowing came into his orbit sooner or later. So when Eliza saw Clement in conversation with a stranger, her spirits rose. He was a tall man, like Clement in his thirties, but with a weary air that made him look much older than his friend. *I have experienced a hundred similar occasions*, his dull eye seemed to say. *I have seen a score of girlish beauties. I have exerted myself to dance the self-same steps in every flower-decked hall from Vauxhall to the Pantheon.*

The bored gentleman, having been introduced to them as Lord Stanhope, saluted Clement's betrothed with perfect chivalry, Mrs Edgcumbe with impeccable respect, and Eliza with restrained gallantry. Sarah would, as usual, have been overlooked had it not been for his insistent good manners. Though she was the youngest and least important, he expected an introduction to be made and Sarah was propelled with a nudge from her mother into the centre of his attention. And here, in an instant, she was fixed, for Stanhope thought her as beautiful as the darkness between the stars is beautiful. He had possessed the stars, those alluring women, married and unmarried, who dazzle the salons and assemblies with their brightness. The stars are beautiful, yes, but they all look the same, and there are so many of them. Girls like Sarah, gazing on society with a disgust that matched his own, were rare. Though her boredom was instinctive, his the result of a lazy mind and an atrophied soul, it appealed to him a hundred times more than Eliza's chattering eagerness to please.

He was still considering the effect Sarah had on him when a brilliantly dressed girl, hanging on the arm of a showy young man, jogged his elbow. "Stanhope! Bertie has found a table. There's a fellow keeping it for us now."

He frowned at the newcomer and said, "Mrs Edgcumbe, may I introduce my sister, Lady Helen?"

The girl started and blinked at the company as if she had only just noticed them. "Charmed," she cried, presenting them with her bare shoulder. "Do come, Stanhope, or we'll lose our place."

He ignored her impatient tugs on his sleeve. "Would you and your party like to join us, Mrs Edgcumbe?"

"There won't be room for us all," Lady Helen protested.

"I am sure you are mistaken. Lord Bertrand and his friends have made their own arrangements, have they not?" He eyed Bertie, who reddened and agreed. His sister pouted at Bertie's departing back but dared not prevent his going.

They followed a flouncing Lady Helen towards the table, which an anxious waiter was defending from a party whom she contemptuously described as "chandlers!". They were in fact Mr Roscoe and his family, who lived in a crenellated mansion in Leigh Woods. From their windows, they could watch the seagoing ships from the Roscoe yard as they were towed up and down the Avon. Mrs Edgcumbe, who had often discoursed on the age, character and prospects of the heirs to the Roscoe fortune, followed the example set by Lady Helen and was barely civil to them as they apologetically retreated.

The orchestra started to play a popular song. Lady Helen clapped her hands. "*The Beggar's Opera*! I adore MacHeath. Don't you, Miss Edgcumbe?"

Sarah, the startled recipient of her attention, stammered, "I have never seen it."

"But it's delightful. You must see it the next time you are in London."

Sarah, who had never been to London but knew when she was being teased for a provincial, said nothing.

"Mr Edgcumbe does not approve of the piece," Mrs Edgcumbe said. "He has never allowed his girls to play from it. But if you have seen it, Lady Helen, then there can be no harm in it after all."

"Your daughters only ever play what is a credit to you, and

to them," Clement said, gazing adoringly at Charlotte. She simpered back at her betrothed.

"It is a hideous concoction, neither opera nor play," drawled Stanhope.

Lady Helen tossed her head. "Oh, opera! Who wants to listen to an Italian castrato warbling like a girl, or some fat French lady threatening to fling herself off a cliff?"

Sarah, who had often thought the same thing herself but had never dared to say so, asked shyly, "What is *The Beggar's Opera* about?" An angry look from her mother forbade her to draw any more attention to herself and her voice faded to a whisper.

"Miss Edgcumbe wonders what *The Beggar's Opera* is about," Stanhope said.

Lady Helen gave her brother a curious look, half surprised, half knowing. She turned back to Sarah and, friendly all at once, said, "It is about a highwayman who is in Newgate until the jailer's daughter, who is in love with him, helps him escape."

"Oh, I would like to see it!" Sarah exclaimed.

"A play set in a prison? I would never wish to see anything so low." Eliza fluttered primly at Stanhope.

But now the orchestra had finished playing and the dancing was about to commence. It was high time, as the looks that passed between Mrs Edgcumbe and Eliza signified, for Lord Stanhope to ask Eliza to dance. Eliza was mortified, and Mrs Edgcumbe no less so, when Stanhope addressed himself instead to Sarah. Sarah responded with a frightened shake of the head and a timidly stammered refusal.

"What an honour you do the child!" Mrs Edgcumbe said as graciously as she could. With a squeeze of her matronly fingers on the girl's arm, she compelled Sarah to accept.

Then Lord Stanhope requested the second dance from Eliza, and Mrs Edgcumbe was able to breathe again.

"Of course, it only shows what kind of man Lord Stanhope is," Mrs Edgcumbe murmured in Eliza's ear when he led Sarah away. "What condescension! What kindness! And what delicacy too. He knows that the eyes of the world are upon him. Don't turn your head, but from here I can see half a dozen mothers at least, all staring as if their eyes would fall out. It is rare to see a man take such great pains to avoid compromising a young lady who has caught his eye as you have. It would not do if he were to be seen monopolising you all evening. And remember, the first dance is not the most significant in the programme. Think too of the effect of the contrast when he sees how well you dance."

While Lady Helen struggled to stifle her laughter at the mother and daughter's doomed interest in her brother, for she knew from past experience of Stanhope's stratagems where his interest lay, Stanhope struggled to dazzle his partner. He had thought to flatter a clumsy child by convincing her that she danced like an angel, but soon saw that his praise had no effect on her. She danced well enough, but cared little for the skill. He attempted conversation next, thinking it an easy trick to make a tongue-tied sixteen-year-old believe that he was charmed by her every word.

"I believe," he remarked, "that the coolness of the waters here makes them particularly efficacious in cases of fever."

"The waters are not cool," Sarah answered. "They come from the spring at a constant seventy-six degrees."

Could anyone be so impervious to his attractions? A less subtle approach might be required.

"Cool or warm," he said, ogling her significantly, "it seems to me that any man who comes to Bristol in the hopes of a cure is only in danger of being thrown into a worse fever, an incurable fever."

"Oh no, the risk is quite small. It is true that the spring

used to be polluted by high tides, but the pipes into the Pump Room have been designed to allow waste water to run out of the well and prevent tidal water running in. You are in little danger here."

You are in little danger here! Was it his imagination or was there a hint of scorn in her voice? Looking at her more closely, he decided that it was his imagination. She really did think he was interested in the qualities of the Bristol spring. He had forgotten that girls could be so unaware of a man's meaning before they discovered sexual intrigue. After that, they were like all the others. But before!

The dance ended and he exchanged Sarah for a palpitating Eliza, returning a little while later with an effortlessly, for he had made no effort, dazzled Eliza.

"Do you like the Gardens, Miss Edgcumbe?" Lady Helen asked, her gown rustling and her jewels sparkling.

"I like the lanterns strung out in the trees," Sarah answered.

"I like it all!" Lady Helen confided in a piercing voice. "The music, and the dancing, and being looked at by all the people." She rustled and sparkled again, succeeding in catching the eye of a gentleman who happened to be passing. Sarah marvelled at her precocity. They were the same age but Lady Helen dressed, drank and flirted like a woman twice as old and no one, least of all her brother, Stanhope, seemed to mind it. There was no mother or other female relative in charge of her, and had not been for some time. Her only example was her brother's, an example she occasionally remembered to imitate. "Of course," she added in a bored drawl, "it's only a secondary Vauxhall, and not at all like the London one."

But a moment later, she was revelling in the brazen admiration of a knock-kneed, warty-nosed lord as he sauntered past their table.

141

"Sarah, ask Lady Helen if she would like to eat some more strawberries," Mrs Edgcumbe commanded.

Lady Helen wrinkled her nose and waved the dish away. "No, I'm bored to death with them. I'd like to go for a walk."

"A walk! What an excellent idea!" Mrs Edgcumbe cooed and, in a minute, the company was broken up. Clement and Charlotte walked together as usual, and Lord Stanhope attended Eliza and her mother. Lady Helen put her arm through Sarah's as if they were the best of friends, though Sarah had hardly spoken ten words to Lady Helen's hundred. But perhaps that was what made her such a desirable companion.

No one as determined as Lady Helen to enjoy attention could fail to attract it. She sauntered along with a triumphant smile on her face, glancing now over her right shoulder, now her left, her eyelids lowered and her head thrown back. Gentlemen sighed and gentlemen bowed, and the responsibility for keeping to their path and negotiating the crowds fell to Sarah. But Lady Helen did not like to be directed. Gradually, her pace slowed so much that they fell behind the others and, after a short while, Sarah lost sight of them altogether.

"They must have gone down here," Lady Helen suggested carelessly, directing Sarah onto one of the paths leading away from the orchestra stand. The way was narrow and not so well lit as the main routes and, rather than leading to any public entertainment, led only into a maze of shadier ways between tall hedges. They turned to the right, to the left, but could not find a way out of the labyrinth. It was odd to be so lost and bewildered when they could still hear music and voices.

"I can hear someone talking!" Lady Helen said.

Sarah too could hear men talking. It was difficult to tell whether the sound was in front or to the side. The girls were continually frustrated by the impassable hedges. Sometimes they seemed to have lost the sound altogether, but with another turn it was amplified until it became so clear they could almost distinguish what the men were saying. Sarah felt a growing sense of unease. The men were well-spoken, but there was a hint of coarseness in their tone, and more than a hint of insobriety.

At last there were lights ahead. Drawing near, they saw that a fixed lantern dimly illuminated a small arbour. One man sprawled on the bench, his legs spread out in front of him and his hands crossed over his stomach, another perched on the arm of the bench with his feet on the seat. Standing in front of them, a third brandished a champagne bottle at a slim, delicate-looking youth.

"I don't think I should have any more." The boy's voice was high and nervous.

"Don't be such a baby," growled Sprawler. "You said you wanted to come out with me and my friends. Since I have brought you along, you had better not be a millstone."

The man with the bottle thrust it into the boy's hands, forced it to his lips and held it up while he drank. After a mouthful, the lad signalled that he had swallowed enough, but the man kept the bottle there. Coughing and spluttering, the boy succeeded at last in pushing the drink away. The man held up the bottle. "He's had a good swig!"

"Give it to me," said Percher, while the boy wiped his chin and dabbed at the front of his shirt.

Sarah did not like the look of them. She whispered, "I think we should try another way," but Lady Helen, seeing only an opportunity for eliciting more adoration, pulled Sarah after her and hurried towards the gallants.

Sprawler was the first to see them. "What's this?" he cried, heaving himself into a sitting position. "Look here, boys. I told you our luck would turn."

143

Percher jumped to the ground. "My God, it's those actresses. The ones we saw at the Hotwell last night. How d'ye do, ladies. Ed, manners." With a kick he encouraged Sprawler to stand up. They surrounded the girls, executing exaggerated bows.

Lady Helen smiled and batted her lashes, but Sarah shrank from their leering faces. She started to back away, tugging a resistant Lady Helen with her, but one of the men leaped forward to block their path. Sarah moved to the left. The path was blocked that way too.

Lady Helen smirked and preened as the men edged them in. She thought that this was all part of some complicated ritual of worship of which she was the object. Sarah was filled with contempt for the obsequious female vanity that interpreted bullying as homage.

"Gentlemen," she said, her voice cold and steady, "let us pass."

"You aren't going to leave us when we have only just met?" slurred Sprawler, grabbing Sarah's hand.

"Do not touch me, sir!" Sarah snatched her hand away.

"Hoity toity!" he laughed, lunging at her again.

"Oh, sir!" Lady Helen tittered. "We aren't actresses! I am – "

Sarah did not give them time to discover the name of the lady they importuned. The young boy with the damp front was the weakest link in the chain and it was towards him that Sarah, dragging Lady Helen behind her, made a dash. With the flat of her hand, she shoved the unsteady boy in the chest as hard as she could. He staggered. Sarah let go of Helen's hand and lifted her heavy skirt. Then she was running, away from the light, away from the voices, into the darker pathways, until the blood roared in her ears and she could not draw another breath. Her ribs felt as if they would break against her tight bodice.

She slowed down and turned to look behind her. None of the roughs had followed – but neither had Lady Helen!

Sarah shut her eyes and squeezed them tight. Everything was spinning around her – she was going to faint –

"Where are you running to?"

Sarah opened her eyes on muffling darkness. She put up her fists and battered the chest and arms that enveloped her. Through her panic she heard, "Calm yourself, Miss Edgcumbe! There is nothing to apprehend." It was Lord Stanhope. "That's better," he said. If his arms encircled her more tightly than was necessary, she did not notice.

"Lady Helen!"

"Sir Clement has gone to look for her. Sit here and collect yourself. You have run yourself into a fright, quite needlessly."

He drew her into a convenient arbour and she sank down onto the stone seat with Stanhope beside her, one arm protectively around her shoulder.

"Dry your tears," he said, drawing her close to him and dabbing at her face with a lace handkerchief. If there were no tears on her face, she did not notice that either.

"I'm not upset," she declared as soon as she got her breath back. "I'm angry."

"Angry?" he repeated. "How magnificent!"

"Yes. How dare they think they can treat us like that!"

"Shocking, shocking," he murmured, drawing her closer still.

"What right do they think they have…"

"I am glad that it was you, and not Eliza, whom my sister led into these byways," Stanhope murmured.

"… except the right of superior numbers and superior strength – "

"Yes, men are very strong," agreed Stanhope, tilting up her chin and pressing his mouth over hers.

Unable to move, Sarah endured having her head pressed back in the crook of his arm, the closing of his eyes to the shock and outrage in hers, and the strange, wet, pressure of his lips. She thought the kiss lasted for ever. He thought it very brief.

"No, you really must learn to do it properly," he said, releasing her. "Your lips are like wood. We haven't enough time now and, besides, you're too young to be trusted not to advertise your new condition to the world. Even your mama would notice, I think. So let us use these precious moments to understand one another. You know I admire you, Sarah."

"But Eliza!" she gasped.

"Eliza is pretty," Stanhope said, "and vivacious and charming, etcetera, etcetera, though a bit long in the tooth. But I am captivated by your dark and sullen beauty. Don't you like sullen? I do. I like the way your eyes glower at the world and the rareness of your smiles. It's true, there aren't many men who are capable of seeing you as I do. There is a very special feeling between us, Sarah, that no one else suspects."

Sarah understood that he might just as well have said *that no one else will believe*. Who would think he was interested in her?

"No," she said.

Stanhope shrugged. That *no* meant very little to him. It was simply the response of a startled girl, a flattered and a fascinated girl, to his overtures. Give her time to get over the shock of being found attractive, and by such a man as himself. It would not be long before she came to terms with the danger and the excitement.

She rose to her feet and he made no effort to detain her. She would take his arm because she had to – to keep up appearances – and they would return to their party. The hand that rested on his would tremble and he would apply a secret pressure as he released it. Their eyes would meet and the rest would follow, for they would already be tied by deceit.

He stood up and held out his arm. She stood before him,

head bent, hands clasped together, thinking. He liked her attitude. He looked forward to being the one to influence those thoughts.

"Miss Edgcumbe?"

Her head jerked up, she gave an anguished cry and, before he could stop her, she was off, twisting and turning into the maze. She was lost to his sight long after he had given up the effort of following her. Let her go! It was not his place, nor was there any need, to chase after her.

Thirteen

Maria Lambert and Monsieur Favet had timed their arrival at the Gardens to avoid the queues. With a flourish, the Frenchman helped the lady descend from her carriage and led her between huddles of liveried drivers who were sharing jugs of beer over dice and cards. A few chairmen stood about, hoping for early fares.

The couple passed into the gatehouse where two waiters lolled on one of the high-backed benches around the walls. They were baiting a young woman who stood before them, her dress snagged at the hem, hair tumbled down from a style that was far too elaborate for her age, her satin shoes filthy and torn. Catching sight of the arrivals, the waiters abandoned their game and scrambled to attention.

Their first impression of the girl was that she was one of those women who please paying gentlemen in the ill-lit walks and bowers of the Gardens. They were about to pass without noticing her when she wailed, "Oh, will you please get me a chair!"

It was the voice of a gentlewoman, a young one, in distress. At once, Monsieur Favet halted. He bowed, a bow that Mrs Lambert thought put every Englishman to shame, and quietly enquired if he could be of assistance. Terrified, the girl shrank from him.

But now Mrs Lambert, coming up to Monsieur Favet, recognised her. "Why, Miss Edgcumbe! What has happened?"

The girl looked at the older woman, doubtfully at first but at last remembered her and blurted, "Mrs Lambert! I am trying to get home and I want a chair but I haven't got any money and so they cannot fetch one for me!"

"Cannot fetch one!" Monsieur Favet rounded on the waiters. "How dare you, ruffians, treat a lady in this fashion!" His hand was on the hilt of his sword, the churls quaked.

"Monsieur," Mrs Lambert murmured with pride in her voice, "do not waste any time on these fellows. We must take Miss Edgcumbe home."

Sarah was still too nervous to trust her arm to Favet, so Mrs Lambert led her to the carriage.

"Miss Edgcumbe," she explained to Favet as they travelled back into town, "is Joseph Edgcumbe's youngest daughter. Before you came to England, I often attended his musical evenings. Miss Charlotte sang, and Miss Eliza played, and – " squeezing Sarah's hand, "Sarah used to hide behind doors and curtains in an effort to avoid the company. Which was hardly flattering for us!"

Sarah laughed, as Mrs Lambert had intended. The tears had dried on her cheeks and, in the moonlight, it was possible to get some idea of how the awkward child had grown up. Her mother died shortly after giving birth to her, having provided Joseph Edgcumbe with a son eight years previously. Mrs Lambert remembered them as a charming pair of children and thought it marvellous to see how Alex cared for his little sister. She often saw Sarah sitting on his knee while he let her look at his books. They were full of interest for the young child, as his reading consisted almost exclusively of books about ships, which were enlivened by diagrams and drawings. Or he would teach her from his book of maps. How gravely she stared up at his face, trying to follow the strange words!

"This is the Atlantic Ocean. Here's America. It takes six weeks or more to cross. Bristol is here. Put your finger on the page, that's right. Here's India, and China. Batavia, which is owned by the Dutch. This is New Holland. No one has sailed along the eastern coast yet. And here, all this empty space, that's the Pacific Ocean where you can sail for weeks without seeing land. You can sail past land and never know it's there. And there's a new land waiting to be discovered. It's called the Great Southern Continent. And, one day, I shall sail southwards and I shall find it."

It is very doubtful that she understood everything he told her at the time. All that mattered for Sarah was that he paid her so much attention, for she got precious little from anyone else. Her father was writing a *History of Music* and spent his days in his study. When Sarah was two-years-old, he emerged long enough to remarry. Why he chose Clara Hutchinson when – here Mrs Lambert checked herself. Clara, she continued after a brief pause, brought two girls to the match, Charlotte and Eliza, both as selfish and silly as herself. Where Sarah suffered from too little attention, those girls suffered from a good deal too much.

Sarah must have been very lonely after Alex left home, when she was four and he was twelve, to go to the naval Academy in Portsmouth. His visits home were rare after that, for he started his training in the middle of a war and the Navy needed all the sailors it could get to man its ships. By the time the war ended, he was sixteen and had already seen active service. Even when the peace came, there were still British interests to protect and he was more often at sea than on land.

Favet waited in the carriage while Mrs Lambert took Sarah into the house in George Street. The door was opened by Mrs Edgcumbe's housekeeper who shrieked when she saw Sarah sinking in Mrs Lambert's arms.

"Miss Sarah has come home early, that is all," she snapped, and sent Sarah to her room while she explained to the flustered woman that a glass of wine was needed. When at last the domestic seemed to understand her, Mrs Lambert went upstairs. She passed the room that Sarah's stepsisters shared, with its clutter of discarded dresses and ribbons, its smell of powder and perfumes, its echo of giggles and gossip so strong that the words *ridotto, rout* and *assemblies* seemed to whisper over the loops and frills. Next door, Sarah's room was smaller, the bed neatly made, clothes put away, nothing but a hairbrush and comb laid out on the dressing table.

She was sitting at her desk in the dark when Mrs Lambert entered with the candle. In front of her lay her sketchbook, open at a study of a rose. The original, picked from the garden, stood in a glass of water nearby. Even by the flickering candlelight, Mrs Lambert could see that the drawing was very fine.

"Do you like to draw flowers?"

"Yes, when I am in my own room," Sarah answered listlessly. "When we are drawing downstairs, we have to make copies of ruined abbeys under moonlight from the print books that Mother buys. She thinks my flowers are too botanical and botany is not a fit subject for a woman."

It was only one more instance of the woman's stupidity and Mrs Lambert made no comment as she put the candle down. As the shadows fled, she saw that almost half the desk was taken up with a model ship. It was not a toy as its size and the detail with which it was fashioned proved – every sail, every block, every coil of rope was represented. It was one of those models that naval students use to teach themselves a ship's rigging.

"That's a strange ornament for a young lady's room."

Sarah smiled. "Alex gave it to me before he went to sea." She pointed. "The main topgallant. The mizen topsail. The fore topsail."

"You are almost a tar yourself! I had almost forgotten the handsome boy and his ships. Where is he now?"

Sarah sighed. "He is in Newfoundland, surveying the coastline. He will not be home until next year. I have not had a letter for months. Would you like to read his last one?"

She opened a drawer in the desk. It was full of letters, all done up with ribbon like billets-doux. She took out a packet and handed the latest one to her guest, who skimmed over it for politeness's sake. *Hope that Madame Edgcumbe's temper is improved... When I'm home, I'll take you down to Avonmouth to see the pilots... Now, you asked how I set about my surveying work. It is done by means of triangulation, which is when you divide the area you wish to survey into triangles...*

"But you must tell me," she said, handing the letter back, "what happened in the Gardens?"

Sarah's face hardened. "I was ill, that was all."

"Why were you on your own?"

"I felt faint and lingered behind the others, and then I could not find them."

"It sounds as if they have found you."

Downstairs, the hall was full of people all talking at once. Mrs Lambert recognised Mr Edgcumbe's voice amongst the rest. He had just returned from an evening at his glee club when their carriages pulled up. Usually, his wife and her daughters greeted him coolly after his singing parties, which were held in an upstairs room of a tavern. They would complain that he came home reeking "as if he had been brought up on a tobacco plantation", a consequence, Mrs Edgcumbe would suggest, of mixing with "music teachers and organ players" and singing "songs which must be low since no women are present". But tonight they clung onto his arm, pouring out their tale.

"I shall send her away!" Mr Edgcumbe thundered.

Mrs Edgcumbe's footsteps clacked across the tiles. "Do you hear your father, Miss?" she called. "Come here at once."

Quickly, Mrs Lambert tidied Sarah's hair. "You had better go down."

She started out bravely, but quailed at the top of the stairs. She swayed and clutched the banister, looking down at the angry, upturned faces.

"We have had to come away because of you!" Eliza screeched.

"You deserve to be whipped! Let me go, Clement!" Charlotte struggled to free herself from her lover as if she meant to administer the chastisement herself.

"Come down," Mrs Edgcumbe commanded. When Sarah set her foot on the hall floor, her mother caught hold of her arm and shook her. "Your father will send you off to school after this my girl, and don't think that I shall be able to stop him!"

That allegedly stern parent looked on, frowning as if he were trying to follow a particularly confusing scene in an Italian opera.

As Mrs Lambert started after Sarah, another girl darted forward from the shadows around the front door. Her dress was showy and her manner brazen, and it was likely that the bloom in her cheeks came from wine. Lady Helen giggled. "La, Sarah, what did you run away for?"

Mrs Edgcumbe rattled Sarah again. "Now tell me what you mean by this? Putting your friends to the trouble – "

"To the shame!" interposed Charlotte.

"To the shame of having to make enquiries – "

"Public enquiries!" Charlotte again.

"– of having to make public enquiries about you! To discover that a waiter had more idea of the whereabouts of her daughter than her own mother! And then to be informed that you had joined another party and taken yourself off home! Oh, I know that you have to be different and dislike what the rest of the world enjoys, but when I say you are to go to the Gardens then to the Gardens you go. You do not take yourself off at your own pleasure."

The shaking was severe and the grip on her arm tight. Sarah could not have answered if she had wanted to. Giddily, she pressed her hand to her head, but her fingers were hot and did not bring any relief to her flushed brow.

From the shadows came a new voice, calm, soft, courteous.

"Mrs Edgcumbe, if I might be permitted to suggest. It may be that Sarah had a reason for her flight."

A low hiss escaped Mrs Lambert's lips. The man looked up. Their eyes met.

Lord Stanhope mastered his surprise, dismissing her with an insolent flick of his eyelids. "Sarah was alarmed by the high spirits of Lady Helen's friends," he continued smoothly. "There was an embarrassing moment before recognition when I fear they were perhaps a little more jocund than they should have been."

"What a scared cat you are, Sarah!" Lady Helen laughed again, a gross, grating sound Mrs Lambeth thought it. "When it was only Bertie's mob. We would have come after you only I was scared of the dark and they had to help me find my brother. But they said they are sorry."

So she was Stanhope's sister, Mrs Lambert thought. If he'd had the care of her upbringing, then he had produced a female libertine.

"I don't know how anyone can be so foolish," Mrs Edgcumbe snapped. "But even if she was frightened, for no good reason, it does not account for leaving without us, and causing Mrs Lambert," Mrs Edgcumbe reluctantly bowed to her visitor who had reached the bottom of the stairs, "such embarrassment. Do you think there is no one else in the world but yourself? You bold, stubborn, unsociable girl!"

Stanhope cleared his throat. "It may be, Madam, that Sarah, after wandering around on her own, came to the conclusion that her friends had left the Gardens. Quite properly, she realised that it was out of the question that she should remain there. Some acquaintances happened along and she explained her situation with all the exaggeration her confusion suggested to her. I do not doubt that she did the best she could under the circumstances."

"Is this true, Sarah?" Mr Edgcumbe eagerly took up Stanhope's lead. He had begun to realise that having to fulfil his threat to send his daughter away when she was, on the whole, a quiet and peaceable little thing would involve him in the trouble of choosing a school, transporting the girl to it, and posting regular banknotes.

"Yes," Sarah murmured. "I thought you had all gone home."

At this, Mrs Edgcumbe released her grip. Sarah tottered and would have fallen if Sir Clement had not caught her and helped her into the footman's chair.

"Why you could not tell us this yourself without leaving it all to Lord Stanhope to divine, I don't know," Mrs Edgcumbe grumbled. "You really have been very foolish, Sarah."

"Can I have a glass of water please?" Sarah whispered.

"There now, you have gone and made yourself ill," Mrs Edgcumbe rejoined. "Let that be a lesson to you."

"Here's the water," said Sir Clement.

"Thank you," said Sarah, and burst into tears.

"Oh dear, child, what are we going to do with you?" Mrs Edgcumbe, moved to pity at last, bent over the girl.

A diffident cough. "Might I suggest?"

"Of course, Lord Stanhope."

His eyes sought out Mrs Lambert's. "The girl needs putting to bed."

*

Mrs Lambert called on the Edgcumbes the following day and was told that Sarah was ill in bed. It was a week before she came downstairs, and before Mrs Lambert was able to take any action.

Uncle Jacob stood by the hearth boasting about his new carriage. "I got it for no pounds, no shillings and no pence! Yes, no pounds, no shillings and no pence, nor halfpence neither! He took one chance too many, did Jon Bowood. I warned him when I gave him the loan. But, I promise you, there's a lot to be made from our Clifton Green house-building venture. I say, Joe, you won't sign the deeds with a crotchet, eh? Or a quaver?"

Joseph, who may have taken to music to drown out the din of his elder brother's teasing, sighed. "Shall we go to my study? We can have our Madeira in there while we deal with my investments."

Jacob started after him. "Where d'ye buy yours? Jackson's? Why, he's the most expensive wine seller in Bristol. Don't buy from him again, brother, or you'll end up as bankrupt as Bowood. Tim Tatton!" he roared as they passed through the door.

"Coming, sir!" cried the clerk who was sitting on a hard chair in the hall with the Edgcumbe papers on his lap.

Mrs Lambert smiled at Sarah. "I heard you were ill and have come on purpose to see you."

"That is very kind," said Mrs Edgcumbe stiffly. "Sarah has had nothing but a slight chill."

"A slight chill," Mrs Lambert replied, "if it is indeed a chill, is not very pleasant all the same, is it?"

Sarah blushed. To set her at her ease, Mrs Lambert endured Mrs Edgcumbe's and her daughters' conversation for several moments – "I hear the King has given the Queen a gold shuttle for her lace work. Isn't that a lovely gift, girls?"

As soon as she could, Mrs Lambert introduced the purpose of her visit. "I have come to invite Sarah to spend an afternoon with me. Perhaps, Mrs Edgcumbe, you could spare her tomorrow if she is feeling strong enough?"

"Invite Sarah?" exclaimed Eliza.

Charlotte dropped the mote spoon, with which she had been poking leaves out of the teapot spout, onto the tray.

"Oh, I do feel strong enough!" Sarah cried.

"I… I am not sure. We may have engagements," Mrs Edgcumbe objected.

"I am not engaged to anything," Sarah said.

"How can you be," Mrs Lambert said with a smile, "since you have been ill all week? I meant to be the first with an invitation."

"Well, Sarah is grateful, I'm sure. But a social gathering may be too much for her in her present state."

"I have not invited anyone else, nor shall I receive any other visitors if I have Sarah for company."

"I think it would do me good to go," Sarah said.

Mrs Edgcumbe could not deny that the girl had brightened up at the prospect. If her guest was happy to lift the burden of looking after the convalescent from the busy mother's shoulders for a few hours, why should she refuse? So she did not.

Fourteen

On a June day a year later, Sarah sat in the garden of Maria Lambert's house on Clifton Hill, an unread book open on her lap. The few hours of that first invitation had soon been extended to entire days, then to weekends, then to weeks at a time. It was an arrangement that suited everyone except Stanhope, as Mrs Lambert privately remarked to Monsieur Favet with satisfaction. He must have been frequently disappointed by the removal of the girl from his society, the more so since he knew that he was being deliberately thwarted. His determination to best Mrs Lambert had driven him to desperate measures, and if Mrs Edgcumbe had been inclined to grumble about Sarah's Clifton visits, she was reconciled to them now.

Sarah had chosen her time badly. Going to Eliza's room on the evening that the engagement was announced was not wise, but she had been so alarmed. The thought that Stanhope would soon be a member of the family, claiming a brother's rights of intimacy, filled her with dread. Her fear was not just for herself. Eliza had to be warned.

"You don't really know what he is like," she said.

Eliza laughed. "And you do, I suppose?"

"I know something of his true nature. Prior to making his declaration to you, he… he… made a proposal to me."

"He asked you to marry him?"

"Not exactly."

"Not at all!" Eliza sneered.

"He has behaved inappropriately towards me."

"What do you mean? What nonsense! You ugly owl! Stanhope has never shown the least interest in you and neither will any other man. You will remain a spinster all your life!" Eliza's voice grew shriller and louder until, at last, Mrs Edgcumbe burst into the room demanding to know what the noise was about.

"Tell her, Sarah," Eliza cried, flouncing into a chair.

Sarah had not been able to repeat her hints, and Eliza would not, so Sarah had been sent to her room to await a scolding about attention-seeking and spoiling other people's happiness and always going against the grain of her family.

Sarah was not thinking of that now. A tall, elegant figure made his way along the path. There were more flowers on his waistcoat than in the bower, and his perfume drowned out their fragrance. The care he lavished on his appearance often fooled other men into thinking him an easy target for insult, but Favet was a brilliant swordsman who practised and trained every day.

"Here you are!"

"I hope you haven't been put to a great deal of trouble to find me, Monsieur Favet." Sarah returned his smile.

"Not at all. I thought you would be here. I regret to tell you," he added, "that the carriage has arrived."

Sarah jumped to her feet. "Has it? Thank you, Monsieur."

"I don't think you are so sad to leave us this time."

Sarah laughed. "I'm sorry. Do I look so eager to be gone?"

"There is no need to apologise." He offered his arm. "It is good to see you smile. Ah, here is Madam."

"Sarah, your mother is waiting for you," Mrs Lambert announced as she came up to them. She linked arms with her favourite. "Remember, you are to come back to me on Wednesday."

"I remember!" Sarah answered. She kissed Mrs Lambert

159

goodbye, ran into the house, seized her things from the hall table and hurried into the waiting carriage.

"I thought you would never come out," said Mrs Edgcumbe piercingly. "Don't wave, that foreign monkey is standing next to her. Are you going to greet your mother?"

"How are you, Mother?" Sarah pecked her mother's cheek.

"Tut, this driver is so slow," Mrs Edgcumbe fretted. "And I am so busy! Really, when he knows I have so much to do, what with Charlotte's Condition and Eliza's Wallpaper to think about, I don't know why Alex has to bring a visitor home with him."

Her mother's remarks could not spoil the joy of the day for Sarah. After two years in Newfoundland, Alex was coming home, and bringing his friend George Fenwick with him.

"Why, Sarah, you are radiant tonight!" Mrs Lambert exclaimed, as Sarah shrugged off her outdoor things in her hall on the following Wednesday. "And which is Mr Edgcumbe, and which Mr Fenwick?"

"But don't you remember, Alex?" laughed Sarah, proudly presenting her brother.

Recalling the charming boy he had been, Mrs Lambert was little surprised to see how distinguished a young man he had become. At twenty-five, he already had more than ten years' sea-service behind him. The experience showed in his self-assurance and poise. He was tall and strong, and the cut of his coat emphasised his broad shoulders and straight back. He wore a blue jacket lined with white, a white laced waistcoat, and white breeches. The colours suited his tanned face and his thick brown hair, bleached almost fair by wind and sun.

George Fenwick was no less attractive in his civilian's dress, unostentatious but unmistakably wealthy. Two years older, he was a head taller than Alex with dark hair and brown eyes. His face was equally weather-beaten, though in his expression was more seriousness than in Alex's, a more learned air, and also the look of a man used to being indulged. All this Mrs Lambert noted as she watched George's head turn towards Sarah and astonishment spread across his features. Eyeing her young friend, she guessed the reason for George's surprise. She thought, You wonder at the transformation from the dull, silent girl you have passed the last two days with in George Street, Mr Fenwick!

George Fenwick marvelled at his own obtuseness. Had he not learned enough about transplantation by now? Take an exquisite bloom from between the windswept rocks where it grows, plant it in the richest soil, shelter it from wintry blasts, water it daily, and watch it turn into a slimy tangle of brown stems. There are places to which living things belong and places where they cannot thrive, and he had made the error of thinking that Sarah belonged to the home where he had first encountered her. A very different home from this one. Here there were books on the shelves open to all to peruse not, as at Mr Edgcumbe's, shut away in one person's private study. There were magazines on the tables – journals of essays, letters, poems, gossip, scandal, and controversy. George had seen nothing but fashion plates and sentimental picture books in Mrs Edgcumbe's drawing room.

There was the foreigner too, who George knew would never be suffered to cross the threshold of any establishment which Mrs Edgcumbe controlled. George turned and held out his hand to the 'French secretary', who Mrs Edgcumbe had mentioned with a suggestive little smile and a twitch of her shoulder, confiding to George that Favet "had to flee his own country after killing a nobleman in a duel". George thought that if the Clara Edgcumbes of this world are to be believed, it was a wonder there were any swordsmen left in France since the only ones anyone ever heard about had either been slain or were on the run.

George later confided in Mrs Lambert that he was already plotting, at this early stage, how to extricate himself from the visit. Alex had certainly not benefited in George's eyes from his transformation from shipboard companion to landsman. For two years, George had been hearing about Alex's sister. There was no other girl like Sarah! You could explain to her how a sextant worked, she could solve the mathematical problems Alex set her in his letters, and she knew as much about a ship's rigging – more in some cases! – as any young officer.

And what a brave little thing she was! Often, when Alex was home on leave, he took her down to Bristol Quay, or to the sail loft on Wapping Wharf, or to the shipyard where he told her how a ship would rise in glory from the slime of the mud and the grime of the smoking fires and the foul language of the carpenters, caulkers and blacksmiths. He pointed out the exact spot from which John Cabot had sailed to his discovery of Newfoundland. He took her to Goldney Hall and paid the gardener to lead them down into the grotto where the cold, dripping walls were encrusted with South Sea shells. All done in strictest secrecy mind, not the sort of outings Madam Edgcumbe would have approved of, but you could rely on Sarah to be a merry, smart, sensible girl.

What a picture George had formed in his mind! Then, after hours of travelling, they had arrived in Bristol and George was ushered into an ugly pink drawing room where a pompous old dilettante with a frivolous wife, one vain married daughter, one vain engaged daughter, and one plain daughter neither married nor engaged had greeted him. George did not see the youngest's plainness at first. In the flurry of throwing herself into Alex's arms, he had an impression of a slender girl with large dark eyes brilliant with happy tears and a smile that a man might think it worth coming home for. Then the lady of the house, her feathers wobbling angrily, scolded, "Sarah, you are not the only one Alex has not seen these two years!" The girl faded away into a corner, along with George's first impression of her. There she had remained for the rest of the evening until prodded out of her place by her mother to greet her brother-in-law to be, which she did with a marked lack of grace.

Now, as George bowed and murmured, "Bien le bonsoir, Monsieur. Vous m'honorez," he could not help his chagrined gaze straying to where Sarah stood arm in arm with Alex. George Fenwick was rarely humbled because rarely wrong. He had been wrong about Sarah – he was delighting in his humility now!

"Champagne!" Mrs Lambert cried. "Unless you would prefer sherry."

"Champagne is the thing I missed most during our voyage," George declared.

Alex laughed. "He is a terrible humbug, Mrs Lambert! There is no man so oblivious to what he eats or drinks as George."

"I kept quiet about my suffering for want of champagne, my dear boy, as I know that none of you grog-swilling tars know the taste of good wine."

"Bravo, monsieur!" Favet exclaimed. "Now you will taste an excellent wine." He waved the servant aside and dealt with the bottle himself, while he and George exchanged views on grapes, vintages and how best to drink a good wine.

At dinner, Mrs Lambert placed George Fenwick on her left, Favet at the head of the table on her right, and Sarah and Alex opposite to her. She exchanged a smile with Favet, sharing her pleasure at the sight of Sarah – captivating without being coquettish, beautiful without being self-conscious, and intelligent, yes, very intelligent! Yet never strident. She had a thrilling voice, low and sweet when she spoke, light and gay when she laughed. The girl could have made two or three good matches from amongst the gentlemen to whom she had been introduced in her friend's society. Mrs Lambert had sympathised with the lovers' complaints of indifference, wondering what ideal of manhood blinded her to their qualities. But then she had not met Alex Edgcumbe, nor George Fenwick who was so worthy to be his friend.

Alex had been describing, in a light-hearted manner, some of the discomforts of shipboard life. Glad to see that George's appetite had not been ruined by maggoty bread and portable soup, Mrs Lambert asked him, "And now the amenities of life are restored to you, what are your plans, Mr Fenwick?"

"My plans are to escape those amenities at the first opportunity. I plan to take ship to Iceland just as soon as I can obtain a berth."

Favet shivered. "Brr! Iceland! The very name freezes my bones. If Alex said he was going to Iceland, I would understand it. He belongs to the Navy and must go where they send him, isn't that so?" Alex acknowledged the truth of the remark. For a moment, the reminder that she and Alex must sooner or later endure another leave-taking brought sadness to Sarah's face.

"But you, Monsieur Fenwick," Favet continued, "what compels you to go?"

"I go to study nature."

"To study nature? Plants, and rocks, and creeping things and crawling things?"

"Yes. Do you know there are fish that can fly, birds that spend their entire lives in the air, animals that keep their young in their pockets?"

"And mermaids and Cyclops and antipodes?"

George laughed. "Who knows? There is so much yet to discover."

"But what do you hope to discover? How the flying fish flies?"

"Well, it would be worth knowing. But the natural sciences mean much more. To study nature is to study God through His creation. By striving to understand the laws that govern nature, we strive to discover God's immutable, eternal laws."

"But nature is not eternal," Favet returned. "The Bible says that God does not mean it to last. Isn't the world expected to end on the Day of Judgement? How then can you discover eternal laws from something that is only temporary?"

"But there are eternal principles. Since God is eternal, how can it be otherwise? Of course the world will pass away in its due time. Everything has its place. There is an order to everything."

"And you can observe this order when you study a fish?"

George, ruffled by Favet's searching questions, began to suspect him of atheistical tendencies. "I do not confine myself to fishes on my travels. I also study humankind. The aim of science is to distinguish the divine in us from the earthly, to identify those qualities that belong to man as God created him and those that are merely incidental. We all know how much variety of law and custom exists between one European country and another. Imagine, if you can, how much greater the difference between the people of one continent and another. Yet some things are common to all. How better to determine which than by observation?"

"Where we have just been," put in Alex, "the ladies get married in gowns perfumed with train oil." He grimaced. "I hope Eliza will carry a sweeter nosegay!"

They all laughed. "But it is only habit," George said. "If you had been brought up to it, you would not find the smell noxious."

"And I suppose," said Mrs Lambert sharply, "had I been

born in Turkey, I would be glad to live in a harem since it is only our European habits which prevent us from making slaves of our women."

"When I say that some of the things we believe in are only habit, I do not mean to say that we should abandon them on that account," George replied. "There may be very good reasons for obedience to the rules by which we live, which comparison with those of other nations will only strengthen."

Favet, out of respect for George's earnestness, dropped his argument.

Mrs Lambert now put her question to Alex. "Do you have any idea where you will be sent to next?"

Alex hesitated and glanced at George.

George laughed. "Come, come, Alex, I promise you your wish will come true! Lord Sandwich will not refuse my father. You will have your place on the next Pacific voyage."

Mrs Lambert kept herself up to date with the transactions of the Royal Society. "I have heard that Mr Banks is planning a second expedition but I would have thought his voyage would have been of more interest to you, Mr Fenwick."

George shrugged. "I have no desire to serve under Mr Banks."

"But he has been greatly honoured since his return last summer. He is a favourite of the King, an honorary doctor of Oxford, a Fellow of the Royal Society. Even Doctor Johnson speaks well of him. And he has the reputation of being a charming, as well as a learned, man."

George smiled. "He is indeed a Lion but I have no wish to be cast in the role of one of his cubs. There is more to botany than Mr Banks."

"And this voyage will no more be under Mr Banks's direction than the last one, which was under Captain Cook's command," said Alex. "Like all supernumeraries, Mr Banks will be under the authority of whomsoever the Admiralty appoints to lead the expedition."

"An expedition to where?" asked Favet.

"To the Great Southern Continent!" Sarah breathed.

Favet raised his eyebrows. "Do the English really believe in this Great Southern Continent?"

"And the French do not?" Alex retorted. "Did you not send your own ships to look for it only a few years ago under the command of Bougainville?"

"And Comte Louis Antoine de Bougainville found no such land. No one has ever seen it."

"It's been sighted on many occasions," Alex corrected him. "Byron saw it in '65, but was unable to make a landfall. As did Wallis who went out immediately after him."

"*Far, far to the south in a vast ocean, they saw snow clad peaks, and then the fog came down and the ship drifted until they arrived at King George's Island.*" Sarah dreamily recited the navigator's account of the tantalising sighting.

Favet glanced from sister to brother. "An ancient fog that has come down from the time of Pythagoras! This Terra Incognita is nothing but a fictitious land invented to fill the gaps in ancient maps."

Alex shook his head. "Not in ancient maps. Alexander Dalrymple published a chart of the South Pacific two years ago in which he demonstrates that the Continent is there and that it descends below the sixtieth parallel."

"And how does this Dalrymple – what a strange name! – know it is there?"

"The name is Scottish. By scientific study. He is an astronomer, a cartographer and a surveyor. He is also a Fellow of the Royal Society who appointed him as one of the advisers for Cook's voyage. In fact, he wanted to go but only as the expedition's commander and, as I said, His Majesty's ships sail under the direction of His Majesty's Navy."

"I suppose they cannot expect Captain Cook to undertake such an arduous task again?" Mrs Lambert wondered.

"If they wish it, they could," Alex replied. "But I hope they will not choose Captain Cook this time."

She was astonished. "Not choose Captain Cook? You two seem determined to pluck the claws from our Lions! Why would you not wish to see Captain Cook in command?"

"Oh, Captain Cook is a competent sailor, and no doubt a good man," Alex said. "In fact, I applied to sail with him in the *Endeavour* three years ago, but unluckily I was sent to Newfoundland instead."

"Unlucky? You met me!" George gaily protested.

"Unfortunately," Alex continued, "Cook did not achieve what he was sent to do. That is why a second voyage is necessary."

"But he was sent to observe the Transit of Venus and he did observe the Transit of Venus," Mrs Lambert objected.

"Yes, he did, and his observations are extremely valuable. But the Admiralty did not send him all that way to make an observation that could just as effectively have been made from other, more easily obtained sites."

"For what, then, did they send him?"

"To find the Great Southern Continent. Captain Cook, you see, may be a fine navigator and an excellent surveyor of coastlines and islands but he is no true explorer. He sailed as far south as his orders bade him and no further. He did not go beyond the fortieth latitude and so he did not find the Great Southern Continent. He turned back too soon."

Favet snorted. "How can you miss a continent?"

Alex, with a look that showed how he pitied the landsman's ignorance, smiled. "The ocean is vast, and hides many things."

Fifteen

Unfortunately for George, his charm was such that it was not long before the Edgcumbe family desired to pay him every attention, curtailing the time he could spend with Sarah and Alex. He hit on the solution of inviting them to Overcombe. There were some awkward moments when Mrs Edgcumbe thought herself included in the invitation, but luckily when she learned that Mrs Lambert and Monsieur Favet were to be included in the company, she remembered that Bristol society could not do without her.

In honour of George, Mr Edgcumbe organised one of his musical soirées, complete with Charlotte's screeching and Eliza's hammering at the harpsichord. Mrs Lambert was invited for the first time in many years, largely because George expected she would be. Monsieur Favet, of course, was not which at first inclined her to refuse the invitation. But George, Sarah and Alex begged her to help make their evening bearable, and Favet assured her that he did not feel the slight in the least. Besides, she relished the shock that Stanhope would have when he saw Sarah girded with the triple protection of his future brother-in-law, his brother-in-law's friend, and his enemy.

When the performances had ended, the company gathered in the drawing room for refreshment. Mr Edgcumbe collected a modest amount of praise for his "little composition" that ended the musical interlude, and Charlotte and Eliza garnered a smattering of raptures. However, the company's – or at least the female half's – principal interest was in the two travellers who were surrounded by inquisitive beauties.

George responded good-naturedly to all their simpered enquiries. "Have you ever seen a merman?"

"I have not. I do not believe that the half-man, half-fish creature exists."

"Is it true that the African kings live in golden palaces with diamonds in the windows instead of glass?"

"I have never been to Africa, but it may be the case that what is a rarity here is present in such abundance there that it is put to the most mundane uses."

"Have you heard of the mad old man who wrote to the King claiming that he can steer a ship by his watch?"

"Oh, but he is not mad at all! Perhaps Captain Edgcumbe can explain the principles behind Mr Harrison's excellent timekeeper."

Alex reddened. "Um. Ah. Steering a ship... well, it's... ah... a question of navigation... latitude and, well, longitude... Does anyone want any more tea?"

With that, he ducked away, leaving George to entertain the designing ladies with a story about how his dog saved his life when he was caught in a snowstorm while out walking near St John's in Newfoundland – a touching instance of brute fidelity that made many an eye shine. Every now and again, his gaze roamed hopefully about the room, returning with a disappointed air when he saw that Sarah was not there. Mrs Lambert could not see her either and was dismayed to notice that Lord Stanhope was no longer standing where she had seen him last in conversation with Sir Clement.

Alarmed, she went to look for Sarah. She was not in any of the reception rooms. It was a mild evening. Perhaps she had – unwisely, given her experience with Stanhope – gone into the garden. Mrs Lambert went downstairs, passing Mr Edgcumbe's plunge bath which was close to the housekeeper's room. Servants scurried to and fro. None of them had seen any of the guests go into the garden.

She made her way back to the house, so anxious by now that she decided to draw George into the search. Crossing the landing, she noticed that the door of a small drawing room at the rear of the house stood ajar. It was a room the family occupied when they were in what Sarah called their "unsaloned state". It was not a favourite of Mrs Edgcumbe's, who considered its prospect of the harbour vulgar. There was someone inside. Mrs Lambert heard voices. A man and a woman. Puzzled, she drew closer.

The only light came from the low fire and a single candle on an occasional table next to the armchair by the hearth. The top of a man's head was just visible above the back of the chair. His right elbow rested on the arm of the seat and a dainty pair of feet peeped out from the other side.

"You can sail for weeks without seeing land. You can sail past land and never know it's there. And all you would see, all around you, is the ocean."

The voice was Alex's, and his situation surprising. Then after all, Mrs Lambert reflected, he would not be the first man to be more comfortable in the company of servants than eligible ladies. She was tiptoeing away when the girl on his lap spoke.

"I'd like to be on that ship, Alex. To be a captain, like you."

Mrs Lambert had found Sarah.

Alex laughed. "We couldn't have two captains on board. You could be my lieutenant."

"I shall not. I shall be an Admiral."

"If you aren't careful, you'll have to be a monkey boy and see how you like that."

Mrs Lambert stepped into the room. Sarah snuggled into Alex's chest, their heads touching over a large atlas. Perhaps it was the one on which she used to trace, with a solemn little finger, the sea routes he described to her.

"Why, look at you two playing like children!" Mrs Lambert cried.

Sarah started, struggled free from the arm about her waist and leapt to her feet. The book slipped to one side. Alex caught it.

"Yes," he said smoothly, "we were remembering how we used to hide from the din when we were little."

Sarah giggled. "We were being very silly, weren't we, Alex?"

He grinned up at her. "Very. Please don't scold, Mrs Lambert."

"I am not your mother," she protested laughingly. "But it is really wicked of you to abandon George like this."

"Poor George! Alone with the savage tribe." Alex sighed and shut the book. "Oh well. Back to the fal-de-rol."

In the salon, Stanhope's affianced moped in the corner. Her lord had gone and Mrs Lambert was now at liberty to return to Monsieur Favet and a late supper. She found George and they arranged to meet for a walk along the river path at the bottom of the Gorge on the following day.

In the morning, George was detained. Alex explained that he had been closeted with Jacob Edgcumbe since breakfast. His uncle had some ideas about managing the Fenwick estate that he could not keep to himself, although George had advised the banker that his father had his own man of business in Stroud and that he himself had no thoughts of changing the arrangement when the responsibility passed to him. It is remarkable how patient George was with the elder Edgcumbes. Only yesterday, he had spent an hour in Joseph's study listening to an interminable, droning extract from his *History of Music*, a subject in which George had only a feigned interest.

The walkers left instructions with Mrs Lambert's servants to send him after them if he arrived in time, otherwise to ask him to wait until their return. They had only just reached the top of the Zig Zag Walk down to Hotwells when there was a loud "Hoy!" and George ran down the steps, waving his hat. They waited for him to catch up, moving to the side of the path to allow a family party to ascend.

The father pointed into the Gorge and opined, "It would be a charming prospect were it not marred by the snuff mill above, the lime kiln below and those rough fellows in their rowboat." His daughter yawned and his wife fanned her red face with flabby fingers.

George, catching sight of something in the bank, exclaimed, "Oh look! *Ophrys apifera*, near perfect!"

"A bee orchid? Where?" cried Sarah.

George leaned over the fence and pointed out the little flower growing on the edge of the drop. "See how the lip resembles a bee. Oh, I have not got my sketchbook!"

"I have mine," Sarah said, "but we cannot stop here without blocking the way."

George frowned. "What a shame."

"I will pick one." Sarah thrust her sketchbook into Alex's hands, knelt down and crawled through the wooden railings.

"Miss Edgcumbe, for heaven's sake, be careful!"

George's cry attracted the attention of the family, who had not climbed very far. They looked back, the man poised to run down and offer his help. When he saw Sarah, he shooed his family upwards, fearful that his women might be contaminated by the sight of her ankles, her dusty skirt, and her disregard for propriety.

"Give me your hand!" said George.

Sarah, who had her prize, looked down at his outstretched

arm. Her brother, who knew better than to treat her like a drawing room miss, gazed calmly at the river, measuring its depth with a mariner's eye. Sarah hesitated, not sure whether to laugh or frown at George. When she saw how pale he had gone, she realised that either would be too cruel. His distress was not to be trifled with. The colour he had lost suffused her own face. She put her hand in his and allowed him to help her back from the verge onto the path.

Alex chuckled. "What a fright you've given George!"

"But I was in no danger. Look."

She was right; she had never been near the edge of the chasm. But George still clutched her hand and she still permitted it. It was some moments before he could be convinced that they had not nearly lost Sarah.

When at last fluttering hearts were stilled – if indeed they were – they continued on their way to the foot of the stairs.

"Alex, I forgot to give you this!" George said. "It came for you just before I left. I thought you might want to read it at once. It's from the Admiralty."

Alex snatched the letter. They crowded around while he broke the seal. Sarah hung onto his arm, the eager anticipation in her face matching that in his. His eyes narrowed and instantly her smile vanished.

"Alex, what is it? Have they turned down your application?"

"No, they haven't. They've appointed Captain Cook to command the second expedition – had appointed him within a month of his return last summer! He's sailing next month."

"And you are going with him, are you not?"

He shook his head. "He is the worst man to send. Everyone knows what he thinks of Dalrymple's map. 'Very doubtful,' he said when he saw it. Very doubtful! Cook won't find the Great Southern Continent because he's not looking for it. I shan't go now."

He tore the letter into tiny pieces. They fluttered about his feet, or were caught by the breeze and floated down to the muddy riverbed exposed by the low tide. A despairing, dramatic gesture, but not one that had George's attention. He was watching the tears brimming into Sarah's eyes, watching them prepare to fall like a man waiting for the axe to come down on his neck.

He gripped Alex's hand. "If Cook won't look for it, Alex, then you and I shall! We will get our own ship, we will find the South Land, and you shall survey it and I shall botanise it! We will be the most famous explorers in history! I'll write to Lord Sandwich at once."

George had won a stay of execution.

Of course, an expedition of this kind requires lengthy preparation, and it was the following summer by the time that Alex and George were in Bristol making their last minute arrangements. Cook's ship *Resolution* and her consort *Adventure* had set sail the previous July, a few weeks after Alex had withdrawn his application for a place on the voyage. By now, Alex calculated, they should be in Tahiti.

Joseph Banks was not on board after all. Having complained that there had not been enough room on the first voyage for his people and paraphernalia, he had insisted that another deck be added to Cook's ship. It was badly designed. The first time they tried to sail her, she almost capsized under the extra weight. Cook had the deck demolished, Banks protested, angry letters passed between Banks and Lord Sandwich, and Banks withdrew from the expedition.

Banks's resignation proved awkward for no one but himself. A man called Forster was appointed in his place. But Banks had not done with making a fool of himself. Three weeks after leaving Plymouth, Cook arrived in Madeira. Here he learned that he had just missed a botanist called Burnett who had been waiting for Mr Banks, having been appointed some time previously as his assistant. Burnett had passed the time as any good botanist should, gathering flowers, but when the news that Banks was not sailing with Cook reached the island, he had hurriedly taken a berth on the first vessel home. When the *Resolution* anchored in Funchal three days later, the place was still chuckling over the exploits of this Mr Burnett, who was so obviously Mrs Burnett. Banks, embarrassed by the exposure of his plot to smuggle a mistress on board a vessel he had almost sunk, fled to Iceland, setting sail for the north while Cook proceeded on his way south.

All this sea-gossip they heard from a busy, excited Alex who had come to Bristol to oversee the final alterations to the *Miranda*. Sarah was his clerk, inventory maker and bookkeeper. She toiled away in her room late at night in order not to disturb Mrs Edgcumbe, although Mrs Lambert thought it questionable that the woman had any but the vaguest notion that her stepson was going on a perilous voyage. She was content to believe with the rest of the world that they were fitting out for a trading voyage to the East Indies.

"Do you still abstain from sugar, Sarah?" Charlotte paused with the silver tongs poised over the teacup. Having dismissed her child to the care of nurses and governesses until she should be of an age to be of interest, she was on her daily round of visits.

Mrs Edgcumbe, lowering the letter she had been about to open, said, "It is really very odd of you, Sarah, to persist in taking against something as innocent as sugar in this way."

"But Sarah does not think it is innocent," said Charlotte, stirring her sweetened drink.

"I don't know what terrible crime you think us all guilty of I am sure," Mrs Edgcumbe said.

"It is because of the slaves," said Charlotte.

"Slaves! Do you see any slaves here? Are there slaves in the kitchen? Are there slaves in the stables? Perhaps Mr Edgcumbe is hiding them in his study."

Sarah accepted the tea with thanks, making no attempt to defend herself against their sarcasm. She moved back to the table and resumed her examination of the objects laid out upon it. Equipment had been arriving at George Street nearly every day – telescopes, charts, bedding, shirts, barometers, chronometers. There were books too. They would have on board Dalrymple's *Account of the Discoveries Made in the South Pacifick Ocean Previous to 1764*, Dampier's *New Voyage Round the World*, John Narborough's *Account of several late Voyages and Discoveries*, and – a gift from Favet – Bougainville's *Voyage autour du Monde*.

Sarah ran her fingers over a dark wooden case. Inside was a glass circle bounded with brass, beneath the glass an eight-pointed star, pointing to the east, to the west, to the north, to the south. Soon, too soon, Alex and George would be following that star.

"What are you doing?" Mrs Edgcumbe called out irritably.

"Looking at the compass."

"Put it down before you break it." Mrs Edgcumbe tutted, rolling her eyes at Charlotte in a manner that signified, *You see what I have to put up with!* "Come and sit down while I read Eliza's letter."

Sarah did as she was told but, rather than reading the letter, Mrs Edgcumbe summarised its contents for her listeners.

"She says that Stanhope has taken a dislike to the wallpaper in the morning room and it is all to be done again – I did say that stripes were not a good idea. They entertained Whigs last evening and will be entertaining Tories tonight… And there is a postscript from Lord Stanhope himself. Can I spare Sarah? He writes: *It is time for her to make a visit to us. She will be company for Eliza during the day and an addition to our society during the evenings. I would suggest that she join us at Grosvenor Square the weekend after next.* Grosvenor Square and only a fortnight to get ready! Charlotte, ring the bell. I shall send for the dressmaker at once. You might look a little more grateful, Sarah. It is very kind of Lord Stanhope to take such an interest in you."

Later that day, Mrs Lambert received a visit from a distraught Sarah. Her news did not surprise her friend. With her brother's departure imminent, she had been anticipating something of the sort from Stanhope. She had already given the question of how Sarah was to be kept out of her brother-in-law's society some thought.

"Sarah was running away from Stanhope?" Ben exclaimed, as Mrs Edgcumbe finished her story.

"From all that her future held for her if she remained here."

"That's why Alex took his sister on a ship to the Pacific?"

"There was nothing else he could do. He could not challenge his brother-in-law to a duel, and it would have been futile to issue a warning to Stanhope since he would not be in England to enforce it. He did offer not to go, but Sarah would not allow him to make the sacrifice. The sea was his life, and all his life he had dreamed of making that voyage."

"But why didn't she talk to her parents?"

"Pah! Her father was too wrapped up in his musical projects and her stepmother was too dazzled by her Lord son-in-law to listen to Sarah. They have blind eyes, all of that family, blind still to the pregnant serving girls, the dismissed governesses, the actresses and whores."

She caught Ben's eye and laughed bitterly. "Yes, perhaps I exaggerate a little. Nevertheless, Mr Dearlove, Stanhope is a corrupt man and Sarah loathed him."

"Couldn't you have taken her away somewhere? To London, or the country?"

"Do you think Mrs Edgcumbe would have allowed her to come with me instead of going to Grosvenor Square?"

"But for Alex to expose his sister to such dangers!"

"She was already in danger. You have heard her story. A woman can be as safe at sea as on land. It is only exchanging one peril for another, one party of savages and monsters for another."

So Sarah had gone to sea because she was afraid of Stanhope. But what was all the fuss about? A few unwanted advances, a little teasing, some inappropriate hugs and kisses from a sister's husband?

"If Sarah was so maidenly, how could she bring herself to put on a sailor's outfit?"

"I have already told you that Sarah did not run away dressed as a man. I supplied her travelling wardrobe."

"Then how did they disguise her when she was on board?"

"They did not. George had appointed a secretary, but the expedition still lacked an artist. Sarah filled the vacancy. It is not so rare as you seem to think. Mr Banks was willing to take a female assistant, and there was a female botanist on board Bougainville's ship. Women have been to sea before, Mr Dearlove."

Sixteen

In that land, Ben remembered reading, *men and women are free to contract and cancel alliances by mutual consent. No parent forces their union and no laws hinder their separation, although the forging of the nuptial bond may be preceded by parental consultation where the partners are young, and in every case is accompanied by celebrations in the form of feasting and gift-giving. In spite of this freedom, or perhaps because of it, the young do not lightly sacrifice their chastity, and unions, once formed, tend to be long lasting. There are as many old, comfortable couples there as in Europe but fewer men and women plaguing one another's lives. If a union should prove unhappy, they have the remedy of speedily terminating it.*

This is not to say that the disturbances, both private and public, that are liable to accompany misplaced affections do not occur. There are as many unrequited loves and jealous lovers in this land as any other and, though there may be no Montague or Capulet to endanger the common peace since recourse to violence is extremely rare and regarded as the greatest crime a man can commit, resentment and hatred may lodge in these as in any other hearts.

Nor is this freedom wholly happy in its moral consequences for, although in general the people achieve a standard of constancy that many in our own society fail in, there is a class of people who, rejecting even these gentle bonds, live in a state of unbridled licence. These, the Travelling Dancers, are a peripatetic society, open to all who wish to join, of men and women who live by the performance of plays and dances and the dissemination of news and telling of tales from township to township. During their visits, a town takes on a festival appearance – the people deck themselves out in their finest clothes, their houses are adorned with flowers and streamers and all work, save the most necessary, ceases. When the Dancers leave, they may take with them one or two others who have a desire to essay their mode of existence, and may leave behind the consequences of their amours. This is considered no shame on them or the people who adopt the infants, none of which are suffered to go uncared for. Should any unions bear fruit after their departure, the child is as welcome as any other and no opprobrium directed at the mother.

In their relations with the crew, the people are chaste. The men do not offer their womenfolk for nails and knives as in the South Sea lands, nor do the women barter themselves away for a bit of cloth or a string of beads.

Which must be a disappointment for the sailors, Ben thought as he avoided three lurching mariners blowing rummy kisses at any shop girl or barmaid who had the temerity to peek out of doors.

Mrs Lambert's elaborate concoction of a hell-fire aristocrat had not convinced him. Stanhope was a man, not a devil. He could not turn himself into a cloud and pass through a keyhole. He could not sprout wings and fly in through a window. The threat he presented was nothing compared to the perils of the

South Seas. If Sarah had the courage to face the one, she would certainly not have fled cravenly from the other.

George loved Sarah, even if Mrs Lambert did not want to admit anything so commonplace. How could Sarah fail to return the love of the man who was "so worthy to be her brother's friend"? Mrs Lambert's buggybow Lordship had been a convenient invention for the lovers, lending their flight a veneer of necessity. And Mrs Lambert, who ought to have proved herself a better and wiser friend, had abetted the young people in their wild project, her judgement skewed by her detestation of Stanhope.

It was Mrs Lambert – who insisted that she scorned romanticism! – who had come up with the tale told to the world. Alex had been gone three days when Sarah disappeared from George Street. Of course, a message was sent to Avonmouth, but the *Miranda* had already set sail and the family believed that Alex never learned of his sister's disgrace. Two weeks later, they received a letter from Sarah herself, sent by the obliging Mrs Lambert who happened to be on a tour of Kent, telling them she had married an ensign and was living in Chatham. The family cut her off and, as far as anyone knew, she was living in Chatham still.

The three sailors on the Quay, who could hardly be described as able-bodied, staggered through the busy people at the waterside, attracting laughter and cheers. Ben, welcoming the diversion, stopped to watch their progress – forward one step, back two steps, reeling to the right, rolling to the left, now one down, now another, their attempts to help one another bringing all three down in a heap together. They drew such a crowd that he was not surprised when he felt his arm jostled, nor when something jabbed him in the back. But the jabbing became insistent. He turned to confront the nuisance and a voice announced, "Benjamin Dearlove, you're under arrest!"

Half an hour later, he was in Newgate.

"No, Father, I did not assault an officer of the Press Gang," Ben said wearily. "I only pretended they were press officers to get away."

"Then why have they arrested you?" The little apothecary wiped his eyes, which were watering as much from the stench of the jail as strong emotion. He cast another look of horror around the streaming walls and the dank green flagstones, careful not to catch the eye of any of its stinking, drinking inhabitants wallowing amidst overturned pisspots and filthy straw. Already his son looked as if he had been in the place for weeks, his clothes grimy and his face pale.

Ben had asked himself the same question, considered motives of revenge, coercion, intimidation, but had to face the fact that the most chilling possibility was also the most likely – to get him out of the way for a while.

But he did not want to alarm his father. "It's a mistake."

"But you were there? The officers saw you?"

"Yes, on the road from Stroud. But it was not I who attacked them." He did not add that it was the other way around.

"Then the other people – the farm workers – will be able to say so."

"I doubt they will come forward to incriminate themselves," Ben snapped. But then he was sorry for the pain that twisted his father's face and said gently, "Mr Fenwick will help me."

"Mr Fenwick! Mr Fenwick! Who is this Mr Fenwick and what trouble has he got you into?"

"Mr Fenwick is a gentleman. He will be at the White Hart in Broadmead this afternoon."

"I will go for him myself!" The old man pushed his hat onto his head.

"No, Father!" Ben clutched his arm. Christopher Dearlove

stared at his son, dread and disappointment mingled in his expression. "Dear Father," he said tenderly, but the words wrung his heart, weakened him. Quickly collecting himself, he said, "A note will suffice. And when you have written it, lock up the shop and go and stay with the Shackletons. I don't want you to sit at home alone worrying about me."

"I am used to being alone, and to worrying about you," Mr Dearlove said sadly.

Ben thought the weight of his guilt could get no heavier. "Promise me you will spend the night with the Shackletons."

"Very well, son. If you think it best."

"I see you have had some adventures since you left Overcombe," Antony Fenwick said, turning away to flick dust from a wooden chair. There was no dirt on the seat, the action was to hide his disgust. After only a day in the crowded pit, to which more reeking low life had been added every hour, Ben stank appallingly.

Ben, believing that Antony had deserted him, had been miserably settling down for the night when the warders came for him. Antony, who had been delayed on the road by a slight accident to his coach, had paid for the privilege of a private interview in the sheriff's room. The light from the candle on the desk played over a litter of writs, seals, spilled tobacco and ash. In one corner of the wall was a cupboard full of bottles of spirits, any one of which Ben would gladly have swigged had it been offered to him.

"What have they told you?"

"That you were the ringleader of a gang who attacked two travellers on the road."

"That's a lie! They attacked me! The others were rescuing me. They were the men I told you about, Hay and Beale. The ones who are looking for Anon. They followed me to Bristol and I led them to Overcombe."

"Then they will know George is not there. I am at a loss to understand what it is they want with him – and no, I do not believe in your Fair Land! Whatever it is, we must find him first before they can do him any harm."

"I don't think they can hurt him. I… I think that nothing can harm George now."

"What do you mean?"

Ben knew that there is only one merciful way to inflict pain. The blood-dried bandage must be ripped off the wound in one swift movement; the cup must be clapped onto the skin, not lowered gently; the veins must be nicked with a decisive stroke. "It wasn't George who wrote the book. George is dead."

There was a long silence. Antony broke it with a bitter laugh. "And how did my brother, who was alive yesterday, come to die last night?"

"I made a mistake."

"A mistake?"

"I'm sorry."

"But you are not mistaken now?"

Ben looked away. "Not this time. I know who did write it. Sarah Edgcumbe." He took the note with Matthew's transcription out of his pocket and handed it to Antony. "There was no ensign in Chatham. She was on the *Miranda*, and I have seen her. I saw the drawings for the book in her room and I assumed she was merely the illustrator. But she is also the author."

"If she survived, it is possible that George also – "

"No." Ben would not foster false hope again. "I've seen her grief. She lost him somewhere on that voyage. They must have been married. I don't see how Alex would have helped George otherwise, although Mrs Lambert refuses to admit it."

"What has Mrs Lambert to do with this?"

"She helped them plan Sarah's flight. She is helping Sarah still. It was to her Sarah turned when she was taken ill."

"Then Mrs Lambert knows what happened to George?"

"She says not. She says Sarah will not talk of it."

"Perhaps Miss Edgcumbe was not on board the ship."

"You have George's note."

"It tells us only that she was on the *Miranda* when they set sail. It is not likely that George or Alex would have taken her with them into the Pacific. They will have left her somewhere safe to await their return."

"But the book – "

"Ah, yes, the book. I read the copy you left with me. I sincerely hope it was not written by Miss Edgcumbe."

"Mrs Lambert says it was."

Antony shook his head. "I never understood George's fondness for Mrs Lambert. All that you have told me proves me right. When a woman sets herself up as a wit, she is a danger to herself and to her sex. I fear it is her influence on Miss Edgcumbe that lies behind the whole sorry adventure. She considers herself strong-minded, but really she is only baleful. I remember Miss Edgcumbe as a modest girl. It is hard to imagine her the author of this book."

"I don't think Mrs Lambert had anything to do with writing it."

"Because she told you so? She has hardly demonstrated her probity."

"The only way to be sure of anything is to find Sarah and ask her."

"True. But how are we to do that?"

"I don't know. Perhaps you could persuade Mrs Lambert to help."

"I could try, though I don't hold out much hope. Like all

186

women, she is stubborn in her wrong-headedness. But if Sarah is George's widow, then it is my duty at least to make the attempt. I don't say I believe that she is, mind. I don't believe George would have encouraged a respectable young girl to ruin herself by running away from home and then abandon her while he went on a long sea voyage. Nor can I see any reason for it. There would have been no objections to the match on either side." He paused. "You have killed my brother a second time, and you have made it impossible for me to let him rest with *that* slur on his reputation."

"I'm – "

"Sorry. Yes, you look sorry indeed. We must see about getting you out of your plight. We will need to find your bucolic Samaritans and ask them to stand witness for you. It shouldn't be difficult, I know all the landowners thereabouts. Has your bail been fixed?"

"Yes, but Father cannot pay it."

Antony stood up. "It's late, but I am sure I can persuade the sheriff to deal with me now. If I can secure your release tonight, I will. Go home and clean yourself up. Come and see me first thing tomorrow and we will discuss how to proceed in the search for Miss Edgcumbe."

"Is – are your son and – and Miss Fenwick with you?"

"No. They wanted to come, but I thought it would serve no purpose. They sent you their best wishes, however."

Seventeen

Sent you their best wishes, not sent you *her* best wishes. But George, though amiable, is a careless lad. It must have been Rachel who remembered to send best wishes. Or perhaps their father put it into their heads to send them? Or perhaps neither of them remembered me. Perhaps Mr Fenwick made up the best wishes while we were talking, out of mere politeness.

It was nearly eleven o'clock and Ben had just been released from Newgate. He was lucky that Antony had been so generous with the jailer, who might otherwise have made him wait until morning. He hurried along Baldwin Street, quickened his pace as he passed Marsh Street, where every other building was an inn. Most of them were still open, for no nightwatchmen ventured to cry the hour in that quarter. They let alone any man foolish enough to stay late toping so close to the quayside. After an evening of dancing and drunkenness, he was liable to wake up on a slave trader bound for the West Indies, or locked up in one of His Majesty's holding vessels awaiting transfer to one of His Majesty's ships. It was a profitable sideline for the innkeepers.

On Broad Quay, the lamps burned but the ships were in darkness, no candles being allowed on them while they were in port. From time to time, the guards who protected the vessels from theft and arson made their rounds of the decks, stopping to investigate the *plop* of a rat in the water or the tapping of a broken barrel bobbing against the ship's side. Sometimes they called across to one another or chaffed the slinking nightwatchmen.

The lamp over the apothecary's porch was unlit. Good, his father had obeyed him and gone to the Shackletons. Ben put his key in the lock. The door yielded to his slight pressure. He pushed it wide, his heart thudding with sudden fear. The shop smelt of ginger, cinnamon and bark – familiar scents, but very strong. He leaned over the threshold and listened. Nothing moved. He was sure that the house was empty, but went in on tiptoe anyway. Near the counter a shard of glass broke beneath his foot. He caught his breath, stood still and waited. Nothing.

He opened the parlour door. The fire was nearly out, reduced to a dull red glow of cooling embers. As his eyes adjusted to the shadows, he saw that their two armchairs, his and his father's that usually stood on either side of the fireplace, had been overturned. He groped across the room, fumbled on the mantelpiece for a spill and a candle. The spill was slow to catch. He crouched over the coals, shaded the flame with his hand as he lit his candle. He rose and held up the light.

A candle had been left to burn out on the dining table. Scattered around it was a litter of letters, bills and receipts. Ben glanced towards the window. The locks on the old desk were broken and the drawers gaped open. On the floor next to the desk, in his nightgown and old woollen robe, lay Christopher Dearlove. He lay on his side, a dark stain beneath his head, his thin legs curled up, a massive book hugged to his chest. Ben crashed to his knees, pressed his fingers against Father's neck. After a few seconds, he moved his hand down and pulled the robe up around the exposed chest, protecting it from the cold night air. Father's eyes were already closed, which afterwards Ben was grateful for. It meant he did not have to face his gaze. Perhaps it would have been better for him if he had, for ever after he was haunted by the sorrowful accusation he imagined there.

He was dimly aware of a low moaning. It came from his

189

own lips as he gently prised his father's fingers apart and removed, as if from a child who has fallen asleep reading a favourite tale, his *Recipe Book*.

"I don't want to go to bed."

Mrs Shackleton sighed. Ben sat on one of the righted chairs by the fireplace, had been sitting there for hours while Mrs Shackleton and one of the neighbours laid out his father on a trestle table in the shuttered shop. The coroner had been and gone. Ben knew everything there was to know about his father's death. It was clear enough what had happened, yet still he could not comprehend it.

He had stumbled into the street yelling "Help! Murder!" In minutes, the quay was full of people in their nightgowns waving lamps and nightlights, along with the watchmen from the ships with their carefully shuttered lanterns. The shop was suddenly illuminated, revealing the mess the murderer had made. Blue and white fragments of medicine jars lay on the floor, their aromatic contents criss-crossed with footprints.

The peruke-maker from next door was the first to run into the back room and see what had happened. It was he who had the presence of mind to send one of the watchmen for the coroner, though someone else – probably one of the wives – thought of sending for Mrs Shackleton.

They huddled around the doorway, all talking at once.

"Who would do such a thing?" "Always such a polite man, a hard-working man, a God-fearing man." "No, I didn't see anything." "There was a man hanging around, I thought he was taking a piss." "I heard glass break, but I thought it was someone throwing a bottle into the water." "And his son just taken into Newgate."

Murder, of course, the coroner said, peering suspiciously at the son with the stench of the jail still upon him. A villain, come home to rob his father? No, he was not in the house at the time. Strangers, then – motive, robbery. No sign of forced entry – the peruke-maker's wife remembered hearing someone knocking on the front door but had thought nothing of it. It was not unusual for the apothecary to receive late callers, and he always answered a summons from his patients no matter the hour.

Too late for the hue and cry, though there were many willing to go on a hunt for Mr Dearlove's killer. The assailant or assailants would be miles away by now or holed up in some drinking den. There was no trapping him where, if only for the sake of defying the law, a score of people would be ready to swear he'd been all night. The coroner would put a notice of the murder in the national newssheet, *The General Hue and Cry*. There was not much more he could do.

"Looking for the old fellow's money," the coroner concluded. "If only he had handed it over. He might be alive now."

But Father did not know what it was they wanted him to hand over so they had turned the place upside down. Ben had seen their handiwork before, in Poland Street. They had not come to steal Father's money nor his medicinal secrets. Powdery footprints on the stairs led to Ben's room. The chest where he had hidden George Fenwick's papers had been ransacked, and the case of letters was gone. Thinking they had what they wanted, Hay and Beale had ended their search there. The leather satchel was still underneath the mattress where Ben had left it.

Mrs Shackleton rested her hand on his shoulder and repeated, "You ought to sleep." He did not answer and, after a moment, she moved away.

There was a steady stream of visitors all the next day. At mid-morning, Ben left Mrs Shackleton to deal with them and went into the parlour. The room was tidy now, with a fire burning. It gave Ben no sense of comfort. He crossed over to the dresser and glanced at the gap in the plates. Mrs Shackleton had taken the fragments of *The mercies thou receive* to her husband to mend. Ben grabbed a bottle of claret and a glass, filled it to the brim and, still clutching the bottle, sat down opposite his father's empty chair.

There was a knock on the door. Matthew had already called. The dear fellow was heartbroken but, hurried about his business by his own father, had to promise to return later that day. Ben did not care who came or who didn't.

"Go away!" he snarled, but rose when Antony Fenwick stepped into the room.

Antony grasped the young man's hand, pressed it gently. Ben turned away, croaked, "Sit down… will you have a drink?" Pottering about at the dresser gave him the chance to wipe his eyes.

"I came as soon as I heard. I cannot tell you how very sorry I am. I will always regret not having had the chance to meet your father. I was listening to what people outside are saying about him. One man said, 'When my wife was ill Kit Dearlove let me have medicine for nothing, until I could pay for it.' Another told how he sat up with his boy for three nights in a row. I would like to stay for the funeral."

"Of course. You know that Hay and Beale took George's letter case? I still have the wallet."

"You think Hay and Beale killed your father?"

"They threw me in jail. Then they came here."

Antony shook his head. "You have no proof of that."

"George's papers are all they took. I told you. They are looking for whoever wrote *A Voyage to the Fair Land*. For Sarah Edgcumbe."

"Because the Fair Land is real?"

"It is."

Antony was silent for a moment. "Ben, you know that this

is something that George's papers could never prove, for it is not true."

"Then why do they want them?"

"I really do not know. Perhaps they do believe in this mythical continent. There are dreams that lure men on, rumours of lost lands and hidden cities, hidden treasure, fabled gold. The facts speak against such chimera, and the world labels the man who seeks them mad, but he will not abandon his quest. The thought of wealth or power is too much for him. That is your Fair Land. But the age of exploration is over, Ben. There is nothing left to discover."

Ben stared doggedly at the ground. "Sarah Edgcumbe went on that voyage. She can be found. She can tell you whether or not the Fair Land exists."

"She certainly set sail on the *Miranda*. What she did after that we cannot know unless we find her, or unless Mrs Lambert tells us."

"She says she does not know."

"Do you believe her?"

Ben shrugged.

"I am on my way to call on her and make one final appeal to her good nature. Though I am not sure that female hyena has one. Will you accompany me?"

"No, I'll stay here. Do you want George's maps?"

"Will you take them to your sea captain?"

"No. I'm not going back to London."

"But Miss Edgcumbe – "

"I can't help you. I have to look after Father's business now. I'll go and get the satchel."

"What is it?" demanded the thin-faced girl.

"It is a paregorick draught."

"A what?"

"A potion, a soothing potion."

193

"What's in it?"

"That would be telling."

"Nothing poisonous?"

"No, nothing poisonous." Though I wish there was, Ben thought savagely, then you and your mistress would stop pestering me for medicines you have no intention of paying for. He signed a sheet of paper with an angry flourish and handed it to the servant. "My bill."

The girl snatched the paper, wrapped it around the bottle and left with a perky, "Good day". He turned to tidy the shelf. The bell over the door jangled. He lowered his stiff shoulders down into his back, forced a smile and faced his next customer.

"Antony! Come in... let me fasten the door... come through... Mrs Shackleton! Wine, please."

Antony Fenwick followed him into the back room. "Don't shut up shop on my account."

"I was just about to have my lunch anyway. Will you join me?"

"No lunch, thank you. But yes to a glass of wine, to see me on my way."

Fenwick took off his hat and gloves and sat down. Mrs Shackleton placed a bottle and glasses on the table with a look that plainly said: *And I hope no harm will come of it!* The household wine bills had never been so large under Mr Dearlove, only a week in his grave. Ben ignored her unspoken reprimand. He had inherited a good business and was in no danger of ruining it by running up accounts he could not pay.

"You intend to stick to your resolution?" Antony Fenwick said, when the wine had been tasted. "You will not go back to London?"

"No. That is all finished with."

"You could get a good price. My man of business would gladly invest your funds for you." Fenwick spoke with little expectation of the offer being accepted. He had made it before, and been refused before.

"Thank you, but I could not sell my father's shop."

Fenwick sipped as he eyed the young man in his sober suit and plain wig. After a moment he said, "You were right about Mrs Lambert – an intelligent woman, but not a cooperative one. Can you guess why she was absent when I first called on her?"

Ben swirled the wine in his glass and did not answer.

"She said she had gone to take a friend to Southampton, taking a roundabout route in case a certain young man tried to follow."

Even this brought no response from Ben, but Antony decided to carry on with his story despite the lack of encouragement. Mrs Lambert, he went on, had added archly, "Though I was sad to wave farewell to Miss Edgcumbe when she set sail for Le Havre. She will be in Paris by now, I expect. And from there..."

"Where?" Antony had prompted her.

"That I cannot tell you."

"Mrs Lambert, you do know that a murder has been committed?"

"I did not. I am shocked and grieved to hear it. But you do not think it connected with this business of Sarah's book?"

"Mr Dearlove's son thinks so."

"I hope he is wrong. It is doubly shocking that a man might die for such a silly reason."

"Then you do not think the Fair Land exists?"

"Mr Fenwick, if I thought that I would have to believe that Sarah had cheated me, for you know I was one of the *Miranda*'s investors."

"You think her honest?"

"Honest enough not to make claims that might be to her advantage. She did not run away with your brother, they were never lovers, and they were never married."

"Does she know how he died? Was she on the ship when it foundered?"

"All Sarah would tell me when I asked her how she escaped its awful fate is that she was not on board," Mrs Lambert had answered, and with that had declared their interview over.

"So I was right," Antony ended his account of the meeting. "Miss Edgcumbe was never in the South Seas. And now she has gone, and I am glad. Glad too that there was no connection between her and George. His fame is as spotless as it ever was, her own less so I fear. Obscurity is after all her wisest course."

"Another way of saying good riddance?"

"I own I am glad to be free of any obligation to find the woman." He drained his glass. "I must be going. If you are ever in Painswick, you will call on us?" He thought he saw a glimmer of interest – or hope? – in Ben's eye. Then Ben looked away again and with a gracelessly mumbled "Thank you" said goodbye.

Eighteen

There were very few conditions for which a cure was not to be found in Christopher Dearlove's *Recipe Book*. It was the work of his lifetime and more, incorporating knowledge handed down to him by his mother. She had it from her mother, a woman no wiser or more knowledgeable than any of the other goodwives of her village, except that she saw that their old learning would be forgotten if she did not take pains to pass it on. As experience taught him, Christopher had added to or subtracted from the recipes, but the base of many of them was still those traditional, empiric treatments. It was no longer necessary to pick sage before sunrise as herbalists had done in more superstitious times, yet it was still the most effective gargle for sore mouths and throats, as Kit Dearlove's customers could testify.

Conning the familiar emetics, preservatives, preventives, expectorants, diuretics, and embrocations, Ben sat alone in the room behind the shop two or three evenings after Antony Fenwick's visit. Mrs Shackleton had gone home to her husband, taking with her the substantial remains of roast mutton followed by baked apples and cream flavoured with orange flower water. He had done his best to swallow the food, knowing the trouble Mrs Shackleton had gone to, but it was impossible. When, by your own foolery, you have led your father's murderers to your father's house, everything must taste of ashes.

The door between the parlour and the shop was ajar, the shop faintly lit by patches of light from the lantern over the porch. He glanced up when a long shadow slowly traversed the next room, breaking up the chequers of dark and light. There was someone walking along the quayside, a nightwatchman or customs officer perhaps.

There was no cure for his despair amongst the recipes and he had not been looking for one. Nor was it necessary for him to revise what he had never forgotten. If anyone had asked him, he could not have explained why he was turning the familiar pages that his father's hands had turned, or tracing with an imaginary pen letters his father's hand had formed. It was the self-torture of the bereaved.

He closed the book, yawned and stretched. He was tired of reading, he might as well go to bed. But he did not move from his chair. In London at this hour, he and Campbell would be leaving the theatre, laughingly criticising the performance as they were swept along with the gaudy throng of Covent Garden. Was Campbell thinking of him now? He doubted it.

There was a tap on the shop window, timid but clear. Did they think apothecaries never slept? But Father never turned anyone away, and he was determined to uphold his practice. He rose to his feet, put the book on the desk and strode into the shop. He did not take the candle. There was sufficient light to see a dark figure standing in the doorway – a servant girl, her hood drawn about her to protect herself from the harbour-side miasma seeping from dark mud and glistening stone. He drew back the bolts.

"Ben Dearlove?"

"Yes. What can I do for you?"

"Can I come in?"

He stood aside and let her into the shop. She threw back her hood. "Do you recognise me?"

He did, although her looks were much improved since that

198

night at the theatre. She was better dressed, well wrapped up against the night air in her new travelling dress and cloak. Her movements were quick and impatient, not weak or nervous. Her face had filled out a little; some of its shadows had gone. Yet there was still the look of distress in her great dark eyes, a look, he guessed, that with her was permanent.

Recovering from his surprise, he invited her into the parlour. She looked about her, taking in the lonely homeliness of the place. She pushed her cloak back from her shoulders, sat down close to the fire, her hands held out to the blaze.

"So you are the young man who was looking for me."

"I thought you had gone to France."

She shrugged. "As you see… I was sorry to hear about your father."

Her pity angered him. "Perhaps if you had come forward sooner he would not have died."

She flinched, feeling the hurt he intended. It was not habitual with him to inflict pain and he wished the words unuttered. Awkwardly he said, "Can I get you something? A glass of wine?"

"No, thank you. It was quite impossible for me to do so. I bitterly regret your father's death, but only secrecy will prevent many more deaths. I want you to understand that."

"Secrecy. About what?"

"The Fair Land."

He sat down. "Then it is real?"

"Yes, Mr Dearlove. For five years, the only happy years I have known, I lived there. So did George Fenwick."

"But how can it exist and men not know?"

She smiled sadly. "The ocean is vast and hides many things, things that must remain hidden."

"Why? If it is anything like the land in your book – "

"It is exactly like. That is why. What do you think happens to a land when it has been *discovered*? What do you think it becomes once it has been exposed to our greed and cruelty? Its wealth plundered, its people turned into slaves, Vannir and Tinyar chained to a plank in a stinking ship – " She paused, struggled for self control. "These are a gentle, generous people, not used to defending themselves. With their own hands, they'll give away all they possess. Of their own will, they'll serve without realising that they are being made slaves of."

"If you wished it to remain a secret, why did you write the book?"

"I needed money, Mr Dearlove. Though if I had only myself to care about, I would not have taken the trouble to keep myself alive. I thought no one would recognise the truth at the heart of the text. Everyone believes that fool, Cook."

"He turned back too soon."

She glanced sharply at him. "I said that?" Her features softened. "And then, it did me good to write it. It made me feel close to him, for a while."

"To George."

"But the work was also a strain. I became ill."

"And you turned to your confidante, Mrs Lambert, for help."

"Yes. Do you see now why the Fair Land must be kept secret?"

"Because you think we would turn your friends into slaves."

"I know we would. You have met my uncle. Even a man like him has dreams. A Great Southern Trading Company with an army of merchants, agents, and overseers to run it; a country called Jacobiana, capital city Jacobsville; and money, made by any means."

"But your uncle didn't believe me. He all but threw me out of his office."

"My uncle had you followed. I saw the man when you called on

Maria Lambert in Clifton. I remembered seeing him when I was a child. His name is Bowood. He's a sailor when he can find a ship that will take him. He works for my uncle when he can't." She drew her cloak about her shoulders, rose to her feet. "I don't imagine that anything I say can make the loss of your father any easier for you, but I hope that now at least you will understand why I cannot speak. The Fair Land must not be found."

He stood up. "It cannot be kept a secret forever. Surely, George should have the credit of discovering it, and his nation the first claim to it? For what else did he go on his voyage if not to make discoveries? Why did he take the trouble to send his maps back if he did not want the world to know about the Fair Land?"

"To send his maps back? What maps?"

"The ones he sent home from Batavia."

She staggered. He put out a steadying hand, which she thrust away. "Where are these maps? Do you have them?"

"His brother, Antony, has them at Overcombe. There was a box of letters, but Hay and Beale took them when they broke in. They were written before the voyage. It was from them that I learned you were on the *Miranda*."

"Hay and Beale?"

"French spies. I thought at first they worked for the Admiralty. They followed me in London."

"The Admiralty!" Dismayed, she pressed her hand to her forehead. "Mr Dearlove, I beg you – "

She was interrupted by someone pounding on the front door. She span round and fled into the kitchen. She flung open the back door and stumbled across the yard, through the gate and into the alleyway. Before Ben could go after her, the shop filled with the sound of splintering wood and the crunch of heavy boots. The parlour door crashed open and two dark shadows burst in.

Ben slammed the kitchen door, wedged his back against it

and turned to face the intruders. They grabbed his arms and dragged him away. He lunged out with his right foot, hooked it around the leg of the chair behind the desk and jerked it over. It hit one of them on the back of the legs and he buckled, losing his hold of Ben. Ben swung back his freed arm, aimed his fist at the other man's cheek. But he had lost his balance, the blow was weak and easily deflected. The man let go of him and scrambled into the kitchen. His footsteps receded into the dark alley behind the house. His accomplice was still down, struggling to disentangle himself from the chair. Ben grabbed hold of his pigtail, shook, pummelled, kicked, and punched the kneeling man.

"You bastards – you murdered my father – you bloody bastards!"

"No I didn't – Help! Help!"

"Lying son of a bitch!" Ben swung back his arm. A huge hand clamped his wrist and jerked his arm behind his back. A voice grated in his ear.

"It wasn't us who killed your father."

Ben wriggled round, spat in his assailant's face. "Well, if it wasn't you, who was it, Mister Hay?"

Hay, still clasping Ben's wrist, ignored the question. "Where's she gone?"

"I wouldn't tell you even if I knew."

"Are you telling me you don't know where she is?"

"Are you telling me you didn't kill my father?"

Hay stared at him. After a moment he released his painful grip. "We did not kill your father. But if you help us, we can help you find out who did."

"By helping me to another prison cell?"

"You're more use to us out of prison now."

Beale struggled to his feet, gingerly feeling his scalp with his fingertips, and reached in his coat pocket for his pistol. The other man shook his head and Beale's hand fell to his side.

Hay moved towards the fireplace, flung back the tails of his black coat and sat down. Ben slowly followed, sank down opposite him. Hay removed his hat and ran his hand over his coarse black hair. He looked calmly around the room, his heavy head turning slowly on his muscular neck. He had a cruel, stern look about him: it was the look of a man used to winning obedience by the application of the rattan.

"Mr Beale, look in that there dresser and see if there's a drop of something to ease our yarning."

Beale found and uncorked a bottle of claret and filled three large glasses.

"Help yourself," Ben said nastily.

"Thanks. Don't mind if we do." Hay took his drink from Beale.

His hands shaking, Ben did the same. Beale slunk into the shadows behind the other man's chair. Ben rubbed his bruised arm and eyed the pair warily. Over Hay's head, the pugilist mouthed vengeful threats at him.

Hay lowered his glass and smacked his lips. "Now, Mr Dearlove, about your father. It is true that we had you arrested – "

"So you could break in here! He was an old man – there was no need to hurt him."

"And we did not hurt him. I don't deny that we may, if need be, turn housebreaker, but we are not murderers. I sent Mr Beale here with orders to search the place. He's the quiet type is Beale, used to mum and tiptoe, not a bludgeoning blunderer. Mr Dearlove would never have known he was in here. Except he didn't come in."

"The old man – I mean Mr Dearlove – had visitors. An elderly couple. I thought they were going to be here all night!" Beale whined.

"The Shackletons," Ben murmured. "Father was supposed to go home with them. He shouldn't have been here."

Hay glared a warning at Beale. "The quiet type, as I said. Since we'd gone to the trouble of getting you to a place where we thought we could keep you for a good few days, Mr Beale judged it more prudent to delay the attempt until the following day when the gentleman might be out." Another look of displeasure directed at Beale. "He left the quayside and I, unluckily as I see now, did not send him back to watch through the night. If he had been here, your father would have come to no harm."

"Why should I believe you?"

"Because we would have been more interested in the housebreaker. He was looking for something, wasn't he? What was it? Something you brought from Overcombe?"

Ben said nothing.

"We know you went to Overcombe because George Fenwick was on the *Miranda*. You think Fenwick wrote the book, don't you? And we agree, it's very likely."

"But George – " He broke off. If they did not know George was dead, he was not going to tell them. He covered the outburst with a sneer at Beale, who was pointing at him with one hand and drawing the index finger of the other across his throat. "You do, do you? What great scholars you are!"

Hay smiled blandly. "Well, I'm not so much a reading man myself, but my betters tell me it is so, and I am sure they are right."

"Your betters in Paris?"

For the first time, Hay seemed rattled. "In Paris? Who says we serve the French? I'll have his damned liver out!"

"So you do work for the Admiralty?"

Hay clicked his tongue. "So you thought we worked for the French. I see now why you refused our invitation to a quiet word on the Stroud road."

"A quiet word!"

"Very good trick you played too, and if it had happened to someone other than ourselves, we might have had a laugh over it."

A choked snarl from Beale suggested that he had not found anything humorous in the situation.

"So, where is Fenwick now?" Hay continued. "Does the woman know? What's her involvement in all this? Is she his wife? His doxy?"

The question amazed Ben. The information it had taken him such time and trouble to find – that the *Miranda* existed, her destination, details of her captain, crew and supernumeraries – would have been easily available to them if they worked for the Admiralty. So how did they not know who Sarah was?

Of course. She had eloped with George. Her presence on the *Miranda* would not have been admitted in official reports. Besides, women rarely found their way into naval records. Although they did sometimes travel on ships with their husbands or lovers, and might be given tasks such as washing, mending, cooking, or even helping to load guns and bring powder up from the storeroom during a battle, their names never appeared in the crew lists. No rations were apportioned to them, and if they died at sea no note was made of it in the ship's log.

Even so, he was still wary. Hay had not actually said they were naval agents. Apart from a folded piece of parchment waved at a bunch of farm workers, they had offered no papers, no warrants and no sealed orders to prove that they were connected with the Admiralty. Should he ask for proof? But it might be unwise to let them know he was still suspicious. It is easy to get rid of a man in a maritime town, and he did not want to wake up with a sore head in a dark hold somewhere far out on the ocean.

"She has no connection of that sort with George. She was employed to do the illustrations for the book. That was why

I went to see her in London, because I thought she might know where he was. I was wrong. She never met the author or learned his name."

"So why did she run away?"

"She was in debt. She couldn't pay her rent."

"Why did she come to see you tonight?"

"She wanted to borrow money."

"She followed you all the way to Bristol to ask you for money? Are you such a generous man?"

"I gave her money in London." This was true. "Besides, she has other friends in Bristol." This was too close to the truth, so Ben hastily added, "They won't help her. So she came to me. I don't know any more than you do where George is." That was no lie either!

Hay was silent for a moment, thinking all this over. "So that brings us back to your father's murderer."

"And you say it was not you. Then who – " He bit his lip.

Hay leaned forward. "Do you have an idea, Mr Dearlove?"

Ben hesitated. He had to be careful to appear helpful while not giving them anything useful. "You said you would help me find my father's murderer if I cooperate with you?"

"Yes."

"George's brother gave me a case of letters about the voyage. That's what I brought back from Overcombe and that's what the thief took. But they won't tell you much. They were written before the *Miranda* sailed and concern arrangements for hiring the crew, buying supplies, that sort of thing. They won't be of any use to you." No point in lying about that, though he carefully omitted to mention the maps in the leather wallet now in the possession of Antony Fenwick.

Beale grunted. "We can't rely on his say so. Our orders are to find them."

Ben glanced up at him. "Orders from the Admiralty?"

Hay shrugged. "Now, think. Who else is there that has an interest in the *Miranda*?"

"A man who wants to make money by any means."

"I heard about your father's death. A terrible business. These rogues get bolder every day. The judges are too soft. I'd transport the lot of them and leave them to take their chances amongst the cannibals." Jacob Edgcumbe shook Ben's hand. "And now you wish to deposit your money with the Bank? A sensible decision, Mr Dearlove. Let them dare to rob us!"

Ben snatched his hand away. "I was not robbed of money, but of papers."

"Family documents? A will, perhaps? Mortgage deeds? Such things are not easy to replace. Still, the Bank will do what it can to help you."

"They are letters connected with the voyage of the *Miranda*, and you've got them."

Edgcumbe's unctuous smile disappeared. "Mr Dearlove, I fail to understand why you insist on intruding your wild theories into that old business." He reached for the handbell on the desk. "Now, if you and your – friend – " he eyed Hay with distaste, "would not mind, I have work to do."

"My *friend* is Mr Hay of the Admiralty."

Hay neither denied nor confirmed this, but it impressed Edgcumbe whose hand hovered over the bell. "Naturally," he said after a pause, "I am glad to cooperate if the matter has become official. Tim Tatton!"

The clerk clattered into the room.

"Bring us some wine. Sit down, gentlemen."

No one spoke while Tatton, casting curious glances at the visitors, bustled about with their drinks. Edgcumbe leaned back behind his imposing desk and rested his chin on his steepled fingers. Ben noticed that those fingers trembled slightly. He seemed to be calculating something and, by the time he dismissed Tatton, had decided to adopt a bold, candid attitude.

"You are aware, Mr Hay, that mine was the major investment in the *Miranda*? I am sure that whatever the Admiralty's interest in the vessel, no just claim will be forgotten."

Hay raised a diminutive glass to his lips. "I'm not here to divvy out the profits. Do you have the letters?"

Edgcumbe brightened at the reference to profits and chose to ignore the man's insolence. "As a matter of fact I do, though I had no idea they came from Mr Dearlove's house. They were sold to me by a man called Jonathan Bowood."

"And how did he come by them?"

"He found them in a tavern. A few nights ago he was staying in The Seven Stars near the docks when he came upon the case under the bed. Presumably, it had been put there by the thief after the robbery, with the intention of returning for it at a later date. Bowood is not a great scholar, but he managed to read the names on some of the letters. The names Fenwick and Lambert meant nothing to him, but the Edgcumbe name is, of course, well known in the city. So he brought the letters to me. I could not allow Edgcumbe correspondence to be left in the hands of strangers, so I agreed to his price. I admit I was puzzled by their appearance in a quayside tavern, and my next step would have been to contact Mr Fenwick and Mrs Lambert to see if the case had been stolen from either of them."

"You believed Bowood's tale?" asked Hay.

"I had no reason not to believe it. Bowood has occasionally worked for me, run errands, delivered notes, and so on. Do you think his story false?"

"I'm a Dutchman if it's true," Hay answered.

Edgcumbe sighed. "He lost what little money he had, you know, and I was glad to help him out with employment from time to time. I am saddened to think that the man is a villain after all."

Ben's self-restraint gave out. "It was you – you murdered my father! You sent Bowood after me! You told him to steal those papers!" He lunged across the table and seized the banker by the throat. The decanter fell over and smashed onto the floor. The silver tray crashed on top of it. Jacob bellowed murder. The door flew open and Mr Tatton, followed by an excited crowd of bank clerks, tumbled into the room. "Mr Edgcumbe – are you alright, sir – oh, Lord, it's robbery and murder, boys!"

The words 'robbery and murder' penetrated Ben's hearing. With a roar, he tightened his fingers and shook his sputtering victim from side to side.

"That's enough, my lad!" cried Mr Hay, pulling Ben off and shoving him down into his chair. Edgcumbe fell back into Tatton's arms, panting and clutching at his throat. The clerks sidled forward, but quickly edged back when Hay rounded on them.

"There's no harm done," he said. "Let's clear the room and start again, eh?"

Edgcumbe, torn between fear for his safety and fear of indiscretion, shook his old servant off. Tim Tatton knew a little too much about the *Miranda's* business – and in particular a certain insurance settlement, nothing of which ever found its way into Mrs Lambert's or George Fenwick's estates – to be allowed to remain in the room. "It's alright, Tim. Only a misunderstanding. Just tidy up the mess and leave us."

A few moments later, the door closed and the three men sat facing one another as before.

"Feelings are bound to run high," Mr Hay remarked philosophically. "A murder has been committed."

"Of course, I make allowances – " Jacob began, but a growl

from Ben persuaded him that it would be better not to elaborate the point.

"Is this Bowood still at the Stars?" Hay resumed.

"He is not. He signed on for a whaling voyage last week."

"Damn the son of a bitch!" Ben thumped the arm of his chair. "I'll track him down and I'll see you and Bowood swinging side by side for this, Edgcumbe."

"Mr Dearlove." Jacob's voice dripped sympathy. "You are – and very understandably too – upset and I will ignore these accusations, for the time being. If I had known that Bowood had broken into your house to get the documents, of course I would have notified the justices."

"You're lying – "

Hay laid his hand on Ben's arm. "Leave it, lad. As for the papers, Mr Edgcumbe, I'll requisition them if you please."

Jacob, who had read the letters and found them of little value, easily relinquished them. He rang the bell and gave the order to Tim Tatton. Ben watched in disgust as a receipt was prepared and signed. No wonder Sarah ran away from home, he thought. What a family was hers! He looked at the painting of her father Joseph's querulous, self-absorbed face mooning above a sheet of music. As weak as Jacob was strong, but his equal in selfishness. Joseph was dead, but what a jolt Ben could give the rest of them – that stepmother, too partial to her own daughters to notice the young girl's difficulties; those two vain, selfish girls with no sympathy for their more original and independently minded stepsister; above all, her uncle, that getter of money by any means. All he had to do was reveal that Sarah still lived. Let the Edgcumbes face the world then!

No. He was glad he had kept her secret. He understood now Mrs Lambert's assertion that Sarah would not shame them but that they would shame her. Edgcumbe rose from his seat to see them out and Ben ignored his proffered hand.

*

"You said you'd help me get the man who killed my father!" Ben slammed his glass on the table.

"So I did," Hay replied, calmly topping up the young man's brandy from the dusty bottle.

They were sitting in The Rummer in St Nicholas Market, just around the corner from the Edgcumbe bank. The place rang with the chatter of sailors, carters and porters. No one paid any attention to the aggressive young man in the corner, nor his tough-looking opponent. If a chair hurtled towards them, then they would duck; if a broken bottle rolled along the floor, then they would dodge; if a stray punch or kick came their way, then they would brawl. Not before.

"You don't believe that rubbish about Bowood finding the case and offering it to him?"

"No. But we can't prove anything against him without Bowood."

"Then you have to find Bowood."

Hay reached in his pocket for his snuffbox. "Bowood has gone, else Edgcumbe would have been a lot less confident of his tale. I'll send Beale to find out what whaler he's on and where she's bound if you like. But, you know, there's no point in following. The man's probably jumped ship already." He put two pinches of snuff on the back of his hand, sniffed loudly into each nostril.

Ben wrapped his fingers around his glass and stared into the cloudy liquid – it was not the best quality brandy. He had spoken rashly when he said he would follow his father's killer. Shipping out on the next available whaler would be a hard journey of ice and slaughter, and the chances of catching up with the man at the end of it were slight. And what would he do when he had him? He had no means of dragging a man back to the gallows. That only left killing him, which would put the rope around his own neck.

"Unless Bowood comes back to Bristol, I'll never catch him. And Edgcumbe goes free."

"For now, I fear that is so."

Ben sighed. What now? He had not misled Hay and Beale about the value of the letters, but he was glad he would not be witness to their disappointment when they studied the contents of the case. That still left George's maps. If they should learn about their existence, there was no telling what they would do to obtain them. He thought of these ruffians hanging around Overcombe... near to Rachel... Antony had to be warned, and the maps put into safekeeping. Ben did not expect him to be pleased when he learned the fate of his brother's letters, but he hoped he would understand that he had sacrificed them in order to protect the ultimate prize and George's legacy – the Fair Land.

All he wanted now was to be rid of the pair and get to Overcombe as soon as possible.

"Will you leave for London soon?" He tried not to sound too eager.

Hay's eyes flickered, but he answered with a shrug. "May as well go today as we've got what we came for." He dropped his snuffbox back in his pocket and scraped back his chair. "I'll bid you goodbye, Mr Dearlove."

When he had gone, Ben pushed the glass away. He waited half an hour and then hurried down to the stables to arrange for a horse to be ready for him at first light in the morning.

Nineteen

"But where on the world could this Fair Land be, when all has been charted?" Antony demanded.

"That is what George's maps will tell us," Ben answered. "We must take them to Captain Brine at once."

"I agree that, once and for all, they must be deciphered by an expert. I doubt that they will reveal the existence of a hitherto-unknown continent. However, I will get them."

He crossed the study and opened the door. George was in the hall examining, as if he had never seen it before, *The Battle of Naseby*.

"People who listen at doors are apt to hear disagreeable things about themselves," his father said. "Since you know what we are talking about, you may as well make yourself useful. Go upstairs and fetch Uncle George's maps."

George, conscious that he had got off lightly, skipped across the hall, winking at his grandfather's portrait as he passed. "My uncle, the discoverer of a new land!" he whispered gleefully. "Just think of it, Grandfather! Perhaps I shall go there one day and help build a new country. Oh, aren't you proud?"

The old gentleman, who had held his own views about the kind of people who ended up in the colonies – dissenters and convicts for the most part – remained voiceless and George pranced on up the stairs.

"Do you have a description of this man Bowood?"

"I could obtain one. No doubt he's well known in the dockside taverns."

"You could lay it before the port authorities. If he is still on the whaling vessel when she returns, they may be able to apprehend him."

"A good suggestion. I will look into it as soon as I get back to Bristol, though it will be a year or more before the ship comes home."

George's footsteps clattered down the stairs. He burst into the room. "It's gone! Uncle George's wallet is gone!"

"Gone?" they repeated, following up the exclamation with anxious questions: *Are you sure? Could one of the servants have moved it? Did you look in...?* – which served only to confirm that the wallet had indeed disappeared. They gazed in consternation at one another.

"Have there been any strangers about the house lately?" Ben asked.

"Rachel would know. George, go and find her."

He returned after several minutes with his sister. "Had to stop and tidy her hair," he muttered.

She darted a furious look at him, avoided meeting Ben's eyes, and fixed her attention on her father as he put his enquiry. She recited the list of workmen and laundrywomen who had visited Overcombe Park in the last few days. They were all villagers and well known in the area.

"Peddlers? Knife grinders? Beggars?" Ben suggested.

Rachel shook her head.

"There was a gypsy this morning," George said. "But she didn't come into the house."

"Yes. A curious, dark little creature. You praised her eyes."

George blushed. "Yes, well, they were very fine."

"What did she come for?" asked Ben.

"She knocked on the kitchen door and asked for a cup of milk," Rachel answered. "Then she danced for us, barefooted, and sang in her own language – strange music, tuneful without being anything like a tune. Her voice was so sad."

"A Travelling Dancer!" Ben exclaimed. Antony looked at him in puzzlement. "She is Miss Edgcumbe's companion... Who witnessed her performance?"

"We all did," George said. "Except Father, who was out at the time."

"Did the servants watch her?"

"Yes, most of them."

"And while you were all distracted by the performance Sarah Edgcumbe came in and took the papers."

"But how did she know where to find them?" George looked unconvinced.

Ben, remembering Mrs Lambert's story, said, "She visited Overcombe, didn't she? With Alex. Doubtless your uncle showed them his workroom, entertained them with a few experiments, his collection of curiosities... She guessed that the papers would be there. And now she will destroy them."

"Destroy them?" George repeated, his dreams of governorship in a far land dissolving. "But why?"

"She thinks that we will rob the people of the Fair Land and turn them into slaves."

"If they do exist, they cannot long remain unknown to the civilised part of the world," Antony said. "The French, the Spanish and the Dutch also wish to expand their territories. If anyone is to govern them, it is better for the natives that they should be under British rule."

The civilised part of the world! Ben shifted uneasily. Perhaps Sarah's fears, knowing her Uncle Jacob as she did, were understandable. But we are not, he said to himself, a nation of Uncle Jacobs. Still, Sarah's pleas haunted him – "They are a gentle, generous people." But Antony was right, the Southlanders could not remain hidden forever.

"Why don't we go after her?" George cried impatiently.

"Let us think for a moment before we rush off in all directions," Antony answered. "Perhaps one of the estate workers noted which way your gypsy went after her performance. Possibly the women passed through Painswick. It could be that someone remembers something that might help us."

"Then I will go there at once," Ben said. "If you can lend me a fresh horse."

"Of course. And I will ask Cales to gather the men together so I can question them."

"What about me? Shall I go with Mr Dearlove?" asked George.

"If he thinks you would not be a hindrance."

"No, that's fine. But let's hurry."

At The Falcon, they were still recovering from the lunchtime rush. A boy knelt before the fire, building it up with fresh wood, while two barmaids ran back and forth clearing dirty dishes from the tables. One of the girls stopped in her tracks when she saw the new arrivals. Her face lit up with recognition. Ignoring the young gentleman from Overcombe Park, she smilingly asked Ben what she could get him.

George cast a look of admiration and envy at Ben, who beamed at the landlord's daughter. "A glass of ale apiece," he said, seating himself at a nearby table.

"We haven't got time to sit and drink." George hissed.

"I'm not sitting and drinking. If you want help from an innkeeper, spending some money is the only way to get it."

The girl came back with their ale and lingered by their

table while her companion bustled resentfully past with her hands full of beer mugs.

"We're looking for two women," Ben said. "A thin, nervous looking lady in her middle thirties and her servant, a small, dark-skinned woman. Have you seen anyone like that in the village?"

"They stopped here last night. They went out walking early this morning, and when they came back, the lady said her carriage was to be made ready immediately and ordered a pint of wine. I took it in to them."

"They had a private carriage?"

"Yes. A fine one."

"Do you know where they went when they left?"

"To Gloucester to take a coach to London."

"To take a coach? I thought they had their own carriage."

"It was borrowed. The driver told me. He had to take it back to Bristol when he had dropped them off. He said he'd be glad to see the back of them. He was sure the servant was a witch, she was always talking mambo-jomba." Her eyes rounded. "Is that why you are after them?"

"No, they are friends of ours and we have missed one another, that's all. The servant isn't a witch. She's a foreigner."

The girl looked as if she thought they were the same thing.

"I can guess who lent Miss Edgcumbe the carriage," Ben said when the tapstress had been summoned back to her cleaning by her father. "It was Mrs Lambert. Drink up, George. We're going to Gloucester."

They went directly to the Coach Office on Northgate Street. A pimply-faced clerk sulkily left his computations in the counting-house to come to the door and tell them that the London coach left nightly at ten o'clock, arriving at the Bolt and Tun Inn in Fleet Street at seven in the morning.

"Has a lady with a foreign servant taken a seat on tonight's coach?" Ben asked.

"There isn't a service on Wednesdays."

"But you said nightly."

"Nightly, except Wednesdays," the clerk answered, as if only a fool would not know this.

"Well then, has the lady taken a place for tomorrow?"

The clerk thoughtfully picked the top off a crimson swelling on his chin. "I wouldn't know. I'm accounts, not bookings."

"Where are London passengers likely to stay?"

The clerk shrugged. "There're lots of inns in Gloucester."

Ben turned away in exasperation.

"What shall we do now?" asked George.

"Sample Gloucester's inns. Sarah Edgcumbe must be staying in one of them, waiting for tomorrow's coach. Besides, we need to find somewhere to stable the horses."

"There might still be places on the four o'clock mail coach if you're interested." The remark came from a stableboy who slouched against the wall near the archway into the coach yard.

"There's another coach to London? But the clerk never said."

The lad sniffed. "He wouldn't, would he? Not one of theirs. Run by the landlord of the King's Head."

"Is it running today?"

"Yes."

"Which way is the King's Head?"

"I'll take you."

"Thank you, but I don't want to get you into trouble with the Coach Office."

"Don't work *here*," the ostler replied with a shudder that suggested he would rather be destitute. He levered himself from the wall and, hands in pockets, swaggered off. They followed him into Westgate Street, passing half a dozen inns before arriving at the King's Head. The ostler pointed. "Coach parlour's in there! I'll take your horses."

They glanced into the crowded parlour. It was as shabby and grimy as such apartments usually were and smelled of wood smoke, tobacco, damp coats, broiled chicken and ale. The air was further weighted with the perfumes of eaux, powders and pomades which a travelling salesman was attempting to sell to a sailor in his best land togs: blue jacket, petticoat breeches, and buckled shoes. A gentleman seated by the fire squinted at the labels in the voluble salesman's hands and, in asides to the squire who stood in front of the flames warming his backside, claimed that he could read them. He was, he avowed, a famous eye-doctor and had just completed a tour of the West Country, leaving behind five hundred people whose sight he had restored. In the corner a noisy, good-natured family, the youngest child on the mother's lap, shared food from a basket.

Ben was not surprised that Sarah was not there. "She'll be waiting in a private room."

He shut the door on the racket and stepped back into the corridor. A latch rattled and a maid carrying a tray of dirty dishes hurried out of the room on their right. They moved towards the smell of hot dinners, but stopped in astonishment when the girl shrilled, "Get out!" confusingly adding, "Go through if you please, gentlemen."

She disappeared into the kitchen as they realised that the dismissal was meant for a skinny boy lurking on the doorstep. He bobbed out of sight but, as soon as she had gone, skipped over the threshold.

"If you're looking for a coach to London, I can find you a place. The ones Mr Phillpott runs are cleaner and better sprung than the King's Head's too."

"Mr Phillpott?"

"Landlord of The Bell Inn. Coaches every day at four o'clock, no exceptions. The original and best London and Gloucester post coaches. New and elegant. Arriving Gloucester Coffee House, Piccadilly every morning at seven."

"Yet another London coach?" Ben exclaimed.

"Original and best." The boy cast furtive glances at the door through which the girl had passed, anxiously expecting the appearance of a boot black or scullion to see him off the premises.

"We'd better go there at once," George said.

"Wait!" Ben pulled him back. "There isn't much time. You had better look for her here and I'll go and see if she's at The Bell."

The Bell was a large, seventeenth-century building on Southgate Street. A sign in one of the windows announced: *For one night only Signor Rossignoel the famous copier of the finest notes of the feathered tribe will perform a concert in the Great Room. After the concert will be a ball. Tickets 2s 6d each.* In the lobby, Ben was almost mown down by scurrying waiters, their arms full of punch bowls, tablecloths, glasses and chairs, frenziedly preparing the assembly room for the evening's entertainment.

He removed his hat, shook off the first raindrops of a shower, and beckoned to one of them. "I'm supposed to meet a lady here. She is travelling with a foreign servant and may have booked a place on the London coach. Can you tell me how I might find her?"

The servant, flustered by so unusual a request, replied, "I'll fetch Mr Phillpott." His colleagues, overhearing this, exchanged scared looks and redoubled their efforts, racing up and down the stairs as if bets had been laid on their performance.

Mr Phillpott appeared, ordered the men to look lively and stop dawdling, and Ben repeated his enquiry.

"You're a runner, aren't you?" the landlord exclaimed. "And she's a trickster like Lady Hall! Damn the impudence of these jades! I thought there was something suspicious about her, though her money looks real enough. That servant of hers is no more a French maid than I am." He snapped his fingers. "Bob, run for the constable."

"No, no!" Ben cried. "I have no connection with Bow Street and nothing to do with any adventuress like Lady Hall. I am employed by Mr Fenwick of Overcombe Park, Painswick. The lady is a friend of his and it's important that I see her before she leaves for London."

"A gentleman of Painswick? Bob, how many times have I told you not to spread rumours about respectable guests? It's no way to do business, sir, no way to do business. And don't stand there like a fool. Show the gentleman to the lady at once."

"There's no need to announce me." Ben dismissed Bob with a few coins and waited until he was out of sight before opening the door. The chamber was indistinguishable from those found in any other old, respectable inn – the furniture dark and solid, a dull patterned rug on the floor, heavy curtains at the leaded windows. An inner door led to the bedroom.

Sarah Edgcumbe sat in an armchair huddled over a blazing fire, like a traveller who has grown used to hot climes. She had a sheaf of loose papers on her lap. One by one, she was throwing them into the flames, watching each page writhe against the glowing coals before adding the next.

She turned her startled face towards the door, recognised Ben and with a cry of dismay grabbed the remaining sheets and flung them into the hearth. Her aim was poor and most of the papers fluttered to the ground, lodging against her shoe. Ben recognised them – the roughly-drawn maps, diagrams and astronomical readings from George's wallet.

"No!" he rushed towards her.

She snatched up the pages, brandished them over the flames. "I will if you come any closer."

He stopped. "They aren't yours to burn. You have no right to destroy them."

"George had no right to keep them. He knew that we could never go back to the Fair Land."

"Why do you say that? We have ships, we have men... perhaps none so brave as Captain Edgcumbe and Mr Fenwick, but British ships will sail to the Fair Land again." He dared not look at the papers she dangled over the hearth, tinged red by the firelight. "You know the language, the customs. They'll need your help. Think of it! You could be on one of those ships... you could see Mervidir again, and the waterfall, and drink *maran* with Tinyar and Vannir."

She moaned. Her hand sank, the papers twisted between her fingers. "I can't go back. No one can ever go back."

"You cannot keep the Fair Land hidden forever."

"The ocean hides many things, things that should stay hidden. You would help me, if you knew."

"You came to me for help in my father's house. You said the same thing then: the ocean is vast and hides many things."

"I remember."

He took a cautious step forward. "Then why don't you tell me what is hidden? And then, perhaps, I can help you."

The ruddy light flickered over her pale face. He saw the lines that grief and anxiety had drawn there. He pitied the woman, worn out by the keeping of her secrets.

"In the Fair Land you were happy and healthy," he said gently. "You could get your strength back again."

"Yes," she whispered.

"Then tell me."

She was silent for a moment, hunched over the flames, her arms crossed over her stomach, as if she felt a bitter cold. Then she began to speak.

Twenty

Awbray had managed to get the fire in the great cabin going but the wood was damp and produced more smoke than heat. Everything was damp – the walls, the table, the chairs, our clothes, our breath on the cold air. The floor was damp too, although it was weeks since it had been washed. Every morning, after he had emptied the chamber pots, heated water for the gentlemen to shave in and tidied the great cabin, Awbray used to slosh the baize floorcloth with salt water, leaving it to dry without taking it up. But now it never dried, so Awbray had stopped washing it. It was astonishing to see how quickly its colour had changed after only a few weeks' neglect – the gay red grimed by the marks of our boots, the ash from the stove, spilled wine, ground-in crumbs, dog hairs, scrubbed patches where George's hound Twinger had relieved himself.

It was altogether a more dismal place than when I first came on board. Then, I had thought it fresh and quaint. George had paid to have the walls painted pale green and the beadwork picked out in gold paint. He had brass hinges fitted on the door and dark green velvet curtains hung over its half-glazing. Alex protested at so much extravagance, but George only clapped him on the shoulder and laughed. "The *Miranda* is your first command, and she shall be fit for you to sail!"

Now the green velvet had gone to stuff the gap in a broken stern window and there was nothing to veil the marine on guard duty outside, slumped miserably against the wall. The brass fittings were tarnished, the gold was flaking off and the light paintwork was scuffed and stained. The tablecloth was filthy, but not quite so filthy as the ones that had gone into the laundry bag waiting, with heaps of our clothes, for conditions favourable for cleaning. Drop the bag into the sea now and it would come out as a big frozen ball and, though it might thaw, it would not dry. The ship looked as sad outside as she did inside – her bright blue and yellow dulled by angry oceans, her varnish chipped by furious wind and rain, her deck bleached white – yet the sailors were constantly painting and mending.

There were two of them working in here now, sitting cross-legged on the cold floor repairing a sail. Davy Davies and Josh Twitty. The two men were inseparable in their mutual hatred. Wherever one worked, the other worked. Wherever one messed, the other messed. Wherever one danced and sang during the sailors' recreation periods, the other capered too. Not an opportunity was missed to insult each other.

"Leek eater," Twitty would sneer at the Welshman.

"Croaker," Davies would spit at the Yorkshireman.

And indeed Twitty was a terrible complainer, always grumbling about something or other. He was grumbling under his breath now, casting angry glances at Davies who only lifted his buttock higher and grinned at the mephitic results. All this was carried on when they thought I was not looking, and I did my best not to look. But I do have other senses. If only Davies, and the rest of us, had some leeks to eat, or any fresh vegetables. We had been living on salt beef and sour cabbage for far too long.

There was a sudden creak of wood as a gust of wind slapped against the stern. The windows rattled, the sails flapped and the voices of the men on deck were picked up by the tempest and whirled about the ship before disappearing into the waves.

The draught dislodged the faded green velvet and a blade of cold air entered the cabin. Nathaniel Davenport, who sat at the table writing, coughed but did not look up from his journal. He was bundled up in one of the blankets from his cot so that only his thin hand and wan face were exposed.

Nathaniel had made an unwise match and wedded against his father's wishes. He had been cut off not only from his father's wealth but, when his money disappeared, his wife's affection too. Blithely ignoring the fact of their marriage, she had left him to go and live with a lord. In his hopelessness, Nathaniel had applied to be George's secretary. The voyage had done nothing to heal his broken heart and much to weaken his lungs.

Awbray, emerging from the captain's larder where he worked by day and slung his hammock at night, hastened to stuff the fabric back into the holed glass. He knelt on the window seat and fiddled with the frozen, sodden cloth. He started back with a cry of alarm. Something dark tumbled down and landed with a click on the bench.

"Ugh!" the lad cried, his face twisted with disgust. "A scorpion!"

Nathaniel looked up. "A scorpion? Is it alive?"

The boy cautiously poked the insect that had been caught up in the folds of the velvet. Its arched tail wagged feebly. "I think so."

Nathaniel put down his pen and, trailing his blanket, went over to the window. "How curious," he said, examining the creature.

"Where has it come from?" Awbray looked anxiously at the gap in the window as if he was afraid that more of the beasts would fly in.

"It must have come on board with some supplies. Could it have been in the baskets of fruit we took in at Rio? How could

225

it have survived the cold? It is as if it is in a state of frozen vitalisation." Nathaniel looked around the cabin. "Fetch me one of the specimen jars."

"Are you going to keep it?" Awbray's face fell in dismay.

"When we return to warmer climes, as I hope and pray that one day we will, it will be interesting to see if the animal's full spirits are restored."

Awbray did as he was bid, standing well back while Nathaniel manoeuvred the scorpion into the bottle, which was provided with a perforated lid.

This done, Nathaniel resumed his place, Awbray went back into his cubbyhole, the sailors bent their heads over their work and I took up my pencil and once more attempted to make a sketch of the mottled petrel George shot yesterday. The fire was beginning to look a little brighter but the room was still bitterly cold. Nevertheless it was warmer than my cabin, which had an inch of icy water washing about in it when I woke up this morning. Luckily, I had stored my boots and outer garments in a cupboard above the bed and they were dry, or what must pass for dry. I had not removed the sailor's trousers and quilted petticoats I wore under my skirt when I crept under the cold blankets last night. I had not removed them for days.

Kitty appeared from under the table and jumped with an imperious squeak onto my lap, circling and pummelling with her paws until she had made herself comfortable. I rubbed her under her chin where the fur was soft and warm, which she allowed while staring greedily at the dead bird.

The cabin door opened. The smoke swirled around the room. George stepped in, knocking snow from his shoulders. Nathaniel frowned at the puddle of icy water collecting around George's boots, though really it made no increase in the dampness of the cabin. Awbray, with an eager smile, ran to help George out of his wet oilskin coat.

George's face was chapped and pinched by the freezing air. His breathing was raspy. He had not fully recovered from a bout of feverish sore throat, swollen neck and fever. Many on board the ship were similarly affected. It was due, Alex said, to drinking iced water. More nutritious food and milder air would soon restore the sufferers. For now, like the rest of us, George felt the effects after weeks of living on preserved food, damp bedding, and in perpetual cold.

No one who has never been cold from the moment of rising to the moment of lying down, and through the hours in between, can appreciate the lowering effect on mind and body. The chilled, aching limbs are only a little relieved by rubbing with flannel. The head and teeth ache. Nothing can relieve the melancholy of the mind but the sight of a roaring fire and, on the worse days when the howling winds and mountainous waters penetrate every seam of the ship, a fire is the one thing you cannot have since all have to be extinguished on the onset of a storm.

Of melancholia, however, George exhibited no symptoms.

"Why don't you come on deck?" he cried. "Don't you know you have just missed a whale blowing?"

"We watched a whale blowing yesterday," Nathaniel muttered, his eyes fixed on his book.

George regarded the pale, dejected man for a moment. "It would do you a great deal more good than sitting in this fog."

Awbray glanced anxiously at the window. "Why, sir? Is there another one coming down?"

"No, my lad. I mean the fog in here. I don't know how anyone can breathe. You need some air, Nat."

A man who relies on another for his wage does not ordinarily allow himself the luxury of insolence. When that man finds himself in a pitching ship in the most miserable portion of the globe, where the sun is seldom seen through the mists and the thermometer rarely rises five degrees above the freezing point, prudent considerations are apt to be forgotten.

"Antarctic air is the very last thing I have any need of," Nathaniel snapped.

"It's only a cold, man. Take a diaphoretic. And ask Mr Nock to give you some antimony."

A fit of wheezing and coughing prevented Nathaniel's reply. As the ship's bell began to clang, the door opened again to admit Lieutenant Sloper. Alex and Lieutenant Nightingale were just behind him.

Davies nudged Twitty and hissed, "Look sharp, here comes the Old Man!"

Sloper overheard but did not rebuke the seaman. Rather, a faint smile crossed his thin, weathered face, although it failed to diminish its sourness. He threw his soaking wet coat into Awbray's arms. The boy staggered under the weight.

The title the 'Old Man' had no relation to Alex's age but to his position as captain. Sloper, nearly twice as old as his commander, had been passed over for promotion many a time. He had experience at sea, and many years of it, but *he* had no rich friends to help him, *he* did not mix with families who could count the Lord of the Admiralty amongst their acquaintance, *he* had not, as the sailors said of the favoured, come on board through the cabin windows. Let the sailors call the captain what they liked!

Eight bells rang, the bosun's mate piped the men to dinner and Davies and Twitty scrambled to their feet and hurried away to join their mess. Having hung the gentlemen's coats to air as best he could in his little room, Awbray ran down to fetch our portable soup from the stove on the mess deck. While he was gone, Mr Nock arrived. The surgeon had been making an inventory of his medicines. He told us that a great deal of his bark supply had gone to treat feverish patients but, to his relief, there was no shortage yet.

The table was cleared of our work, including the lifeless petrel, and the dinner laid. We might dream of beef and plum pudding, new-laid eggs, asparagus, cherries, fruit tarts, almond cakes, oranges and apples, but we ate thick soup made from cubes of dried meat, and damp bread that had been re-baked so many times it crumbled into powder when broken. This was followed by a tasteless pudding made with musty flour and stale raisins. When we had finished the dreary meal, the table was cleared of plates and crumbs. Apathy gripped us. Everyone was reluctant to start work again. Even George, sitting with his arms folded across his chest, could think of nothing to say and stared morosely at the stains on the tablecloth.

Alex exchanged glances with Lieutenant Nightingale, cleared his throat and said, "I have something to discuss with you."

Mr Nock, with a lingering look at the stove, started to plod back to his dingy cabin below deck.

"No, I shall need your opinion." Alex motioned to the surgeon to stay. "Mr Nightingale, the charts please."

The lieutenant rose and opened a long, narrow chest on top of the sideboard, selected two or three of the scrolls inside it and brought them back to the table. Alex stood up, picked one of these and opened it out before us.

"This is Mr Dalrymple's chart showing the Pacific portion of the Great Southern Continent."

There was no need for him to tell us, we had perused the document to the point of boredom many times. Yet something in Alex's voice re-awoke our interest. The atmosphere in the room changed. The fire seemed to burn higher. The light falling through the stern windows turned a fiercer white.

Nathaniel poked his head out of his blankets and peered gloomily at the vast blanks. Mr Nock stroked one of his thick eyebrows with his index finger, a habit he had when he was perplexed. Lieutenant Sloper glowered at the map as if he blamed it for all our troubles. Nightingale stood at Alex's elbow, his hands behind his back, reverently gazing at his captain. There was an expression similar to Kitty's when she gazed upon the dead bird in the eye George fixed on the geographer's theoretical map.

"Mr Dalrymple has suggested that lands sighted by the Spaniard Juan Fernández in the 1560s, Quiros in 1606, and Davis in 1685 are part of the Great Southern Continent." Alex joined the points as he named them, sketching a vast coastline with his finger. "Our course is south west, and our current position is here." He rested his hand on a spot somewhere in the foothills of Dalrymple's continent. "We are sailing," he said quietly, "across the Great South Land."

"Dalrymple has put the coastline too far to the north," George objected. "The land is here but does not extend as far as was thought."

"We are nearly seventy degrees south. We have sailed further south than any ship, and we have met with no land."

"We could sail over the pole and take a trip round the world in five minutes if the ice wasn't in the way," Nathaniel sneered.

George glanced angrily at his secretary then said to Alex, "You know how misleading sightings can be in these regions. Distances are hard to judge. Wallis reported seeing land to the south of King George's Island. It is only that it is further away than he realised."

"And you know how misleading sightings can be," Alex replied. "How many times have we seen what we thought was land only to discover it is fog or an ice island? The ice field is thickening, it is becoming mountainous, and the ice islands as they break off from it are numerous, clustered together and larger than any we have yet met. When the next fog comes down, we will have no idea of the extent or quantity of ice that surrounds us. We will only know that we are surrounded and likely to collide at any moment."

"But the ice is proof that there is land nearby. Seawater cannot freeze, the water the floating ice renders is fresh to drink. It comes from rivers and lakes. We cannot be far from the land of its origin."

Alex shook his head. "The ice is a barrier we cannot pass. I do not say it is impossible to navigate through it but I say that I will not attempt it."

"You will not attempt it?" George cried. "You would come this far and, at the end, give up the search?"

"What we are looking for is worthless. Should the land exist, it is surrounded by ice, it is covered by ice, nothing can grow there, nothing can live. It can be of no value to anyone. It is madness to continue to risk our lives for such a useless prize."

"You are thinking of turning back?"

"I have decided. We cannot remain in this frigid zone."

"God be thanked!" Nathaniel cried.

Even when he was ill and drawn or cold and pinched, George's face was a pleasure to look upon and I had never imagined anything could mar his looks. At this moment, shock and anger made him ugly, drawing the skin tight around jaw and cheekbone, dulling his eyes to murderous darkness, twisting his shapely mouth. Alex, as if embarrassed by the transformation, turned away and sought the surgeon's advice.

"Mr Nock, what is your opinion of the health of the crew?"

"The men's health is surprisingly good in the circumstances.

231

I have treated only minor cases of injury – strains caused by heavy work, hands lacerated by the ice on the ropes and rigging. Most of them are suffering from colds and chills which they cannot rid themselves of. The carpenter is my main concern. His chest is congested. Most importantly, we have not yet had a single case of scurvy thanks to the preservatives they are eating."

"No scurvy!" George cried. "Isn't that the worst we have to fear? And you can treat it, should it occur?"

"I said there has not *yet* been any scurvy. And while there are effective antiscorbutics I can use – I have a good stock of wort – it is better to prevent than treat the disease. You have not, I dare say," Mr Nock eyed the young man from under his bushy eyebrows, "ever seen a man with his limbs swollen and ulcerated, his agony intensified by the ceaseless pitching of the ship."

George impatiently waved this pathetic image away. "But the men are fit? They are able to continue the voyage?"

Mr Nock's thickset face took on a disapproving expression. "None of us have eaten fresh food for nearly two months, and the food we have is stale and not as fortifying as it was when it was packed. So far, this has only resulted in a general gloomishness, and in some costiveness, in others looseness. However, I do not doubt that continued exposure to these conditions, on such a low diet, will bring about a steady deterioration of well-being."

"Thank you, Mr Nock," Alex said. "The new course I determine – "

George interrupted. "Do you agree that the ice is unnavigable, Nightingale?"

The lieutenant looked at Alex.

"Can't the man answer?" George snarled.

"The lieutenant's agreement is irrelevant," Alex said. "However, you may answer Mr Fenwick's question, Lieutenant."

232

"I do agree."

George turned away from him. "Lieutenant Sloper?"

"You are asking what I think? It was my opinion that we should not have come this far. But no weight was given to it, although I have sailed in the waters near Greenland and have some knowledge of the property of ice islands. Even to sail close to them puts the ship at risk for they are as liable to collapse and engulf us as they are to hole us."

"You see, George," said Alex, "the dangers are too great. You cannot think it is wise to risk our lives any further in this cruise. You will not allow," he added persuasively, "that Miss Edgcumbe should be exposed to further hardship."

"But you want to continue, don't you Miss Edgcumbe?" George appealed to me.

I was sorry for George clinging onto a hope Alex had long ago abandoned, but the thought of leaving this awful region almost made me weep with joy. Yet how to tell George that he had not one ally in the room, that I too thought the time to abandon our quest in these waters had come?

Alex put a decisive end to my dilemma. "We shall put about and sail east to the thirty-eighth latitude where we will look for the land said to be discovered by Juan Fernández, or for Easter Island."

"All we will find are more islands!" George said.

Alex shook his head. "There is still room in the ocean for a land of great size to be discovered between Cape Horn and New Zealand. We may find the continent yet, and it will be a useful discovery if we do for it will have a productive climate and ships will be able to sail there without danger."

He waited, but seeing that George had no more to say, he called for his coat. Awbray, who had been in the pantry all this time, came running out with the still-damp garment. He had heard everything and could not disguise his smiles. He almost skipped across the cabin. If he could have yelled *Three cheers*, I think he would have done. I think we all would have done. The lieutenants donned their outdoor clothes and followed the captain out of the cabin. In the doorway, Alex paused and glanced back at George but his friend did not meet his eye. Alex put on his hat and went out. The bright optimism in the sentry's face as he saluted the captain showed that he too had heard every word.

Cold air shrieked around the room, fell flat when the door closed. For a moment, no one spoke. Then Nathaniel flung off his blanket, jumped to his feet and retrieved his journal and pens from the sideboard. "I have some news to record in my journal today!" he crowed.

With a strangled curse, George rose from his chair. He rounded on Awbray. "Where's my coat, boy? Look lively, won't you?"

The door slammed behind him and he was gone. But where could he go on this small ship to hide his raging disappointment?

Twenty-One

We knew that many more weeks must pass before a landfall. Nevertheless, on the day we put about we rejoiced as if we were already within sight of breakers washing gently on a hospitable shore. The sailors, who had previously gone about their arduous duties in sullen silence, shouted and laughed at one another as they toiled on the icy deck.

Alex opened half a dozen bottles of his best wine with dinner in the great cabin. It may have been thrown away on salt meat and sauerkraut but it felt like a banquet. He had just raised his glass to toast the King when we heard singing coming from the mess deck, the first in a month. Immediately, he ordered the purser to serve an extra ration of rum to the men. The cheers that greeted this announcement almost shook apart a ship that had survived the hurricanes off Cape Horn.

Mr Nock was a heavy man with a somewhat forbidding face under eyebrows tweaked into horns by his habit of fiddling with them. He was not married, and at this period of his life – he was near his fiftieth year – had either abandoned or had never had any ambitions in that direction. He was a solitary, self-sufficient man who spent a great deal of his time in his cabin. What did he do in there besides take inventories of his medicines? Sometimes he treated patients, sometimes he wrote his journal, sometimes he studied his medical books. He also wrote poetry.

In the early days of our voyage, his verses often contributed to our after-dinner entertainment, but the muse had not visited him for a long time. Tonight, however, she had communicated to him a verse on the occasion of our southern explorations, entitled *English Heroism*. It began, "*The brave bosoms of Britannia…*" and was of such a rousing nature that, after one hearing, Mr Nightingale declared he would turn it into a song on the spot. When the lieutenant accompanied himself on his guitar, he had a fine singing voice, especially for soft airs and ballads. Many weeks ago, with tears in his eyes at the harsh twanging that emanated from the damp-warped wood, he had set the instrument aside. Now, with only his wine glass and a pair of spoons, he managed to produce a creditable tune.

Our singing may not have benefited our sore throats, nor our ears, but it was balm to our hearts. I put my arm through Alex's and was rewarded with the pressure of his hand and an unguarded smile, unshackled for once from the cares of command. Mr Nock rumbled out the notes. Nathaniel croaked. Awbray, a pile of dishes in his hand and a dirty cloth over his arm, added his treble to our performance. Even Mr Sloper, whose usual response to Mr Nock's verse was a sneer, beat time with his hand and tunelessly mouthed the words.

And what of George? Did he sit glowering at Alex, or resent our celebration, or feed his disappointment with strong wine? He did not. He joined in the singing with the same goodwill he had shown the company since sitting down for dinner.

The song finished in laughter and applause. "Again!" cried Lieutenant Nightingale, using his knife as a baton. I shook my head. I was thirsty. George, who sat on my right, filled my empty glass for me.

"Thank you," I said, taking advantage of the noise to address George privately. "And thank you for singing with us."

George smiled. "I do not sing particularly well."

"You do. But you know that that is not the reason I thanked you. I know the song is very far from expressing your feelings and I am sorry for it."

"I cannot stand out against the desire of the many."

"But you do see that turning north is the right thing to do?"

He hesitated. "Yes. Alex is right. There is no land and, even if there were, it would be of interest only to philosophers."

I was relieved to hear the admission and said eagerly, "There are other places to look. Even if the Continent is not on this side of Cape Horn, it may be on the other. Mr Dalrymple has placed a gulf there – St Sebastian."

George glanced at Alex. "If he chooses to go that way."

"You know he will go if he can. Much will depend on the condition of the ship, the strength of the crew, and the season. A captain has to take all these things into account."

"You are right, of course. I do not command the ship."

There was bitterness in his voice but nothing a smile and a sympathetic voice could not dissipate. I gave him the smile and my sympathy, I thought, would always be his. "We may not need to sail towards the Falklands. We may already be on course for the land we seek."

"Are *you* glad that we have turned back, Miss Edgcumbe?"

"I am."

"Then so am I."

"What has happened to our chorus?" Nightingale rebuked us. With apologetic laughs, George and I once more raised our voices.

The celebratory mood could not last. We were still amongst the ice islands. Sometimes they were like floating palaces with turrets of marble. Sometimes they were blue, glittering masses, hardly moving as if they were rooted to the ocean floor. Sometimes they were fast-sinking rafts made of spongeous ice,

237

rapidly dissolving. Once we saw a shaggy white bear pacing on one of these in ever-decreasing circles as the surface beneath him crumbled away. The sailors wanted to shoot him but it was not safe to launch a boat and he was swept away to another death.

The ice islands could seem as solid and silent as rock yet, if the ship passed too close, we could hear them groaning as they succumbed to the mighty internal forces that caused them to explode in upon themselves. Sometimes a fissure appeared without warning and, before the *Miranda* had time to veer off, there was a horrible sound and huge chunks of ice crashed into the ocean. Then we braced ourselves for the rocking caused by the impact of the waves against her side or, if the ship was very close, the thud of ice boulders on the deck.

The boulders were collected and melted, but we did not rely on chance for our water supply. Regularly, boats were launched and rowed to the ice and the men hacked off as much as they could carry back to the ship. One calm morning, George accompanied them, taking his guns with him. Albatrosses – birds that can be studied and then, after careful dressing, eaten – had been seen around the ship.

"Some fresh meat will do you good, Miss Edgcumbe," George said, buttoning his coat.

I nodded wearily. I could not think George's excursion on an icy ocean in a tiny boat comparable to what I endured at that moment. Nevertheless, I thanked him as graciously as I could. I had a heavy cold and, in addition, I was suffering from the woman's condition, a great inconvenience on board a ship even though I was allowed the comfort of fresh water for washing and not salt, which was often all the gentlemen could obtain. I still had some clean strips of linen left, torn from one of my sheets. The rest had been rinsed in salt water and put away until such time as thorough washing would be possible.

Nathaniel gagged. "Albatross. Disgusting meat!"

George, ignoring his secretary's remark, left. Nathaniel's pen scratched across paper. The fire crackled and smoked. I fell into a light sleep in which I was aware of my aches, the cold in my bones, the sound of men's voices, the rattle of chain and rope, and the bumping of the lowered boat. After a long time of dozing, I heard rapid footsteps. The door opened and closed. Someone came into the room, his breathing laboured.

"What's the matter?" Nathaniel cried.

"We've lost the cooper," George answered, his voice flat.

I opened my eyes. "The one they call Bungs?"

His real name was Gemaliel Sprat. He was a young, soft-spoken Scot with a wistful manner, as if he were constantly brooding on some great loss.

"Yes, I'm afraid so."

"What happened?" Nathaniel hurried over and helped his employer out of his coat, a service he did not usually render. George gratefully allowed him to peel off the frost-rimed garment.

"We rowed the boat to the mouth of an ice cavern. We thought it a safe, sheltered spot. Sprat was leaning out to chip some ice away. There was a swell. He overbalanced and went overboard. I think he lost his senses almost immediately. We tried to reach him but the roof of the cave collapsed. We had to push off with our poles. There was nothing we could do to save him. We stood off and waited for the fall to end. It seemed to go on forever – the dreadful roar and tumble, the water slapping against the madly bobbing boat. We rowed back to the spot as soon as we could. We could see him buried under the ice. It was impossible to dig him out."

Nathaniel clicked his tongue. "You must drink some brandy. Sit down."

George sank into a chair, rested his elbow on the table, his head in his hand. He looked a hundred years old, his face white and full of lines like cracks in the ice, the ice that was liable to fall apart without any warning and engulf a man. The awfulness of our situation smote me then as it had never done before. I was cold and in pain, trapped on this stale ship, surrounded by men with death in their faces. I felt dizzy and tears blurred my vision. The men's voices seemed very faint. Alex came in. It seemed to me that he floated above the floor and his outline shimmered.

"I've ordered soup to be served to the boat crew and sent them below to rest. I've asked Mr Nock to attend you." He put his hand on his friend's shoulder. "You must not blame yourself."

"We were shouting directions to one another, our voices echoed around the cave. The roof was unstable. We should not have made so much noise."

"You did not know the structure was weak. George, it is no one's fault."

"Sprat was a good man."

"He was and we are all sorry he is dead."

A good man gone, trapped in the ice, unable to move, unable to speak, left to float endlessly alone, his glassy eyes fixed on the ship as she sailed away from him.

"What if he is not dead?" I shrieked. "What if he is in a state of frozen vitalisation?" I was aware of their startled faces turned towards me. Then I lost consciousness.

I was in the dark. There was a burning smell under my nose and a red light close to my eye, which vexed me. I was warm down my left side and there was a comforting weight across my shoulders. I liked the warmth and moved towards it, away from the crimson spot. The circle grew large and hazy. I coughed. The spasm forced my eyes open. Mr Nock wafted the smouldering feather away. I was still sitting by the fire.

Alex knelt beside me, supporting me in his arms. "She's awake," he said.

"That's better," Mr Nock answered, his voice a comforting grumble. "Nothing but a touch of hysterics brought on by exhaustion and strain. Give her this to drink."

Alex took the cup from him and held it to my lips. It was mulled wine and sugar, warmed over the cabin stove. I put my hand around Alex's, steadying the vessel as I drank.

"You should have some too." Mr Nock handed a cup to George.

George waved the drink away and dropped to his knees before me. "Miss Edgcumbe, please forgive me! I had no intention to cause you any distress. I should not have spoken of – " He broke off.

I let my head fall back against Alex's shoulder. "You are not to blame. I am weak and tired."

"We all are," Mr Nock said grimly. "The sooner we can get some vegetables and provisions, the better it will be."

Alex nodded. "We will make what speed we can."

But the voyage went on, and the gentle Scot's death destroyed the optimism that had enlivened us since the *Miranda* turned about. George got rheumatism from going out in the wet boat. Awbray fell a prey to fainting fits. Alex had chilblains on his fingers and toes; his hands were red and raw. Nathaniel's eyes became so inflamed he could not read or write. The crew, worn out by the constant watching for danger, suffered from the same complaints. There was an epidemic of colds. Mr Nock ordered that malted wort liquor should be drunk with every meal as a preventative, but it was not long before signs of scurvy began to appear in the men – bad gums, livid spots, swollen feet.

Their tempers were as bad as their health. They grumbled at the officers whenever an order was given and there were loud complaints about the food, in particular the bread, which was all but inedible. Alex did not say anything to us but he doubled the guard of marines on the great cabin. Discipline was hard to maintain. It was only the knowledge that there was no other way out of our predicament that kept the crew going. As for what went on amongst themselves, it was impossible to regulate.

There was on board an able-bodied sailor by the name of Mutloe – the sailors called him 'Tripes'. The man was almost a giant. No Navy issue shirt or trousers would fit him so he had to sew his own from fabric bought from the purser. Despite his huge hands, his needlework was excellent. His main problem was footwear. In warmer climates he could, like most of the sailors, go barefoot, but on this voyage he suffered a great deal from cramming his enormous feet into boots and shoes that were too small for them. Eventually, he took to hobbling about with strips of wool and hide bound over his feet. He was constantly tripping, and his favourite oath could be heard all over the ship – "Blister me tripes!"

Inadequately shod as he was, it was not safe to send him aloft and so he was employed on other duties where his great strength was useful. Some of the men began to resent the fact that he was excused from rigging duties while they were still compelled to clamber over the slippery ropes and battle with the stiff canvas. "Tripes had a proper pair of boots before sailing," they muttered, "but sold them to pay a gambling debt. He did it on purpose, in order to shirk the most hazardous work."

One of Mutloe's critics, Nathan Joliff, could project his voice by a sort of ventriloquism. His skill entertained the men hugely at the start of the voyage. Lately, he had got into the habit of mimicking Mutloe's "Blister me tripes!" The mockery got on Mutloe's nerves, but the big man could never catch Joliff out. "Which of you said that?" Joliff would demand, his face a picture of innocence, while the men guffawed at Mutloe's spluttering, thwarted rage.

One morning, Joliff failed to respond to all hands. A search was made. He was nowhere to be found. The last sighting anyone remembered of him had been on the previous afternoon when he went to the heads. He must have fallen overboard and drowned.

"Well, blister me tripes!" Mutloe exclaimed.

And the men, with downcast eyes, shuffled back to their duties.

Alex was convinced that there had been foul play but could prove nothing. The crew refused to accuse Mutloe and no one complained about the distribution of duties again, not even when a popular man called Tudway, sent aloft to take in the topsails, lost his grip during a hail storm and fell from the yards to his death.

One day, a bundle of seaweed went by with some petrels feeding on it. Another day we passed a bed of broken ice. Penguins could be heard croaking but it was too foggy to see them. The thermometer was at thirty-five degrees, the rigging still frozen, the air freshening. A gale blew up and it was impossible to sleep. The fore topsail split. All the time, had we but the energy to appreciate it, we were sailing north. The thermometer reached forty-four degrees and we saw shearwaters and blue petrels. At fifty degrees, it was calm and George and Nightingale went out shooting in the boat. They brought back albatrosses and a Port Egmont Hen.

Then the thermometer stood at seventy degrees and I opened the scuttle of my cabin to let in the mild air. George called me on deck to watch a shoal of porpoise leaping high into the air, their sleek forms teasing our battered, labouring ship. In the distance, we saw several white birds. A speckled sea snake came alongside. As Alex pointed it out, it slithered away under the ship. We saw dolphins, shoals of fish, birds of all kinds – terns, gannets, noddies. We sighted more clumps of seaweed and excitement shivered through the vessel. Land could not be far off. But where? The sky clouded over, the birds disappeared. Had we missed it?

The wind abated. We advanced scarcely a mile and a half in the hour. Sloper swore he could smell land. The claim aggravated the rest of us. More than once, the cry of "Land!" turned out to be false – it was nothing but a trick of the haze. A little breeze sprang up and the *Miranda* began to move forward again. And then, about fifteen leagues distant, land was sighted from the top masthead.

Twenty-Two

It was the first anniversary of our landing. We sat on mats arranged in a semi-circle around a temporary platform at the edge of a clearing on the outskirts of Mervidir. The air was filled with the scent of the sweet oil the men rubbed on their skin and the orange flowers women wore in their hair. In the row in front of me, a girl poured frothing drink into her lover's outstretched cup. I breathed in the vanilla-like aroma of *maran*, a kind of sherbet made from fruit and milk. Every now and again, the smell of wood smoke from the dampened cooking fires drifted into our circle, or on a light breeze came whiffs of pine, grass and the ocean.

Children walked up and down passing round trays of sweets they had spent the afternoon making. Bright insects – blue, yellow, orange – hummed overhead. No one minded them: they were quite harmless. Gaily coloured birds chirruped in the trees around the glade. There was an excited babble of voices, interspersed sometimes with a sudden peal of laughter or the wail of an impatient child, quickly hushed by a soothing murmur.

The late afternoon sun shone gently on my neck and arms, caressing limbs still tingling from bathing. I reached up to my shoulder to adjust my dress. I had dressed quickly, so perhaps the tie was loose. The light material felt cool on my skin. I glanced down and admired the pattern around the hem. The blue swirls matched the polished stones on my sandals. Like everyone else's, the robe was new, specially made for the occasion. Tinyar, who had given it to me, felt my movement and turned to smile her approval.

There was also a glint of amused remembrance in her eye. A few weeks after our arrival, she had been deputed by the other women to introduce me to the bathing pool. It was in the woods on the edge of the town, a basin some five or six feet deep, surrounded by ferns, filled with fresh water by a stream on its way to the ocean. Women sat or stood about, some dressed, some dressing, some whose nakedness shocked me. They crowded round me gazing solemnly at my clothes. One or two recoiled, their noses wrinkled and, to my shame, I realised that they were as appalled as I might be by a ragged urchin tumbling in a kennel. Yet theirs was the greater tolerance for, in our towns, we haughtily pass the filthy beggars.

Although they were puzzled by the complicated arrangement of buttons and ties, they did their best to help me undress. I had abandoned stays long ago but I refused to take off my chemise. Still clad in the stained garment, I let them lead me into the water up to my ankles. At first, I would only splash my head and arms but, little by little, they drew me on until the water came to my knees, then to my thighs and finally to my shoulders. Alarmed, I clung to Tinyar's wrists, my petticoat billowing around me, like a gouty old woman in a spa. But I had never been in a spa, had never known what it was like to feel rocked by the water yet held by it, to spread out my arms and let them float in front of me, to feel tiny eddies wreathe about my legs and ankles and rush between my toes. I watched in wonder as the others swam and dived and splashed, sure that my limbs would never be strong enough to imitate them.

When I came out, I refused the dress they offered me. It revealed too much flesh. They shuddered as I clambered back into my own clothes. I was surprised when Tinyar called for me on the following day. Surely it was unnecessary to bathe again? But my clothes were wet under the arms and around my breasts, my skin was sticky and I remembered the feel of the water on my skin. This time, Tinyar offered me a longer dress. Again I shook my head, again I resumed my own dress, but I shrank from the feel of it.

"You look like a Greek goddess." Alex's breath was soft on my ear. I turned to smile at him but he had turned away, had presented me with his burnished shoulder, his hair curling about his neck. He was listening to George, pretending that he was innocent of whispering compliments when no one was looking.

Tomorrow, George was going away. It was the expedition into the interior he had long dreamed of making. Hutan would be his guide. George's dark face was tense, yet I knew the journey held few fears for him. He would be well provided with men and weapons and, although the people of the town did not know what lay beyond the distant hills which marked the boundary of their own land, they had never had any reason to believe it populated by a hostile nation. Invasion was unknown to them.

"I will return," he said with a sudden passion. "No matter what, I will be back."

"Rest assured," Alex promised, "we will not leave the Fair Land without you."

No one thought of leaving the Fair Land, then. Often Alex said, "The *Miranda* is ready, we should set sail." Always George pleaded with him, "Another few weeks, then the dictionary I am compiling will be complete. Another month, and my history of this nation will be finished. Another quarter of a year, then we will have surveyed all the coast roundabout. We will not be a Dampier going back with wildly exaggerated reports of fertile soil and good anchorage, or a Dalrymple relying on conjectural charts. We will be able to provide the

Admiralty with trustworthy information about where the harbours are, where the minerals are to be found, which plants are medicinal, where mast-tall timber grows."

Time passed. Stars began to appear. Voices grew sharp with impatience. *After the welcome we've given them, you'd think they'd be eager to repay us. But then you can never trust the Travelling Dancers. I've heard tales of them refusing to play at all, or stopping a performance because someone in the audience was talking.* In the distance, a pipe began to play a simple tune. It could have been a child playing. No one paid it any attention.

Slowly the music drew nearer, a compelling, repetitive melody. It made me think of the sea – a wave coming in, a wave going out. We craned our necks. Where was it coming from? The player was behind us, a tall, muscular youth with, unusually for a man, short hair and clad in a starched linen skirt, his upper body bare. He looked neither to the right nor the left as he advanced. He was like a wave passing over us. He stopped in front of the platform, playing out the last notes. The branches around the stage rustled. One by one, the other players stepped out of the trees, moved slowly towards the stage, stood in a silent circle waiting for the piper to finish. He lowered the instrument and pirouetted to face us.

"I am the ocean," he announced, "and today our play comes from the ocean."

With a mischievous grin, he placed the pipe to his lips again and played – a bosun's whistle! At his signal, the actors clambered up onto the stage and split into two groups. The characters on the left shuffled forward clinging to one another, fearful, bent and weak. The group on the right went about its business – weaving, fishing, making bread – oblivious to the travellers drawing nigh. Between them, children played. One of the girls saw the newcomers and called her parents. The commotion spread through the village. Everyone dropped what he was doing and ran to see. The stage was the Fair Land, and the drama a re-enactment of our arrival.

The British sailors, starting with fright at every sight and sound, landed. They were suspicious. They threw up barriers and huddled comically behind them, while the southerners, by dance and mime demonstrating the beauty and plenty of their land, tried to entice them out. The *Miranda*'s crew, several of whom were here with their wives, roared with laughter as they recognised their captain, the officers and themselves.

And it was all true. We had made our camp on the shore, much to the perplexity of the southerners who had dragged Alex and George to the town and, by signs, conveyed that one of the long houses was at our disposal. Alex shook his head – the risk was too great. He would build an enclosure, sharpen stakes, make an armoury, and have the marines patrol our boundaries all day and all night. The people watched in amazement as the weak sailors toiled to bring materials from the vessel, smite iron, saw wood, hammer nails. They groaned with pity when they saw the sick carried ashore. They watched in admiration as the ship was careened. Several planks were found to be damaged; she needed patching, caulking, scraping, and painting.

George was played by a handsome, swaggering man, full of charm and self-confidence. He climbed over the fence or sneaked past the sentinels, powerless to resist the urge to explore. Contrary to Alex's orders, George had often wandered about on his own, speaking to the people, accepting invitations into their houses, tasting their food, watching their entertainments and games, and returning from these unauthorised expeditions to admonish Alex: "Your precautions are needless. None of us will suffer harm from these people." Every morning when we opened the gate of our enclosure we found baskets of fruit, baked fish, coconuts and sweet potatoes.

Alex insisted that relations should be established between our nations on a formal basis. He accepted an invitation to a feast in the town, expecting that it would be an occasion for dignitaries to meet. He and his officers dressed with particular care. They looked stiff and uncomfortable as they set off in their heavy blue jackets, blue breeches, and buckled shoes. Their discomfort was increased when they arrived in the town to discover that accommodation and food had been prepared for a hundred men – the invitation had encompassed the sailors. For a time it seemed that hopes of a friendly alliance were ruined for the Fairlanders were offended. In the end, Alex sent back to the camp for the most presentable of the men. They were on strict orders to behave well. They were so overawed by the occasion and the excellence of the food that they acted with perfect decorum.

Gradually, we had come out of our enclosure. The play ended with the joyful mingling of both groups and a song of amity. When the applause finally died down, the audience dispersed, the elders to drink and talk late into the night, the young people to dance, the younger children to sleep, the rest to play at British sailor, marine, or lady. The Travelling Dancers passed amongst them, now leading wild dances, now singing love songs, now telling stories to entranced listeners, increasing happiness and joy wherever they went.

"Miss Edgcumbe, may I speak with you?"

I had been following Alex to the area set aside for dancing, a square of wooden floor hung about with garlands and ribbons, when George spoke to me. Some of the Travellers had infiltrated the orchestra. Their inspired, virtuoso performances on flute, drum and lute left the ordinary musicians behind, made the dancers whirl faster and faster in a blur of tangled limbs and laughter.

George and I turned aside into a quiet path. A couple stood close together whispering endearments. The girl caught my eye as I passed. Hers were filled with contentment. I remembered the Bristol Vauxhall and the danger in its secluded walks and thought it nothing but a vile parody of these woodland paths, these lovers' meetings.

We walked on in silence away from the gaiety and the music. The darkness was mild and fragrant. A small animal rustled across our path. A bat flitted overhead. A firefly glowed between the trees. We stopped in a dell. The trees deadened all sound. There was nothing but silence and the softness of night between us.

George looked awkward in his robe and sandals, his hair loose about his face as the men of the Fair Land often wore theirs. It was odd that for all the fineness of his frame, their style of dress did not suit him as it did Alex. He looked better in European clothes. Perhaps a sense of this added to his embarrassment now.

Nervously, he snatched my hand. "I shall leave early in the morning and will not have another opportunity of speaking to you before I go."

I pressed his fingers. The coming parting was painful to both of us. "I had planned to join you and Alex for breakfast," I said, trying to smile. "I did not want our goodbye to cast a shadow on this night."

"It does cast a shadow. I do not know how long I shall be away or what dangers I might face and, when I get back, there is still the voyage home with all its perils. Perhaps it is unjust of me to ask but I cannot leave without knowing. Miss Edgcumbe – Sarah – will you tell me – is your heart your own?"

"Is my heart my own?" I repeated in astonishment.

"Perhaps it has been given away, before we left England? Yet

251

I have not observed any sign that this is the case and I know that there has been no opportunity since. Forgive me if I am wrong, I do not seek to force your confidence. All I ask is if your heart is still your own, would you consider exchanging it for mine?"

Was my heart my own? The question had never before occurred to me. First, the horrors of the voyage, and then the wonders of the Fair Land had left no room for the imagining that usually consumes a young woman's energies. With nothing else to do, she will dream of love, plan for love, imagine herself into love. She will long for that great change in her circumstances. But I had already made a change in mine more fundamental than the mere swapping of one family for another. I did not want to change them again. I was content to remain what, at that time, I still was – the maiden sister keeping house for her brother.

To part with George was agony: he was very dear to me. Yet, though we mingled our tears, I could not give him the answer he desired. He listened respectfully to my commonplace excuses.

"It was unfair of me to expect it when the future is so uncertain," he said. "There is a possibility I may not come back, though all my hopes and my determination fix me to it. Will you allow me to put the question to you again on my return, when you have had time to consider the idea? It is not, surely, such an abhorrent petition?"

"Oh, George, there is nothing abhorrent about it."

This brought a glimmer of his old self-confidence back to his eye. His courage was restored by the tears I should not have allowed myself to shed. They were shed in love, but it was not the kind of love he sought and I was wrong to let him mistake them. But he was going away in a few hours. I could not send him away uncomforted.

It would have been better for us all if, that night, I had trampled on the heart he offered me.

Twenty-Three

"You practise this ritual daily?"

"It is not a ritual. It is a useful activity."

Vannir looked doubtfully at the paraphernalia on the desk from the captain's cabin – the pens, paper, sand for blotting, ink from our dwindling store. Alex had already started experimenting with manufacturing his own ink. So far, a solution of gunpowder and the sap of a plant the Fairlanders regarded as a weed promised to be an effective substitute, but we did not know how long it would last without fading.

"What is its use?" Vannir asked.

"It is a way for men to speak to one another even when they are apart. I could send this book to someone on the other side of the world and he could tell from it what I have seen, what adventures I have had, even what my thoughts are. I will show you. You have been here all the time I was writing this page. You agree that Sarah has not seen it?"

Vannir nodded. Alex handed his book down to me, pointing to the place where he wished me to begin reading. I was stretched out on a mat with Kitty purring at my side. Vannir glanced distrustfully at the dozing animal. None of the Fairlanders liked the ship's cats. Their detestation dated back to their first encounter with my pet when a group of them came across her basking in a splash of sunshine. Smiling, I showed them how to pet her. They took it in turns to run their fingers along her back, amazed by her throaty purring, her velvet paws, her green eyes half-closed with pleasure. Then one of them, laughingly ignoring my instructions, stroked her fur the wrong way. There was a hiss, a flash of claws and the youth clutched his wealed arm, the long streaks oozing blood. Before he realised where his wounds had come from, Kitty had settled down with a yawn of indifference.

The Fairlanders had never been able to understand why we kept such dangerous and foul-tempered animals about us. It was unfortunate, then, that many of the cats had gone ashore and their numbers were multiplying. So too had a number of rats and other vermin that had escaped death when the *Miranda* was fumigated.

Kitty made a low mew of protest when I put her aside to read as Alex directed:

And Dannyadd looked out over the battlefield and wept over the bodies. The defeated dead still clutched their statues and amulets, while the victorious slain yet clutched their clubs and lances. The tattered banners of Amraho fluttered on one side of the ground, and the red flags of Dannyadd waved on the other.

And Dannyadd caused the bodies of the defeated to be stripped of their swords and icons, and the corpses of the victors to be stripped of their clubs and lances, and victor and vanquished were laid side by side on a great pyre and sprinkled with perfumed oil and, as the flames were kindled, Dannyadd caused every object which bore the Face of Amraho to be cast into the flames, and every weapon spotted with the blood of those slain in the War of Amraho to be thrown into the blaze.

And Dannyadd ordered that every temple that had been built to the Face of Amraho should be pulled down, but every private room or chapel belonging to the worshippers of the Face of Amraho should be allowed to stand. And he decreed that anyone who wished to show in any form whatsoever, whether in picture or carving, statue or tapestry, the Face of Amraho should be allowed to do so in their home without hindrance. But any person who did not wish to represent Amraho in painting or sculpture, talisman or ornament, should be free to do so without molestation.

And Dannyadd decreed that no man should arm himself except with a spear for the fish or a bow for the hunt, and no woman should carry weapons except for a knife for the catch or a needle for the hide. No dispute should be settled by private argument or fight, and no opinion should be proved by one faction taking up arms against another, but all matters should be laid before a council, and any who attempt to settle a dispute by sharp words or sharp weapons are to be outcast.

Vannir shrugged. "She is remembering the story that Fanvay told us last night."

"Not remembering, but reading," said Alex. "There is a difference. In time memory fails, stories are forgotten. Writing them down is like storing them up, the way you store fruit or grain over the winter. I have stored up the story so that it can be told again exactly as I first heard it, as many times as I like."

"Why would you want to tell the same story over and over again? There are always more stories."

The two men stared at one another at a deadlock.

"There's something to be said for Vannir's way," I laughed. "Books are nothing but trouble. Reading them weakens the eyes, writing them strains the shoulders, and then there's all the anxiety of finding somewhere to keep them safe from fire and damp... Alex, it's too hot for a serious conversation. You've been scratching at your journal all morning. Why not come for a swim?"

"Very well." Alex smiled at me.

Vannir put down his cup. "Now that's a pastime that makes sense to me."

"Will you join us?" I asked him.

"No, I've promised Fanvay I'll help him in his garden." He rose to his feet. "I shall tell him about our talk. Perhaps he would like to look at your writing."

"I could teach him, or you, how to do it," Alex said.

"I'm not sure I – what's that noise?"

Someone ran up to the house, sandals flapping on the dusty ground. The curtain across the door was flung back without any ceremony of *Are you at home?* or *May I come in?* and Nathaniel burst in. Ruddy from his exercise, the secretary presented a very different figure from the coughing, wheezing invalid of the voyage. English wife, weakness and woe were forgotten. He had married a girl from the town and they were expecting a child.

"It's Mr Fenwick!"

"George?" Alex sprang up. "Where is he?"

"On the outskirts of the town. Can you hear the people running to meet him?"

Having delivered his news, Nathaniel span on his heel and sped back into the street, Vannir following closely behind.

Now we could hear the horns blowing, the rattles whirring, the drums beating, and the hurry of many feet. Twinger's great hound-bark boomed over the yapping of the village dogs. Children shrieked and adults cheered. But all I remember is the steady drip drip drip of the ink that Alex had knocked over, the dark drops dribbling down the side of the desk and bubbling away into the ground.

Alex moved towards me, holding out his hand. I put my fingers into his – how steady they seemed, but cold – and looked up into his face. So pale he was, and his lips were white as if frozen. But he smiled at me, a very different sort of smile from that of a moment ago, which I see now only in my dreams of the happiness that has gone. He said gently, "Come, Sarah."

I tried to rise but my legs failed me and I sank back, gasping and half-blind. Alex stooped and lifted me up.

"But Alex – "

He laid his finger on my lips. "Let us go and welcome our friend."

George had not changed in fourteen months except to look stronger, bolder, and prouder. Girls and women clung about him. He ducked his head and allowed himself to be kissed, but all the while his restless eyes scanned the crowd. The marines marched smartly behind him, petals raining down onto their shabby coats. Captain Williams, out of national and military pride, had kept his men well drilled, their faded uniforms patched and repaired. Bilby, the little drummer boy whose travels had turned him into a stout lad of eighteen, gave up beating his tattoo and blushed at the garland of girls about his neck.

Hutan strutted at George's side. He had one of the marine's guns slung over his shoulder – the first Fairlander ever to carry one. He relished the adulation, catching hungrily at the women who danced about him. He punched the air and roared like an exultant predator about to sink his claws into his prey. Sloper was there too, enjoying his share of caresses, although he had never been popular.

After them came a long line of men – the Fairlanders

who had followed Hutan, the men of the *Miranda* who had volunteered to go with George. They carried packs on their backs but were not overburdened, for most of the spoils of their expedition were slung over sturdy ponies they had picked up on their travels. The townsfolk stared in wonder at the strange, shaggy beasts and their friends who led them with such nonchalant skill. No pack animals had been seen in Mervidir before.

Families flung themselves onto brothers, cousins, sons, marvelling at the half-strangers who had come back to them. The sailors called out to their old messmates: "Here's Bottle Belly – without the belly!" and "Joe Moulding!" and "Yellow Sam!" Hawbuck, and Dog Head… Jonny Bone and Jawing Tom… Pig Hog… the strange nicknames and raucous shouts filled the air.

Davies found out Josh Twitty. The two men had endured a long separation, for Twitty had stayed behind with his wife. "You never saw such places. The land beyond the hills is as beautiful as Wales!" Davies declared, gripping the other's hand.

"Then it must be an ugly, poor place!" Twitty retorted, wiping the tears from his eyes.

"Any lost? Any dead?" The greeters were eager to know.

"Yes, one lost. Mutloe did not come back. Died of a colic ten days from here," Mr Nock reported. "Brought on by over-indulgence in garva-fruit."

He had died then from greed, for everyone knew that the garva, though delicious, should only be eaten in small quantities. His strength had been useful but his temper dangerous, and his loss did not restrain anyone's joy. I span giddily through the crowd looking for one face, listening for one voice.

"Oh, Alex, such cities we have seen – such people! They

have houses and temples – machines for drawing water – carriages – markets!"

They were in an embrace, George's tanned hands resting on Alex's shoulders. "Where is your sister?"

He caught sight of me and ran towards me with outstretched hands. I could not move, not to meet or to speak or to smile. He interpreted my stillness as censure for his over-familiarity and, faltering, recollected the manners of a gentleman. He bowed. "Miss Edgcumbe."

To dash his spirits at such a moment! No one who loved him could have done it. I could not do it. I burst into tears and threw myself into his arms.

The sun had set, the torches were lit, the pelts, jewels and carvings put on display, and the feast eaten, but the conversations going on around the mats in front of the town house showed no signs of ending. There were so many things to tell. The sights the explorers had seen, the dangerous mountain paths they had traversed, the wonderful nation they had discovered. This people's chief town was built on a cliff above a river, and in it they lived like lords in white houses with furniture of ebony. The men could all have been sons of Dannyadd, and the women – the women could only be whispered about later when the wives and sisters and aunts and mothers were out of the way.

"You should see that city," George said to Alex. "It makes this place look like the collection of huts it really is, and as for its idle, shabby inhabitants…!"

I twisted the gold bracelet around my wrist. It was very heavy and smooth except for the hinge where it opened; the fastening was hidden inside. George had given Alex a torc, also of smooth, thick gold, which Alex was not wearing. There was no chasing on either piece, nor any patterns on the brilliantly coloured textiles George had brought back. I wondered if everything the foreigners made resembled their jewellery and cloth – plain and imposing, a celebration of the precious materials of which they were composed rather than the artistry of craftsmen.

Alex, George and I were sitting on the town house veranda. Vannir was with us, and Tinyar, and other friends. Hutan was there too, his skin gleaming with oil, clutching a huge goblet also of heavy, unadorned gold. They had brought back enormous jars of wine, heavy and sweet. Hutan brushed away the *maran* whenever the jug came his way but kept his cup filled with the wine, as did George.

"It has walls all around it," George continued. "Orchards and vineyards outside it and, inside, there are gardens and parks where they hold their concerts and games. Wrestling and a kind of jousting with short spears seem to be their favourites, even small boys play it. They're also very fond of watching their soldiers parade up and down. The people gather along the city walls to cheer and wave banners while the men drill on the plain below. It's an astonishing spectacle – the men in their polished breastplates with circlets of gold around their heads, accompanied by the beat of drums and wail of the pipes, like the Scottish bagpipe. I do not think any men are exempt from military service, but I could not be sure.

Their king lives at the summit of the town. His house is grand and always full of supplicants, but he mingles with the people. There do not seem to be any *taboo* laws. No one bows to him, no one carries him on their shoulders as they do in Tahiti, he doesn't have a guard. He takes part in the games too. If he loses he has to abdicate, but it's not the man who beats him who takes over. Their laws of succession seem very complicated, I couldn't understand them."

"They are a warlike people?" I shivered at the thought that they now knew about the existence of our peaceable villages near the coast.

"They are organised to defend themselves," George answered. "Without organisation, there is no civilisation. They even have a kind of writing. It's on the walls of their temples, but I couldn't begin to decipher it."

"They have statues of Amraho in temples?" asked Vannir.

"Yes, but they don't call him Amraho."

"We could have statues too," growled Hutan. "It is allowed."

Vannir frowned. "In private, yes. No one here would go back to the days of public carvings and statues, and arguments about the true appearance of the Face of Amraho."

"Because there was once a war?" Hutan asked mockingly.

Vannir nodded. "No one wants that again."

"And who are you to say what people want?" Hutan snarled. "You do not speak for us. You are not our leader."

George, bored by their exchange, said, "I hope the *Miranda* will not sink under the weight of the specimens I have collected."

"I dare say she will manage," Alex said coolly.

"I shall write such a book when I get home! I shall dedicate it to you, Miss Edgcumbe, with your permission."

"I should be honoured," I said, glancing nervously at Alex.

George sighed. "If this is what it is like to come back to Mervidir, then I am impatient to see Overcombe again! I wonder what Antony is doing now, and Father. Sitting by the fire reading the newspaper I expect. And here am I, feasting on baked fish and sweet potatoes in this squalid little square. I often thought of you both when I was away. Do you know where I was on June the fourth? Huddled in a cave, listening to thunder and rain, a howling wind, trees crashing down, and boulders tumbling into the ravine. I was far from here, even further from home, and had no idea what lay ahead. I don't think I have ever been so miserable. Then, I remembered it was the King's birthday. There was nothing to drink, only water collected from the storm. But I filled my travelling cup and raised it up to the tempestuous sky and, as I made my toast, I pictured you two sitting on the veranda of your house raising your glasses to His Majesty. It was foolish of me, but I felt sure that we were drinking his health at the very same moment."

Alex shifted uneasily. "We didn't celebrate the King's birthday this year."

George stared at him in astonishment. "Why not?"

"We forgot," Alex said. "There was some confusion over the dates."

"Well, I suppose these things happen," George said, mastering his disappointment. "It's easy to lose track of time when none of our clocks or chronometers have worked since we left the Antarctic."

There was an awkward pause filled only by the popping of the torches on the wall behind us. The silence that fell between us seemed universal and, looking about me, I saw that all of the sailors had vanished, together with the Fairlanders who had been on the expedition and most of the young men from the town. The stay-at-home crew members had perfected a method of brewing beer from the fruit of a certain tree, rough and ready stuff which they usually only drank in small quantities. Having eaten their meals, the men had taken several casks of this potent drink and gone off to celebrate in true naval fashion. Deserted families sat disconsolately around the empty baking dishes and crumb-spattered mats.

Somewhere behind the town house the sailors started singing.

Of all the delights that a mortal can taste,
A bottle of liquor is surely the best,
Possessed of that treasure my hours sweetly glide,
Oh there's nothing like grog! Says sweet Tommy McBride!

"If the men carry on like that, they won't be fit to attend Sunday service tomorrow," George remarked.

"We do not always have a formal service," Alex replied, hastily adding, "It's not always possible to gather everyone together now the men are dispersed about the town in their new families."

"No Sunday service? No King's birthday? Is there anything else of civilisation you have abandoned?" George's voice was taut with disapproval.

"We read prayers. Sarah and I." Alex bit his lip, shrinking from his friend's anger.

I lowered my eyes, unable to look at George or Alex, to compound or betray the untruth. It was many months since we had read from the *Miranda*'s prayer book or opened our Bibles. The religion of the land was irresistible. It was all around us. It was in the sand, the grottos, the wood, the scrub, the mountains, the waterfalls, the rivers and the sky. It was in the breasts of the people. There was no comfort for either of us in a creed that condemned those who dwelt in the Fair Land to eternal damnation.

"As if I have any right to censure you," George said after a moment. "We were not much better on our journey. Religious observances were too often forgotten. It's humiliating to realise how easily we let things fall by the wayside. If only the Navy had given us a chaplain."

"It is not often a priority with their Lordships." Alex forced a smile.

The defection of the sailors and the guests of honour marked the end of the feast. The women cleared away the dishes, the old men rolled up the mats and carried them back to their homes. The smaller children had fallen asleep, the older ones yawned. No one was in the mood for storytelling or gossiping. Vannir and the others said goodnight and moved off. They had not gone far before Fanvay came up to speak to Vannir.

Vannir beckoned to my brother. "Fanvay would like to look at your writing in the morning." Alex went to speak to them. George and I were left alone.

"We went for a moonlit walk once before." George smiled. "Will you accompany me on one now?"

I knew that George meant to repeat his offer but I agreed. It was not too soon to undo the mistakes I had made on the last occasion.

We walked under the trees in silence for a time, until the lights of the town were behind us, and stopped when we caught a glimpse of the sailors' lamps through the branches. The men were singing and dancing, would be singing and dancing for hours yet.

George clutched my hand in both of his and pressed it to his lips. "I asked you once if you could love me," he said. "From what I have seen today, I flatter myself that it is possible."

"It is not," I said, though I trembled to say it.

"But when you saw me you embraced me – "

"You are a dear friend."

"Friend!" He let go of my hand, half turned from me. "You did not forget your modesty so far for a friend."

"If you think me immodest, I am sorry for it. I could have dissembled my joy at seeing you safe and well again, but I thought we had learned to be more honest in this place."

"This place!" he exclaimed bitterly. "Yes, it is this place.

You are confused – overset – by it. These outlandish manners do not become you. I do not reproach you, Sarah. We have all forgotten ourselves a little. But my love for you is unchanged."

"And mine for you." He attempted to retake possession of my hand but I avoided his grasp. "I do not – I cannot – love you as a wife would do."

"How can you know that?" He shook his head. "All this hesitancy! When the confession has already fallen from your own lips." He gathered me in his arms, possessive, confident.

"No!" I pushed him away.

He staggered back, overbalanced more by his surprise than my strength. "But you said love – "

Someone crashed through the bushes, disturbing the sleeping birds, releasing clouds of tiny bats. Two men, swearing at the darkness, blundered to within a few feet of where we stood. There was a pause then a loud stream spattered on leaves. Embarrassed and surprised, George and I did nothing to betray our presence.

"I'm surprised you don't piss sitting down like one of the natives!" A Welsh voice – Davy Davies. Who else could his companion be but Josh Twitty?

Twitty grunted. "It's not me who's gone native."

Davies chuckled coarsely. "I don't believe you."

"It's true, man. Awbray heard them at it. He came and asked me if they were really brother and sister and I said, why do you ask? So he told me."

"Awbray's a booby! He doesn't know his arse from his elbow."

"Maybe not. But why do you think they built their new house on the edge of town, away from prying eyes? And why hasn't he taken one of the native women in all this time?"

"He's the captain."

"He's a man. He must be getting it somewhere, eh?"

"She didn't share his cabin on the voyage."

"No, but she shares his bed now. He's gone native, I tell you. The way they pass their brats round, they don't know who's related to who and they don't care either. They'd do it with their own mothers if they wanted to. He's taken a leaf from their book. She's his doxy." Twitty lowered his voice. "I tell you what, I wouldn't fuck my sister if she was the last cunny on earth."

There was an angry rustling of leaves. "That's enough! Stow your filth, you bastards." A swish of a cane was followed by a cry of pain from Twitty.

"Lieutenant Sloper, sir, we meant no harm, sir," he whimpered.

"I'll do you harm, d'ye hear me, if I ever hear your damned blabbation again, you son of a whore. By God, I'll have you flogged around the fleet if I ever see the two of you whispering in corners again. Cut away you dogs, get out of my sight."

"Yes, sir. Straightaway, sir. Thank you, sir." The sailors scurried off, leaving the forest trembling as they fled.

The bats went back to the tree tops, the birds' confused trilling faded away, the branches whispered back into place. Sloper remained where he was. He hummed softly to himself, gently slapping his rattan cane against the palm of his hand. Suddenly, he laughed out loud and then, with slow, deliberate steps, he moved away.

"What exactly did George say to you?"

Alex turned away from the doorway. Behind him a pale, metallic light sliced into the darkness. Streaks of red, like raw flesh, were beginning to appear in the east. The sailors had only stopped carolling an hour ago, although their choir had been gradually thinning out since midnight.

"He said he knew sailors were coarse but what we had heard went beyond that. It came from unspeakably depraved minds, dangerous and mutinous minds. They could not be allowed to spread their poison amongst the rest of the crew. You must assert your authority – have them lashed, have them hanged. I said you couldn't."

"I couldn't? Because I don't have the authority, or why?"

"I simply said you couldn't. He was going to run back here to you but I caught his arm, begged him not to. He said I had been grievously insulted. I said it was only drunken men talking, it was of no importance. And then he looked at me – oh, for how long a time he held me in his gaze! I had to look away. A change came over his face. He flung my hand off his arm and rubbed the spot where my fingers had been, his mouth twisted with disgust as if he was contaminated by my touch. His voice was not like his at all – it was rasping and ugly – and in his face there was such horror and hatred. He said, *The stench of you!* and then he retched."

I shut my eyes but it only made the image of George bent double, clutching at his guts, all the sharper. I hurried on with my tale, which I had repeated a dozen times through the night. "Then he cried out."

Children woke up in terror, men armed themselves and rushed out of their houses to defend the town from the beast that threatened it, the sailors' music wound to a halt in a squeal of discordant notes. But after one long, maniacal howl, there had been nothing more. The children were soothed back to sleep, men laughed at their alarm, the fiddles started up again. The sailors danced and whooped like devils and I was alone in the forest.

I sobbed at the remembrance of it. Alex stood behind my chair and put his hand on my shoulder. "Hush! He doesn't know. It's the pain of his rejection, that's all."

I rested my face on his hand. My tears smeared the back of it and trickled between his fingers.

A dark figure in the doorway blotted out the dawn.

"There is no need to afford me further proof," said George. He wore a coat, breeches and boots, his sword fastened to his side. His eyes were red and underscored by dark circles. There were welts running down each side of his face where he had dragged his nails through his own skin.

He was accompanied by Lieutenant Sloper. The lieutenant was in uniform, his hat tucked smartly under his arm, the buttons on his blue jacket gleaming.

"George, where have you been all night?" Alex started forward, full of concern. George stepped back as if avoiding a leper. Sloper grinned.

"I do not intend to curtail your freedom in the time remaining to us on the Fair Land," George announced without any preamble. "Nor will I keep you in irons on the way home. You will sail the ship as her captain. However, when we arrive in England, I will make a full report to the Admiralty and I will give evidence at your court martial. I will do everything in my power to ensure that you never disgrace His Majesty's command again. More than that, I will publicise your crime to all the world and I will make it my task, so long as you and I both live, to ensure that you never mix in society again. Every door will be closed to you, every employment refused to you, every avenue of preferment will be denied."

Alex staggered back. "George," he whispered. "George – "

"Don't call me that."

Alex swallowed. "We can't go back, you know we can't go back. You cannot mean to expose Sarah – as you are a gentleman – "

"She is beyond the pale of my protection – of any decent man's protection."

Alex groaned, shook his head blindly. Groping for words, he could only repeat, "We can't go back."

"But you will. Don't think I will allow you to remain here wallowing in your crime."

"What is a crime in the old world is no crime here. We are not going back."

"You are not staying," George flashed back.

"The ship is under my command. She will not sail unless I say so."

"Then Lieutenant Sloper will take command. You cannot detain His Majesty's ship or crew in the Fair Land."

Alex, comprehension dawning in his face, looked from Sloper to George. "So, you were prepared for this! I shouldn't be surprised. You've resented the fact that I am in command often enough. But I think you'll find that the crew are content to remain. They have wives and families, they've settled down here. They don't want to go back to England any more than I do. See if they obey Sloper or follow me."

Sloper brandished his cane and snarled, "They'll obey – "

George signalled to him to be quiet. "We will see," he said and, turning on his heel, left the house.

Twenty-Four

Half an hour passed. The sun rose. A door opened and slammed. Women's voices, cheerful and bright after an innocent night's sleep, reached us on the clear morning air. Light footsteps passed close to the wall of our house: girls on their way to the bathing pool. From the centre of the town came the faint jingle of harness, the clopping of hooves, the protesting whinny of ponies dragged from warm straw. British voices, urgent and businesslike, rumbled through the streets and in through the windows, disturbing the sleepers. Floorboards creaked, water splashed in bowls, doors opened. People stood yawning on their thresholds, called in puzzled tones to one another.

Alex rose to his feet. He moved slowly, awkwardly, like a dying man. His eyes were wide in his face, a cold, dead blue as if desperation had murdered something in him. He staggered across the room, opened his sea chest, took out his white shirt, shoes, jacket and breeches. He pulled his robe over his head and stood naked before me. I gazed upon him like a woman who knows her lover will soon die and there is little time left for storing up the memories. His shoulders were wide and strong, his waist and hips narrow, his legs muscular and shapely. I could see, as I had often felt, the smoothness of his skin. Then the linen shirt billowed down and covered him, like a curtain falling.

I stood up, my limbs cold and cramped. With numb fingers I buttoned his shirt, shook out his jacket and held it for him while he put his arms in the sleeves and shrugged it on. He pulled on his breeches and, wincing, thrust his feet into shoes stiff from disuse. He bent his head and I combed his hair, pulled it back, and tied it up with faded black ribbon. He put on his hat and strode out of the house.

In all this time we had not spoken. He had not told me to stay, but he had not told me I should not follow. In the end, I did go after him. I hid behind the trees near the town house.

George stood on the veranda supervising the removal of his collection from inside. He had woken the sailors to do the work. Bottle Belly, Joe Moulding, Yellow Sam, Hawbuck, Dog Head, Jonny Bone, Jawing Tom, Pig Hog. These and the rest of the men who had travelled with George on the expedition stumbled about cursing the sunshine, unshaven and reeking of beer.

Some of the sailors who had stayed in Mervidir helped them. Josh Twitty was there, working beside Davy Davies. Others stood by, unsure of what to do. Josh looked dazed, both by drink and the crisis he had precipitated. Others stood about, scratching their heads and blinking stupidly as their fuddled brains tried to understand what was happening. Lieutenant Nightingale, looking self-conscious in his robe when all the other officers were in uniform, moved irresolutely between the veranda and the labourers, doling out half-hearted instructions in one breath and countermanding them in the next.

The Fairlanders who had travelled with Hutan mingled with the workers. Hutan himself stood between George and Lieutenant Sloper. Every now and again he threw out an order, which the British sailors obeyed after casting sullen glances at Sloper who ratified the commands.

Awbray, his bare feet dirty and bruised as if he had been tramping sleeplessly all night, sat on the ground. He still wore his festive gown. It was crumpled and grubby. He was the first to see Alex striding down the narrow path into the square. He rubbed the back of his hand across his tear-stained face and made a weak, mewling sound, an incoherent plea for forgiveness. Alex ignored the boy.

The sailors nudged one another as the word quickly passed amongst them. There were a few guffaws, some booing and hissing, but a gesture from George silenced the demonstrations. The men shuffled aside to let Alex through. He came to a halt a few feet from the house.

"Where are you going, Mr Fenwick?"

"To make the *Miranda* ready to sail," George answered, "and then to England."

There was a murmur of astonishment amongst the men. To England! How long had that been in the air?

"I have not given orders to set sail."

"No, but I have," Lieutenant Sloper snapped.

"The ship is not under your command."

"She is when her captain is a disgrace to the British Navy."

George cast a warning look at Sloper who fell silent.

Alex smiled. "I see where the authority lies. You are in error, Lieutenant, to accede command of one of His Majesty's ships to a civilian. To sail under those conditions would be nothing more nor less than an illegal seizure of the vessel and any who sail with you would be guilty of mutiny."

"And any who refuse to sail, guilty of desertion!" Sloper retorted.

The crew shifted uncomfortably. They did not like all this talk of mutiny or desertion. They were terrible alternatives for a sailor to have to choose between, knowing he could not come well out of either.

George, sensing their unease, laid a restraining hand on Sloper's arm. "There is no need for this kind of talk," he said smoothly. "There is only one man here who has any reason to dread returning to his own country." He raised his voice. "A hero's welcome awaits the rest of us! It is time to go home, to go back to our families – the rosy-cheeked children asking why they have no father, the mothers weeping over boys they fear they have lost, the aged fathers praying for one last glimpse of their sons before they die, and the faithful wives who gaze morning and evening out to sea and wonder when their husbands will come back."

Nathaniel Davenport's hand crept from his side and caught hold of his wife's. One hand resting on her swollen belly, she glanced up at him, her pretty face creased with misgiving. She had never learned more than a few words of English. Only a few of her people had studied it: Vannir was one of them.

"It is time to go home!" George repeated, his voice trembling with the effect of his own oratory. "Who is not weary of dirt tracks, and coconut trees, and sleeping on a grass mat in a hut? It is time to go home to British lanes, and British oaks, and British houses."

Davy Davies clasped his hands to his breast and gazed over George's head, over the roof of the house and the tops of the trees. He was lost in a vision of his homeland and saw none of these things. Twitty stared at him incredulously but the Welshman was blind and deaf to him when Twitty jeered, "What's up with you?"

"What man would remain poor in exile when he can go home and be rich?" George continued. He gestured towards the heaps of goods. "What benefit to you are these things here? Your gold and spices and carvings, obtained by bitter toil and hardship, have no value in this place. You cannot sell your prizes. You will never be rich men here, and yet you are in possession of untold wealth!"

The sailors shifted restlessly. In London, their booty could buy them anything – carriages and clothes, houses and whores, food and furniture, tipples and tobacco.

"Home?" Twitty hawked and spat onto the ground. "Back to the lash and climbing the rigging with a bosun's rope tickling your feet and working all hours for bread full of vermin and a fourteen inch of hammock to call your own? Back to a nagging wife and pewling children, back to the clap, back to the cold? When here the women are kind, the bread grows on trees and all a man has to do is pluck what he wants!"

There was a murmur of agreement from the sleek men who had stayed behind when George marched away. But the lean travellers, who had dreamed of chops and porter on their hungry march, and had brought back nutmeg, pepper and cinnamon thinking of the savour they would add to English puddings and ale, had not acquired an idle taste for bland food easily obtained. They had no wish to settle for an easy poor man's life when they had the means for an easy rich one. And what was the labour of a few months on board ship to men who had trekked across mountains?

George saw his advantage. "The ship will sail as soon as she can be made ready," he said, turning away with an air of finality.

A chorus of cheers greeted his words and George's men resumed their labours. A few of the others glanced at Alex but he did not speak. It seemed he had lost the will to command. One after another, the married men, some with a backward glance and others glibly abandoning their women, shouldered cargo. Perhaps they were thinking that there was still time for them to collect a few treasures of their own. The mats, trays and vessels that adorned their homes would fetch a good price in England.

Lieutenant Nightingale dithered at the foot of the veranda steps. Awbray shakily rose to his feet, picked up one of the bundles and, with slow, tragic movements, began to pack it away. Twitty folded his arms and planted his feet firm on the Fair Land. The men, who had growled assent to his words, clustered about him.

"You are deceiving these men." Alex did not raise his voice; his determination to be heard carried his words to George's ears. "What you promise, you cannot perform. The ship is mine and she will not sail."

The perplexity flew from Nightingale's face. He pushed his way through the crowd and placed himself at the captain's side. Several of the men, inspired by his shift of position, dropped the work they had reluctantly taken up and sidled after him. Twitty swaggered over. Nathaniel pulled away from his wife's clutching hands. Awbray, glancing timidly at Alex, stumbled after them.

The two parties regarded one another in hostile silence. On one side, Twitty fingered the handle of his knife. On the other, Davies clenched his fists.

"But the ship is ours," said George. "Williams and his marines are down there now." He smiled, enjoying the shock this gave Alex. "Any man who wishes to go home can come with me," he announced.

He descended the steps, followed by Hutan and Sloper, and moved across the square to oversee the final adjustments to the loads. All was hurry and flurry now as the burdens were parcelled and tied onto the horses' backs. Orders were shouted, harnesses tightened. The confused beasts snickered nervously as they were pushed into a line. Everyone was talking, flinging out challenges, pleas, and farewells. "Come with us!" "Stay with us!" Dust swirled around the men passing and re-passing between the two groups, some to join Alex, some to join George, some still undecided, some decided but dragging their feet, fearful of the consequences of their choice.

"Mr Nock!" Alex smiled as the grave-faced physician lumbered towards him. "Do you come to join me?"

"I do not," Nock answered. "I came to perform the duty required of me by my profession and nothing more. There is no child, I hope, nor one expected? I ask," he added hastily, "as a medical adviser."

Alex hesitated. "Would there be danger to... to the mother if there were?"

Nock shook his head. "No more than ordinary. But the child – "

"There is none."

The doctor nodded. "It is well." He paused, examining Alex as if he were a diseased limb he had just lopped off in a dissection room or an organism riddled with a corruption his science could neither explain nor forgive. "We know that it is not impossible for natural consequences to arise from an unnatural union. If this should happen, smother the child rather than let it live a deformed and idiot life. This is the only advice I shall give you."

He turned on his heel and disappeared into the eddying dust.

"Hutan!" Vannir's voice pierced the throng. "Why are you and your friends going? What has the foreigners' quarrel got to do with you?"

Hutan, shouldering his musket, met Vannir at the edge of the procession, the head of which was already leaving the town. All of the young Fairlanders who had been on George's expedition and a few others enticed by the tales of their adventures had taken leave of their dazed families and were marching away too, their backs set towards their peaceful homes. They were going to Britannia where they would be treated like princes!

Hutan gestured contemptuously at the forlorn group around Alex. "They give us nothing. Fenwick will go back to his land and bring back other men like him. For just a few spices, they will give us machines to tend our fields, coaches to travel in, houses of stone to live in. And they will give us ships so that we too can go to other lands and bring back good things."

Vannir frowned at the foreign words in Hutan's speech: machine, ship, coach. "But we don't need their things."

Hutan's thin lips curled. "Life is not only about need. If you had seen the country beyond the hills, you would understand that. They build temples filled with gold. We make nothing living as we do, with no man commanding another."

He noticed then that his party had nearly all gone and, unwilling to walk at the end of the line, he left Vannir standing and ran off to catch up with George and Sloper.

"What's the condition of the *Miranda*?"

Lieutenant Nightingale, who was now in uniform, considered Alex's question. "Well, she's been in dry dock for nearly a year, she's demasted and though she hasn't been neglected – her hull's been inspected, her sails regularly aired, her paint freshened – she'll need a thorough overhaul before launching, caulking between decks, ballast. They've got to take water and supplies on board. There's only half a crew to do the work and only one of the carpenters with them, though they do have the armourer."

"Then they'll want to rebuild the stockade while they're working. We'll have to move before they have time to complete it."

"To take her back?"

Alex's eyes slid away from the young officer's.

"But I don't understand," Nathaniel Davenport said. "Why not just let them go?"

Before Alex could speak, Josh Twitty growled, "Because they'll be back, sooner or later."

Alex pressed his lips together, overlooking the common sailor's interruption. Twitty had elected to stay with Alex because he did not want to go back to England, not out of respect for his authority. Every insolent look and word told Alex that his obedience was only on sufferance.

"Twitty is right," Alex said. "We will only enjoy a temporary respite. We won't be left in peace forever."

"But we haven't done anything wrong. They're the ones who are stealing the ship," Nathaniel wailed.

"That's not the tale they'll carry to their Lordships at the Admiralty," Twitty said.

"Well, why don't we just go somewhere else?" the secretary demanded.

The same question was in my mind. I sat on a chair at the back of the room, listening to the men around the table. My presence embarrassed them. No one looked in my direction, no one wanted me in the room, none of them wanted to hear my voice. I made myself as still as I could, as silent as I could, but I wondered that Alex did not hear my thoughts screaming to him. We could move to another town, or disguise ourselves as Travelling Dancers, or go over the hills and far away until we found another country!

"We might as well go back with Fenwick as live like fugitives," Alex said.

Vannir tapped his fingers impatiently on the top of the table. "Why did you ask me to attend your council?"

"Because it does affect you," Alex replied. "If George sails home with news of his discovery, more ships will come. In two, three years perhaps, but they will come. Everything will change. Europeans will come to trade with you and they will stay until they have taken everything you have to exchange, including your land. Then they will plant sugar cane or tobacco and you will be forced to work on their plantations because you no longer have anywhere to grow food or build your houses. You have plenty now. You will be poor then."

Vannir smiled. "What nonsense is this? We are not traders and, if we were, we would not trade on those terms."

"They will bring guns and money and their own laws. You won't have any choice."

Vannir's smile disappeared. "You never said anything about this before."

"Because it could not happen as long as we stayed in the Fair Land. For your people's sake as well as ours, we have to prevent their homeward voyage."

"So we are going to recapture the *Miranda*," Nightingale said.

"No. We are going to destroy her." Alex turned back to Vannir. "I have men and I have guns, though not enough to go around. Fenwick has the marines on his side and the powder store and a defensible position, even without a stockade. But if you join us, then I know we can succeed."

Vannir clutched the edge of the table, splaying his fingers across the rough surface. His fingertips and knuckles were white.

"You know our history, our laws. We do not fight battles. We do not go to war." He rose, clutched his robe about him and stalked out of the house. Alex groaned and sank his head into his hands. The offence was given and there was nothing he could do about it until after the battle.

Alex was wrong and Vannir was wrong. We could win without Vannir's aid, and the people of the Fair Land did fight battles. George's party occupied the site on which we had first landed five years ago. By late afternoon, they had already revived the camp. The hammers rang at the forge, the saws whined in the carpenter's workshop, the smell of paint and pitch lay over everything, the grass was trampled by hurrying feet. There had not, of course, been time to replace the stockade if indeed George meant to do so. The fact was, that though sentries had been posted as a matter of routine, no one really expected their crewmates to take up arms against them. They thought it more likely that the crew would gradually be reunited as those who had stayed with Alex realised the hopelessness of his cause and his unfitness to command. One or two stragglers arriving in the camp during the day had reinforced them in this opinion. And then there was the natural reluctance of the men to fight one another.

But the defenders had miscalculated the strength of our desire to stay. Less than an hour after the council, Alex led the attack. Night was falling on a long, long day by the time George, Sloper and the others had been disarmed and herded into a sullen group in the centre of the camp. Three of Hutan's friends lay dead, their prowess at arms insufficiently developed for their first-ever experience of combat. The only other fatalities, also on George's side, were Jawing Tom and Bilby, the drummer boy, who had been caught in the blast when a keg of powder went up. Mr Nock was already at work under a shelter made from a sail, removing bullets and dressing knife and sword wounds. Awbray assisted him; I had offered but the men would not let me touch them.

I looked up as Alex's footsteps drew near. He had come to speak to the injured. Though pale and exhausted, they grinned up at him, for they would all live.

George forced his way from the huddle of prisoners. The guards tried to push him back but Alex signalled to them to let him through.

"Well, Captain, what do you intend to do with us now? Are you going to build a prison to keep us in? Or do you expect us to give you our parole?"

"Neither," Alex replied.

"What then?" George's eyes widened in sham terror. "Is it to be a massacre?"

Alex shook his head.

George regarded him for a moment. "Your actions are ludicrous. You cannot detain us. We will take the *Miranda* and we will sail to England and we will come back and hunt down you and every one of your miserable cut-throats."

"I have no intention of detaining you beyond this night," Alex answered. He raised his voice in command. "Pack the remaining powder kegs in the hold. Put the barrels of pitch on deck. Prepare the fuses." He smiled humourlessly at George. "No one will take the *Miranda*."

George laughed. "What do you see around you? Timber! Acres of timber! Burn the ship if you like. We'll build another."

"George, we can't live in enmity – " Alex's voice cracked. He was about to make an appeal – to what? Their former friendship, the love George once had for me, the well-being of the people of the Fair Land?

"Sir, the Natives!" cried Nightingale.

They came towards us much as they had on that first day on the beach: well-formed men and women, some tall, some short, some with straight hair, some with curled. Some wore their hair loose to their shoulders, some fastened it back with ties ornamented with shells, coloured stones and feathers. They were all, men and women, clad in robes fastened at the shoulders and finely woven with hems patterned or fringed, some falling to the knees, others almost to the ground, but none breaching the rules of modesty. Some went barefoot, but most wore sandals decorated with beads.

We knew all of them by sight, most of them by name. Vannir and Fanvay were there, as were Tinyar and my other bathing companions. Girls whose weddings we had danced at. Elders to whose tales we had listened. Women the sailors had married, babies they had fathered.

Yet there were no words of greeting.

They came to a halt, wordlessly gazing upon the scene lit partly by the brazier in the surgeon's tent, partly by the lowering sun. The surgeon's instruments glowed red hot in the fire. The light from the flames fell on the bloodied men, danced over the buckets of ruby water. The edges of the weapons taken from the defeated men were dark with gore, the eyes of the vanquished bloodshot with hatred.

A faint breeze blew wisps of smoke into the trees. The sea washed against the shore. Fanvay took a basket from one of the women, stepped forward and placed it on the ground in front of Alex.

"We have taught you how to use these healing herbs."

"Thank you – "

He interrupted. "When your hurts are treated, you will leave. All of you will leave. You will take nothing with you but food and water for your journey. Neither you nor your kin will ever be welcomed here again."

"Leave?" Alex repeated. "But we can't leave. That was the reason for all this – to protect you – "

Fanvay cried, "Hutan!"

Hutan pushed his way forward. He attempted a defiant smile but his face only distorted into a stiff grimace.

Fanvay announced his doom. "You, Hutan, and those with you are outcast. You will leave now. By morning, you will be far away, with huntsmen at your heels to prevent your return."

This was a rare and terrible punishment, the harshest that could be meted out. The Fairlanders did not punish men by executing or imprisoning them, for their traditions forbade violence against one another. But an outcast was an animal and could be killed like an animal if need be, if he attempted to break the terms of his sentence. The condemned groaned, some wept, some begged their relatives to plead for mercy for them. None did. Fanvay and the others turned their backs and walked away in silence.

"Manny!" Nathaniel shrieked, stumbling after his wife. Her parents put their arms about her and hurried her along, burdened with her child as she was. Once she looked back, her grief-stricken face white in the gloom. But she did not stop.

George burst out laughing. "Congratulations on your victory Captain Edgcumbe! We're all going home!"

Twenty-Five

Sarah stopped speaking, her head sunk in grief. Downstairs in The Bell, a door opened, releasing a babble of voices. It flapped shut, the latch rattling in the draught. Heels tapped on the flags of the passage and out into the street. A man cleared his throat and spat. His footsteps plashed away through dirty puddles.

So much, Ben thought, for Captain Braveman, Mr Noble and the gallant girl who ran away to sea to be with her lover. But that is what she had done, except her lover was her brother. He had heard of such things happening in the crowded rookeries of London where families wallowed together like brutes, crowded promiscuously into one room with their ignorance, filth and gin.

In the room next door, the bed creaked. Bare feet slapped gently to the floor. Someone had been sleeping in there – the woman he had thought was Sarah's servant.

He shivered with revulsion. "You did have a child."

She looked at him, surprised by his accusing tone. "I am childless."

Sarah's companion quietly entered the room. She must have heard them talking for she betrayed no surprise at the sight of him sitting across the hearth from Sarah. The two exchanged words that he could not understand. After a while, he recognised one repeated word – Manny.

"She is Nathaniel's wife," he said wonderingly.

"Widow."

"And the baby?"

"He died before he was two days old."

Sarah finished speaking, put her hand on the other's arm and guided her to a seat between her and Ben.

"I can't pretend to understand the manner in which you and Captain Edgcumbe lived, " Ben began hesitantly.

"We disgust you. Say so and be done with it."

"Very well," he said slowly. "I am appalled. But the crime you committed does not make your discovery any less valuable. There are no survivors left to tell tales against you. The world need never know what passed between you, Alex and George. Let me have George's papers and I promise that I will keep your secret."

"You do not know what secret to keep," she snapped. "Even if you did, we cannot go back to the Fair Land. On this they were inexorable. In the morning, they came back to the seashore and removed the bundles and crates of specimens, took away all the shells and plants and animal skins that George had collected. And when, a few days after the *Miranda* had been launched and was almost ready to sail, we discovered that Twitty and Nathaniel had deserted, it was the Fairlanders themselves who tracked them into the hills and brought them back."

As Sarah continued her story, Manny gazed into her face, following the words she could not understand, though she knew their import only too well.

A voyage has hardships enough but you can have no idea what that voyage was like. Half of the men had to be cajoled or bullied into working, the other half sang as they laboured. Hardly a day passed without the marines being called to a fight between sorrowing and joyful men.

Sloper expected that he would be given command of the ship but George said that, since Alex had got us to the Fair Land, he was the only person who could safely navigate us home. But he insisted on keeping Alex under close watch. Alex had to take all his meals in his cabin and, even when he slept, a soldier was posted at his door. For the rest of us, George had the great cabin divided into two. We would take silent meals, each party constrained by the presence of the other behind the thin wall.

On the third day out, Nathaniel was caught stealing bread. Sloper was for forcing him to run the gauntlet, there being nothing sailors hate more than theft at sea. Nor are they very fond of stowaways; he was taking the food to Manny who was hidden in his cabin. Sloper wanted to turn back and return her to Mervidir but George refused. He could hardly disguise his delight in managing to bring away one specimen from the Fair Land and was always extremely solicitous of Manny's health. Her labour was almost as much of a trial to him as it was to her husband.

In other circumstances, we might have considered ourselves fortunate during those weeks in the Pacific when the ocean, for the most part, lived up to its name, sometimes more than George would have wished. There were whole days when the wind dropped and we made no progress. It was true that, before long, we had little fresh food. All that was left was dried fish and meat, and that had to be rationed. We were always hungry, but not starving. Occasionally, we sighted birds and George took out a shooting party. The meat made a welcome addition to our diet. We had ample water, the sweetest in the world.

Nevertheless, by the time we reached New Zealand, it was high time to replenish our water supplies and we could not have remained free of scurvy for much longer. Twitty was one of the party sent ashore. When a wind sprang up in the evening and they were unable to launch the boat they were benighted. We could see their firelight on the beach and the boat drawn up nearby. Sometime towards the end of the night, the fire went out. We wondered at it but could do nothing until daybreak, when another boat was launched. Other than the ashes of the fire, they found no trace of the ten sailors who had spent the night on land. Their boat had gone but there were no footsteps and no sign of the vessel having been dragged along the sand. They called out their names but were too few and too ill-armed to risk making a broad search.

That night, another fire was sighted on land. We fired off the ship's guns but received no answering signal. In the morning, Alex sent a larger party with a complement of marines to protect them. They discovered the remains of a huge feast, the stone and ashes still warm, gnawed bones scattered about the ground. Nearby was a deep basket. When they lifted the lid, they discovered a human hand inside.

A few casks for our immediate needs were quickly filled by the fearful men but, not knowing if the people who had made the banquet were still in the vicinity, we dared not linger. We sailed further up the coast. Two or three days later, we found anchorage in a bay sheltered by white cliffs and guarded over by two great white rocks shaped like haystacks. Here we were astonished to discover a field of turnips, onions and carrots, straggling and uncared for but growing nevertheless. They had been planted by some other explorer; perhaps Captain Cook himself had sown those seeds. He could not have known the effect his experiment would have. Nothing could have been more heartening. Even the men who had no wish to go back to England were cheered by it and, for the first time in weeks, there was harmony on the *Miranda*.

Seven months after leaving New Zealand, a Dutch ship came into view. We were two days out from Batavia. It was October 1779.

"She's signalling to come on board sir," said Lieutenant Nightingale.

Sloper, who was always annoyed by Nightingale's deference to the discredited captain, frowned.

"Very well." Alex looked up from the charts. "Sarah, you and Manny had better go behind the screen."

George stood up, distrust in his face.

"We do not want to have to explain where Manny is from," Alex said impatiently. "And, if you don't want the Dutch to be the first to know about your great discovery, I suggest you have all these charts and every journal collected and put into safekeeping. I also recommend that, before we go into port, you remind the crew that they are under naval discipline and are not to speak about where we have been to anyone outside the ship."

George glanced doubtfully at Sloper who said, "It is a wise precaution."

"Captain Williams, gather every scrap of paper on the ship. Letters, diaries, if it's writing, seize it. No one is to keep anything back."

The soldier left at George's bidding.

George looked about the cabin, or the half of it we occupied during the daytime. "Where shall we store the charts?"

"In the captain's cabin is customary," Alex said dryly.

George sneered and turned his back on him. "They will go into my quarters."

Williams returned accompanied by two marines carrying the papers they had confiscated. A sea chest was dragged out from under the window seat and the men packed away Mr Nock's medical notes and poems, drawings Nathaniel and I had made and forgotten years ago, half-written letters home, even

Awbray's mathematical exercise books. George added his own books and drawings just before the lid was closed.

"Is that everything?" he asked.

"We could not find Captain Edgcumbe's journal," Williams answered.

"I destroyed my journals, notes and sketches before we left the Fair Land and have kept none since."

"As did I," I said.

"You are a fool, Alex," George retorted. "There are others on board who can draw and other skilled navigators in England. We have enough information to get back without your help."

"God's blood!" muttered one of the soldiers who had poked his head out of the open window. "What a parcel of scrubs is this?"

The boat from the Dutch ship bobbed towards the *Miranda*, the men labouring wearily at the oars. Their faces beneath their caps were white, cheeks sunken, eyes hollow. No one sang nor spoke. All their efforts were concentrated on keeping their emaciated bodies in motion.

"Bullbaggers!" Awbray trembled.

"They are not ghosts," Mr Nock said grimly. "They are sick men."

"Should we allow them on board?" George asked.

"We cannot turn them away without exciting suspicion," Alex said. "And it is necessary that we put into Batavia for supplies and repairs."

The doctor worriedly stroked his eyebrow. After a moment, he said, "We should not allow them to mingle with the crew more than is necessary."

The boat drew alongside and, as our men lowered the ladder, they teased: "Careful you don't overturn the boat, pot-gut!" "Sit down, *mijnheer*, or you'll be carried away on a sea breeze!" "Anyone for roast beef and plum pudding, or have you forgot how to eat?"

Alex seized his hat and went out of the cabin, followed by the lieutenants and George. A few moments later, silence fell on the deck.

"It is time for us to retire," I said. I put my arm around Manny's shoulders – following the loss of her child she was still weak and low in spirits – and helped her to the other side of the partition. Awbray busied himself in his cupboard with cups and jugs, Nathaniel brushed and buttoned up his jacket, Mr Nock put his arms behind his back and whistled softly.

I spied on the meeting through a gap in the boards. The Dutch captain was, like many of his nation, a tall man, but no longer sleek. His wrists, his shoulder blades and his cheekbones protruded from his pallid skin. His jacket hung off him as if it had been made for another man. Sweat started from his forehead and above his lips. His hand shook whenever he raised a cloth to wipe his face. A strong smell of arrack entered the room with him. He was accompanied by a petty officer who was no more robust than his commander.

Alex introduced Captain Van Ruysdael to Mr Nock and Nathaniel. For the sake of appearances, George and the others let him play his part as captain and host. Awbray brought the tray out. Van Ruysdael's eyes lit up, if such a dull flicker could be called a light, at sight of the cups. He was disappointed when all that flowed from the jug was water.

"Our stores are depleted. We have no wine nor spirits," Alex explained with an apologetic smile.

"Cats!" Van Ruysdael cried. I wondered for a moment if he had an aversion to the animals and Kitty had got into the cabin. His lieutenant stood limply to attention. An order was given in their own language and, within half an hour, beer, wine and spirits were on board and the sailors were drinking the health, in uncomplimentary terms, of the Dutch Commodore of the East India Company.

With the polite formalities over Van Ruysdael, who had been curiously eyeing the partition, the broken windows, the scuffed furniture and the worn, colourless floorcloth, began his enquiries. "Where are you from and where are you bound?"

"We are bound for England," Alex answered.

"From?"

"We have been at sea for a long time."

The Dutchman eyed the faded British uniforms. "I can see that. But where are you from?"

"We have been at sea for many months," Alex repeated.

The captain leaned forward. "You're not a privateer, hoping to pick off some Company ships?"

Alex laughed. "You can see that my ship is in no condition to take prizes, even if I wished to do so. The *Miranda* is no privateer. She belongs to His Majesty King George the Third and she is in need of refitting."

The captain ruminated for a moment. "It is good. You can spend your money in Batavia. We are not at war with England!"

"What do you mean by *we are not at war with England*?" demanded George.

Van Ruysdael's eyes narrowed. "How long did you say you had been at sea?"

"My friend is teasing you, Captain," Alex winked at George who, compelled to accept the title of friend, forced a sickly smile in return. "Of course we know who our enemies are. But there's no Frog who is a match for British tars!"

Van Ruysdael smiled. "That is what you say, but with the combined fleet in the English Channel, will your Navy be strong enough to prevent them landing on your island? We will see if you succeed in beating the Armada this time, eh?"

Alex nodded. "In the meantime, it's trade as usual?"

"We are a trading nation. French, English, Spanish… it's all the same to us." Van Ruysdael stood up. "Your money is good."

"How did you know we were at war with France?" George demanded of Alex when the Dutch sailors had departed.

"Who else would it be? They have been looking for the chance since Admiral Hawke destroyed their fleet at Quiberon Bay. And that the Spanish should join them for this war, as they did for the last, is no surprise."

But what was cause for surprise was the information the crew had gleaned from their Dutch visitors.

"We are at war with America?" George repeated, his astonishment shared by the rest of us in the great cabin.

"Yes, sir," said Isaac Fisher, the mate who was reporting what the men had learned. "The French have allied with America, and the Spanish with the French. The colonies declared themselves independent of us three years ago."

"All of them?" Sloper asked.

"Seems that way."

There was a shocked silence, which the mate broke. "The lads are a bit worried about it, sir, not wanting to be pressed into service the minute we get home after such a long time out. Do you think you'll be able to obtain protections for us, sir?"

Alex smiled derisively at the man's faith in George Fenwick's influence. His followers seemed to think he was omnipotent, and George was happy to play the plenipotentiary. He waved his hand regally and said, "I will see what I can do when I speak to Lord Sandwich."

Reassured by this lofty promise, Fisher unsteadily – the men had drunk no spirits for months – left the cabin.

Everyone was talking at once. Did the colonists really think they could survive without home support? What battles had been fought at land or at sea? Could Britain lose her American possessions?

"The war will interfere with your plans," Alex said quietly to George under the babble of voices. "There will be no spare ships to send after your great discovery."

George threw a murderous look at him but made no answer.

"There will be English newspapers in Batavia," Mr Nock's sensible voice rose above the clamour.

George thumped the table with his fist. "Let the colonists strike out on their own if that is what they wish!"

Everyone looked at him. "What need do we have of America now? We are bringing home a far greater prize. Nathaniel, find paper and ink. I shall start drafting my despatches immediately."

Nathaniel slowly opened his writing case, his eye on Alex. Alex shook his head and the scribe let the lid fall.

"You intend to send an announcement of your success to England?" Alex's manner was restrained but I, who knew him so well, could see that his thoughts were far from tranquil.

"Of course," said George. "I shall send a packet home on the first available ship."

"I would recommend that you do not do so."

"I know what you would recommend. You would much prefer the Fair Land to remain a secret."

"But, as you have so often pointed out to me, I must bow to the inevitable. I only counsel you against committing anything in writing to another ocean-going vessel. There is too great a risk of it falling into enemy hands."

George scowled. "Sloper?"

The lieutenant rubbed his jaw. "It sticks in my craw to agree with him but there's truth in what he says. It's too risky to send despatches to the Admiralty while there's a war on. We don't know that another captain will not sell or surrender the papers, and to have two sets of documents on the seas instead of one doubles the chances of an enemy seizing them. It would be better for us to protect our prize ourselves. We'll be able to re-arm the ship in Batavia."

"Very well," George said, anger and disappointment darkening his eyes. "But this is only a respite for you, Edgcumbe. Don't think that you will be able to stop me."

Alex smiled. "Oh, I know that, as ever, you intend to have your own way."

Twenty-Six

"Were you trying to delay news about the Fair Land reaching England when you prevented George from writing his letter?" I asked.

"Yes," Alex answered.

"But why? We will be home soon. What difference will a few weeks make? Or do you hope to find an opportunity to destroy the logs?"

Alex stared morosely at the dusty ground and made no reply. I studied his thin face, the lines around the mouth and eyes and across the forehead. Alex had aged but so, I supposed, had I. I had lost so much weight that, when I looked in a mirror, I was reminded of the existence of the skeleton beneath the skin, and how one day it would be all that remained of me.

Two Dutch merchants strolling home from their warehouse nudged one another and gawped. I had grown used to being stared at. There were very few white women in Batavia and people could not help wondering how I got there. They had not so far forgotten their manners as to omit bowing to us, but Alex did not see them or, if he did, did not care to return their courtesy. The men reached the end of the line of trees where they spoke some sharp words to the *kedisall-boys*, as they called the lads they employed to follow them with umbrellas to protect them from the sun.

I looked across the water. "You could think yourself in the Netherlands."

The opposite bank mirrored the scene on our side of the canal. Steps led up from the water onto a wide pavement lined with trees under which were benches like the one on which we sat. Beyond that, there was a road and, along that, a row of brick houses with tiled roofs and elaborate gables. Here and there church spires reared above the skyline.

There was a low splash and the sound of jaws snapping. I glimpsed something slithering at the water's edge – a hint of reptilian scales, the eddying of murky water. The disturbance sent shimmering waves up into the hot air and, with them, a terrible stench: stagnant water, decaying greenery, excrement. I shifted uncomfortably, suddenly aware of the weight of my clothes, the heat prickling between my breasts, my throbbing feet beating against the wall of their leather prisons.

Batavia was nothing like Amsterdam. Here were Chinese men with faces made cadaverous, the sailors said, from smoking bang and opium; dark-skinned Portuguese maddened by the fumes from their arrack distilleries; sunburned Dutch sailors with the venom from centipede or scorpion coursing through their veins, the bites sometimes so ferocious that limbs might be lost when infection set in.

Malay men with oiled black hair drove the hackney carriages. Barefoot Malay women sat behind the stalls in the bazaar, anxiously adjusting the awnings to cover meat and fish to stop it spoiling in the sun. Half-naked African slaves laboured in the shipyards. They were labouring now on the *Miranda* at the Ondrust wharf on one of the islands in the harbour. The Dutch would not let the English sailors do the work of repairing her, which was just as well since most of our men lay shaking with fever under the tents that had been erected for them on the shore. All of the *Miranda*'s people had been ill to a greater or lesser extent. Harried by mosquitoes at night, with nothing safe to drink but arrack, breathing in air heavy with the vapours of the sluggish canals or the noxious steams of the monsoon rainfall, even George had been grievously sick. Perhaps it was because of his illness that his vigilant wardship of Alex had been relaxed. No effort was made to confine the *Miranda*'s captain to the house that had been hired for the gentlemen, nor to prevent our meetings.

Had George lost interest in revenge? I had begun to hope that the ruin he threatened might be averted. There was a war on, the Admiralty needed experienced sailors. Alex would have an opportunity to redeem himself by heroic deeds.

Alex did not share my optimism. Even if the Admiralty Lords were disposed to mercy, no crew would serve under him. The only reason the *Miranda*'s people obeyed him now was because George, Sloper and their marines sanctioned his orders. And, now that we were in charted waters, Alex was not needed to guide the vessel home.

"Why don't we get away?" I said impulsively. "In one of the Dutch ships. We could go to Japan, China, Bengal… anywhere. We could learn a language, we could trade, we might even grow rich. People do make fortunes from nothing… perhaps that is what George wants. Perhaps he wants us to get away. He loved us once."

Alex smiled gently. "I can't go. There is still the Fair Land to think about."

"Then you do mean to destroy the papers?"

"I don't know what I intend. I only know that I cannot leave the fate of that nation in George Fenwick's hands. As it is, I can hardly bear to conjecture what will be the outcome of Hutan's rebellion. We have taught him greed, ambition, how to command other men. Things will be a hundred times worse if colonising Europeans arrive to exploit the situation we created.

Yet how to stop them? I do not know."

"I don't think we can. Destroying the charts will only hinder, not prevent, their settlement. Alex, we have done all we can. Why shouldn't we think of ourselves now?"

"I know you have a better nature than that."

The Dutch sugar ships set sail for Europe. As well as sugar they carried coffee, pepper, nutmeg, cinnamon, cotton, teas, silks and, so it turns out, George's papers. He addressed them to his home and not to the Admiralty to divert suspicion from them should the ship be seized.

Why did he send the documents in spite of Sloper's warnings? Was it for fear of the *Miranda*'s capture by the French or fear of loss or damage to the locked sea chest? Or was it nothing more than the desire to defy advice because it came from Alex? Whatever was in George's mind when he scorched his name and address into that leather case, the precaution was taken, and in secret.

The men who were strong enough were employed on mending the *Miranda*'s sails and making rope. Sometimes only a dozen were fit enough to muster. Meanwhile, she was caulked and repaired, then moved to another wharf where her paintwork was scraped and repainted, her rigging mended. She was loaded with ballast and coal. Then, on a day of squally rain, she was taken down to Batavia Road to take in stores and water. One afternoon, Alex and George took leave of the Commodore and we went on board for a final sleepless night in Batavia. In the morning, we weighed anchor and, with not one regret, we slipped away from that graveyard, weaving our course through the islands in the harbour where the Dutch had their arsenals and storehouses and the burial ground where lay four of the common sailors, next to Mr Nock and Nathaniel Davenport.

The garrison fired a salute which, having reprovisioned, we were able to return; we had not been able to do so when we arrived. The twenty or so who remained sick smiled feebly in their beds, convinced that now they would improve. But, a week later in the Sunda Strait, eight of them were dead and many others had fallen ill of the flux. If it was not the noxious air of Batavia, then what could it be? The water, we conjectured, and at our first opportunity stopped to replace and replenish our stock. At Princes Island we were supplied with turtle and fowls, rabbit and fish, and no barrier was put on the men trading for themselves. With fresh coconuts, plantains and limes, the crew's health seemed to improve.

We put out to sea again, but once more the ship's health declined. Was the water we took on at Princes Island also unclean? We put lime in the casks to purify it and the decks were washed with vinegar. Mr Nock's assistant, a young man too fond of rum, talked of blistering and bleeding but was, in truth, at the limit of his skill and did very little for the men in his care. The ship stank and the men died. We lost the cook, a carpenter, the sailmaker, boatswain, midshipman, marines, and still the deaths continued.

"The *Miranda* is dying," Alex said as the bodies of marine Captain Williams and the sailor the men called 'Bottle Belly' disappeared beneath the swell. "She is already half dead."

Those of the men who could stand – less than half of the crew – shuffled back to their duties. By now, they were either too apathetic to bother auctioning the deceased men's belongings, which they usually did to raise money for the bereaved families, or they had nothing left to barter with, there having been so many of these sales over the last weeks. The ship groaned with the moans of the men below, sweating in their own blood and shit. A gust of air caught in the rigging: the *Miranda*'s death rattle.

George pushed a lock of his dark hair away from his sallow face and offered his arm to Manny. "You must rest now."

She accepted his support, and who could blame her? Sometimes she drew back from him, agonising over her loyalties, afraid of betraying her own country where now she would have the status of an outcast. But he promised the exiled widow a home in England, protection, food and clothing for her lifetime, which was more than Alex or I could offer her with our own future so precarious.

There was no longer any guard kept on Alex. There was no one to guard him. Sloper had been dead a fortnight. Of the dozen marines who had sailed from England with us six years before, half were dead. Three of those who remained were sick, and three only were well enough to watch in turns over George's cabin where the box of journals and charts was kept. But Alex never went near the room except by necessity, and then he cast not one glance at the sentinel or the locked door. Yet he did roam about the ship, disappearing from the quarterdeck or the great cabin for hours together. With a reduced crew meaning that routine repair work was virtually at a standstill it was, he said, important to keep a constant eye on things. George, sitting up in the great cabin – the partition had been dismantled in Batavia – weak and bad tempered, merely grunted when Alex explained his long absences and went back to his writing.

"Land ho!"

The call drifted down from the lookout. A score of pale faces exchanged glances, animated all at once, hopeful all at once.

Alex shook his head. "It can't be," he said. But the next morning, land was sighted and smelled too, if only in our imaginations, stimulated by the thought of grass and trees and fruit.

"Is it the Cape?" asked George, gripping the rail and peering hungrily through the morning haze.

"No," Alex answered. "It's Madagascar."

"Madagascar?" George rounded on him. "How can that be?"

"We're off course. You try navigating a ship with only half a crew," Alex snapped, yet his anger was perfunctory as if something else preoccupied him. "We will land."

"What if there are French warships here?"

"I doubt if there are. The French have never been made welcome."

"Then who built that fort?" George pointed towards the shore. We could just make out a listing wooden structure rising above the trees at the tip of the bay.

Alex shrugged. "Madagascar was the pirate capital of the world. It's a good place from which to harry shipping rounding the Cape."

"You are taking us into a den of outlaws?"

"I said *was*. Most of the pirates left years ago. But we will take that chance. We need fresh food and water. I understand," he added slyly, "that the land is a botanist's paradise. You can make up for your lack of specimens if you like. The *Miranda* is at your command."

"We will stay only as long as it takes to buy stores," George retorted. "If this is an attempt at delaying me – "

"How much gold do we have left?" Alex interrupted.

We drew closer to a rickety wooden pier. Once the town must have rung with the cries and laughter of carousing pirates, the chink of coin, the squeals of whores. Deals were struck, fortunes changed hands, trade was brisk and no one cared that the merchandise was stolen. Now the houses were as dilapidated as the fort. Only one was of brick, set on a hill above the town and uninhabited now, as could be seen by its gaping windows and overgrown grounds. Perhaps some bold buccaneer, having made his fortune, had tried to set himself up as a gentleman here.

Several of the buildings around the quay still displayed inn signs but most were empty and boarded up. One Dutch ship lay at anchor, her meagre cargo of casks already unloaded onto the quay. A desultory market had been established nearby. The Dutch ship's crew, a mix of nations and none of them the best representatives of their kind, bartered ill-naturedly for scrawny chickens and shrivelled fruit. A group of ragged men watched as the *Miranda* slid into the bay. She must have looked impressive with her fresh paint and new guns – a British ship, formidable and well-armed. If the inhabitants of the place considered trying to challenge her, they must have decided the odds were against them. By the time they realised the state our crew was in, our money was enough to guarantee our welcome.

A boat was lowered, and Alex and George went ashore. They returned late in the afternoon, their business speedily transacted. Casks were already being ferried to and from shore. The men unloaded coops of squawking fowl and baskets of fruit from the boat. Alex climbed on board and threw his bulging satchel at Awbray. "For our dinner," he said.

Awbray scampered off to begin dressing the meat for the great cabin.

"What is it?" I asked, looking forward to a change of diet.

"Fowl, a bit skinny but fresh," Alex replied. "But I've arranged something better for you and Manny. I've taken lodgings for you. You can spend tonight on shore. I've ordered hot water for you to bathe in. It's quite safe. There were French settlers here, a little way down the coast, but they abandoned the place three or four years ago."

Manny looked at me enquiringly; I translated. She clapped

her hands together in delight. For the first time in weeks, a smile transformed her sunken face.

"You never told me you had taken rooms," George objected.

"The women need some proper rest," Alex answered. "Look at them! They will benefit from a night ashore. Or are you willing to gamble with Manny's health?"

As she fell silent once more, Sarah's fingers played amongst the papers on her lap. Ben eyed them nervously. The coals, neglected during her narration, had collapsed in the hearth but still glowed. A tense silence lay between the women. Their eyes did not meet and yet Ben had a sense of some common experience shared but not so far spoken of.

"And it was after you left Madagascar that the storm blew up," he prompted.

"There was no storm."

"But I thought – "

Her head sank to her chest. His questions wearied her. He fell into an embarrassed silence. She was indifferent to his feelings as she took up her tale, her voice weaker now...

Alex had taken rooms for us in one of the quayside taverns. We were nervous at first about going ashore alone, for Alex said he could not spare an escort. But he said we would come to no harm. The thought of the money he might yet spend in the town was enough to guarantee that. The chance of a bath and a night away from the ship was too tempting to pass up. The innkeeper, a descendant of the pirates who had once ruled the district, was an old dark-skinned man with bright blue eyes who communicated with us in a curious mixture of languages – French, English and Portuguese. He was thrilled to have paying guests in his tavern, which was none too clean but it was quiet. A slatternly servant heated water for us and poured it into a leaky old barrel. Threadbare towels were provided. There was no soap. But how gentle was the water on skin chafed by washing in salt water! How soothing was the heat of it, seeping into aching limbs and stiffened joints!

Afterwards, we wrapped ourselves in musty grey sheets and sat by the window combing one another's hair. Because our clothes had been taken away to be cleaned, we took supper in our room. It suited us to be alone: we did not want to mix with strangers. The room seemed safe and close. Manny sang for the first time since Nathaniel's death, a lament for her child and husband.

I sat by the window gazing out across the bay at the lanterns on the *Miranda*. A man stood motionless on the quarterdeck, silhouetted against the yellow light. He was still there when we extinguished the candles and climbed into bed. But now I think it was only a fancy of mine.

Sleep came immediately, was deep and dreamless, but with waking came dread remembrance. Today we must go back to the *Miranda* and resume a journey that was, for Alex and me, devoid of hope. Yet on board the ship, between the horrors of present and future, was all that I loved and I knew I would go back willingly. Manny was still sleeping. I rose from my bed, wrapped myself in my blanket, padded over to the window.

The *Miranda* had gone.

Twenty-Seven

"Gone?" Ben exclaimed. "How could she have gone? What about the storm that sank her?"

"I said there was no storm," Sarah answered sharply. "Alex sank the ship."

The ocean hides many things.

The *Miranda* had not been off course when she had sailed to Madagascar. Alex had arranged the whole thing. Putting into that old pirate port, getting Manny and Sarah off the ship, slipping away before they were awake. When Sarah looked in the overnight bag Alex had carried in for them, she found that he had left them the *Miranda*'s gold. They bought passage on the Dutch ship as far as the Cape, where the *Bellona* picked them up.

Ben imagined George Fenwick woken just after dawn by the rattling of the anchor chains, feeling the ship begin to move, flinging on some clothes, running onto deck, demanding to know what was happening. What had Alex told him? That, during the night, local fishermen had brought news that French sails had been sighted further along the coast – why else would George consent to their sudden departure? That, on hearing this, Alex immediately sent for the women who had come on board while George slept and were resting in their cabin now – George would not have gone without Manny. That it was necessary for them to put to sea at once and manage with the supplies they had.

Alex had not been prowling about the ship to check on her condition. He had been laying fuses, collecting combustible material, weakening timbers. What had he said to himself as he set about his fatal work? That the *Miranda* was already dying, he was merely hastening that end, and the Fair Land was safe.

"And that is the secret you want me to keep? That your brother is a murderer?"

"If it were that, I would not have told you. There would be no need, you said so yourself. There are no other survivors. I could tell you any tale I liked about the loss of the *Miranda*. Will you not see? It was not one side or the other that was banished from the Fair Land. It was all of us." Sarah sighed, a low and hopeless sound. "We cannot go back there when even the best of us can commit murder and believe we are doing good."

"The best of us. Alex Edgcumbe."

She shook her head impatiently, refusing to defend her brother and her lover. Ben's contempt meant nothing to her. Before he realised what she was doing, she gathered the last of the sketches from around her foot and dropped them into the fire. Their edges began to brown and curl as they sank down into the red coals. The pages turned black, fragments broke off and flew up the chimney.

"You have just destroyed the only evidence that might have helped me catch my father's killer," Ben said quietly.

"I am sorry for that." She let her head fall back against the chair, shaded her eyes with a thin hand. "But there are other lives to consider."

"Your Fairlanders." He glanced at Manny but quickly looked away again, steeling himself against the appeal in her beautiful eyes. "I give you due warning, Miss Edgcumbe, I intend to go to the Admiralty with this. I will tell them about the Fair Land.

And, unless you agree to tell what you know of it as well, I will also reveal the truth about Alex Edgcumbe."

"They will not believe in the Fair Land while they have faith in their hero Cook. As for Alex, he is dead now and they cannot touch him. I will not tell my story again."

He stood up. Her languor enraged him. She talked about murder, suicide, and massacre as if they had no meaning. "I don't know how you live with your shame."

She smiled bitterly. "I don't know how I live."

The frantic activity in the hall had ended and the waiters were going about their normal business. On the stairs, one passed Ben at a sedate pace. He carried a tray with a note on it.

Young George Fenwick jumped up from a chair near the door. "Where have you been? I watched the London coach at the King's Head load up but the women didn't get on it. Have you found anything?"

"She is here."

"Have you seen her? You are shaking... you look ill. What has happened?"

"I can't tell you, George. Don't ask me. I need some fresh air."

George followed him to the doorway where he gulped deep breaths of the damp air. He raised his face to the drizzle and rubbed the water across his eyes before putting on his hat.

"What are we going to do?" George asked.

"In the first place, eat. I haven't had anything since breakfast and I need fortification. Then, when we and our horses are rested, we will go back to Overcombe."

"What about Miss Edgcumbe? And Uncle George's papers?"

"The papers are gone. Don't ask for explanations now." Ben put his hand on the lad's shoulder. "Come. Let's go back to the King's Head. The air here has made me sick."

They stepped out into the street. Ben grabbed George's arm and pulled him back inside. A man stood with his back to them; a wispy pigtail hung down his back.

"Beale!" Ben hissed.

"One of the spies you told Father about?" George's face was bright with excitement.

"Yes. Then where's the other bastard?" He glanced back up the stairs. "Miss Edgcumbe! Stay here."

"But – "

Ben raced up to Sarah's room and flung open the door. Hay knelt beside the fire, jabbing the coals with a poker. Sarah Edgcumbe had not moved. She watched the man with complete indifference from beneath the shade of her fingers. Manny sat on a low stool beside her, chafing her other hand, crooning softly.

"You won't tell the Admiralty but you'll tell the French, is that it?"

Her head jerked up, pain in her eyes. Ben had no pity for her. George came up behind him, stared goggle-eyed into the room. The boy's mouth fell open at the sight of the pale, fragile woman who was Sarah Edgcumbe.

"George, fetch the constables!"

Hay calmly replaced the poker on its hook beside the fire, rubbed his hands on his breeches and stood up. "Now, now, Mr Dearlove, there's no need for that. Stay where you are, lad." He reached into his pocket and drew out a sealed paper. "Here's my commission. Beale's is the same. Signed by Mr Philip Stephens, First Secretary to the Admiralty." The man preened as he added, "For special duties."

"It's true." Sarah's voice was weary. "Mr Hay works for the Admiralty."

Ben glanced down at the paper. It looked real enough, but he had no experience of forgeries. For all he knew, it was a fake.

"How do you know?"

"He is in possession of certain facts that prove as much."

"Then you have her!" Ben cried. "And now she can tell you the story she told me."

"And I'm sure it will be an interesting tale."

"What? What tale?" George demanded.

Ben took the boy's arm, steered him towards the corridor. "Not now, George." He paused on the threshold to look back. "Nothing salvageable?"

Hay shook his head.

Ben was not surprised. Hay could not have expected to save anything. All he had succeeded in doing was breaking up the charred remains.

"Never mind. Their Lordships will hear her evidence now. It will all come out about Jacob Edgcumbe and Bowood, and I will swear to what she told me. You know where to find me."

"If we need you," Hay agreed affably.

"Will you take her to London?"

"Yes. We've a carriage ready."

Ben looked down at Sarah Edgcumbe. The ruin of those responsible for his father's death was inevitable now. He could afford to be merciful. "I will testify about the Fair Land, and about how George and Alex quarrelled about coming home, and about the storm that sank the ship, all as you told me. Nothing else."

Whether she understood his promise or not, she gave no sign. She lay back in her chair as if in a faint. Only the fluttering of her wet eyelashes told that she was still alert to events around her.

Twenty-Eight

Spicy tendrils of steam rose from the glass between Ben's fingers. He felt the wine cooling, losing its comfort and savour. Gusts of wind swirled leaves through the air and spattered raindrops against the windows, which were snug and did not rattle. An owl hooted. Drowsily he thought, it's the cry of a lost soul, George's lost soul, fluttering against the window of his home.

A long time passed before Antony spoke. "And this is the story she told?"

"Yes."

Antony rose from his chair, kicked the log in the hearth, watched the flecks of red shoot up the chimney, sat down again.

"It is vile, vile. The product of a diseased mind, an unnatural, vicious mind."

"You think Miss Edgcumbe is mad?"

"Most certainly I do. The strange life she has led has unbalanced her. She must be hysterical to believe men are in love with her when they are not. Her brother-in-law Stanhope, George, her own brother! She has overburdened her faculties with the writing of *A Voyage to the Fair Land* and can no longer distinguish truth from fantasy. What sort of woman could have written such a book? Only one who has entirely lost all sense of feminine delicacy. The best place for her is an asylum."

"She is not mad," said Ben. He had given the question much thought during the ride back from Gloucester with George sulking at his side because of his refusal to tell him what had happened in the room at The Bell. Ben had tried to understand how a girl brought up as Sarah had been could have descended into such a pit of sin. He guessed that religious observance had been more a matter of fashion than fervour in the Edgcumbe household, but religion there had been, religion with its laws and duties and sanctions. *And if a man shall take his sister, it is a wicked thing.* No wonder Alex and Sarah had stopped reading their Bible. But it had not been madness.

"Sarah is a woman who has abandoned European habits," he said slowly.

Antony frowned. The phrase was familiar to him. "George used to talk about *European habits*."

"Yes. The words are George's, spoken at a dinner party a long time ago. He said, *When I say that some of the things we believe in are only habit, I do not mean to say that we should abandon them on that account.* But Sarah did abandon them."

"And is the blame to be laid at my brother's door?" Antony demanded. "Is he to be held responsible for leading weak minds astray?"

"I do not think Sarah's a weak mind." Ben blinked. The fire was making his tired eyes sore. "She was telling the truth."

"And if she was then she and her brother are savages, monsters, murderers. Would any sane woman accuse herself of such crimes?"

"If they had been committed, yes."

"And you think that the Admiralty will hold an inquiry into the loss of the *Miranda* on the strength of Miss Edgcumbe's delusions?"

"My father's death is no delusion. Edgcumbe murdered him, caused his death at least. I can't prove it myself, but after the inquiry the world will know it and I will see him hanged."

"I'm sorry, Ben. I think your faith in the woman's testimony

311

is misplaced. You cannot possibly believe her. Their Lordships cannot possibly believe her."

"You once thought it possible that your brother had been to the Fair Land."

"No, I told you that there is no Fair Land. I did snatch at the little hope you brought me that my brother might still be alive."

Guiltily, Ben remembered the hurt his mistake had caused. "Even if Miss Edgcumbe's tale is not true in all its particulars, the very suggestion that the *Miranda*'s loss was no accident will be sufficient to force an investigation. Only let that happen and justice will follow sooner or later."

"I think and hope you are wrong. Let no one look further into this abomination. Here the matter ends."

"It is not ended. The truth – "

Antony raised his hand. "It is not the truth. I will hear no more. As you value our acquaintance, you must give me your word that you will not repeat the creature's story. It must never come to the ears of my children, nor shall my brother's name be sullied by her filth."

"As for that, I have already decided that I will not reveal the details of their relationship. That story is for Miss Edgcumbe to tell or not as she chooses."

"And brand herself mad if she does!"

Ben let the subject drop. Antony might feel differently when he had had time to think about it. Besides, it was out of their hands. They could only wait now on their Lordships of the Admiralty.

*

On a wintry day four months later, Ben put down his pen and read what he had written.

Hail the Ruler of the Waves! Salute the Guardian of the Seas! Bow before the Champion of the Oceans! Long live the nation – that unchallenged, undisputed nation – whose magnificent ships ride the unfathomable deeps, whose undaunted mariners brave the unknown places of the world. Vive la nation that will people the unclaimed continents with poissardes, sans-culottes, muscadins and ouvriers. Join with the Admirals of Britain in paying homage to the new Ruler of the Waves: France!

It was a fair start, though little to show for the time he had spent on it and not half scurrilous enough yet. He would go on to accuse the Admiralty Lords of cowardice, sloth and a lack of patriotic fervour for neglecting a great British discovery and leaving the Fair Land to fall into foreign hands. As a first venture into pamphleteering, it might do.

He rubbed his cold fingers and listened to the by-now familiar sounds of the Soho streets. Carriages clattered over the slippery road, pedestrians' feet slithered on the icy pavements, another nuptial battle raged overhead and, next door, the prostitute's bed thumped rhythmically against the thin wall behind his own. After a moment, he gave up trying to warm his hands, stood up and crossed the bare floor to rake out the puny fire.

He took down his greatcoat – his one extravagant purchase – from the nail on the wall. A glance around the room sufficed to check that all was in order. There was not much to check, only one chair which was at the desk, a washstand, a few yellowing prints on the dingy wallpaper, a shelf with the remains of his lunch – a shop-bought pie and a jug of ale – and a few books on the mantelpiece.

He unlatched the door and went out. He walked briskly, his breath puffing white on the air. The way was familiar to him as he trod it every week. When he first came back to London, he had trodden it every day.

He had been in London since the beginning of the year, living on the proceeds of the sale of his father's shop. He had no idea how long the money had to last and, now he was planning to venture into a pamphlet war on the Admiralty, there would be printing costs to pay. So he was more frugal than he had ever been before his father's death – living in a garret, eating in the cheapest chophouses, going early to bed to avoid having to burn coals and candles.

As usual, the Whitehall traffic was at a standstill. Brewers' drays and farmers' wagons mingled with crested carriages, one of which broke away to sweep under an archway into a cobbled courtyard. Ben followed it.

In the high-ceilinged hall, three porters sat in black hooded armchairs. Icy air rolled along the ground, but their feet were snug in the drawers that slid out from beneath their seats. There was a fire in the hearth at which they could warm themselves if they got chilled with sitting.

One of the men half rose when Ben came in, recognised him and sank back. "It's Ben Dearlove."

A second man swivelled his neck to peer around the wings of his chair. "Tut!"

The third merely watched through slitted eyes.

Ben gritted his teeth and addressed the porter who had spoken his name. "I am here to see Secretary Stephens."

The man droned the usual response. "D'ye have an appointment?"

"No. But I have written to him."

"Can't see you without an appointment."

"Then can I wait?"

"Not unless you have an appointment."

"Then can I make an appointment?"

"No."

"How can I have an appointment unless you let me make an appointment?"

The man grinned. "Now there's a riddle, eh?" He winked at his companions.

Ben knew better than to linger in the hall. They would only throw him out. He dragged his feet, hoping that they would call him back, that this time his persistence had softened their hearts sufficiently to allow him to pass into the waiting room and join the captains and lieutenants petitioning for commands.

One of the oaken doors off the entrance hall opened. The porters, kicking the drawers back with the smoothness of long practice, shot to their feet. An elderly man in a dark green suit and thick black stockings approached them, the raised heels on his gleaming shoes rapping sharply. He had hard bright eyes, a thin line of a mouth. Weak and wizened as he was, he was king of this realm. The doormen leaned deferentially towards him to catch his whispers. He pointed at Ben and the three porters turned and stared at him in surprise.

Encouraged by their unwonted interest, Ben took a step forward. One of them broke away to intercept him. The old man, meanwhile, trotted off down the corridor.

"If you please, sir!" Ben called after him. "I have important information – "

The porter's hand was on his arm, the front door stood open, the steps were hard and slippery... but instead of pushing him outside the man said, "If you will come this way,

His Lordship will see you now."

His Lordship! Which Lordship did he mean? His awed tones suggested that it was someone very high up indeed. Could it be the Earl of Chatham, the First Lord of the Admiralty, himself?

With stately steps, the guide led him along the corridor, took his coat and hat, and showed him into a large rectangular chamber panelled in dark wood. A fire blazed in a brown marble fireplace, above which was a rack of rolled-up charts. On the opposite wall was what Ben took at first for a clock until he saw that it only had one hand. It had a map of Europe on the dial, marked with the points of the compass instead of hours. The pointer was in almost continual motion, but he could not tell what it was supposed to measure.

Two people stood behind the table in front of the middle of three windows. One was the man from the hall, the other a tall figure in a high-collared jacket who had his back to him. He was staring out at the stable yard, humming a tune. As he drew near, Ben recognised a theme from Handel's *Water Music*.

"I am Secretary Stephens," announced the man in the green suit.

His companion broke off in mid-note and turned. Ben was surprised to see how old he was; the straight back had not prepared him for it. A pair of deep lines ran down from the corners of his mouth, another pair emphasised his long nose. His forehead was high and there was probably little of his own hair left under the light wig. The skin around his dark eyes bagged and he was jowly. Ben guessed that he was in his early sixties. In fact, he was seventy-one.

"This," Stephens continued, "is Lord Sandwich."

"Lord Sandwich! Where's Chatham?"

The Earl smiled. "The present First Lord of the Admiralty is not such an assiduous attender at the office as was I. Mr Stephens

316

has taken the liberty of appropriating the boardroom for this interview, knowing we will not be disturbed." He sat down, signalling Ben to take one of the chairs on the other side of the mahogany table. Stephens took his place at his side.

"You've been writing to the Admiralty, demanding an inquiry into the fate of the *Miranda*. Mr Stephens has your letters here."

"And why haven't the Admiralty answered any of them?"

The secretary took the letters from his pocket and placed them on the table. "Nothing goes to their Lordships that has not first passed through my hands."

Ben leapt to his feet. "No one has seen my letters, have they? I shall write to the Earl of Chatham at his private address – petition him at the House of Lords – wait on him until he agrees to see me, if I have to wait a hundred years!"

"And tell him what?"

Ben swung round to face Sandwich. "About the *Miranda*. That the Fair Land exists."

"You would be wasting your time. The Admiralty has no interest in the *Miranda*."

"No? Then why did they go to such lengths to find Sarah Edgcumbe? Setting spies on her and me!"

"It was not the Admiralty," Stephens answered for Sandwich. "Mr Hay and Mr Beale were acting privately for His Lordship. I recruited them myself. I was happy to do so, having served under His Lordship during his time in office here." He cast a worshipful glance at the Earl.

Ben sank back into his chair. "They were working for you? But why? And what have they done with Sarah Edgcumbe?"

"Why would they do anything with her?"

"They arrested her in Gloucester."

Sandwich smiled. "Come now, Mr Dearlove. No one has

been arrested." He fluttered his fingers, interrupting Ben who was about to protest. "Well, there was one unfortunate occurrence in Bristol, for which I do apologise... but Hay and Beale have no powers of detention, you know. Even if they had, burning documents is not a crime." He nodded at Stephens who pulled a sheaf of papers from under Ben's letters and slid it across the table towards Sandwich.

"Before she left London," the Earl went on, "Miss Edg – "

"Left London? You let her go?"

"Why would anyone keep her here? As I say, before she left London, she gave me a statement she had prepared. In it she confirms that she was on board the *Miranda*, but she did not sail to the Pacific. Mr Fenwick established her in Madeira before continuing his expedition to the South Sea. She waited for his return but, when it became clear that he was not coming back, she had to make her way back to England bereft of her lover's protection. Here, outcast by her family and reduced by her poverty, she hit on the idea of blending her experiences with her imagination and produced her astonishing book."

Sandwich pushed the pages towards Ben.

Gratified as I am by a romantic young man's reaction to my tale, there is yet some mischief in his attempt to unmask the author. I wrote with no immodest desire to enter into the world of letters, and nothing but the direst necessity could have induced me to seek publication of a book, the merits of which have been exaggerated by an indulgent public. I have no wish for my authorship to be exposed, yet I fear that Mr Dearlove's misunderstanding of my little romance, while it flatters my skills, should it become universally known will, by heightening curiosity, force me to reveal myself in order to affirm that the book is fiction...

Ben flung it aside, the rest unread. "This is nonsense. She is still trying to keep the Fair Land secret. But the papers she burned prove it exists. Why else did she destroy them?"

"She burned private letters." The old lecher smiled coyly. "Love letters between herself and Mr George Fenwick. It is all there in her statement."

"There were no letters in George's wallet. It contained maps and sketches of the Fair Land. And Miss Edgcumbe's companion, Manny, is a Fairlander herself."

"The servant? She's from Tahiti. She was picked up in a French ship, I believe, and later made her way to Madeira where Miss Edgcumbe took her into her employ."

"That's a lie. She's the widow of a British explorer, one of the men who was on the *Miranda*. Find her and ask her."

Sandwich smiled. "I am afraid my Tahitian is a little out of use. It does appear, Mr Dearlove, that you have been thoroughly hoaxed by Miss Edgcumbe's book. Indeed, I thought it very good myself. I wish I had thought to ask her who helped in the writing of it… but we are not here for a literary debate. I want to put a proposal to you. You see, your insistence on exposing the history of the *Miranda* puts me in an awkward position."

Sandwich bent his head and polished one of the large gold buttons on his jacket between his finger and thumb. "When I became First Lord of the Admiralty the accounts were in chaos. Inventories never matched expenditure. Timber no sooner went into the shipyards than it went straight out again, crews were supplied with casks of watered down beer and half-empty barrels of pork, and the muster rolls were filled with non-existent sailors. Little corruptions that cost the Admiralty dear. I worked every waking hour during my periods of office to change this."

"And change it you did, my lord," Stephens murmured appreciatively.

"All I am remembered for now is being a member of the administration that led the British to defeat in America. I am," he grimaced ruefully, "the man who lost the nation a colony. You know I have political enemies, that I have often been the subject of pamphleteers' innuendo, the inspiration for a lampooning pencil. I am in debt – that last election cost me dear – but no one has ever doubted my honesty in financial matters, and especially in relation to the Admiralty's funds. Clarity in the accounts, that was my watchword, Mr Dearlove. However, in the case of the *Miranda*, a little – shall we say – obfuscation crept in. With one expensive expedition already underway, I could not justify the granting of funds to a second, almost contemporaneous, one. Yet I was anxious to secure for the nation any discoveries that the ship might make. So funds were provided – confidentially."

"You embezzled money to help finance the voyage of the *Miranda* to oblige a friend," Ben said.

Sandwich sighed. "You see, it is that kind of ill-informed exaggeration I have to fear. There was never any doubt that the ship was owned by the Admiralty. The fact that George's name appears on the bill of sale is irrelevant, though I do not suppose for a moment that I could persuade anyone of that should the document come to light. The *Miranda* was simply one asset that the government was not aware it possessed. If the voyage had been a success, I would have been praised for my foresight. As it is…" He left the sentence incomplete.

"Then you have nothing to fear. The voyage was a success. The Fair Land exists."

Sandwich shook his head. "Impossible. By the time Captain Cook came home from the Pacific in '75, he had utterly disproved the existence of any Great Southern Continent."

"Captain Cook was wrong. Send ships. See for yourself!"

"Send ships? Do you think the British government would send ships to the other side of the world on the say-so of a young man who has not even the most rudimentary grasp of geography?" Sandwich smiled. "No one would be more delighted than I if it were possible to expand British territories, but I fear we must make do with the continents we have. Even if we had the vast resources needed to launch such an expedition, we could not waste them in such a cause. The upheavals in France have shaken the balance of power in Europe and we cannot afford to relax our guard. I am not alone in predicting that war will come, and one day soon. So you see, even if you succeeded in laying your claim before Chatham, he would have neither the leisure nor the inclination to act upon it. This is no time to go looking for Cyclops, sirens and one-footed Antipodeans."

Stephens sniggered.

"It may suit you to believe Miss Edgcumbe's statement," Ben retorted, "but she told me a very different story."

"Yes. But you have no proof, whereas I have her letter."

"No, I have no proof. Hay wasn't trying to salvage the papers from the fireplace! He was making certain that they had been destroyed, wasn't he? You told him to make sure that there was no evidence left of the *Miranda*'s voyage. He was to destroy anything he found."

"As you say," Sandwich said calmly. "About my proposal – "

"You can keep your proposal. I shall go to the newspapers – petition the Houses of Parliament – the King himself if I have to! My father died because of the Fair Land and I will see his killer brought to justice."

"Then hear me out."

"Why should I?"

"Mr Dearlove, you can waste your talents on a career as a pamphleteer if you wish, but you will never avenge your father's death that way. Lacking proof as you do, the best you can win for yourself is the reputation of an eccentric, the worst an accusation of slander and, once the novelty of your claims has worn off, you will sink into scribbling obscurity."

Ben could think of no answer to this. It was an all too dreadful possibility.

"Miss Edgcumbe has provided me with a description of Bowood, and Beale has discovered that he shipped out on the *Friendship*. There is only one power in the world capable of bringing him home – the British Navy. We can follow any ship anywhere, board vessels on the high seas, detain any man we choose. Now, if Mr Stephens, with his usual admirable discretion, arranges for a vessel to be sent to bring back your father's murderer, will you consent to end your petitions?"

"What's the point of bringing Bowood back to England? I can't prove he's the killer unless there's an inquiry."

"No, it's unlikely that a judge would convict him. But he will not come home. He will be pressed into the Navy. There are naval captains who can make a sailor's life very miserable indeed."

"Why should I trust you?"

"Why should you not? I give you my word. If Bowood can be found, the Navy will have him."

Ben bit his lip. What, after all, had he to put his faith in except the unsubstantiated story of a woman who many would think was mad? He thought back to the first time he saw Sarah, muttering in the theatre, antagonising the audience to the point at which her very life was at risk. She had been ill then. She had been in a fever at Clifton, speaking in her delirium a language Mrs Lambert did not recognise. She could have been speaking in tongues for all anyone knew. And in Gloucester – worn out, huddled over the fire, shielding her eyes from the light that pained them – she might have been suffering from some unbalancing distemper of body and mind.

He was no expert in diseases of the mind to prove her sane or insane. No expert in navigation either. How could he insist on the truth of a claim for which he not only had no written proof but no rational proof? And then, what other chance would he ever have of avenging Father's death?

"How will I know when Bowood is found?"

"You can look for a letter from Mr Stephens."

"It might never come."

Sandwich said nothing. There was nothing more to say. Ben reached across the table for his letters. On his way out of the room, he flung them onto the fire.

Twenty-Nine

Ben watched the decanter make its slow journey around the table, the cut glass reflecting each candle flame a score of times, a row of silver cutlery for a single knife, a dozen silver dishes for a solitary one. His gaze fell on the fruit platter heaped with pineapples, figs, grapes, oranges. A sight to make a scorbutic sailor's eyes water!

But Ben was not thinking of sailors, or ships, or anything very much apart from the taste of the wine, the winter rain spattering against the windows behind the red velvet curtains, and the pleasant warmth of the room. He watched as the others helped themselves to a drink. Mr Dowling, the publisher, took a prudent half-glass; not old Mr Dowling, who had retired to a country house in Bayswater, but his sour-faced nephew who had inherited the business.

Campbell filled his glass to the brim and dolefully watched the bottle continue on its way. Not so much the Scottish poet these days as the *sottish* poet. The last ten years had not seen the fulfilment of his ambition. Barlow, the fat critic, was no more, but there was no shortage of pomposity to replace him. One Mr Jackion sat at the table, his manner becoming ever more portentous as he swilled his wine around his mouth. Mr Jackion's appreciation of Ben's last book had been as enthusiastic as his appreciation of Ben's claret. At least Jackion's readers had interpreted his impressive but unintelligible periods as praise.

There was no lack of hopeful young authors either. Two

gorged fellows sat at the far end of the table, one completely overwhelmed by the company and desperately gulping for Dutch courage. The other, convinced that he outshone the luminaries on either side of him, airily waved the decanter along. Mr Rigg the poet had disappeared from the view of literary society years ago, and the whispering revolutionary Mr Hart had gone joyfully to France in 1790 to perish in The Terror three years later.

Ben's brother-in-law caught his eye and jerked his head towards Dowling. Ben returned the signal with a shrug. He had invited the publisher: there was little more he could do. George Fenwick was a lawyer now, though he spent more time scribbling romances than studying cases. No publisher had yet accepted his first production, a lurid tale of Tahiti. Ben had read it and thought it unlikely that any would. Nevertheless, he had set up this meeting between Dowling and George at his wife's pleading. You could bring publisher and author together, Ben thought, but you could not force commerce to make a proposal to literature if literature brought no hint of a dowry. He had failed to make the match for more deserving works than George's.

"Do you remember Parmeter?" he said suddenly to Campbell, who was sitting on his left.

"Preposterous Parmeter? You tried to get him published didn't you? I hear that he has set up a press at his house and prints his books himself at the profitable rate of five a time."

"Indeed he does," the airy young man eagerly put in. "His latest production, *The Annals of Albion*, is magnificent and deserving of a wider circulation. Are you of that select band that appreciates his work, Mr Dearlove?"

"I am, but Mr Parmeter is not an easy gentleman to help."

"And what, pray, is *The Annals of Albion*?" demanded Jackion.

"It is a mythology, the epic history of a non-existent land," Mr Airy replied.

Jackion snorted. "Humph! For it to have any worth, a book must be true to nature. A non-existent land! Such stuff is nothing but the outpourings of a childish imagination."

"But it is the age of imagination," said the shy young man. Jackion turned an indignant gaze on him and he blushingly silenced himself with another swig of wine.

"A non-existent land?" Campbell repeated. "Ben, do you remember that book that caused such a sensation when it came out, oh, how many years ago? No one reads it now... what was it called? *Travels in the Free Land... Journey to the Far Land...*"

"*An Account of a Voyage to the Fair Land*," Ben said quietly.

"That's it! The book was written in a manner that made it seem as if it was a true story. Very convincing it was too. Some people actually believed the Fair Land existed somewhere in the Pacific. You did, didn't you, Ben?"

"George, help yourself and send the bottle around again... no I didn't," Ben answered, meeting Campbell's bleary eye with his own clear gaze. But, even as the lie fell from his lips, the image of a letter, long since destroyed, rose into his mind – an anxiously looked-for letter from Mr Stephens of the Admiralty telling him that a sailor called Bowood had been pressed into service on one of His Majesty's warships, the *Windsor Castle*. Ben hoped that the man's life would be as miserable as Sandwich had promised. Then he realised that his bargain with Sandwich was cemented.

Even after the Earl's death, Stephens kept the agreement in place, writing to remind Ben that while he, Stephens, continued to ensure that Bowood remained in his naval captivity the contract was not void. A year later came a third letter, with the news that the *Windsor Castle* had been with Admiral Hood at the

British withdrawal from Toulon and Bowood had perished there.

By then, the *Miranda* had dwindled to a distant dot on the horizon of new interests and concerns and, since committing Stephens's final letter to the flames, Ben had ceased to think of her. If he remembered her at all now, it was only as a foolish obsession that had gripped him when he was young.

Ting – ting – ting! Ben started. Campbell, hunched over the table and staring up into his face, was beating his glass with a fruit knife. He was drunker than Ben had realised.

"Ben, aren't you listening to me? You definitely said you knew who wrote it. You can't deny that."

Ben laughed insincerely. "I said I might find out. I never did though."

"Huh. I wonder why the author never wrote anything else. He could have made a fortune." The decanter hovered unsteadily over Campbell's glass.

Ben caught the glass stopper before it rolled off the table and replaced it in the empty flask. "Perhaps there was some secret grief in the writer's life that prevented it."

"Wasn't that about the time that your father was murdered?" slurred Campbell.

There was a rustle of interest around the table.

"Yes," Ben answered shortly, half-rising from his chair. No one followed his lead and he sank back.

"I was very fond of that book," Campbell mused. "Read it over and over again. Copied whole passages out. Do you know, it occurs to me now that your own writing is very like that style."

"No, it isn't," Ben said evenly.

"But it is," Campbell persisted. "It's exactly how you write. Your earlier work was nothing like it. Do you remember your *Almira and Ethelfreda*? A plodding, plagiarising thing."

"You never said you thought so. What did you think was

wrong with *Almira and Ethelfreda?*"

With a drunk's tenacity for sticking to his point, Campbell refused to be diverted. "Now how did it go?" He held up one hand and shut his eyes. He thought for a moment.

"The ladies will be wondering what's become of us all," Ben said, but no one took the cue. Slowly, Campbell opened his eyes and took a deep breath. His voice was suddenly clear and deep. It rolled impressively about the silent room.

With the stars twinkling through the masts, and the moonlight turning the dark wood to silver, the ship would sail and sail and sail into the night, under the stars and the black sky, until the black turns to grey and the sky is pearl white and soft pink and pale yellow, and rainbows dance in the white foam around her prow. And then the water changes colour, from deep blue to pale green, and birds wheel around the mast, and ahead lies a long, low purple belt of land, and drawing closer they see snow-capped mountains and ancient forests, golden meadows and green pastures, beaches of black sand, cities of dazzling white stone. Smiling people garlanded with flowers wait to greet them; there is music, laughter, and no going back.

THE END

Glossary

Batavia: Former name of Jakarta, capital of Indonesia on Java.

Bosun: Or boatswain; the officer responsible for the ship's sails, rigging, anchors and cables, who also pipes the hands to their duties.

Brightsmith: Maker of shiny metal fittings for ships.

Chaffering: Trade; buying and selling.

Doldrums: Parts of the ocean where calms prevail; also used of someone who is miserable.

Glee club: A club or society for singing part-songs or glees.

Gleeted: A gleet is a discharge of pus or mucus from a wound or the urethra.

Great Southern Continent: Also known as Terra Australis Incognita or the Southland, from ancient times a continent believed to exist in the southern hemisphere, and the goal of voyages of discovery from the Middle Ages on. Captain James Cook disproved its existence during his second voyage in 1772 – 1775.

Grog: Rum and water mixed. Half and half is equal measures of each.

King George's Island: The name given to Tahiti by Samuel Wallis who landed there in the *Dolphin* during a search for the Great Southern Continent in 1766. Tahiti was originally spelt Otaheite, the name Captain Cook uses in his journal.

Mercury: Used to treat syphilis.

Mote spoon: A teaspoon with a long, narrow handle, the narrow end used to unblock leaves from the spout of the teapot.

New Holland: The Dutch name for Australia.

Pizzle: Animal penis, usually of a bull.

Pox: Syphilis.

Rattan: A climbing palm, and also a stick made from the tough stems.

Ridotto: An assembly with music and dancing, sometimes gambling too.

Rout: A large evening party or soirée.

Shipwright: A man employed in the building of ships.

Taboo: Objects set apart for use by gods, royalty, priests or others, or which certain groups are forbidden to use; sacred.

Lightning Source UK Ltd.
Milton Keynes UK
UKOW051351130612

194328UK00001B/4/P